MAVERICK

Lilly Atlas

For my sister wife. Sorry I turned you into a club whore. Okay, I'm not sorry. Love you!

Stephanie Little firmly believes the world exists in two states: right and wrong, good and evil, unlawful and law-abiding. She chose her side the moment she joined the FBI and pledged to rid the world of as many criminals as possible.

Maverick is everything Stephanie isn't: inked, pierced, flirty, masculine as sin, but most of all, an outlaw. When corruption in Stephanie's crime-fighting world lands her in the clutches of a dangerous gangster, Maverick is there to keep her sane and battle for her protection.

With Stephanie's neat existence so turned around that she can no longer distinguish the good from the evil, she finds herself thrust into a world so gray she can't see three feet in front of her face. To survive the confusion, she turns to the only person who keeps her grounded—the sexy outlaw who melts her heart and weakens her knees.

But law enforcement and criminals can never mix. Not in the way her body and heart are begging for. At some point, someone is going to learn her secret, and when that happens, her fierce protector could become her greatest enemy.

CHAPTER ONE

Was there a reason the men in her life—the important men who'd educated her, trained her, guided her—had all turned to the dark side? Was she the connection? Or was it just a coincidence that her father turned criminal and now her partner at the FBI seemed to have done the same?

Only on a much more sinister level?

Once again, her world had been smashed to bits by a man she'd trusted. And it hadn't been smashed with a sledgehammer either. No, a damn wrecking ball in the form of an undercover assignment crashed through the glass house she lived in, launching millions of sharp shards at her delicate skin.

And it hurt.

God, did it hurt.

"One more chance, bitch. What the fuck are you doin' here?" some dead-eyed brute asked her about five seconds after his fist connected with her face.

For the second time.

The additional punch disoriented her for a second, long enough to lose her sense of upright and meet the ground. Crash landing on the rock-and-twig-filled ground of the Tennessee forest felt about as wonderful as being socked in the face. Shit, she was going to feel this for quite a while.

If she survived.

On all fours, with palms and knees throbbing from the bits of gravel and dirt embedded in her skin, Stephanie spit out blood that had pooled in her mouth from the split lip. Fear clawed at her throat, but there wasn't time for it. She had to think and think fast. "Hiking," she said, the sound a bit muffled from the swelling. She stared up at the man who was as comfortable hitting a woman as she was lounging on her couch and watching Netflix. Not a good sign. It meant he truly didn't give a shit about her life. "Got lost."

And...damn...who knew talking with a split lip would hurt so damn much? Tears pooled in her eyes, but she'd rather die than let one of those suckers slip free. She wasn't the toughest of chicks out there...physically at least. A few arrests during her time as a beat cop had resulted in physical altercations with significant bumps and bruising. She'd always put on a tough mask in front of her fellow officers but bawled like a baby in the privacy of her own home.

Dead-Eyes threw back his head and laughed before turning to his buddy, a guy so overweight Stephanie was pretty sure she could outrun him even if they broke both her legs. She'd never outrun Dead-Eyes, though. He was big, muscled, and packed a wallop of a punch. "You believe this bitch, Top?" he asked the larger man.

Top grunted and shook his head, his many chins wobbling like Jello. "Fuck no. No reason for a bitch to be hiking out here, Shark. Ain't even any fuckin' trails."

Like he spent much time trekking through the great outdoors.

Stephanie bit back the smart-assed remark on the tip of her tongue. Silence was her best bet. Plus, this little gangbanger pow-wow gave her a second to reorient and breathe through the pain.

This entire thing had been a huge mistake. She wasn't a field agent, but basically an FBI desk jockey for the Cybercrimes Investigative Division. Daniel Rey, her partner of the past two years, had been an undercover agent for the Human Trafficking Task Force for years. When the Bureau sniffed a case here in

Maverick

Townsend, Tennessee, they dragged Rey away from his cushy job and threw him back in the field. That was a year ago. She was his contact in DC.

Nothing more. It kept her plenty busy, investigating leads, following financials, learning all the players. But she wasn't an undercover agent.

Yet here she was because he'd missed two check-ins with her in a row. Not uncommon for an agent deep undercover, but it was his first. So the Bureau had sent her to Tennessee. And she'd been the idiot to go off in the woods by herself.

"Get the fuck up, bitch," Shark said. He grabbed her hair and started to yank her to her feet. She may not be out in the field often, but she'd been trained like any other agent. Reflex and hours of rigorous instruction kicked in. She reacted without thinking, ramming her elbow into his hard gut.

Shark grunted and released her hair. "Fuck!" he yelled.

Her heart raced and, for one second, she froze. Then her brain screamed *run*, and she took off like a rabbit.

She'd made it five steps when a strong arm tagged her around the waist and lifted her off her feet like she was a small child. And like a child, she freaked the fuck right out, kicking, screaming, trying to bite. But it was all in vain. Whoever held her was bigger, stronger, and meaner than she was. He squeezed her until she felt her ribs would pop right out of her sternum.

"Settle the fuck down, bitch," he growled in her ear, and her breath seized.

Daniel Rey. Her partner. Known as King to these assholes.

Her muscles went limp with relief, and she sagged in his arms. Thank God. Nerves still had her insides quaking, but some of the fear had gone. Rey was here, and he'd make sure she wasn't harmed.

All he had to say was that he believed her. Saw her tromping around like a bewildered idiot. Spotted her looking lost and stupid in the woods. He could volunteer to drop her somewhere and scare the piss out of her so she wouldn't talk.

Then Stephanie could find out what the hell was going on and why Agent Rey had missed his last two check-ins.

He turned around with her still in his arms and trudged back the twenty feet to where Shark and the Top dude waited. Shark had the creepiest smile, making all the hair on her arms stand straight on end. She shivered despite the hot sun shining through the trees. She wanted to be gone in the worst way.

Take a breath, Stephanie. Rey won't let them hurt you.

Right? He wouldn't. Sure, sometimes undercover agents had to commit heinous acts to work their way into a gang, but that wouldn't involve hurting their partner. Would it? Stephanie would make the worst undercover agent ever. She'd never be able to break the law, even in the name of good. The ends didn't always justify the means. Her ingrained sense of right and wrong came from growing up with a strict as hell police officer single-father.

"No fucking way this bitch was just out in the woods," King said, releasing her. Two seconds later she felt something hard press between her shoulder blades. His AR-15.

What the fuck?

What was going on? Why hadn't he just let her outrun him? Let her escape? They'd never know. He could have feigned falling down or something.

"I say we waste her now. Bury her and get back to those bitches we left naked and needy." As he spoke, he circled until he was standing in front of her, weapon leveled at her head. She blinked back her surprise at the sight of him. Gone was his thick head of blond hair he kept in a neat and professional style. Now, he was cue-ball bald and had a scruffy goatee. He'd bulked up, too.

What. The. Fuck.

His own wife might not recognize him.

A cold wave ran through her from the very top of her head straight to her toes. Stephanie had never worked so hard in her life as she did to keep the shock off her face and the vile words in her mouth. Could he mean it? Was there a chance he'd been swallowed up by Shark's world?

Calm down.

King wasn't serious. He couldn't be. Her partner was a veteran FBI agent, for crying out loud. They didn't just throw away everything they'd worked for, throw away their families for a life of crime. There had to be an extraction plan bouncing around in his head.

That knowledge helped her relax despite the fact one twitch of King's finger would splatter her brains all over the Tennessee woods.

"Nah," Shark said. "Where's the fun in that? Let's take her with us. A few hours hanging with the boys, and she'll be ready to talk."

Fuck. Fuck. Fuck.

These men were suspected of human trafficking. They'd have no qualms about raping her.

She tried with all her might to send King a mental message, but he wouldn't meet her gaze. This was as bad for him as it was for her. They'd torture her for information, and she'd crack. His identity would be revealed, and the shit show would commence.

Everyone cracked.

Especially if they had zilch training in enduring torture. The Bureau told her it would be no big deal. Lay eyes on Agent Rey, and she'd be home in two days.

Wrong.

Why the hell wouldn't he make eye contact?

"Who gives a fuck why she's here? Let me kill her and be fuckin done with it," King said.

Stephanie was in grave danger of puking all over the forest floor. As she stared at her partner of two years, the partner who taught her everything she knew about working for the FBI, the partner who teased her endlessly for her opinions on the black and white nature of the world, the nausea became unbearable.

When he'd regaled her with tales of his undercover days, King had told her working undercover would change her view of the world. That undercover agents often had to live the life of a criminal and learn to deal with living in the shadows for the sake of doing good. Even though she'd heard it before, she'd rejected the notion of living in a gray zone.

Finally, he met her gaze. His eyes were flat, emotionless, nothing like the man she knew and trusted. He winked, but it wasn't an I-have-your-back kind of wink. It was evil. A promise of horror and pain.

And she knew.

There were no fucking shades of gray.

She'd been right all along.

Only black. Only white.

And King had officially been swallowed by the darkness.

But this wasn't a case of doing what he had to, to maintain cover. This was a monster who wore human skin for a time and managed to fool even the most skeptical. Her knees wobbled and her head spun. She had to leave. Had to get out before they killed her...or worse.

"What the fuck did I say, King?" Shark asked. "I want her at the compound. You can kill her eventually, but it's been a shit week. The boys need some fun first."

Stephanie swallowed. Boys? Fun?

There weren't too many ways to interpret that.

Without thinking, she took two steps back on legs that could barely hold her.

"Don't even think about it, bitch," King said. He stepped closer, and she flinched as the barrel of his rifle made contact with her forehead. "Swear to God I'll explode your head all over this fucking forest." There was no way the hatred in his tone was fake. He wasn't acting.

She believed him.

Why? What was so appealing about this lifestyle that a decorated FBI agent would do a one-eighty and betray everything he once stood for?

Sure, he and his wife had a few money troubles, but enough to do this?

Frustration with the system?

Sticking it to the man?

It seemed too dramatic to be merely making a point.

The ultimate hissy fit?

"Let's roll," Shark said, turning on his heel and trudging toward the building she could see through the trees in the distance.

Top leered at her for a second longer before waddling after his master like an overfed but well-trained dog.

If there was any chance for escape, it was now or never. She was somewhat alone with her partner. Maybe she'd misinterpreted Rey's actions and he really was an amazing actor and undercover agent. Maybe so good he'd even fooled his partner. "Please, Daniel," she whispered as she started to back away again. "Let me run. Tell them I tripped you. You can call in later when this blows over."

"Don't. Fucking. Run."

"Why are you doing this? What happened to you?"

"Bitch," he practically growled at her. "If you don't fucking move, I'll shoot out your knee. It'll hurt like a bitch, but it won't keep you from what's coming."

Her stomach lurched, and she gagged as bile climbed high in her esophagus.

For one second, she had the insane urge to call out to Shark. To yell as loud as she could and let the scumbag know his precious King was an undercover FBI agent.

It wouldn't matter if he pledged his loyalty to Shark forever. He'd be killed. That's how it worked with gangs.

Nothing less than he deserved at that moment.

But she didn't give into the urge. It wouldn't be justice; it would be an act of vigilantism. It was the job of law enforcement and the legal system to handle his actions.

If she lived long enough to report back to her superiors.

"You can still leave," she whispered as she started after Shark. King's gun remained on her, and even though it was no longer touching her skin, she felt the sight of it like a needle stabbing straight through her skin.

He just grunted and said, "Move."

"Why?" she whispered when Shark was out of earshot.

King grunted and shook his head. "So fucking naïve, Stephanie. You always have been. It's all gray out here."

No. She refused to believe it. This situation was clearly not on any gray spectrum. King was evil. Plain and simple.

"No, Daniel, I'm not naïve. But you sure are a fucking traitor."

"You'll never get it. And you'll never survive this world. Wake the fuck up," King said as he thrust his right arm forward and rammed the butt of his rifle into her head.

His murderous expression was the last thing she saw before her vision went black.

CHAPTER TWO

Maverick tilted his head and stared through his one functional eye at the punk-ass guard Shark left as babysitter. Skippy was his name. A stupid brute who was good for nothing but taking orders and bashing heads. Like Mav was going anywhere with at least ten plastic cuffs anchoring his arms and legs to the thin metal chair.

He supposed he could stand in some sort of awkward crouch and shuffle his way to the door with the chair on his back, turtle shell-style, but then what the fuck would he do? His ribs were so busted he'd be lucky to make it ten steps before puncturing a lung and suffocating to death on the floor of this basement hellhole.

"Don't you feel a little like a pussy, man?" Maverick asked.

Skippy grunted and slipped the strap of his M16 over his head. Another unnecessary precaution because Mav was pretty sure blood hadn't flowed to his hands in almost two days. The straps hadn't been quite as tight before that, but he'd managed to slip a hand out and break some assholes nose. Shark had his minions add a few more ties and cinch 'em down real tight after that.

In no time, fingers on both had gone from mild tingling, to seriously annoying pins and needles, to agonizing burn. Now they were numb. Dead. Fuck, he didn't know what the hell he'd do if they had to amputate.

Half his security business was run from his computer. The keyboard was his livelihood, and the hands that typed on it kept him useful and valuable to his club.

Shit to worry about another time. He had to make it out alive first.

"Funny thing to ask comin' from a skinny man bleeding and tied to a chair." Skippy was built, a mountain of lumpy muscle with a grizzly beard and a bit of a southern twang. Mav had actually met him before at a bar. Back before he'd lowered himself and joined up with Shark, he'd worked on a shrimping boat out of Louisiana or some shit like that.

Mav shrugged the half inch that his shoulders could move as he licked his tongue over a freshly bleeding lip. "Just, you know, it's easy to wail on a dude tied to a chair."

"You run your mouth too fucking much," Skippy said. He had a bulge in his lower lip at all times. The man never seemed to be without a hefty gob of tobacco stuffed in there. "Keep it shut, and I won't hit you."

Mav grunted. Not happening. His smart-ass mouth was the only weapon he had at the moment. "We could make it interesting."

One of Skippy's blond eyebrows rose. "Interesting?"

"Sure. You could untie me and see how far I get."

Skippy laughed and pushed off the wall. "You're fuckin' hilarious. I got at least sixty pounds on you, man. You're damn scrawny."

That was sort of true. Maverick certainly wasn't bulky. He was tall and slender, but he wasn't soft. He might not have the heft that Skippy boasted, but he was still fit and strong as fuck. And scrappy as all hell. Being on the skinnier side his whole life, he'd grown real tired real fast of getting his ass handed to him in his foster home, and he learned to fight dirty. Nothing better than a good gutter fight.

"Well then, you shouldn't give a shit about letting me out to stretch my legs." In his weakened state, he'd never overpower

Skippy, but he wasn't a dumb fuck like the skipper was, so he stood a good chance of outsmarting him and getting away. Or at least he had until that last beating. That one was the killer that had taken a few ribs out of his commission. It'd been harder than he'd imagined to keep his face neutral and throw sass at his captors. But he'd done it. Last thing his club needed while they searched for him was to know just how bad off Maverick was.

He'd been snatched off the street by a horde of Shark's guys—they all ran together—a few days ago. A way for Shark to fuck with his MC. Shark had been trying to move in on the Hell's Handlers' turf but been blocked at every turn. So they'd kidnapped Mav. And they'd been sending pics and videos of him daily just to taunt with Mav's brothers who had to be going out of their minds trying to find him. Hell, he had no fucking clue where he was so he couldn't even give them some kind of clue.

Skippy spit a wad of brown phlegm on the ground. "Nice try, asshole. You ain't stretchin' no legs."

There was a commotion outside the door that had Skippy turning toward it seconds before it flew open and Shark strode in. He was followed by King, the biggest piece of shit Maverick ever had the displeasure of meeting. That guy was a grade-A douche no matter how he looked at it. His bald head was so inflated he practically fell over as he walked.

The guy probably had a tiny toothpick dick. Guys with the smallest dicks seemed to be the biggest bastards. Overcompensation and all that.

King was dragging something—someone rather—under the armpits.

Please don't let it be one of my brothers.

When the Gray Dragons snatched him, he'd been with one of the prospects who'd taken a beating so severe Maverick had to wonder if he was still alive. If he wasn't, not a single one of these gang pieces of shit would be left breathing when the club found him.

And they would find him, of that he had no doubt. He just had to stay breathing long enough for them to have something to find.

When King dragged his struggling captive into the room, Maverick worked to keep any signs of curiosity off his face. If Shark caught wind of the fact he was dying to know who the prisoner was, the sadistic gang leader would find a way to fuck with Maverick over it, probably harming the hostage even more in the process.

It only took a second after King dumped his captive to the floor for Maverick to realize the person scrambling into the corner was definitely not one of his MC brothers, but a woman. A tiny slip of a blonde woman with a split lip and bloodied shirt. She was cute, wholesome looking. Certainly not one of Shark's sluts.

Fuck. Things were about to get ugly.

"We brought you a friend, Maverick. Too bad for you, you won't be the one to play with her. You can watch, though, if you cooperate."

Dread settled low in Maverick's gut. Now, he had no choice but to find a way out. And soon, before his club located him. There was no way in hell he was going to sit by, bound to a chair, while some poor woman was raped by these savage animals. He may be an outlaw and an asshole, but he loved the fuck out of women, and none of them deserved that shit.

"Bored with me already?" Maverick asked in a tone that suggested he was the bored one. Any time he could keep them talking to him was time they weren't focused on her.

Shark scoffed. "Not even close. In fact, I've got something special planned for you after we get our new guest settled."

Fan-fucking-tastic.

"Bring it on."

The woman sucked in a sharp breath, drawing Mav's attention. She was gently prodding her oozing lip while glaring daggers at King.

A woman who didn't cower.

Nothing wrong with that.

"What's the problem, guys? Can't find any willing women to come back here with you? Gotta go out into the woods and trap one like an animal?" He chuckled and shook his head. "Pretty piss-poor game you losers got."

King spun then lunged for Maverick, but was stopped by Shark with a meaty palm to the chest. Shark whispered something in King's ear that had him smirking and nodding. Then he crossed to the opposite side of the room and dragged a rectangular table back toward the woman.

Shark was no idiot. He wouldn't fall for Maverick's lame attempt at distraction, but King? Yeah, that guy was all hot air and bluster. Easy to manipulate because his own pride got in the fucking way. The Handlers had eyes on the Dragons for a while, and Mav was familiar with all the major players.

"Get up," Shark ordered her.

Her fear-filled gaze met Maverick's, and he gave her a quick nod. Whatever they had planned for her would be worse if she resisted. Best save that for the really bad shit. She scrambled to her feet with a soft groan and stood before Shark, squaring her shoulders and giving him one hell of a fuck-you glare.

Shit, she was just a little bit of a thing. No match for these animals. Couldn't have been more than five-feet-three-inches, which wasn't the smallest of women, but compared to Maverick's six-four, it was tiny.

Maverick didn't know the woman, but he was proud of her chutzpah. He was also attracted as hell. Damn but the woman had a banging body. Tight in all the right places with a gentle swell to her breasts. She wasn't the curviest of chicks, actually more on the straight side, and her tits weren't huge by anyone's standard, but she had just enough to fill his hands.

He'd always preferred smaller woman. Someone he could easily manipulate in bed. Start on her back, flip her easily and yank her up to all fours. Hoist her up and fuck her standing in the center of the room if he felt the urge. Couldn't do that with a woman nearing his own height. He liked a big difference between them. Loved feeling the slight weight of a small woman. Liked her to know he was bigger, stronger, could dominate, but also protect if needed. Not that he discriminated when it came to fucking, because let's face it, fucking a woman, any woman, was better than not. But he still had his preferences.

Despite the pain and a room full of gang members who'd love nothing more than to kill him, Maverick felt a stirring in his jeans. A woman that could give him a hard-on amidst the threat of death and dismemberment must be something pretty damn special. He couldn't help the laugh that snorted out.

"Something fuckin' funny?" King snarled.

"Yeah, man, I just remembered your sister's face when I banged her. You know I made that bitch come six times in one night?" Juvenile? Perhaps, but seeing the deep shade of purple overtake King's face made it all worth it.

A strangled sound came from the woman. She had her hand over her mouth, holding in laughter. A woman who could not only give him a boner but laugh at his ridiculous taunt when she had to be scared out of her skin?

Fuck yeah, this woman was special. No way could these pieces of shit be allowed to ruin that.

"Enough," Shark said, grabbing the woman's arm and shoving her toward King. "Get her on the table." Then he looked Maverick straight in the eye as he gave his men orders. "Pants off."

Well fuck. Maverick's foster momma always told him his smartass mouth would get him in trouble one day. Looked like today might be that day.

King's mouth turned up in a smarmy smile as he reached for the woman. Horror crossed her features, and she struggled against him in vain. In seconds, King had her on her back, laid out on the table, arms above her head. Skippy secured them to the table legs with handcuffs.

Then, King made a big production of removing her pants. Tears coursed down her face as she kicked like a pissed-off horse, but Skippy joined in, anchoring her legs to the table. Her slender legs didn't stand a chance at moving a man King's size. Maverick tried to help, yelling slurs and insults at each of the men and their families, but to no avail.

Within seconds, her jeans were on the floor and her legs were spread. A blue terrified gaze met Maverick's. Bile shot up his esophagus. He almost closed his eyes, unable to witness a woman being violated, but forced himself to keep his gaze steady and locked with hers.

She'd need something to focus on, and if he could do that for her, he'd do what he had to, no matter the cost. She bit her already abused lower lip and jerked against the cuffs around her wrists.

The sound of metal clicking against the table reverberated in the room, followed by the chirping of a phone.

Shark checked his cell and frowned. "We got business, boys." Then he loomed over the woman. "Get comfy. We'll be back," he said. And as quick as it all began, Maverick was alone in the room with the frightened woman.

Her body sagged against the table like she'd lost every morsel of energy she had. "You're okay. You're okay," she chanted to herself, almost quieter than Maverick could hear.

Shit, she'd been so brave in the face of the Dragons. To witness her underlying fear put a different kind of ache in his chest.

"What's your name, sweetheart?" he asked after giving her a few minutes to collect herself.

Her body jerked as though she'd forgotten she wasn't alone. Her head turned, and she stared at him. As it was, she was beautiful, but when her mouth wasn't swollen and she didn't have mascara tracks running down her cheeks, she'd be a knockout. Blonde hair that looked to be about shoulder length and eyes the deepest shade of navy blue. Her skin was olive tan, whether from time in the sun or her natural tone, he didn't know. But damn if he didn't want to find out.

"I'm S-Stephanie." She cleared her throat.

"I'm Maverick or Mav, and I'd say it was nice to meet you, Steph," he said going straight for informal, "but it's pretty shitty to meet you, actually."

When she huffed out a small laugh, warmth filled Maverick's chest. "Shitty to meet you too, Maverick," she replied.

As long as she didn't lose her spirit, she'd be okay. And that was the one thing he could help her with. Whatever he could do to keep her distracted, and maybe make her laugh a time or two. "How'd you get so unlucky as to end up here with me?"

"Unlucky is a good word for it," she said. "I'm in town with a girlfriend. Just a getaway to the mountains. She pissed me off so I decided a hike by myself would be a good way to relax and get some perspective. It wasn't. The worst case of wrong place, wrong time that there could be."

Huh. Something about the story didn't ring true. Maybe the way she kept shifting her eyes and biting her lip. Then again, she was probably just freaked the fuck out. Not that it mattered if her story wasn't real. She was here, and that was the bottom line. "Shit, babe, that is some bad luck. Gonna tell you a secret though, okay?"

Cheek against the table, she nodded.

"My boys will be coming for me, and I promise you they won't leave you here. Not sure how long it's gonna take, but they will get both of us out of here. So all we have to do is make sure they have two live bodies to rescue. Okay?"

"Your boys? Like your sons?" She stared at him, hanging on his every word.

He laughed. "Hell, no. I don't have kids. Or a woman, for that matter. My motorcycle club, The Hell's Handlers."

Stephanie's eyes flared with surprise and a tiny hint of unease, but then she smiled. "I think some badass bikers are just what this situation calls for."

Shit, he liked this woman.

"Sorry you have to stare at my mostly naked ass this whole time. At least they left my underwear on. That has to be a good sign, right?" There was a tremor in her voice like she needed him to agree so she could stop worrying about the risk of rape.

Unfortunately, that wasn't a comfort he could provide her.

"Baby, I'm sorry you feel vulnerable and exposed, but I gotta tell you. Being able to stare at that those sexy stems for the foreseeable future just might make being here worth it."

A delicate snort left her. "If I couldn't see how swollen your eyes were, I'd know something was wrong with your vision by your statement. What you're looking at is called chicken legs."

"Woman, you're crazy. I like a woman in a tight little package."

She flushed and rolled her eyes. "Guess you're not as bad off as I originally thought if you can still hit on me."

"I'd have to be dead not to notice that body, babe."

She shifted, and the clamor of the chains on the metal table made her jump. "You're quite the charmer, aren't you?"

"That's what all the ladies tell me," he said.

Man, if they weren't in this shithole, he'd be all over her.

Maybe when they got free, he'd take her out and show her exactly what he could do with his mouth.

First, he had to make damn sure they both got out alive.

And that Shark and his cronies kept their filthy hands off Stephanie's beautiful body.

CHAPTER THREE

Almost twenty-four hours had passed since the men had tied Stephanie spread-eagle to a table and left her in a basement with another captive. Something must be up because they hadn't left anyone to guard them.

At least that was her best guess as far as the number of hours passed. A small rectangular window let her know the sun had set, risen, and was beginning to dip again. So it had to be somewhere around the full-day mark.

At one point, when her bladder had been near bursting, she had to humble herself and ask Maverick what she was supposed to do.

A chuckle and a "let it fly" had been his response. "I've been here three days. They let me eat and piss the first day. Haven't taken me from this chair since."

Fantastic. Well, that accounted for the smell when King first brought her in. She'd held out for another hour then had no choice but to urinate. On the table that she was lying on.

Disgusting didn't begin to cover it.

Neither did mortification. At least Mav had the decency to look away and sing so he wouldn't see or hear her.

Since she hadn't had a thing to drink in ages, she probably wouldn't have that problem again.

However long she'd been there for, it was a very long time to be immobilized, frightened, and freakin' cold. Every so often, she drifted to sleep only to be jerked awake by a screaming pain in her shoulders or wracked by shivers from the cold, dank basement.

Night had been the worst.

Pitch black, icy, terrifying. Her brain ran through every second of the year King had been undercover with the Dragons. Where had she missed it? How had she not picked up on his betrayal? She'd only spoken to him via phone, email, and text. Not enough to determine he'd been lying to her. She shouldn't be surprised. It wasn't the first time a man had betrayed her by going against everything he'd proclaimed to believe in.

Thank God for the man in the room with her.

Maverick.

He was the one reason she hadn't lost her sanity or freaked out. Throughout the night, he'd regaled her with stories of ridiculous stunts his club brothers pulled and tales of vengeful women he'd pissed off throughout the years.

In reality, probably less than half of it was true, but she appreciated his effort to keep her calm more than she could ever express. Because Shark and King were coming back at some point, and when they did, it would be awful.

Gang members didn't tie a woman to a table and remove her pants for no reason.

No, they did it for one big reason, and that was to rape her. During quiet times, like now, when Maverick succumbed to sleep, or maybe just passed out from pain and dehydration, she tried to prepare herself for the inevitable violation. Tried to wrap her mind around what was going to happen. Maybe if she could somehow find a way to accept it before it happened, it wouldn't destroy her.

A very big maybe.

And really, it wasn't working. All it was doing was ramping up her anxiety at every bump or squeak. The "is it them?" thought was always followed by about fifteen minutes of straining to hear any and every noise and discover if her captors were returning.

With a sigh, she rolled her head and stared at the handsome man slumped in the chair. Or he'd be handsome if it wasn't for all the bruising. They'd done a number on him. Shirtless, he was…God, how to even describe the man suffering with her. Tattoos covered his body. And she meant covered. Arms, chest, neck. Only his face was devoid of ink. Then there were the piercings. Lip, eyebrow, tongue, if she wasn't mistaken, and nipples.

She had this urge to go to him and soothe him. Press her lips to each and every bruise and promise him as he'd done for her that he'd be okay. He'd heal.

Something about him captivated her. He wasn't her type. Not at all. She tended to date nice guys, on the rare occasion she actually had a date. Easygoing, laid-back men, willing to put up with her long hours and intense job. After working in a field that taxed her both mentally and physically, she gravitated toward men who didn't do either. Who just let her be and went with the flow.

Of course, she was often bored after the third date, so maybe when—because she was working on remaining positive—she got out of the damn basement, she could take a good hard look at her type.

Piercings on men were something Stephanie had never understood. She could handle an earring if it came along with a guy who caught her attention, but nothing else. Yet on Maverick…it just fit. He should look like a thug or at least a facsimile of the many gang members she'd run across in her career, but he didn't.

Maybe it had something to do with the fact that he was on the leaner side. Not unmuscular, but the long, elastic strength of a runner as opposed to the brute bulk many of these guys used to their advantage. Then there was his hair. It screamed hipster. Long on top, the ebony hair was shaved on both sides. She'd actually seen it in an article at her salon not long ago. It was called an undercut.

Really, what endeared him to her was his personality. Quick wit, charm, and the desire to comfort her made it impossible to write him off as nothing but an outlaw biker. But he *was* an outlaw, a criminal, and she'd do well to remember that. She could come to grips with the fact that she was attracted to him—that was just a combination of chemical reactions and the heightened senses of an adrenaline spike. But make no mistake, she'd arrest him in a heartbeat if she had to.

Because she was the law.

And he was a one-percenter.

Who probably belonged behind bars. She knew a fair amount about his MC, and while they weren't involved in drugs, prostitution, or gun running, they weren't saints. Just because the FBI had bigger fish to fry didn't mean the Handlers didn't break the law.

"You stare much harder, and I just might blush." Maverick's sleep-roughened voice made her flinch, then wince when the abused muscles in her shoulders rebelled against the unnatural position.

"Sorry, babe," he said. "Those arms must be feeling like overstretched rubber bands right now, huh?"

Her face heated at being caught staring without really seeing. Hell, she'd been looking right at him, but so lost in her thoughts she hadn't even realized he'd woken up. "Something like that."

He shifted or tried to as much as his bindings would allow, which was about an inch, then emitted a pain-filled grunt. "Motherfucker."

"You all right?" He looked like shit. There was so much bruising on his chest and torso the tattoos were lost to the deep purple contusions. When he'd been dozing this time, air whistled through his lungs with each inhalation. She didn't know squat about medicine, but she knew breathing was vital and wasn't supposed to sound like that.

"Just peachy, wildcat. Don't worry about me. Got hurt worse

last week when I was between these two hotties with talons for nails. Let me tell you, those bitches could scratch."

Stephanie snorted out a laugh while her mind raced. Was that a true story? Or just bluster to keep her from knowing how bad off he really was? "Two, huh?" For some inexplicable reason, the thought of him with two long-nailed, busty bleach-blondes who were gymnast flexible irked her. Okay, so maybe she'd added the cup-size, hair color, and flexibility herself.

"Yeah. Slow night." He winked, and Stephanie laughed.

"You're so full of shit."

He winked again. "You'll never know. How you doing? You freezing your ass off?"

"I'm cold, yes, but unfortunately my ass is still there. What there is of it to begin with."

Now it was Maverick's turn to snort. "Already told you that was a good thing, wildcat. If you don't believe me, I may have to show you exactly what I mean as soon as we bust out of here."

Heat spread through her even if she didn't believe him. Two chicks in one night was a slow night? Yeah, men like him didn't go for uptight, workaholics who hadn't been laid in years. Not that it mattered. Because, hello?

Criminal.

As in breaker of the law.

Wrong.

Not right.

At least this time she knew up front he wasn't a law-abiding citizen. No chance for the shock of betrayal she'd suffered in the recent and distant past.

She was about to fire back some halfway witty retort when the unmistakable sound of men's heavy footsteps echoed in the hallway outside the door. For one insane moment, Stephanie almost laughed. Chalk it up to fear, exhaustion, and low blood sugar, but she found it hilarious how obvious it was that the men were in the hallway when she'd been straining so hard to hear something, anything, to warn her of their approach.

"Hey, wildcat, look at me." Maverick's voice was clipped, commanding.

She obeyed without thought, rolling her head in his direction.

"Fuck," he said when their gazes connected. "I'm so sorry, babe. I can't do shit for you. I've been trying to get out of here for days, but I'm stuck."

"It's okay, Maverick," she whispered as shakes started to dance through her.

"Whatever happens..." he said. "*Whatever* happens, you look into my eyes. Like you're doing now. The whole time. You understand?"

The eyes he spoke of widened, and she nodded. He sounded like he cared. Like the thought of her being violated was tearing him apart. "I'm sorry you'll have to see—"

"Stop," he said, shaking his head. "I don't give a shit about myself. Go wherever you have to in your mind, but keep looking at me."

Stephanie swallowed a beach ball-sized lump and moved her head in a single nod just as the door swung open and Shark and King filed in. Both men ignored Maverick and proceeded immediately to her, looming over the table.

King sneered down at her, and she swore right then, if her hands were free, she'd commit her first murder and serve the time without a moment of regret. If she survived this, that smug face would haunt her nightmares, but at least there, she'd be free to exact her revenge. Strip him, tie him to this very table, and leave him out in the woods for birds to peck out his eyes and rabid woodland creatures to slowly feast on his balls.

"Fucking stinks in here," King grumbled.

"Happens when you don't let us out to take a piss," Mav fired back.

"No worries." Shark disappeared for a moment, then came back with a bucket he handed to King.

Before she had time to process his intent, King dumped the bucket on her lower half.

Icy water crashed over her, making her shriek in shock. Shit. It was colder than cold. But at least it would wash away the urine she'd been lying in for hours.

King laughed long and loud as he tossed the bucket into a corner. "Miss me?" he asked, hovering over her once again.

"About as much as I miss a nasty bout of diarrhea," she replied. "Which I have to say, smells better than you. What the hell have you been doing?"

Maverick's bark of laughter had her smiling despite the dire position she was in. Words were her only weapon at the moment so the elementary-school taunt would have to do. And it worked. King's nostrils flared, and a vein throbbed in his bald scalp. He fisted a hand in her hair, yanking her head up.

"You're going to pay for that," he whispered for her ears only. "Hope you weren't still holding out hope that I'd be getting you out of this."

It hurt like hell, but Stephanie managed to bite back the yelp of pain. No way would the motherfucker get the satisfaction of knowing he was causing her any discomfort.

"I want first crack at her," King said as he dropped her head back to the table and looked at his master.

"Knock yourself out." Shark waved away King's concern as though he was asking if he could eat the last yogurt in the refrigerator, not be the first one to rape her. "I've got my own piece coming later. But leave some for Skippy and the others. Think I'll watch, though. Get me in the mood for my own bitch." He palmed his crotch and rubbed up and down the length.

Stephanie gagged.

"Fuck, Shark, no one wants to see you grabbing that cocktail weenie between your legs," Maverick said.

"Shut the fuck up," Shark shot back. "Get to it, King."

Stephanie's breathing increased to near hyperventilation as King circled a hand around one of her ankles. With a lecherous grin that made bile rise in her throat, he trailed his large hand over her calf and up to her thigh.

There was nothing she could do about the rapid breathing and the shakes, but she made damn sure those were the only outward signs of distress. Inside her head, she was screaming, crying, hurling every vile insult possible at King. She was also begging him to stop, pleading with him to leave her untouched. But he'd never see it.

Instead of letting the fear and horror out, she clenched her back teeth and turned to meet Maverick's gaze. Those olive-green eyes met hers, and he nodded once.

"Shit, King. I thought it was bad watching Shark touch his-fucking-self. Please don't tell me you're about to whip your dick out." Maverick kept his attention on her as he taunted King.

"You're about to see me stuff this bitch full of my dick." King's hand was inching closer and closer to her panties. Somehow, it was so much worse that yesterday she'd trusted this man with her life. This lying, backstabbing, raping piece of garbage. Tears filled her eyes, and she wanted to close them. To disappear. But she kept her focus on Maverick's solemn face.

"I've heard all sorts of rumors about you guys and the sick shit you get up to, but I didn't realize it was like this."

"Sometimes you gotta take what you need, Maverick. Make it yours. The world will pass you by if you just wait for everything you want," King said.

"Nah," Mav said, throwing her a wink. How he managed to sound like they were just buds taunting each other out on the ballfield she'd never know. "I ain't talking about you doing the woman. I'm talking about how you need a few dudes in the room staring at your dick before you can get it up."

Both Shark and King tensed, and King's hand left her leg. Stephanie's eyes fluttered closed for half a second as the moment of respite registered.

"That's it, isn't it?" Mav went on. "You may be fucking some bitch, but you ain't getting your jollies from her. It's from your boys seeing your dick. That's what makes you hard, ain't it?"

"Shut the fuck up," King roared, leaving the table and

storming toward Maverick.

Oh, God. Stephanie held her breath. He'd turned the attention to himself. Why? He was in way worse shape than she was. Why would he do that?

"Hey, man. Just cuz it ain't my thing, don't mean it's wrong. What the fuck do I care if you boys like looking at dick? You do you, bro."

King hauled off and backhanded Maverick across the face. A sharp cry was ripped from Stephanie the moment her partner's hand met Maverick's cheek. Maverick's head whipped to the side so fast she'd have thought she was watching a movie on fast forward. He spat blood onto the floor then turned and gave King a bloody grin. "Go ahead. Take it out, man. I can look at it all you want if it helps you."

King's breathing snorted in and out like an angry bull. He glanced at Shark, who nodded, then turned back to Maverick and gave him the most chilling smile imaginable. "Don't go anywhere," he said. "Be right back."

Maverick assumed an unaffected expression as King walked out of the room, but Stephanie's stomach bottomed out. Something awful was about to happen.

It felt as though she'd just been tossed straight from a screaming-hot frying pan.

Directly into the fire.

CHAPTER FOUR

The moment the creepy fucker, King, released Stephanie, the pressure in Maverick's chest eased. He'd never sit around and passively watch any woman be harmed but, Christ, when King's hand curled around her creamy thigh. Maverick nearly lost his shit. It was probably a good thing he was restrained, or he'd have shoved that very hand straight up King's own ass.

Stephanie's petrified blue gaze met his once again, and he flashed her his customary grin and a wink. But it wasn't fooling her. She knew as well as he did that their situation might have just gone from shit to shinola. Difference was, the pain train would be speeding down the track toward him instead of Steph.

So, mission accomplished.

Mav could handle pain. He'd been handling it since he was six years old and his old man came home piss-drunk and beat the crap out of him for spilling water on his bed. That was the first of many beatings from his sperm donor. Shit only deteriorated when the old guy croaked and Mav was shipped off to foster care. That wasn't even the lowest point in Mav's life. Not the first time he'd stared down death either. This time, though, he was hoping for a rescue not an ending.

So, pain was fine. But watching Stephanie get raped was not.

They didn't have to wait long to discover his fate. King returned just seconds after leaving, a smirk on his face and a smoldering clothes iron in his hand.

Well, fuck.

Looked like the pain was going to be pretty fucking spectacular.

"What—" Stephanie began only to be cut off by Shark.

"You know anything about the Hell's Handlers MC, Stephanie?" Shark asked.

Her gaze cut to Mav as though looking for permission to answer, and he gave her the most reassuring smile he could muster. He had an idea where this was going and what it was going to cost him.

And he'd take it. He'd fucking take anything these bastards dished out to keep them off Stephanie.

No matter how loud he'd scream on the inside.

"N-no," Stephanie said, her terrified gaze shifting between the three men in the room. He wasn't sure he believed her, but that was the least of his severe worries.

"Well, you see, these assholes have a special ritual when they patch into the club. They get a brand on their left forearm. It's a big fuckin' deal to them. They have to endure the pain without crying like a little bitch, without passing out or puking. Ain't that right, Mav?"

Maverick didn't bother to answer.

"That brand is sacred. They can't have any ink on the part of their arm if they want the brand. And if they can't get the brand, they can't be in the club. So it's a big fuckin' deal. What would they do to you if something happened to the brand, Maverick? Oh say, you lost your arm or something?"

Hatred like he'd never experienced burned inside him, but he kept his mouth shut. The club would kick him out. Harsh, but it was the rule. Brand had to be there to be in the fuckin' club.

"Don't know?" Shark pushed off the wall and shrugged. "Guess we'll find out. King." He nodded at King who couldn't possibly look more eager to inflict some pain.

"Oh, my God. Don't!" Stephanie cried out.

Shark and King ignored her and advanced on Maverick.

When they reached him, Shark withdrew a knife from a sheath on his belt and cut the ties around Maverick's left arm.

Maverick tried to strike out, but the arm had been immobilized for so long it was useless. He wasn't able to do anything but sit there helpless as they flipped his forearm up and re-secured it to the chair.

Then Shark backed away, grinning like a loon, and King advanced on Maverick, iron in hand.

Stephanie went crazy. There was no other way to describe it. She thrashed, kicked, and screamed until her voice cracked. Shouting insults that shocked and impressed even Maverick, she fought against the cuffs until Maverick was worried she'd break her wrist.

He'd been right to call her wildcat.

"Stephanie," he barked out, ignoring the men about to torture him.

"No," she screamed. "Leave him alone. Come back over here. Take me. You can do anything you want. Just leave him alone!"

Jesus Christ, was the woman insane? She was practically begging two sadistic men to attack her. For what purpose? To save Maverick some pain?

The pain would be temporary. Pain faded.

As though transfixed, Maverick watched the hot iron slowly lower toward his arm. King took great pleasure in drawing out the anticipation. Just part of the torture.

"Maverick!" Stephanie screamed.

He tore his gaze away from his fate and stared into her pretty eyes. She held his gaze, still screaming at the top of her lungs and fighting for all she was worth. Bloody red rings formed around her wrists and ankles, and her left hand hung at an odd angle, but she didn't lessen her struggles. At that moment, she was a warrior, and Maverick would never ever forget the way she looked fighting for him.

His wildcat.

When the pain came, it was like nothing he'd ever

experienced. Time had weakened the harsh memories of the branding ceremony until it was nothing more than a story told to make him look badass. But, holy shit, the memories came back to him tenfold.

Fiery pain so severe his vision blurred crawled over his entire body. He was powerless to stop the shaking as shock set in and his body went haywire. Even though each breath was more agony, Maverick's chest rose and fell in a rapid rhythm. He gritted his back teeth to hold in the animal scream clawing at his throat.

Nausea rolled through his stomach, and he fought the urge to vomit. Puking would only be murder on his ribs. He kept his attention on Stephanie who was still yelling and wrenching her body against the metal cuffs. He couldn't hear what she was saying over the ringing in his ears, but her gaze never wavered. Never left his.

After a few moments of such outrageous pain, his mind started to numb. Some kind of protective mechanism. The anguish faded into the background and Stephanie took the forefront. Her beautiful face streaked with tears, mouth moving a mile a minute as she begged Shark and King to turn their attention to her.

As suddenly as it was shoved against his arm, the iron was ripped away, taking with it chunks of charred skin. The fog in Maverick's mind cleared, sharpening the pain and making him aware of the room again.

Stephanie had stopped writhing and lie quietly, tears streaming down her face. Her poor wrists and ankles were bloodied and so raw they looked like uncooked meat.

"Let's see if your bike-riding buddies want you back now," Shark said as he laughed. His phone rang, and he spun away to answer it. "King," he said after hanging up, "we gotta roll."

King nodded and tossed the iron at Maverick's feet. "What? No smartass comments about my dick now?" He threw back his head and laughed like he was watching a hilarious comedy special. "Didn't think so."

With that parting shot, he was gone.

Maverick looked at Stephanie. The skin on his arm screamed with a pain so all-consuming it was challenging to get his brain in gear and think of something pithy to say.

"Mav—" she started, but the words were lost in a sob.

"Shh, 'sokay, wildcat." Shit. Those were some severely slurred words. He rolled his head across his shoulders, trying in vain to breathe through the pain. It was just too damn intense.

Under Stephanie's watchful eye, he closed his eyes, counted to five, then looked at his left arm.

Shit. Fuck. Damn.

There was nothing there. Nothing but singed, over-cooked flesh where his beloved brand had been. His heart squeezed with pain almost worse than the touch of the iron. He'd been so damn proud the day he earned that brand, and never once had he taken for granted the brotherhood, the family he gained when he patched in. He'd die for any one of his brothers. They'd saved him from himself.

And now he might be out. All because fuckin' Shark got greedy and wanted to take over the Hell's Handlers territory.

"If your brothers are as much of a family as you say they are, they'll never kick you out over this, Maverick. It was completely out of your control. You saved me from..." Her voice hitched, like she couldn't bear to say the word. "I'm so sorry."

He couldn't think about it right now. About possibly losing the one thing in his life that he gave a damn about. "Tell me a story, wildcat," he said as a wave of dizziness hit him.

"A s-story?"

"Yeah, babe. Make it a good one. Tell me about when you lost your virginity."

She huffed out a shaky laugh. "Thought you said you wanted a good story."

"Oh, I bet it will be good. How old were you?"

"Fifteen."

"Shit, wildcat, that's young."

"Yeah well, it was just the once, then not again until I was twenty, so that might tell you how wonderful the experience was. Can't I just tell you the punchline? How my cop father caught us?"

Her old man was a cop? Would the man come looking for her? Probably wouldn't like a one-percenter sniffing after his baby girl.

Maverick let his eyes close as he laughed. "Fuck, that hurts. And no, I'm gonna need the whole story."

Stephanie was quiet for a long moment, then she broke out into a lengthy story about how she'd boned a junior on the wrestling team in the back seat of her pop's car only to have her in-uniform father knock on the window five thrusts in.

He had no idea if the story was real or if she'd made up some bullshit to pacify him. Didn't matter.

All that mattered as the pain grew too extreme and the darkness came for him was Stephanie's soothing voice guiding him to oblivion.

CHAPTER FIVE

"Maverick? Mav?" When it became clear he'd passed out, Stephanie lowered her head to the table and blew out a breath. The movement made the hard metal rings of the cuffs rub against her raw wounds, ripping a gasp from her.

God! What they'd done to him. His arm looked like something straight off the set of the *Walking Dead*. The pain he'd endured, she couldn't begin to fathom. And all because he ran his mouth to save her from being violated. The relief she felt when King left without really touching her was staggering. But it was muted by the overwhelming guilt over Maverick's suffering.

Without so much as a grunt of pain, he'd locked eyes with her and rode it out as though the iron was nothing more than a fly landing on his arm.

It had to be excruciating beyond what she could comprehend.

He was brave.

And selfless.

And honorable.

And a criminal.

That last element was becoming murky in her mind, and that wasn't acceptable. Just because he didn't want to watch her be raped didn't mean he was a good man. Didn't mean she wouldn't have to arrest him when this was all over. Once the FBI got involved, the Handlers would be on their radar even if they hadn't been before.

Yet, still, she'd screamed and begged King to return his attention to her. She'd meant it, too. She'd have endured the horrors to keep Maverick from being burned so brutally.

The guy needed a hospital and soon. Infection would set in fast given the raw, exposed flesh on his arm and the conditions around them. Being in a dank, dirty basement had to be the wort thing for him. Part of her was tempted to wake him. Check on him and make sure he wasn't feeling feverish. Or maybe the best thing for him would be to remain passed out until his MC came for him.

She really hoped they'd hurry up and get to rescuing them. At least Maverick. At some point, her contact at the FBI would become concerned she'd missed yesterday's check-in and send the cavalry looking for her as well.

But would it all be too late?

Fatigue pressed down on her like a lead blanket and, within seconds, she lost the battle to keep her eyes open. Sleep was a welcome reprieve from the pain. It seemed as though every cell in her body was shrieking in agony. Both ankles and wrists were sliced to ribbons, and she was pretty sure she'd broken her left wrist flailing like a madwoman in her attempt to help Maverick. Bumps and bruises were popping up in various places, again from the vigorous trashing against the table. Not to mention she was freezing.

But it was nothing compared to what Maverick had endured, so she closed her eyes, tried to block out the discomfort, and let sleep take her.

Hopefully, she wouldn't wake to even greater horrors.

IT WAS PROBABLY time to be concerned.

Mav had no idea how much time had passed since King tried to permanently remove any wrinkles from his arm, but it had to be a good few hours.

He'd woken up awash in his own sweat, alternately freezing and sweating his ass off. The skin around the edges of the burn was angry, red, and weeping mustard-colored fluid. The bacteria weren't wasting any time waging war against him.

Stephanie hadn't stirred since Mav woke up a few moments ago. Her sleep wasn't restful but full of whimpers and twitching. Her left wrist was fucked up in some way. It dangled off the table at an unnatural angle and had swelled so big it filled the extra space around the cuff.

Shit.

What kind of woman fought so hard to keep a man she didn't know from pain that she broke her own wrist?

A pretty fucking amazing one.

Panicked shouts came from the hallway, and Maverick tensed. There was only one reason for Shark or his men to be freaking the fuck out.

His brothers came through.

"Stephanie," he called. A slight twitch and fluttering of eyelids came from her before she settled. "Stephanie!"

She jerked and mumbled something but still didn't wake.

"Hey, wildcat! Wake up, babe. Cavalry's here."

"Huh? What?" Stephanie shot up only to be slammed back to the table when the chains of the cuffs reached their limit. "Oh, shit, ow, fuck." She panted against the table, tears pooling in her eyes.

With a grimace, Maverick said, "Sorry, babe. You okay?"

"Y-yeah. I'm g-good. I'm good. Wow, that hurt. Okay, what do I do?"

The door flung open before he had a chance to answer, and a tornado formally known as Shark flew into the room. For the first time, the man looked like he wasn't entirely in control.

Eyes wide and insane, hair disheveled, hands trembling slightly, the man was frazzled and terrified.

That's right, motherfucker. My boys are here for you.

"Looks like your time's up, Sharky boy."

"Shut the fuck up." He looked between Maverick and Stephanie a few times before heading to the table.

"Leave her the fuck alone, asshole. They're here for me. I'm your only ticket out of here alive now."

"I told you to shut the fuck up." Shark grabbed Stephanie's head between his meaty palms, lifted her head, and said, "Lights out, princess."

"No—"

He slammed her head back onto the table, and Stephanie's body went limp. When Shark released her head, it lolled to the side.

Out cold.

Jesus. He prayed she was only unconscious. Given their size differences, Shark could have killed her. And Mav couldn't do a damned thing about it. His brain wanted to rush to her and make sure she was breathing, but his body was helpless.

"Let's go, Maverick. I've got some bikers to kill." With practiced ease, Shark cut away Maverick's bindings and hauled him to his feet. The pain of standing on unused legs had his knees collapsing. "Get the fuck up and walk." Shark yanked him toward the door, and just before Mav left the room, he caught a slight rise of Steph's chest.

Thank fuck.

Shark shoved him toward a long, dark staircase much faster than his legs were willing to go. He nearly fell twice but managed to remain upright.

Part of Maverick wanted to fight even though he didn't stand a chance at taking Shark out. But he trusted his brothers. Trusted they'd rescue both him and Stephanie. So he hobbled along in front of Shark like a good little prisoner.

Climbing the stairs took almost every ounce of energy Maverick had left. When he staggered and almost faceplanted at the top of the steps, Shark dragged him toward the cabin's front door.

"Don't fucking move," Shark said. He disappeared through the door, and Mav leaned against the wall, trying to keep the world in focus. He could hear Shark talking and could have sworn he heard his best friend Zach answer with some kind of smart-ass remark.

"You mean this friend?" Shark asked as his hand reached through the door and grabbed Mav's upper arm. Shark yanked him through the door and out into the night. The clearing in front of the house was lit up like a fucking stadium, revealing a smattering of his brothers all with weapons pointed at him and Shark.

Damn, it was good to see them. Deep concern marked each of their expressions. Mav must look like an even bigger pile of shit than he'd thought. Shark shoved Maverick in front of him shield-style and held the same knife he'd used to cut him free against his throat.

"I'm thinking you wasted your time coming here, bikers. I've had a shitty week, and Maverick here has been great. He let me work all my frustrations out on him." Shark laughed, a full body laugh that jerked Maverick around. "I'm not ready to give him up."

His head felt too heavy for his body, and it flopped to the side as he sagged a bit in Shark's hold. The knife bit into the skin of his neck, no doubt drawing blood. Shit. Much more of that and he'd be the reason his own throat was slit. He clenched the muscles in his thighs and locked his knees out so he wouldn't fall.

"Enough bullshit," Zach said as he walked forward. "You don't fucking need him, and we aren't leaving without him. Why not hand him over before we shoot you in the face and burn your palace to the ground, princess?"

Shark, being the crazy motherfucker he was, just laughed. "The interrupter. You know, I still didn't get to finish what I was saying. Hey, Mav? You think I like being interrupted?"

He shook Maverick, and fuck if it didn't feel like his insides were rattling around inside his body. What he wouldn't fucking give to put a bullet in the overgrown fish's brain. The knife pressed into his carotid again, way too close for comfort.

"Just get on with whatever the fuck it is you want to say so bad," Zach yelled.

Even though he couldn't see it, he could almost feel the spine-chilling grin curl Shark's lips. "I couldn't fathom how I lost the bet. How did a bunch of idiots find me out here off the grid? Then I got my answer. And I feel better knowing that you are all, in fact, a bunch of stupid fucks."

"What's the answer then?" Zach looked like a caged animal ready to strike the second his handler flicked the lock.

"It's coming."

Two seconds later, King walked out of the woods dragging Zach's woman kicking and screaming with a gun to her head.

Maverick's gaze cut immediately to Zach, who looked both devastated and enraged. He knew his friend well, and Zach was about three seconds from covering the clearing in Shark's blood.

Words were exchanged between Zach, his woman, Toni, and Shark that let him know he'd missed quite a bit in the time he'd been a captive. Apparently, Toni and Shark had a past Maverick was in the dark about.

His arm hurt so bad, following the conversation became difficult. Remaining awake became difficult. He allowed himself to zone out and trusted his brothers to take care of the situation.

That is until Shark offered to trade him for Toni. That woke him up like a bucket of ice water to the face.

"I'll do it!" Toni screamed after Shark threatened to have his guys shoot Maverick on the spot.

Zach lost his shit. He screamed, cursed Shark, and started to charge, consequences be damned. Thankfully, Rocket caught hold of him with a restraining arm across his chest.

King released Toni, and she started forward. When she reached Zach, he made a grab for her, but she darted away from his hold, her expression apologetic.

What the hell was with the women in his life today? Two for two on self-sacrificing. He must have been pretty kind to women in a previous life to have two in one day offer themselves to

Shark in exchange for his safety. Clearly he'd missed something while he'd been a guest at Hotel Shit-show. There must have been some connection between Zach's woman and Shark. Why the hell else would Shark be willing to trade Mav for her? Hopefully he'd live long enough to hear the tale.

It didn't take more than a few seconds for Toni to reach them and stand behind Shark, as requested. Her eyes held a mix of fear and determination, and Maverick tried to shoot her his customary flirty smirk, but it came out as more of a grimace.

So much for reassuring her.

He shouldn't have even tried.

With his arm hanging on by a thread and his breaths getting shallower by the second, he wouldn't fool a toddler into thinking he was loving life.

"Here's how this is going to go," Shark said to the group of bikers. "Mav will walk toward you, and Antonia will come out from behind me and take his place. You shoot my guys on the roof, and I'll slit her throat. We'll stand here until you're gone. If you don't leave, she's dead."

The sound that came from Zach was a strangled choke. Mav knew how he felt. Well, not entirely. He'd never been gone over a woman the way Zach seemed to be over Toni, but he understood his feeling of impotence. The extreme frustration of watching this race car barrel toward the edge of a cliff and be helpless to do a damn thing.

Infuriating didn't begin to describe it.

Please let Stephanie be okay.

"Hope you can stay on your feet," Shark said as he removed the knife from Mav's neck and released his hold on Mav's body. Instantly, his legs Jello-ed and threatened to collapse. Just a few minutes, a short walk across the clearing, and then he'd be with his brothers and could let his body give out.

"Walk straight. No funny shit or she dies."

By sheer will and stubbornness, he advanced one foot, then had to stop and suck in a few agonizing breaths. He was done, spent. There wasn't anything left in his body to give. But behind him, Toni's life depended on him making it to Zach. And back in the basement from hell, Stephanie was counting on him to survive long enough to send someone for her.

That's what did it. Thoughts of Stephanie: her bravery, her compassion, her unselfish attempts to spare him. The tight body and sweet face helped, too. She was someone he wanted to get to know, and that wouldn't happen if he gave up right then.

His wildcat.

So, he manned up more than he ever thought possible and took another step. Pain shot from his foot up through his trunk and seemed to settle in his ribs.

Do it, Maverick.

Another step that shouldn't have been possible.

The sound of a gunshot that couldn't have been more than five feet away had his body jerking with a painful clench of his muscles. For a second, he froze.

Was he hit?

The pain in his arm was so severe it was impossible to tell if there was a new injury, but he didn't seem to be losing blood.

Shark made a sound like a dying animal, and then the world went crazy. A strong arm snagged Mav around the shoulders and swung him against the building. He didn't hit hard, but his body was so battered any touch sent shockwaves of misery through him. "I got you, brother."

Rocket's voice.

Maverick sagged at the realization his brother had him. Dizziness swamped him, and his legs gave up the fight to keep him standing. Gunshots sounded around him along with the sound of boots pounding on the ground and a few pain-filled yells.

"Don't worry, I got you. You can relax now. We'll get you straight to a hospital, Mav," Rocket said.

Safe for the first time in days, it was as though Maverick's mind and body just up and quit. The world wavered, and his eyes rolled back as he seemed to lose control over his muscles.

"Stephanie," he whispered as the last vestiges of his mind clung to consciousness.

"Shh, don't try to talk brother. You look like complete shit."

He grunted and tried once more, "Stephan—" The words died in his throat as everything faded to black.

CHAPTER SIX

How much isolation, immobility, and discomfort could a person withstand before insanity set in? The question had been circulating in and out of Stephanie's head ever since she woke up alone in the quiet basement…some time ago.

Last thing she remembered was Mav's fervent shout waking her from a nightmare-plagued sleep and informing her help had arrived. Then, before she'd even had time to process the news, Shark made his grand entrance and so lovingly bashed her skull against the metal table. It was lights out once again.

Now, she was in the dark both literally and figuratively.

How much time had passed?

Where the hell was Maverick?

Where was Shark, for that matter, or any of his goons?

The basement was so silent, the sound of her own breathing was thunderous. She'd been awake for what felt like hours but could have reasonably been only thirty minutes. Time crawled forward like a sloth when there wasn't anything to do but stare into the darkness and be tortured by her own thoughts.

The back of her head ached and a tender goose egg the size of, well, a goose egg had erupted smack in the center of the base of her head. Every time she stared straight up at the ceiling, pain lanced through her scalp. She was stuck keeping her head pivoted to the side.

Was this it? Would she die, cuffed to a table, left to wither away and starve? Didn't sound like the most pleasant way to go. Insanity was sure to kick in before she perished from lack of food.

No. Mav promised his MC would rescue them both.

Making promises in the heat of the moment was easy when desperation and hope warred for the dominant emotion. But when all was said and done and Maverick was safe with his brothers, would his assurances hold up?

Probably not.

The man was an outlaw for crying out loud, something she seemed to keep forgetting. For all she knew, King ratted her FBI status to Mav…if he was even still alive. Jesus, maybe his MC hadn't even been here.

Steph took a breath. Somehow, she needed to keep from panicking.

With nothing else to do, Stephanie closed her eyes and concentrated on taking deep, even, timed breaths, something she'd learned in the three Yoga classes she'd taken last year. Maybe, if she made it out alive, she'd finally get serious about working out.

Apparently, she'd mastered the relaxation technique well because, within minutes, the strong pull of slumber lured her mind away from the basement. It was either that or the knock to the head caused a severe concussion and brain injury.

"Shit. That ain't a girl. That's a woman. All woman."

Shocked out of her nap, Stephanie's brain was thankfully alert enough to feign sleep. Friend or foe was a mystery when it came to the deep and rich male voice hovering just a few feet away.

There wasn't a response, but Stephanie had the impression whoever Low-voice was talking to had just glared at him.

"What?" Low-voice answered. "Copper said Mav asked if we'd found a girl named Stephanie. I thought we'd be coming here and finding some strung out teenager like Toni was back in the day."

"You might wanna keep your fucking mouth shut when it

comes to our Enforcer's woman, Screw," the second man said. His voice was just as deep, but darker, almost like he was in pain. "Unless, of course, you're looking for a baseball bat to the head."

At the mention of Maverick's name in conjunction with her own, Stephanie relaxed a fraction. They referred to Maverick as though they knew him. Could these be men from his MC? Could he have sent them back for her?

Only one way to find out.

With a quick prayer she wasn't making the wrong choice, Stephanie opened her eyes and blinked against the harsh flashlight shining directly in her face. Unable to lift a hand to block it, she rotated her head then gasped when the knot on her skull rolled across the table.

"Look, Jig, the chick's awake," the one called Screw said. Screw? What kind of a name was Screw? It sure didn't inspire much confidence in his abilities.

"C-can you shine that somewhere else?" Barely recognizing the dry rasp of her own voice, Stephanie squinted and tried to make out the faces looming above her. What were the chances they'd brought some water? Maybe a Motrin or two?

"Sorry, sweetheart," Screw said, redirecting the light so it shone down toward her feet. "You Stephanie?" Even through the dark, she could make out how handsome his young, clean-shaven face appeared.

She nodded and winced as the tender spot on her head was dragged across the table. "Is Maverick okay? They were..." Biting her lower lip, she shook her head. The memories were hideous, though nothing compared to having the actual memory of the pain like Maverick would have. But still...the smell of burning flesh, the hiss of pain, the agony in Maverick's eyes. Stephanie shuddered and squeezed her eyes shut to hold back tears. "They were brutal to him."

The man on her left stared down at her through dark, lifeless eyes as though studying a bug. He was an impressive hulk of a man. Impressive, but frightening. Yet for some reason, she instinctively knew he'd bring her no harm. He'd been through hell if the mess of crisscrossed scars on his left cheek were any indication. This man knew terror, knew pain, knew devastation.

His jaw ticked once before he spoke. "He's at the hospital. Flirting with every double X chromosome in a mile radius. And talking about nothing but us hauling our assess back here and rescuing the sexy wildcat tied to a table in the basement."

Sexy wildcat. Stephanie snorted out a grunt of forced laughter, and then her face burned hotter than the sun. Somehow in all this, she'd forgotten she was clad in nothing but some panties and a T-shirt. And the panties were wet and stunk of urine despite her earlier ice bath. Wasn't a damn thing sexy about that.

"Sorry about the smell," she whispered.

"Ain't a thing," Screw said as he dug in the front pocket of his black denim pants. He held up a small silver key. "Here we go. What do you say we get you free of this place and over to the hospital?"

The hospital was the last place she wanted to go. What she needed was a way to contact her boss at the FBI. The guy had to be minutes away from sending in the SWAT team. That couldn't happen. It would blow the entire investigation out of the water.

"I don't think I need a hospital, but I'd really appreciate it if you could unlatch me and drive me to my hotel."

The two men shared a look, then Screw shrugged. "Whatever the lady wants." He started with her feet and had her ankles released in seconds. As he moved toward her hands, she flexed and pointed her toes then bent her knees drawing her legs to her chest one at a time. Pain shot through the stiff joints, making her bite her lip to keep from crying out. After only a few stretches, the worst of the pain dissipated.

Okay, that wasn't so bad. Uncomfortable, but tolerable.

"Alrighty, ma'am," Screw said, releasing her fourth limb from its metal cage. He was gentle, careful not to jostle her abused hands. "Yikes, that left wrist ain't looking too good there, Steph.

The fuck you do to yourself?"

Free at last, Stephanie tried to lift her arms out of the unnatural overhead position and return them to her sides. Nothing happened. The muscles just wouldn't obey.

"We got you," Jig said, cueing in on the problem without her uttering a word. The men shared another silent eye communication then moved into action. Each slid a very large hand under her shoulders and another under her elbows. "On three. One, two—"

They moved before she even thought about saying three. With much more care than she thought these big men could ever employ, they rotated her shoulders and brought her arms to her sides. Fiery pain burned through the ball joints of her shoulder, so fierce she couldn't stem the shocked cry this time.

"Ahh, shit. Fuck." She panted and went to bite her lower lip until she made the mistake of grazing the cut with her teeth.

This sucked.

Her left wrist throbbed like the heavy beat of a bass drum making her stomach tumble and roll. Good thing she hadn't eaten in days. Vomiting all over these men would be one humiliation too many.

"Shit," she bit out as sweat dotted her forehead and the room spun. "Give me a minute." She closed her eyes and huffed through the worst of the pain. The men stayed with her, massaging her shoulders and upper arms until her breathing regulated. When she opened her eyes, two kind and concerned men gazed down at her.

Who the hell were these guys? They were criminals, outlaws. For all intents and purposes, at least in the eyes of law enforcement, they were the same as Shark. Gang members who'd be investigated and hopefully tried for their crimes. Brought to justice to prevent innocents from being harmed. Prevent the unsuspecting public from enduring a fate similar to hers.

But these two had been beyond caring. Hell, so had Maverick.

He didn't owe her a damn thing, yet he'd comforted her, made promises, and fulfilled them.

"Shark?" she asked after she was able to speak again.

"Not a problem anymore."

Shit. He'd basically just admitted to a federal agent that he, or his club at least, killed a man. She now had first-hand knowledge of a murder. It would have to be reported. Action would be taken. Didn't matter how much Shark deserved it. Didn't matter that these men had protected others from Shark's evil. Vigilante justice, outlaw justice, wasn't condoned. It wasn't legal.

And there were reasons for that. Good reasons. Society would crumble if every Tom, Dick, or Harry were out there enforcing the code of the Wild West.

"Ready to sit up, sweetheart?" Jig asked.

"God, yes. More than ready. And if we could burn this table before we leave, that would be great." She chuckled at her own weak joke, but the men shared another of those severe looks.

What the hell was that one about?

"I'm going to lift you. You ready?"

Stephanie nodded. Jig's long and thick arm worked its way under her shoulders. She tried to help as best as she could by lifting her upper body, but it was a mostly useless attempt. "Just relax, sweetheart, I got you." Weakness wasn't something Stephanie was used to, but at that moment, she was more than happy to let him do the work.

Once he had a solid hold on her trunk, Jig hooked a hand behind her knees and scooped her to a sitting position in a quick swoop.

"Oh, shit!" she cried as the floor and the ceiling switched positions over and over again. The dots of sweat became rivers, and her stomach lurched. She clutched at Jig's arms then cried out again as intense pain shot through her wrists. The left one fell limply to her side, unable to even grasp the man's shirt.

"Fuck, she's gonna pass out. Screw, help me lower her again.

When's the last time you ate or drank something, sweetheart?"

"Sss been few daysss." Her tongue felt like it grew three times in size, and the room spun more than the one and only time she'd binged on tequila shots.

"Stay with us, Stephanie." Screw's voice was right next to her ear, and his hands landed on her back.

One of the men gathered her into their arms and headed for the exit. With her swirling head, she had the sensation of flying through the air. After exiting the building, the men walked her through a clearing.

At one point, a loud whoosh and a flash of heat had her looking back at the house. Colossal orange flames shot from the roof toward the starry sky.

Holy crap. She'd been kidding when she suggested burning the table. But the Hell's Handlers weren't messing around. There were multiple benefits to torching the place.

Revenge.

Eliminating all the evidence.

And sending a message to anyone who fucked with them.

They'd fuck back. Harder and stronger.

Stephanie shivered despite the heat wafting from the burning house.

An intense wave of dizziness washed through her once again, this time blurring her vision. She fought, tried to stay awake, but the pull to nothingness was too strong.

Gray danced around the edges of her vision. A little nap was all she needed. When she woke, she'd feel so much better.

And hopefully, the gray would leave her vision. Because there was no room for gray. It was nothing but an excuse for traveling down the wrong road.

CHAPTER SEVEN

"Excuse me," Stephanie said to the sternest, most pinched-faced nurse to ever exist. Three hours had passed since she'd been brought in, according to the nurse, and she was finally settled in a room.

Now she needed a phone. Pronto.

"What?" It was like she'd had Botox gone wrong, and the doctor had frozen the wrong muscles, immobilizing her frown. She hadn't shown a single expression beyond a sourpuss all morning.

So much for bedside manner. This woman was as fuzzy and comforting as a porcupine.

"I'm sorry, is there a way I can make a phone call? My cell was taken when I was abducted and held for two days." Stephanie sent her a sweet smile. Maybe it was a bit passive aggressive to play on her recent experience, but come on, something had to crack nurse Beverly's frigid exterior.

But sob stories about being held hostage, injured, and nearly raped apparently weren't hot enough to melt her ice. "Next to the bed. Local's free. Long distance is billed to you. Nine first." Even her flat tone conveyed dissatisfaction with life. She left, closing the door just shy of a slam.

Stephanie stared at the phone waiting on a bedside table.

On her left side, of course.

She'd cracked the end of her left radius, and the arm was in a removable splint, mummy wrapped, and elevated on a pile of pillows. The ER doc hadn't wanted to cast it because they needed access to the deep gouges and open wounds struggling against the handcuffs had caused. Once the lacerations healed, a fiberglass cast would be put on the wrist for a few months.

Goodie. She couldn't wait.

There was no way in hell she was going to call Nurse Crotchety back in to ask for a favor so, with a resigned sigh, Stephanie contorted her upper body, stretched her right arm, and reached for the phone. Her back and shoulders protested with sharp aches and pains, but she managed to grip the corded phone and lift it into the bed. Thankfully, no one was around to hear the grunts and groans the simple task wrung from her.

By the time she had the phone in the bed with her, she was sore, tired, and panting like she'd just gone a few rounds with a sexy man. Ha, that was a funny joke. It had been two years since she'd even been in the vicinity of a partially undressed man. And that was only because her friend dragged her to the beach.

When this was over, she needed to find a man.

Maverick's face popped up in her mind, and she nearly laughed. An outlaw biker with more ink than a Bic factory, enough metal to be a lightning rod, and a panty-dropping smile was so far from what she needed. Even if he'd probably give it to her better than she'd ever had it. It was a non-issue anyway. She was short and skinny with an unimpressive rack. Not exactly the va-va-voom men typically hungered for.

Jesus, she was losing her mind. "Get yourself together, girl," she mumbled as she dialed the well-memorized number to her superior.

Stephanie's boss answered on the second ring. "Baccarella," he barked into his end.

After clearing her throat, Stephanie said, "Sir, it's Agent Little."

"Jesus fucking Christ!" Baccarella's voice exploded through the phone. "What the fuck happened? Where the fuck are you?

Where the fuck is Agent Rey? You both missed check-in. Fuck! I've got the Knoxville SWAT team mobilizing as we speak. Shit! Fuck! The whole fucking Bureau is flipping their shit. We thought you were both dead."

Stephanie gave him a moment to rant and rave. Special Agent in Charge Gordon Baccarella was well known for his impressive verbal tirades during times of high stress. He had an infamous flash-fire temper. It ignited in an instant, burned hot and intense, but died out just as fast.

"Agent Little?" he asked, already calming from the initial shock of hearing her voice on the line.

"I'm here, sir. I'm in a hospital in Townsend, but I'm okay. Minor injuries. Broken wrist, mild concussion, and dehydration are the worst of it." She blew out a breath. "It all went to shit, sir. I was abducted and held by Shark for two days."

"Fuck me sideways. And Agent Rey?"

Daniel Rey. King. Benedict Arnold himself. Murdering, traitorous, raping bastard. "I don't have confirmation yet, sir, but I believe he was killed during the rescue of another individual who was held with me."

"Mother of all living fucks." Something crashed in the background, and Stephanie winced. Baccarella's office was already taking a beating, and she wasn't even finished dishing up the shit pie.

"Um, sir…" She couldn't get the words past her tongue.

"What, Little? Just spit it the fuck out. Give me everything."

He asked for it. "Rey flipped. He was dirty. Working for Shark. I have no idea for how long. I also don't know what he told the gang or if any of the information he passed along to us was tainted. He'd been leading me to believe the Dragons were moving away from the sex trade, but now I have to question all that."

Silence greeted her for long seconds, and she imagined Baccarella muting his end of the phone so he could scream every profanity known to man while tearing his office to pieces.

Wouldn't be the first time. The man's secretary was a wizard when it came to replacing destroyed items before he even missed them.

"You sure about this? Be very, very sure, Little. You're confident he didn't just play his role well? I know you think it's bullshit, but undercover agents have to commit unsavory acts to maintain cover every day. It's the only way they survive sometimes."

"Positive, sir. He whispered it in my ear. There isn't a doubt in my mind he was as dirty as mud. He begged Shark to be allowed to kill me. Fought him when Shark wanted to keep me alive. Would have raped me if it weren't for..." She coughed to cover a near sob. "He almost raped me."

"Were you compromised?"

"I don't believe so, sir. There's been nothing to indicate anyone knows my identity."

"Okay," he said, and she could almost hear the gears cranking in his mind. The blaze was dwindling enough to allow him to process and formulate a plan. "I'm sending someone down to bring you back. You'll be debriefed once you arrive here in DC."

Even though he couldn't see her, she nodded. "No rush. I'm going to be in the hospital for a few days. And whoever you send, give them a cover."

"Why?"

"I was rescued by members of the Hell's Handlers MC. They all just think my kidnapping was a case of wrong place, wrong time. Told them I had a fight with my friend, went hiking, and got lost. Had the unfortunate luck of wandering into Shark's path."

His grunt almost sounded like one of approval. Like he was impressed by her quick thinking and maintenance of cover. "Maybe you should think about going undercover. You think fast. All right. Agent Smith will be down there in four days. Tell them she's your cousin from Nebraska. Your douchebag of a friend was with you in Tennessee and returned home when you didn't come back from your hike, thinking you ditched her. Got it?"

Shouts from the hallway distracted her from the call.

"Little?" he barked.

"What? Oh, yes, sorry, sir. Agent Smith. Cousin. Worthless friend. Got it."

"And, Little, as you know, we've looked into the Hell's Handlers, and while we chose to focus our investigation on the Gray Dragons, these guys are no choir boys. Watch your six. You'll be debriefed as soon as you return."

What the hell was going on in the hallway? Sounded like it was right outside her door. "Sir, I have to go. I'm about to have company."

When the line disconnected with a click, Stephanie held the phone in front of her face. "Thank you, sir, for the concern and wishes for a speedy recovery." Then she rolled her eyes and dropped the phone next to her on the bed. No way was she contorting herself to get the thing back on the table.

"Sir, you're a patient from a completely different ward. You cannot be down here at all, let alone in Miss Little's room." Nurse Beverly sounded ready to scratch someone's eyes out.

"Listen, lady, do I look like someone who gives much of a fuck about following the rules? Now I'm getting in that room to check on my woman, so I suggest you move before I move your cantankerous ass myself."

Maverick.

Her heart raced in her chest and butterflies fluttered in her stomach. What was that about? Had to just be anticipation over seeing him alive and well. They'd shared an intense, adrenaline-fueled experience. It made sense her body would react with nerves and anxiousness when about to be in his presence.

"Sir, if you take one step toward that room, I'm calling security, and I'll have to have you forcibly removed."

"Knock yourself out, babycakes," Maverick said to the nurse. Stephanie's hand flew to her mouth to cover the giggle that leaked out. "I'll be waiting for them right in there."

The door to her room swung open, and there he stood in all his inked glory. He wore a pair of dark blue sweatpants that looked soft and worn in. A plain black T-shirt molded to his trim but still muscular chest. Ink covered most of his skin, and while she'd love to examine it all day long, her eyes were drawn to the bulky bandages over his left forearm. She couldn't even imagine what lay under those bandages. He must be in a serious amount of pain. And yet, he'd broken hospital rules to pay her a visit.

"Hey, wildcat," he said, gifting her a megawatt smile that had the power to vanquish panties on sight.

"Your woman?" Stephanie asked, raising an eyebrow.

His smile turned impish, and he shrugged. "Told my nurse—who is way sweeter than yours by the way—that my woman was two floors down, and I couldn't eat or sleep until I checked on her. She practically threw me in the elevator herself."

Stephanie chuckled. She could see it. Maverick had charm pouring out his ears.

"How you holding up, gorgeous?" he asked as he hobbled his way into her room.

"Geez, Maverick! Are you crazy? Sit down. You can barely walk. You should be in bed."

"You offering up space in yours?" He winked and shuffled to the high-back chair next to her bed. Maybe she should scoot over and let him lie next to her. That chair looked about as comfortable as the metal table she'd been cuffed to.

"Sure," she said before she let herself second-guess the decision. She'd clearly lost her mind but would blame it on the massive dose of pain meds for now.

Mav's face lit up with surprise and pleasure, and if she wasn't mistaken, the darkening of his eyes had a lustful quality to them.

Couldn't be. Must have been some damn powerful pain meds to have her thinking like that.

CHAPTER EIGHT

If Maverick weren't so pumped up on pain pills and exhausted out of his mind, Stephanie's offer to share the bed would have had him popping a boner for sure. Actually, the prescription drug-induced high was a good thing. Miss Stephanie probably wouldn't appreciate a primed and ready-to-fuck biker sliding into bed with her. Not after she'd spent two days pants-less and under the terrifying threat of rape.

She was adorable. At least once he was able to look past the dark circles, fatigue lines, and bruises. After she healed and her face no longer bore marks of the utterly traumatized, she'd be gorgeous.

By the time he made the trip from his room to her bed, a journey that felt like three miles instead of the two floor trip, he could have collapsed and slept for the next week. Although the crushing rib pain that prevented him from taking a full breath might have made sleep difficult. At least he could finally set his mind at ease knowing Stephanie was away from danger.

He perched on the edge of her bed, intent on flopping next to her, but the intensity of the pain in his torso prevented him from doing much more than grunting.

"You okay?" Stephanie asked, concern lacing her voice.

"I've got a handful of broken ribs. Can't seem to move from this position."

"Here," she said as she pushed a button on the bedrail. The

head of the bed rose and rose until it was at a ninety-degree angle. "Try to lean against it now and see if you can lift your legs."

He did as she commanded and rested his back against the elevated bed. It took a monumental effort, but he managed to hoist his legs onto the bed. Once he was situated, Stephanie lowered the bed to about a forty-five-degree angle. He groaned as some of the pressure left his chest. Closing his eyes, he enjoyed the warmth of her body heat and the feel of her soft form nestled along his left side. Thank God someone had helped her wash up.

They stayed quiet for a few moments until Stephanie asked in a soft voice, "Maverick?"

"Yeah, babe?"

"Can I ask you something?"

He opened his eyes and peered into her worried gaze. It didn't take Jig's rocket scientist brain to guess where this conversation was heading. "What do you want to know?"

"What happened after I passed out. I mean, is Shark...will he?"

Ice hardened his veins as Maverick recalled how fearful Stephanie looked when Shark's men dragged her into the basement.

"They won't be doing anything. To anyone. Ever." He looked her straight in the eye as he spoke. Fatigue and pain shone back at him, slightly dulled by whatever magic cocktail they'd given her.

"Did you...?"

"Not me." He shouldn't give her any details. It was club business. And the most sensitive kind. If she decided to go to the cops, she'd have information that could take down his entire club. Something about her called to him, though. Told him to trust her.

And he didn't trust anyone outside his brothers.

"Look, Steph, what I have to say might seem counterintuitive, but you can't go to the authorities with anything that happened."

She stiffened against him. Rigid as a two-by-four.

"My club—" he began.

"Is safe," she interjected. "I won't say anything, Maverick. Your club saved me, and I'd never want you to have any repercussions because of that. I just need to know it's over. That I don't have to look over my shoulder or they won't have the chance to do that to someone else."

"Shh." He held a finger over her soft lips, and damned if his cock didn't twitch in approval. He wanted to replace that finger with his mouth. If only he could bend more than one inch without stabbing rib pain.

Lowering his voice to a whisper, he said, "Shark's dead. He was an evil motherfucker who did things to women that would make your skin crawl. We're stilling finding out shit about that man we didn't know. He will not hurt you or any other woman ever again. He's fucking dead, and his whole gang is going to follow."

Stephanie's eyes widened, and she swallowed hard. Her head moved in an up and down direction as he watched her process his words. "Okay," she finally whispered. "Th-thank you."

Her grateful gaze reminded him of how she looked at him when he goaded King away from her after he'd removed her pants. Then, when King turned his attention to Maverick, Stephanie had done the unthinkable.

The ice in his blood turned to a fiery rage as he recalled her fierce struggle against the handcuffs. She'd fought so hard she'd broken her wrist. And, Jesus, she'd practically begged King to return to her and finish the job, all to spare Maverick the torture of the iron.

With their gazes locked, some invisible yet powerful force passed between them. A connection, like they were now linked because of this experience. It made what she'd done, trying to save him, all the more significant. "What the fuck were you thinking?" he growled at her.

She flinched but held his stare and didn't bother to ask for clarification of the question that he'd posed from out of nowhere. "I couldn't." Her eyes squeezed shut, and she shook her head. "I didn't want him to...because of me." A strangled sob left her throat. "You stopped him from hurting me. But the cost to you..." A tear escaped her closed eyes. "God, Maverick. I'm so sorry for what he did to you. I just couldn't lie there and let him do it. I would have done anything to spare you that pain. I shouldn't say this, but a bullet was too easy for him. He deserved so much worse. All of those men did."

Her scrunched face and shaking head told him she was fighting against horrifying memories. Memories that would plague her, both of them, for a long fucking time. No one, until he met his brothers, had stood up for him, had sacrificed anything for him. His own junkie-whore of a mother wouldn't lift a finger to protect him from the johns who wanted more than just a piece of her used-up pussy. None of his foster parents or siblings spared a second glance when he had the shit beat out of him over and over again. No one so much as gave up a snack to make sure his belly didn't cramp with hunger. Not until he met Zach, who'd saved him from making the ultimate mistake.

Yet here was a woman who didn't know him from Adam, willing to withstand the worst torture imaginable for a female, and all to end his pain. Willing to sacrifice her body to save him.

He'd never met such a woman. Didn't know they existed. Because they never had in his world. Something stirred within him, but he shook his head and willed it away. Damn pain meds making him feel ridiculous emotions.

"Shit, wildcat," he said, lifting her chin with one finger. "Let me see those gorgeous eyes."

Her lashes lifted, revealing eyes swimming in tears. "You are fucking fierce," he whispered as he lowered his head. His chest screamed in pain, but in two seconds, when he finally tasted her mouth, it would all disappear.

Just as he was a breath away, the door flew open, and in marched the nasty piece of work who called herself a nurse.

"Sir!" She gasped at the sight of him in the bed as though she'd walked in on him fucking Stephanie six ways to Sunday.

If only he weren't in so much goddamned pain. He needed an orgasm about as much as he needed the drugs.

"I've called security. They'll be here in a minute. They will forcibly remove you if you do not exit that bed."

"Nurse," Stephanie began.

"Don't bother," he whispered in her ear. "Never met anyone who needed a good old-fashioned dicking more than that grump." He turned to the frowning nurse. "Look, my brothers will be by in a bit. I'm sure one of them would be willing to yank down your scrubs and toss you some dick in one of the empty rooms. What do you say? Might make you a little more pleasant to be around."

Stephanie's eyes widened comically, and she coughed while the nurse turned beet red and sputtered. With a huff, she turned on the heel of her white tennis shoe and stomped out of the room.

"That woman should not be allowed anywhere near someone who's hurting. Christ, I bet the only time she gets any action is when her finger breaks through the toilet paper."

A strangled sound came out of Stephanie, and she slapped her palm over her mouth. After a second, she gave up and dissolved into giggles. Damn, she was adorable when she smiled. And the sound of happiness bursting from her was music to his ears. And a stroke to his cock.

His lightness only lasted a few seconds because the bandage around her wrist slipped, revealing the deep, angry gouges she'd gotten from the handcuffs. He captured her hand and pressed his lips to her palm.

A soft huff of air left her, and her pupils dilated.

Steph was right, a bullet *was* too easy for Shark. His death should have been drawn out for days. Mav smiled internally;

King's death wouldn't be so clean. He hadn't mentioned it to Stephanie, but King had survived the raid on Shark's house. Barely, but he was alive, and his brothers would keep him that way until Maverick could arrive and dish out some of his own justice. He couldn't wait for his chance. The pain and fear he'd inflicted on Stephanie was nothing compared to what Mav had planned for King. A little MC justice on her behalf would go a long way toward calming Mav's insides.

He leaned forward and pressed his lips to Stephanie's head. "Sleep, baby. Your body has a lot of healing to do."

"What about security? Think they're really coming?"

"Fuck security. Ain't a thing in this world that could tear me from your side right now. You're safe, and you're gonna stay that way."

Stephanie blinked then nodded. Her eyes dropped closed, and she rested her head on his shoulder. Within seconds she was out cold, her breathing more relaxing than anything the doctors could have prescribed him.

He couldn't wait to get the fuck out of the hospital.

He had a date with a dead man.

CHAPTER NINE

Two days and a few growled threats from Maverick later, the physician declared Stephanie and Maverick ready for discharge. Part of her was thrilled her new biker friend was able to get her released earlier than expected but, of course, it presented a new round of challenges. Mainly that her FBI contact wouldn't be arriving for another day and a half.

"Seriously," Stephanie said as a woman named Toni wheeled her down toward the hospital's exit. She'd visited a few times along with some other members of Mav's club. They seemed to have adopted her into the family. "Just drop me off at a local hotel. I'll manage perfectly fine until my cousin arrives. It's not even two full days away. Between housekeeping and room service, I won't have to lift a finger."

"Fuck that," Maverick grumbled from the wheelchair next to her. "You're coming with us. End of discussion." He dropped his feet to the tiled floor, making the chair stop short. "Get me the fuck out of this thing. Zach, stop pushing me, for Christ's sake." Zach, one of Maverick's MC brothers, was wheeling him and loving every second of having Maverick at his mercy.

"Oh, little Mavy, you need to stay right here until we get to the car. Wouldn't want you to make any of your owies any worse," he said in a high-pitched voice meant for infants.

"Zach, stop harassing your brother." Toni swatted the handsome blond man on his very round and hard bicep. She was

Zach's ol' lady, which Stephanie learned over the past two days meant they were in a relationship. Not officially married but pretty much married in the eyes of the MC.

Toni, Maverick, and a few of the other club members had spent so much time with her, Stephanie never even had a chance to get bored. Or call the Bureau. Baccarella had to be chomping at the bit to find out more from her.

She never had a chance to obsess over the fact that Maverick copped to his club murdering Shark and planning to kill others.

Nor did she have a chance to obsess over the fact she'd almost kissed the man.

Or the fact she still wanted to kiss the man. More than she'd wanted anything in years.

It had to be nothing more than the byproduct of the intense situation. They'd faced down death together. He saved her from being raped. And she witnessed him being burned and tortured. Emotions were running high and were bound to get tangled and confused.

But she was a federal agent, for crying out loud. Emotions weren't allowed to enter into the picture. Now she had knowledge that could put Maverick and his brothers away for life.

What the hell was she supposed to do with it?

Stupid question. She knew exactly what she was supposed to do with it, but the idea of passing the information about Shark's fate up the federal chain was nauseating. But it was her job. More than her career, it was her life's work. She'd taken an oath, and it meant something to her.

Bottom line, it was wrong. No matter how much better off the world would be without Shark. No matter how much taxpayer money was saved by the MC just eliminating him. No matter how many women were spared Shark's abuse. There was a system in place for a reason. A system she was part of. One that worked if used properly.

Most of the time.

"Miss Little? Are you all right?"

Stephanie blinked and looked up into the face of the nurse's aide who'd accompanied their unconventional group to the exit. A few moments ago, the aide had seemed comically intimidated by the mammoth pack of rough men in leather and chains, but now her expression was full of concern.

Stephanie's face burned. "Sorry, zoned out there for a second. I'm fine." She snuck a sideways glance at Mav, who wore a frown. "I'm good. Promise."

Just trying to wrap my mind around sending you to prison after you saved me.

"We're gonna grab the cage," Zach said, slinging an arm across Toni's shoulders as he tugged her along. "Be right back. Don't you two crazy kids run off now."

"Uhh, I just spent a few days as a prisoner in a basement. Not too keen on being in a cage," she said, trying for light when really nerves fizzled and popped along her spine.

Zach burst out laughing. "I really like you, Steph. A cage is what we call a car. Promise there won't be bars. Though for most of us that's what it feels like," he mumbled.

When the laughing couple left, the young aide visibly relaxed. Not that Stephanie could blame her. Zach was the enforcer for the MC and could scare even the most hardened of men. Too bad he also happened to be funny, playful, and clearly head over heels for his spunky and normal girlfriend.

God, she needed distance from this messed up situation. Distance and perspective. Before she started thinking it was okay to let what she knew slide.

"Here you go, you two," the aide said as she handed a packet of papers to Stephanie and one to Maverick. "Discharge instructions and prescriptions. I believe your nurses went over everything with you."

"We're good, thanks," Maverick said, struggling to his feet as Stephanie nodded.

"Sir…" The aide rushed to his side. As if he'd accept her help.

One thing Stephanie learned about Maverick over the past few days was that he was stubborn as could be and didn't take well to being told what to do. Unless the orders came from his club president, Copper. Then he hopped right to it. Copper must be quite a leader to have earned such respect from Maverick.

Quite a leader. What was she thinking? This was a band of felons.

"Don't even think about touching me," Mav barked at the aide. "Unless you're planning to—"

"Uh, thanks for the paperwork. You can just leave him be. He's not going to listen to anything you tell him to do." Stephanie fired a quelling look at him, and he had the nerve to smirk and wink.

Just then, Zach and Toni rolled up in a dark SUV.

"Right, well, good luck with everything. If you have any questions, the numbers you need to call are in the paperwork." The aide scurried off like she was being timed.

"Are you trying to get arrested for sexual harassment?" Stephanie asked.

He laughed then gripped his side. "Shit, wildcat, don't make me laugh."

"Okay, gimps, let's move out." Zach strode around from the driver's side and opened the back door.

"Either of you want the front?" Toni called out the window.

"Nah. We're good in the back, doll. This way we can make out like horny teenagers while you play mom and dad." Mav shot Stephanie another wink, and this time she couldn't contain her laughter. The guy was truly ridiculous.

And so stubborn. He hoisted himself into the SUV ass first, then scooted to the far window. The only indication he was in pain was the clenching of his jaw and a slight tremble in his arms. With multiple broken ribs and a horrific burn on his arm, the pain had to be off the charts. But he didn't so much as make a peep.

One thing was clear: Maverick didn't like to be seen as weak or lesser in any way.

"Zach, help Stephanie," Toni yelled. "This beast is too high for her to be climbing in when she's all banged up."

"I can do—"

"Babe"—Zach rolled his eyes at Toni—"quit handing out orders, or I'm gonna give you a few orders when we get home."

Stephanie bit her top lip to keep from giggling.

"Not a deterrent, big guy," Toni said.

God, this group was hilarious. Stephanie loved hang—

Criminals, criminals, criminals.

"All right, darlin', let's do this." Zach helped her to stand then slid one arm around her waist and the other under her legs. She let out a squeak of surprise when her feet lifted off the ground.

"My legs are fine," she said as he deposited her into the car. Maverick was staring at Zach like he wanted to strangle his friend. Zach just smirked and did a piss-poor job of suppressing a chuckle.

"Just following my woman's orders," he said. "Comfy?"

"Yeah, I'm good. Thank you. Both of you. You've been through some trauma yourself, Toni. You should be resting."

"Nah, staying busy keeps my mind off things," Toni replied.

With a smile, Zach kissed the top of her head like she was his little sister.

Some kind of strange growl came from Maverick and had Zach cracking up. Whatever the hell that was about, she had no idea.

"All right, let's rock and roll," Zach said, climbing behind the wheel.

"Don't think these two will be rocking or rolling for a while," Toni said.

Stephanie peeked at Maverick. His eyes were closed, and his head rested against the back of the leather seat. The poor guy's bruised face and rigid body spoke at how uncomfortable he was. Yet he hadn't uttered one word of complaint. In fact, he'd spent the majority of the past two days in her room, entertaining her, cheering her up, keeping her mind off her own discomfort.

A week ago, if someone had asked her to describe her ideal man, she'd have said athletic, light hair, and on the muscular side. No ink. No piercings. She wouldn't have described a man who looked, behaved, or lived in a way that even resembled Maverick.

Except for one thing.

She wanted a man who cared for her deeply and wasn't afraid to let others see it. Even if it wasn't a romance between them, Maverick had been more than willing to let anyone who came within a mile of her know he had her firmly under his wing and protection.

Kind of a nice feeling.

And at that moment, beat up and sitting in that SUV, if someone had asked what kind of man she was attracted to, she'd have said an alpha bad boy, covered in ink, with a snarky, flirty personality.

Why the hell did life have to put him in her path? There was nothing there but the potential for pain.

And possibly prison time.

"WHERE IS HE?" Maverick asked the moment his ass hit the unforgiving metal chair. He stared straight into his president's eyes. Sure, his body was busted to all hell, but he wasn't weak. Not by a long shot, and he refused to be treated as such.

The club had King in their custody, and Maverick wanted a piece of the asshole. Hell, he wanted the whole thing if Copper would allow it. But Copper would want his own pound of flesh. King killed Special K, one of the prospects about to be patched in. In fact, Special K was recruited by Copper himself. Not something that happened too often. So there was no way Maverick would have free reign to let his fury out on King, but he'd certainly get to play a bit.

"He's in The Box," Copper said, referring to a basement room the club used for sensitive situations like this. "You sure you're up for this now? We can keep him on ice for a few more days until you're feeling stronger."

Blood boiled in Maverick's veins, and he leveled Copper with a stare so searing he was pretty sure his club brothers wouldn't have believed him capable.

A chuckle came from next to Copper. "Okay, then," Viper, the VP, said. "Looks like the boy wants some revenge."

The boy. What bullshit. Mav was a thirty-eight-year-old man. Not a fucking boy. And while Viper didn't mean it—hell, he called anyone under fifty a boy—it still grated. Because Mav had spent his entire youth being viewed as weak, lesser, inadequate. All because he wasn't a mountain of muscle like his old man.

Next to him, Zach shifted. "Look, it's Mav's body. He wants to risk fucking it up further, who the hell are we to stop him?"

Zach was a good friend and an even better brother. Always had Mav's back.

"I'm good, Copper. Promise. Just need to dish out some MC justice."

The smile on Copper's face was hidden by his bushy red beard. The thing was getting downright scraggly. Not that anyone in their right mind would tell the prez he needed a trim. Not anyone but Shell, the spitfire who'd harbored a deep and unrequited love for Copper for the past decade.

Well not unrequited, because the man definitely had a hard-on for Shell as well. But it would never amount to anything because Copper had some fool notion Shell was too young for him and there was too much messiness in their history.

"All right. Soon as we're done here, Mav, Zach, and I will pay King a little visit. Jig, I want you there, too. Help get a read on the guy."

Jig nodded, a vengeful gleam in his jade-green eyes. He'd been a well-respected physicist working for NASA until his wife and kid were murdered in a horrific event Maverick didn't know most of the details about. Rumor had it, Jig went a little crazy afterward. Until he met Copper, who helped get him back on track.

Sort of. Back on track MC style, anyway.

Copper had given him a family of brothers and a helping hand exacting revenge on the men who'd killed his family. Jig was a smart motherfucker, and Copper valued the treasurer's opinion and advice on most topics.

"My pleasure, Prez."

"Next order of business." Darkness crossed Copper's face. "Viper's ol' lady is planning the memorial for Special K. I want all the ol' ladies involved and helping her out. They're meeting here tomorrow at ten to start planning." He cleared his throat and swallowed before inhaling a deep breath. "Questions?"

Heads shook around the room and a few murmured "nos" rose up.

"Good. Next, Zach spent some time with King earlier today. Guy's a bit of a pussy. Didn't take long for him to start spilling Dragon secrets. There are two key players who he thinks will be vying for top dog now that Shark's been harpooned. Lefty and Sixer. King thinks there'll be a civil war inside the gang. I don't want to wait around for these assholes to kill each other. I want 'em and I want 'em now. Alive is preferred, but dead works for me, too. According to our oh-so-cooperative guest, the gang will crumble without one of them leading. No one else has the skills or ambition to take over."

It would feel damn good to rid the world of the Gray Dragons once and for all.

"Anybody got anything else?" Copper asked.

"I want to give Steph a shot at King," Maverick said.

The room fell deathly quiet. Not even so much as a swallow of whiskey was heard as every brother's shocked stare bore into Maverick.

Copper leaned back in his chair and steepled his fingers under his chin. He didn't immediately shoot the idea down, which was promising. Copper may be a hard-ass with a temper and a ruthless streak, but he was fair. When it came to the members of his MC anyway. "State your reasons."

"What?" Someone scoffed. "Fuck no! Bitches do not deserve in on any club business. Don't give a shit what the reason is."

Screw. One of the prospects, the one who was with Jig when they rescued Steph, actually. Prospects weren't usually permitted at church, but with what went down, it was all hands on deck. Still, first meeting or not, the jerkoff should know better than to interrupt the prez.

Copper shot him a look that would make most grown men piss themselves. "You don't like the way I run my club, you're free to walk the fuck out, Screw. Don't see my patch on your cut or my brand on your arm. No skin off my back."

Screw paled. "No, Prez. No problems."

Nodding, Copper focused on Mav again. "Spit it out, brother."

If the situation weren't so fucked, Mav would have laughed at Copper's intentional use of the word brother. Just a quick "fuck you" to Screw who wasn't yet a brother and who would probably be waiting longer than originally anticipated thanks to his outburst.

"King found her in the woods. He brought Shark to her. He tied her spread eagle to a fuckin' table and took her fuckin' pants off. He was seconds away from raping her when I managed to divert his attention. Then she had to watch as he burned the fuck out of my arm. The woman broke her wrist fighting like a hellcat to get his attention back on her. She…" Mav shook his head as an unfamiliar tingle started at the tip of his nose. Flicking his tongue ring against his lip, he stared at the ceiling. "She fucking begged him to come back and finish the job so I would be spared the pain. She deserves a few minutes with him."

The room remained silent as Copper contemplated Mav's request. "Think she can handle it? He sure as hell ain't pretty right now."

Mav nodded. "I think so. I'll prepare her. She told me Shark got off too easy with a simple bullet to the back. That it didn't sit right with her."

"Don't make me regret this, Maverick. Grab her and meet us down there." Copper sat forward and smacked his palm against the table. "Meeting adjourned."

As the brothers filed out of church, Mav's gut fluttered with excitement.

Playtime.

CHAPTER TEN

"Thanks, Michelle. I really appreciate this. Please don't go out of your way to do anything for me," Stephanie said as she watched the younger woman carry a stack of sheets and towels into the room.

"Call me Shell, and seriously stop. This isn't out of our way at all, is it, munchkin?" Shell asked the chubby-cheeked three-year-old trailing her mother into the room, her short little arms wrapped around a pillow.

"No, mama," the adorable kiddo said as she tried to see over the pillow. "Where's the lady? I want to show her my boo-boo."

Stephanie chuckled. "I'm right here, sweetie." She plucked the pillow from the child and tossed it on the bed.

"This is my daughter, Beth," Shell said over her shoulder as she made up the bed.

"Hi, Beth." Stephanie crouched down so she was eye level with the little tyke. Beth's strawberry-colored pigtails formed two perfect arcs off the sides of her round head. "You have a boo-boo?"

"Yes!" The little girl stuck her elbow in Steph's face. "Yook at it. I felled off the slide at Copper's house. I goed sooo fast!" Clearly, the small abrasion on the child's elbow wasn't causing her an ounce of pain because she relayed the story as though it was a great badge of honor.

With a roll of her eyes, Shell scooped up her little girl. "Miss

Stephanie has a boo-boo, too."

"That's right, I do." Stephanie held up her splint. "I broke my arm."

Beth's striking blue eyes that mirrored her mother's grew wide. They beautifully complimented her light red hair. "Let me kiss it and make it better. That's what Copper did to my bow."

"Your elbow," Shell corrected with a chuckle as the little girl squirmed out of her arms.

As gently as possible for a three-year-old, she grabbed Stephanie's splint and gave the bandaging a dramatic smooch. "There, all better!"

If only.

"Why don't you go grab Miss Stephanie a bottle of water from the refrigerator? Remember where they are?"

"Yes! I reached them myself," the child shouted then shot off like she couldn't be happier about the task.

"Sorry," Shell said, "she's never met a stranger."

"Please," Stephanie said, waving her hand, "she's adorable. The perfect distraction right now. So, is Copper your ol' man?"

Steph had met the MC president a few times in the hospital, and if she had to describe him in one word, it would be intimidating. A giant of a man with an unkempt red beard that she assumed was the reason for his name, he could scowl like no other.

A very unladylike snort shot from Shell's nose. "Nope. Definitely not his ol' lady." There was a note of bitterness to her voice.

Oookay. "Hmm, sensing there's a story there."

Shell sighed. "There are about six stories there, none of which can be told without copious amounts of alcohol. Maybe once you're off those heavy-duty painkillers." Clearly, she didn't realize this was a very temporary arrangement. She straightened and looked around the room. "Well, I think this will work. Sorry, it's not very glamorous."

Shell had set her up in one of the spare bedrooms at the

clubhouse. It was fine. Not glamorous as she'd said, but there was a bed, dresser, and a small flat screen television to keep her entertained. What more could she ask for while she stayed with a group of outlaws and waited for her FBI contact to show? Besides, who knew what she'd overhear that would be useful for the FBI.

"So, are you with any of the guys here?" The trained investigator in Steph couldn't leave stones unturned. Shell seemed so normal. So down to earth. A kind, friendly woman who apparently worked at a local diner and cleaned offices in town. Good mother, hardworking, sweet. She sure didn't seem like a stereotypical biker whore. So, what the hell was she doing with these men?

"Nah," she said, sitting on the end of the bed. "I grew up in the club. Actually, my father was the president back in the day. He was killed by an old enemy of the club." She stared at nothing for a moment as though lost in painful memories. "Anyway, they're family. Once you're in, you're in for life. And these guys take care of each other. Good care. They'd let me sit on my ass and spoil me if they had their way." With a shrug, she smiled. "I'm just not built like that. I take care of myself. And my baby girl."

An odd sensation slithered its way into Stephanie's stomach, some kind of combination of guilt, worry, and admiration for this woman. With each person she met, her initial view of the MC was challenged. Yet still, at the core, they broke the law.

Daily.

Without remorse.

And her job was to put them out of business—permanently.

Stephanie had wandered far into unfamiliar territory without any map to guide her.

"Hey, ladies, look what I found." Maverick stood in the doorway with a giggling Beth hanging over his shoulder. One arm was banded across the little girl's legs, keeping her in place, and the other, the one wrapped in thick bandages, covered his eyes.

"Hi, Mommy. Hi, Miss Stepaknee," Beth said through the giggles.

"Hi, baby. Mav? Why are you covering your eyes?" Shell asked.

"Wanted to give you ladies a chance to get your clothes back on and pick up all the feathers from the pillow fight before I brought my sexy self in here. Last time I walked in a room where there were two naked chicks—"

"I think we get the picture, thanks." Shell shot off the bed and grabbed her daughter. "And I hate to burst your bubble, stud, but no clothing was removed in the making of this room."

Maverick lowered his arm. "Oh, come on, Shell, can't you just play along? Fuel my fantasy of you two hopping around, ti—?"

Shell cleared her throat and inclined her head toward her daughter who was in her arms and beaming at Maverick. "Little ears, Uncle Mav."

"Uh, Beth, Uncle Rocket was just in the kitchen eating a cookie," Mav said with a smirk.

The girl squealed and practically dove out of her mom's arms, throwing the bottle of water on the floor. She took off like a track star once again.

"Tits bouncing while you swat each other with pillows," Mav continued without missing a beat. "And then you'll inadvertently bump into each other." He let out a dramatic sigh. "Want to hear this rest? This is where it gets good."

Stephanie couldn't help but laugh. Maverick wasn't like any man she'd ever been around. He was funny, outrageous, and a completely unapologetic flirt. She never knew what was going to come out of his mouth, but it was guaranteed to make her laugh and blush.

Shell rolled her eyes, obviously much more accustomed to Mav's brand of uncouth humor than Stephanie was. "You know, the only thing keeping me from smacking you is all those injuries. I'm off to find my child before she gets too sugared up.

You need anything at all, Steph, just come find me. I'm working tonight, but I'll be here until about five."

Maverick frowned. "Copper say you could go to work tonight?"

Some of Shell's light dimmed.

"Copper doesn't get a say, Mav," she said before giving him a peck on the cheek and disappearing into the hallway.

"Bet you twenty she doesn't go to work tonight."

Stephanie had seen Copper, and she'd seen his eyes on Shell in the central area of the clubhouse earlier. No way was she fool enough to take that bet. "Think I'll wait until I have a shot at winning."

"Smart woman." He stepped close, so close he was right up in her personal space, practically chest to chest with her. Well, chest to stomach if she was honest. He had quite a few inches on her. As though he'd pushed some sort of power button, her body flared to life. Heat rushed to her face and her core. Both nipples puckered like they were trying to close the small gap between their bodies, begging for contact and relief from the developing ache.

Jesus, this man was potent. Apparently, she wasn't the only one who thought so if his whispered reputation was true. Not that it mattered. Nothing was going to happen now or ever.

Criminal meet FBI agent.

"How are you feeling?" he asked as he slipped his hand into her un-casted one.

"Truth?"

"From you? Fuck yes. Always." His gaze was intense, penetrating as though he was going to look through her to determine if her spoken words were accurate.

"Sore." She shrugged. "A little overwhelmed. A little cheated."

"Cheated?" He tilted his head, and she felt the draw to him like a fly to a spider's web.

"Maybe cheated isn't the right word. More like unsatisfied?"

He snorted. "Unsatisfied, huh? Well, baby, I can cure that for you in under ten minutes."

Oh, lord, what had she said? Her skin heated for an altogether different reason this time. "That's not at all what I mean." *Liar*. "I mean…I was unconscious when it all went down. I missed the bad guys losing and the good guys winning." And she had zip to report to her superiors.

Crazy world when she was calling members of an outlaw MC the "good guys."

He lifted her palm and rubbed his lips over the center of the sensitive skin before nipping at the pad of her thumb. Her knees went liquid and she almost swooned. *Swooned*, like some kind of eighteen-hundreds southern bell. What the hell was this man doing to her body?

And her brain.

It was just him. Affectionate. Flirty. He had his pick of slutty woman any day any time. The flirtation was a meaningless habit, and she needed to get her reactions in check.

"What if I told you, you didn't miss everything?" He spoke against the skin of her palm.

"Hmm?" Shivers originated wherever his mouth met her skin, traveling up her arm. Wait. What did he just say? "I didn't miss everything? What are you talking about?"

He lowered their joined hands but didn't let go. "King. The fuckstick who dragged you in and cuffed you to the table," he said.

He was totally in the dark as to how well she actually knew King. She went to his wife's Pampered Chef party, for Christ's sake. Maybe Agent Rey had some kind of mental breakdown. Maybe that's what fueled his departure from everything he believed in.

"Yes? What about him?"

"He's alive."

The world stopped spinning. That was the only explanation for the complete loss of equilibrium.

"Whoa. Easy there." A strong arm looped around her waist. "You good now?"

Stephanie nodded, though it couldn't be further from the truth. He was alive? He could rat her out at any time. "Yes, sorry. Just took me by surprise. Do you know where he is?" Would he tell them who she was? Who he was? Up to now, the MC had treated her like family, disarming her natural suspicion, but what would they do to her if King ratted her out?

They'd kill her for sure.

She needed to remember where she was and who she was with. They may play her friends now, but they wouldn't hesitate to end her if necessary.

Mav nodded. "We have him. I was about to go…pay him a visit. You deserve to be there. Come with me."

The wheels in her head started turning so fast she felt like an out of shape hamster about to keel over. Part of her wanted to run away, her fingers plugging her ears, begging Maverick not to share any more incriminating evidence with her. Another part knew it was her duty to follow him to the basement and report back to her superiors. Report all the illegal activities that would tear this entire MC, this family, apart. And find out why Agent Rey flipped.

And a third part wanted to follow him down to that basement with her head held high and watch with a smile on her face as someone beat the shit out of King. That part of her wanted him to experience the fear, the helplessness, and the pain that she'd felt. That Maverick had endured for her.

That part of her had never surfaced before.

And it scared the shit out of her.

CHAPTER ELEVEN

Maverick clasped Stephanie's tiny hand tightly as he guided her the quarter mile through the woods. Uncertainty had been clearly written all over her face, ever since he made the offer to accompany him to King. Stephanie wasn't from his world. In her universe, people didn't make their way to dark basements serving as makeshift prison cells and sometimes torture chambers. They didn't take revenge in violent ways.

Hell, she'd probably never even imagined violence and fear like she'd experienced at King's hand. And she sure as hell wouldn't have envisioned herself about to help beat and torture a man who was destined for death within the next hour.

But the path of life was winding and fraught with complications. Some of those complications changed a person.

Forever.

Maverick knew all about nightmare experiences that affected someone so profoundly, he swore it changed the make-up of a person's cells. His demons were in the past, but Steph's were present and waiting just fifteen feet below the ground.

"This is The Box," he said, leading her to what looked like a trapdoor in the middle of the woods. "It's used for club business of a sensitive nature."

Her eyes widened as his meaning sunk in. "Oh," she said, her throat rising and falling with the force of her swallow.

"Last chance to change your mind, sweetheart. Not trying to

be a dick, but once you walk down those steps, you can't unsee and unexperience it. You'll be part of it, and it will be part of you."

The wariness in her eyes was almost enough for him to pull the plug. If she didn't answer in the next five seconds, he'd turn around and hobble back to the clubhouse with her before returning alone. Maybe he'd been mistaken and she wasn't cut out for brutal payback, but he'd sworn he'd seen something in her. Something that called to him on a deep, dark level. The need to release the grip of what she witnessed and endured. And what better way to release that beast than to kill it fucking dead?

Steph inhaled a sharp breath, then the damnedest thing happened. The five-foot-three waif of a woman squared her shoulders, steeled her spine, and narrowed her eyes. "Lemme at him."

She'd rallied. Pride surged through Maverick. There was the woman he'd nicknamed wildcat. Despite her misgivings and fear, she'd march down every one of those steps and confront the piece of shit that terrorized her.

That almost raped her.

Fuck, Mav wanted to lose control on the man. Let his own darkness fly free and use King as his punching bag until the man was nothing more than a limp sack of bones. But he couldn't. Hell, this trip through the woods nearly did him in, and he wasn't due for any more pain medication for at least another hour.

He pressed a kiss to Steph's hand before releasing her. When he bent halfway down to pull up the door leading to the underground room, a sharp slice of pain started at his sternum and shot around to his spine, stealing his breath and making him grunt.

"Mav?" Stephanie asked. He loved that she used his shortened name. Meant she was comfortable with him. Familiar.

"I'm good, doll. Just need a second." Like she'd ever believe that. His words were breathy, strangled, and it sounded as though a Copper-sized man was sitting on his chest. Felt that way, too.

"Don't be a hero," Stephanie said with a roll of her eyes. She grabbed the handle with her uninjured hand and hefted.

The door was heavier than she'd expected, and she faltered after she'd gotten it about a third of the way open, but it was enough for Mav to reach and help her hoist it up. Later, he was going to pay for all this activity big time, but later he'd have all the time in the world to lie in a bed in agony.

Maybe Steph would lie with him. He knew a few all-natural pain remedies that trumped Percocet any day. Though, to be honest, he wasn't quite sure he was up for anything more than passing out next to her. Never once had he slept next to a woman for more than a quick thirty-minute catnap before round two. Or three.

But the thought of sinking into his bed while Stephanie relaxed alongside him, both their bodies healing and recovering from the past few days damage, yeah, that sounded pretty damned perfect.

But first…

"Ladies first," he said, gesturing toward the dimly lit steps.

Stephanie cast a wary glance at the dark entrance to The Box. "Not necessary. I'll follow you. Unless you need me to help you navigate the steps. All this walking has to be murder on your ribs."

Mav chuckled then winced. There she went again, trying to step between him and the pain. In reality, she was right, he hurt like a mofo, but both legs could be hanging off him and he wouldn't let her know it. "I'm good, doll." He stepped forward and kissed her cheek, lingering at her ear afterward. "Appreciate you looking out for me, though."

She turned an adorable shade of pink and nodded, not making eye contact.

"Here we go." Maverick descended the steps slowly since it was all his aching body would allow. "Stay close."

The moment the words left his lips, her fingers curled around the waistband of his jeans. When the soft pads of her fingertips brushed along his lower back, a hot stab of lust nearly took him to his knees.

Even at an unusually slow pace, it didn't take them more than a minute to reach The Box, which was aptly named. About twelve-by-twelve, The Box was just that. A large square room with one overhead light and a hose coming from a spigot in the far wall.

The center of The Box sloped downward from all corners, converging in a hole the size of a manhole cover. King wasn't the first guest to stay at Hotel Box, and while it had been some time since the room was used, no one had any problems doing what needed to be done.

No one except Stephanie, apparently.

The moment she reached the ground, a soft, shocked gasp left her, and her hand flew to her mouth. Wide-eyed, she stared at King, or what used to be King. Now it was just a wounded animal bent on survival.

Uselessly.

Mav felt none of what she felt. None of the shock. None of the horror. None of the fear. And sure as hell none of the guilt. Hopefully she didn't feel guilty either. Because if anyone deserved what the man slumped in the chair was getting, it was King.

"He looks…" Stephanie shifted her gaze from the bloody mess of King to Maverick.

Mav slid an arm around her waist and spoke against her ear in a low whisper. "He can't hurt you anymore. You don't have to do anything at all, sweetheart. You can turn around and walk out of here with the knowledge that King won't be leaving here. Won't be hurting another woman ever again. Or you can stay and watch. Or you can participate."

She turned her head until their lips were just a breath apart. Wildly inappropriate, but Mav could barely think beyond the desire to capture those lips with his.

"Has he hurt other women?" This time her tone had a hard edge to it. She was coming alive.

There you go, wildcat.

King barely looked capable of breathing at the moment. Stripped to his boxers, he was tied to a chair, much as Mav had been just a few days prior. Only this time, there wasn't a snowball's chance in hell of a rescue. Blood ran, not dripped, from his nose, upper lip, and a few spots on his chest where it looked like Zach had gotten him with a knife.

Accidentally, of course.

Purple bruises mottled most of his upper body, and his head drooped onto his chest. A slight rise and fall of his shoulders was the only indication of life, and that wouldn't be there for long.

With a nod, Mav said. "We got some intel during the days when I was gone. Three girls have gone missing from Gray Dragons territory over the past year. All late teens, and all three were assumed to be runaways."

"Oh, God. What happened to them?"

"They became property of the Gray Dragons. Pimped out to sadistic sonsofbitches. Used up and murdered. Thrown away like trash. King killed each one of them."

Tears filled her somber eyes, and Mav had the urge to reach out, wrap her in his arms, and hold her until this all passed. But it was a temporary fix. A Band-Aid on a hemorrhage. And now that she knew, maybe she'd purge any compassion lingering for the man.

"Are you positive it was him?"

"One hundred fucking percent. No question. We have evidence. Camera footage, witness accounts. Plus, he fucking bragged about it."

"Okay then." She faced King again and took three steps forward, her tennis shoes squeaking on the wet ground.

Slowly, King's head lifted until he was able to see Stephanie coming toward him. She stopped about three feet away from him.

Open. Close. Open. Close. Her fists worked in a repetitive pattern.

Would she do it? Would she do anything? Hit him? Scream at him? Burst into tears?

Though his every instinct screamed at him to go to her, Maverick held himself still. This was her show. Her purging of demons. And he wouldn't interrupt.

Her legs started to tremble. "I—I don't think I can..." Side to side, she shook her head.

From Mav's peripheral vision, Copper shifted, uncrossing his arms and taking one step forward. Mav sliced his hand in Copper's direction. She just needed a minute to get herself together. The wildcat would win out.

Like a deadly animal sensing its prey had been weakened, King pounced. "Couldn't stay away from me, huh?"

"Why?" she asked in a whisper. "Why would you kill those girls?"

King grunted out a laugh. "Why? Why the fuck not? We had no use for them anymore. But we sure made a pretty penny off 'em." He grinned, blood outlining his teeth. "They liked it. Begged for it. Kinda like you were begging me for it the other day. You here because you're unsatisfied? Huh, Ag—"

It happened so fast, neither Maverick nor his brothers saw it coming. One second they were about to step in and pull Steph back from the sick asshole's taunts, and the next, her small, balled-up fist had plowed into King's mouth.

And damned if that little bit of a thing didn't pack a helluva punch. King's head snapped back then rebounded forward as though rubber. With a groan, he spat a mouthful of blood at Stephanie's feet. Either she didn't notice or didn't care because she didn't so much as step back.

A cry of rage left her lips, and she was on him again. Hitting his face over and over with her one good fist. So engrossed in her anger and revenge, she wasn't aware of the cut on her wrist opening and oozing.

King groaned and Stephanie yelled, "How could you?" over and over as she wailed on him, punching and kicking him for all she was worth. And she sure as hell didn't hit like a girl. When she cocked her left arm, splint and all, both Maverick and Zach rushed forward. No way would he let her injure herself further by slamming her broken wrist into his face.

"Stephanie!" he snapped as he hooked his hand around her upper arm, stopping the broken arm from flying forward.

King's head lolled forward, a trail of bloody saliva dangling from between his busted lips. No more taunting comments came from him. He was done. Ready for death.

"Oh, my God." Stephanie's hand slapped over her mouth and her legs sagged. "What have I done?"

Mav caught her around the waist before her knees hit the ground, gritting his teeth at the excruciating pain in his ribs. An amazing friend and brother, Zach nudged him aside and scooped her up.

Fuck, if seeing her in Zach's arms wasn't a pain worse than what was tearing through his torso. He was the one who should be holding her. He'd brought her to The Box. He set her on this path. He wanted to protect her. Comfort her.

Not his fucking brother.

Although, never in a million years would Zach cross any lines. He had a damn good woman he loved more than anything.

Goddamn Mav's fucked-up body.

Shit, it was probably for the best. Mav had no business getting tangled up with any woman. For the life of him, he couldn't figure out why he cared so much about this one.

From the safety of Zach's arms, Stephanie stared at him with glassy eyes. Devastated was the word that came to mind when Mav looked at her. Maybe this had been a terrible idea. Maybe he had made her trauma worse.

"Mav," Copper called.

He turned and found his president holding a pistol, handle

side out. "Finish it, brother."

With fucking pleasure.

He fisted the gun and risked a glance at Stephanie. Resignation was written all over her face. "Get her out of here," he said. She didn't need this image in her head on top of all the others that would haunt her.

With a nod, Zach turned and jogged up the stairs, even with Stephanie's weight in his arms.

As soon as he was done here, Mav would see to her. Even though he shouldn't. What would be smarter would be to let Toni and Shell take care of her until her cousin arrived tomorrow.

But he wasn't very intelligent when it came to Stephanie.

Just a fucked-up situation messing with his protective instincts and emotions.

That's all.

Mav stepped forward, letting all the hatred and rage of the past week flow through his veins. Tapping the pistol against King's forehead, he said, "Hey. Look at me, motherfucker."

CHAPTER TWELVE

He can't hurt you anymore.

Those words, Mav's whispered sounds of comfort, played over and over in Stephanie's mind. They weren't true. Daniel Rey could still hurt her and nearly had.

Agent Little.

It had been on the tip of his tongue. His way of taking her out with him. Because it wouldn't matter to the Handlers that King was a federal agent; he was already bound for hell. But Stephanie? Yeah, that would have bought her the next ticket down the drain in the damn box.

Was that why she'd done it? To save herself? Keep him from uttering her secret and blowing her cover? Or was it nobler? Payback for the women he'd killed and the pain he had inflicted on Maverick. Because hearing that he'd killed the women he was sent by the FBI to protect nearly put her over the edge.

Not that any of her good intentions made attacking him the right move.

Halfway up the stairs, a loud bang reverberated off the walls of the small room, making Stephanie jolt in Zach's arms.

King was dead. Killed by Maverick. And her FBI contact would be here to pick her up tomorrow. How the hell was she supposed to explain it all?

"Hey, hon, it's all right. You're gonna be fine. A little bit of time, and you'll be able to move past it. This will be nothing but a sour memory."

She didn't respond. Her mind was too busy spiraling out of control with all the potential ramifications of her actions, Maverick's actions, the club's actions. Time wouldn't help. It was actually her enemy because she would be debriefed by the FBI. And part of that debriefing included informing the Bureau the details of Shark's murder, King's murder, and her complacency. Not to mention the Handlers' role in all of it.

Zach carried her through the woods, into the clubhouse, and deposited her on the edge of the bed Shell had made up. Steph stared, unseeing at the floor.

"Hey," he said, lifting her chin and forcing her to look all the way up his six-foot-plus stature. "You were fucking fierce in there, darlin'."

Fierce. Second time she'd been called that in the past few days. She didn't feel fierce. She felt sick.

Without another word, Zach left, and Stephanie was alone with her rampant thoughts. As she sat perched on the edge of the freshly made bed, staring at the re-opened wounds on her right wrist, her chest tightened to the point of unbearable.

She tried to pull in a deep, cleansing breath, but it was as though her ribcage wouldn't expand. Instead of a lung-filling inhalation, a shallow gasp left her feeling breathless. Again and again she tried to suck in air, only to be blocked by some invisible stricture around her chest. Soon, the room spun, and she was all-out hyperventilating.

The door flew open, and Maverick was on her in a flash, gathering her into his arms despite his grunt of pain. "Breathe, sweetheart, just breathe."

She trembled in his arms, still trying to keep from passing out due to lack of oxygen. After what seemed like hours of his large hand stroking a soothing path up and down her back, the snug band around her chest loosened a smidge and she drew in air as if she was dying.

"That's it, babe. Another one just like that, and you'll feel better."

"What—have—I—done?" The question came out stuttered with a whistled wheeze between each word.

"Nothing wrong, wildcat," he whispered against her ear. "Not one damn thing wrong. We gave that bastard nothing more than he deserved. He was a monster, darlin'. And monsters need to be stopped."

Pressed up against her, Maverick was so warm and so comforting she soon found herself relaxing against him. After a few more minutes, she was able to speak almost fluidly save for the occasional hitch in breathing.

"But it's wrong." She lifted her head and stared into his eyes. He was composed, utterly unfazed by what had just occurred. Stephanie had seen death multiple times, but she'd never personally killed someone in the line of duty. And now she'd allowed someone to be executed without a trial. Without due process. Without a verdict and order from a judge.

Mav frowned. "What's wrong?"

"Killing him. We should have called the police. He needed to be brought to justice."

"What we did was mete out some overdue justice, Stephanie. We sure as fuck brought him to justice." A hard edge crept into Maverick's voice, and his face tightened.

"There are rules, laws. There is a way of doing this to ensure he'd pay. I believe in letting the justice system—"

"The justice system? Fuck the justice system!" His grip on her tightened. "You don't think King and Shark had cops on payroll? You don't think jury members would disappear, judges would be bribed, and cash would be passed around like a joint in a college dorm? That asshole would have been home free before he ever had to worry about bending over in the shower."

"But you don't know that for sure. You have to give it a chance to work."

"No buts, babe. We took care of shit. We were the justice system. Because of the club, three families will know the scum that killed their babies is six feet under. Because of us, other teenage girls in the area will be safe. They're fucking trafficking women. We sure as hell rained justice on them. How can you not see that?"

Panic was working itself under her skin, and she fought to keep it from him. "I see it, Maverick, I do, but it doesn't matter. Right is right and wrong is wrong. Murder is wrong. Vigilante justice is wrong. What if everyone thought like you did? People everywhere would be beating and killing others over every little problem."

"Murder and rape of three teenagers is not a little problem." His scowl made his disdain for her statement quite obvious.

"No, I know that. I'm not saying it is. I know he should be punished, the worst punishment the courts can dish out. It just should have been done the legal way. We acted outside the law. Aren't we just as bad as he is now?" Shit, why couldn't he see this from her perspective?

He released her and stepped back. Immediately, she missed the warmth and vitality he'd been sharing from his body to hers.

"We are nothing like that scum." He practically spat the words at her. Fists clenched, his chest heaved. In another circumstance, she might have felt threatened by his aggressive body language, but this stemmed from his worry for her. So, sick as it was, it made her feel cared for. "We don't go popping bullets in people's heads for jaywalking or for generally being a dick. This man burned my fucking arm to the bone. He almost raped you. Would have killed you. Did that very same thing to three girls who aren't even old enough to smoke a fucking cigarette. And you think he deserves to have some asshole in a suit defend him? You think he deserves less than he got?"

Did she?

"No." This conversation wasn't going where she'd thought it would. Instead of convincing Maverick the error of his ways, he was twisting her mind and getting her to see his side. "He got exactly what he deserved. But it's still wrong. And against the law."

She closed the gap between them and collapsed against his chest, the weight of her sins heavier than lead on her shoulders. "And I participated. I knew you were going to shoot him, and I didn't even try to stop it. I believe in following the law, in the process we have in place to keep people safe and punish those who hurt others."

Lightly banging her forehead on his hard pecs, she squeezed him as tight as she dared. How could she do it? How could she go against everything she believed in? Everything she trained for? The oath she took to protect and serve? She needed to leave. Maybe it was some kind of Stockholm syndrome messing with her head or some hero worship for the people who had rescued her.

Mav circled her hips and nuzzled his nose against her hair, inhaling. Stephanie froze. Toni had been kind enough to bring her some floral-scented hair products she'd made use of before leaving the hospital. Was that why he breathed her in?

He continued to stroke his nose through her hair, down her cheek, and into the sensitive curve of her neck, tickling slightly. Stephanie held her breath and didn't so much as twitch, both petrified of her body's reaction to him and just as afraid he'd stop.

Warmth flooded her stomach and bloomed out until her entire body felt heated and flushed. Her nipples pebbled and sent a message straight to her brain, begging to be touched, pinched, sucked. Between her legs, hot wetness made her slick and readied her for something that should never happen. Something she shouldn't even want but, oh, how she wanted it.

Needed it.

Maverick's hand slid from her lower back up to her hair. He fisted it in a tight grip then tugged, tipping her head back until she had no choice but to gaze right into his eyes. Mouth mere inches from hers, he said, "The world doesn't work that way, baby. Right and wrong? That's an illusion. A fairytale. Humans weren't created to pick one or the other. Every one of us falls somewhere in between. You are fooling yourself if you think you can fit everyone into a nice neat A or B category. What we did may have been wrong in the eyes of the law, but we both know King would never have paid for those crimes. It's ugly, it's messy, and it's fucked up, but it's not wrong. Don't you dare lose a moment's sleep feeling like you've done something wicked here."

And damned if she didn't buy right into his impassioned speech. Maybe it was all the sex-hungry hormones coursing through her system, or perhaps it was just the strength of his convictions, but she found some of the weight lifting off her shoulders.

Then, before she could make a mental list of the many reasons she should inch away, Maverick closed the gap until nothing but a sheet of paper could have passed between their lips. His tongue snuck out, the metal ball glinting in the light of the room, and he traced her bottom lip.

Like he'd found the access to a secret door, her mouth opened, and his lips settled against hers. It was gentle, soft, and so maddening she wanted to cry. He kept the pressure light, rubbing his lips against hers more than actually kissing her. It wasn't what she'd expected, wasn't what she'd fantasized about. In her mind, he'd go at it in a frenzied, ravenous claiming. Or maybe that was just her projecting her desires onto him.

But now, there she was, head immobilized by his near punishing hold on her hair, tipped back, helpless to do anything but receive the inadequate touch. As he continued to torture her with a passion just out of reach, she groaned.

Screw this. She grabbed the back of his head and pushed, mashing their mouths together the way she'd been craving. For all of thirty seconds, Maverick's tongue stroked into her mouth and his lips sealed over hers making the world spin and her pussy clench with unfulfilled need. Every few seconds, the titanium ball of his tongue ring would roll over her own tongue, giving her just a taste of what would be in store for her clit should he ever venture south.

Desperate for more, Stephanie moaned and held him tighter until they both flinched and a metaphorical bucket of ice water crashed over her.

Holy shit, she'd lost her mind.

Here he was, broken ribs, busted face, split and swollen lip, and she was assaulting him like some kind of animal in heat. Not to mention her own healing lip that now stung anew.

She released him at once, and her hair slid through his lax fingers as he stepped back. "Fuck," he bit out, the same frustration she was feeling written all over his face. After pressing his thumb to his lip and it came back blood free, he stared at her with stormy, lust-filled eyes.

"I'm sorry," she said as she ran a hand through her hair. It had to be sticking out every which way. And she hadn't worn makeup since before she was taken. She'd need a pound of it to cover the bruises on her face anyway. God, she was a hot mess. Thankfully, there wasn't a mirror in the room. She didn't think she could face it at the moment, knowing what a disaster she looked like in front of the sexiest man she'd ever met. "I seem to have lost all semblance of self-control tonight."

"Don't be. You have any idea what the fuck it does to me that you want me like I want you? Shit, wildcat, I want more of that mouth. Guess fucking is out of the question until we're back in fighting form, huh?"

When Stephanie laughed, it released the last of the tension. The man was nothing if not blunt. "Guess so."

"Can't even eat you like I want with this fuckin' busted lip." He scrubbed a hand over his face, wincing when his palm encountered the bruised ring around his eye.

Stephanie swallowed and closed her eyes. Maybe with enough mental fortitude, she could will away the image of him going down on her. Hard to do with a deep, pulsing ache between her legs.

No. It was useless. She wanted him with a force that scared her.

The whole thing was so fucked up. He'd killed a man less than fifteen minutes ago and here she was, a federal agent, complicit in a murder and wanting nothing more than to be fucked stupid by the murderer.

"Woman," Mav said on a growl. "Stop standing there and staring at me like all you're thinking about is my mouth on your pussy. You're making me crazy, and there's not a damn thing I can do about it tonight." He grabbed her hand. "Come on, wildcat. Let's take some pain pills, clean up your wrist and knuckles, then get some shut-eye."

She blinked and shifted her gaze. Maverick wasn't even trying to disguise the thick bulge behind his sweats, and the sight of it only made her want him more. "I could…" she said, gesturing toward his crotch as her face flamed.

"Fuuuck," he said letting his head fall back on his shoulders. "Don't even say it, babe. Besides, your lip's almost as bad as mine. Ain't how I roll. Hold that thought until I can bury my face between those gorgeous thighs and fuck you properly without needing narcotics."

Then it would never happen. Because she was giving in to the insanity while she was there in his world and in his clubhouse. But the moment she left, all of this was going firmly in a do-not-revisit file in her mind. Never to be reexamined, never to be opened again. She'd never see him after tomorrow and never think of him if she could manage it.

Fifteen minutes later, medicated, knuckles cleaned, and a fresh bandage on her wrist, Stephanie found herself in her bed with Maverick spooned all around her. She hadn't expected him to climb on in with her but couldn't stop the flutter in her stomach when he had. He was solid and warm behind her, and she hoped with every fiber of her being that his presence would keep the nightmares at bay.

Probably not, considering what she'd been party to that day.

Maverick seemed to fall asleep the moment his arm curled around her, and the steady rise and fall of his chest against her back lulled her into a hypnotic state of sleep.

Sometime later, a firm pressure against her lower stomach woke her. Maverick's open palm pressed against her bare skin spanning the distance between her belly button and her mound. Arousal hit, sharp and instantaneous, whooshing the air from her lungs. The moment his splayed fingers began a slow, southward journey, Stephanie's heart started to pound.

When he reached her sex, he cupped his hand and left it there just resting against her cotton-covered pussy. She'd shed her pants before falling into bed and wore nothing but one of Mav's T-shirts and un-sexy panties.

"M-Maverick?"

"Shh," he whispered against her ear as he worked his fingers under the damp swatch of fabric concealing her. He pressed one of his digits against her opening, just holding it there, not entering, not moving, and her eyes fluttered closed.

Fuck me with those fingers. Please.

"I need to make you come," he said. "I might not survive the night if I don't feel this wet pussy squeezing some part of my body. You gonna let me make you come?"

Let him? She was seconds away from begging for it. "Yes," she said. "Please."

"Hmm," he said, chuckling. "Like the sound of that."

He slid a long finger into her, and she sighed in relief as her pussy tightened down on him. "Soaked," he whispered.

No one else was around, but the moment seemed to call for hushed tones. Anything else would destroy the intimacy. Would rip through the cocoon of forbidden desire and emotion that had bound Stephanie so tightly to him.

He curled his finger and rubbed along the front wall, drawing a whimper from her.

"Feel good?"

"Uh huh." She nodded, unable to do more than make the

garbled sounds.

"Want it to feel even better?"

"Y-yes."

Mav inserted a second finger and then, without warning, he stopped playing, stopped teasing, and fucked her in earnest with his fingers.

"Shit," she cried out as a jolting shot of pleasure ripped through her. She gathered the sheet in the fingers of her good hand and squeezed as though it would somehow be an anchor to the bed when her body wanted to fly apart.

While he worked his fingers inside her, his thumb played with the hood of her clit, rubbing in an arch around the nub but never quite touching it. Maverick was tearing away her sanity one stroke at a time.

When Stephanie canted her pelvis, it increased the sensations, so she did it again and again until she was riding his hand without shame.

"That's it, babe, help me fuck this sweet pussy. Christ, I wish it were my mouth on you right now. Bet you taste so fucking sweet."

She groaned and pumped her hips faster. His mouth was lethal without even touching her skin. She might not survive it if he got it on her pussy.

Good thing it would never happen.

After a few more seconds, he switched tactics and pressed his thumb directly on her clit. Stephanie surged toward orgasm and ground herself against him.

"Close, babe?" His breath tickled her ear.

"Yes, yes, yes. Just a little mo—oh!" She thrust against his palm as her pussy clung to his fingers. The climax crested over her like a wave knocking her down and tumbling her through the surf. She fought for breath as though she really was drowning until the sea calmed and her body settled.

"Exactly what I needed," Maverick said as he withdrew his fingers.

Steph couldn't help but chuckle. "What you needed? I think we can both agree I was the one who got what I needed."

"Hmm." Maverick lifted his fingers to his mouth and licked the middle one clean. She watched him over her shoulder fascinated by how open and unabashed he was with his sexuality. "Shit. That was a bad idea. Thought I wanted to eat you before, but now that I've had a taste, I'm fucking dying for it."

After guiding her back down to the bed, Maverick slipped his hand under her shirt and cupped her breast. Spooned around her once again, he settled his face into the crook of her neck.

Stephanie had never felt so safe, so desired, so cared for.

It was a dangerous game. A slippery slope that led straight to disaster.

"Sleep, Steph. All the problems can wait until tomorrow."

Advice she'd take if only because she had no choice. She'd already made the mistakes. Tomorrow would come and so would the repercussions. No use worrying about them now.

"Um, Mav, you need something from me?" she asked. His erection pressed long and hard along her spine. The thing had to be uncomfortable. If he were feeling half the need she was, he'd be in unsatisfied purgatory.

"Nah, babe. Got what I wanted tonight. I'm fucking perfect."

With that declaration, he fell asleep.

Stephanie closed her eyes as well, reveling in the magic that was Maverick. How was it possible that the biggest mistake of her life was also the greatest pleasure?

CHAPTER THIRTEEN

"All right, all right. Settle your asses down." Copper banged his fist on the table and waited for the guys to stop yammering. A few groans had Copper chuckling, the pounding of his fist no doubt echoing through more than one hungover head.

Apparently, Maverick had missed an epic party the night before. A celebration of his return and Shark's demise. While technically, he was the guest of honor, the brothers didn't seem to care that he hadn't graced them with his presence. Typical. Give them whiskey, pussy, and some loud as hell hard rock, and they were good to go until dawn.

On a typical night, Mav would have been right there with them, collecting women by the dozen, but he didn't have a flicker of regret for missing out. No, he'd been perfectly happy draped all over Steph and trying to sleep with his never-ending hard-on.

Hadn't been easy.

But it had sure been worth it.

Her pussy had been soaked.

And tight.

And warm.

The three requirements of a perfect fuck. And even though his fingers were the only part of him to get any action, it'd been perfect.

Man, that sounded sappy. Like he was some kind of chick.

The doctor swore he didn't have a brain injury. But if he was going to keep thinking about Stephanie and perfection, he might need a second opinion.

"Okay," Copper said once the room had quieted. "This is gonna be a quick meeting. Only one item to discuss, then a vote." He scratched his chin through the ridiculously bushy beard. Shell must have been too busy to be around the clubhouse much the past week because she usually bitched at Copper until he trimmed it. The prez always grumbled about her riding his ass over stupid stuff, but he relented and gave her anything she wanted, every time.

Well, almost anything she wanted. For years she'd been after the ultimate prize: Copper himself. The woman had to be crazy to want to take on that growly beast, but Shell had been smitten with him since she was a teen, if rumors were to be believed. For some reason, the red-headed giant wouldn't admit he was just as in love with the sweet, single-mom who'd grown up in the club.

"What's up, Prez?" Jig asked.

"Y'all know what Shark did to Maverick's arm, burning the piss out of it and destroying his Handlers' brand."

Mav's stomach soured. With one violent move, Shark and King managed to destroy the sense of security Mav had found within the club. Despite everyone he talked to promising him they'd never vote him out of the club, Mav felt the same as when he'd been a thirteen-year-old orphan, standing out on the street gawking at his neighbor's family dinner through their window.

Six of them had been gathered around a beat-up old table. The younger kids were fighting over who got to sit next to their father, their mother was swatting them with her dish towel when they made a face at a dish of vegetables, and the whole family was belly-laughing at something the teenage son said. It was so far removed from any experience Mav had with family, he couldn't tear his attention away.

Loneliness and isolation were gut-wrenching feelings at any age, but even more horrible for a teenager. All he'd had to go home to was a fucked-up foster situation where he'd literally fought for his life against other boys the family fostered.

And now, here he was again. Without his brand. Without the most critical link to his brothers. Standing outside, looking in at the family.

"Grateful Toni ended Shark's sorry-ass life but, man, I wish I'd gotten ten minutes alone with him," Jig said, rubbing his knuckles.

You and me both, brother. Though no one probably felt that way more than Zach, whose woman had been abused by the bastard. He was quiet, but cracked his knuckles under the table, a telltale sign their club's enforcer was pissed and looking to let his fists fly free.

"Second that," Rocket said. Rocket wasn't much of a talker. Tended to live in his own head more than anything, so for him to speak up at that moment meant something to Mav.

Agreements went around the table, each man looking Mav straight in the eye when they expressed their sorrow for what he'd endured.

"We all know what's in the bylaws. No brand, no patch. But I think it's safe to make an exception in this case. Plastic surgeon told Mav there was no way in hell the skin graft would ever survive a branding. Even if it would"—he shook his head then looked at Mav—"I don't feel right about touching you with heat after what those scum-suckers did to you."

Felt good to have his president behind him, but Mav would get rebranded in a heartbeat if the option was on the table. Hell, he'd get it anywhere on his body, but there was limited ink-free real estate and the bylaws said it had to be left arm, so he'd just be putting himself through more torture for no reason.

"Doc did say he could ink it after it heals. If the vote goes for him to stay, Mav said he wants to ink the brand in the exact same spot, if that's cool with everyone. Anybody got problems with that? Now's your chance to say your piece before we put it to a vote."

No one made a peep.

"Okay then, vote on the table is for Mav to remain in the club, keep his position as road captain, and have the brand inked. I'm one hundred percent for all of it." Copper raised his meaty hand. "All in favor."

Maybe it was stupid and chicken-shit, but Mav couldn't watch. He closed his eyes and held his breath.

"All against."

Copper chuckled. "Open your eyes, asshole. Vote's unanimous. You ain't getting away from us that easy."

The sense of relief was dizzying. Blinking his eyes open, he came face-to-face with his entire laughing MC.

"You were seriously worried about this, brother?" Zach asked, laughing loudest of them all.

"Screw you." Man, he loved his family of brothers. They could heckle him until they turned blue, but none of them had grown up the way he had. Alone, disconnected, unloved. Screwed with a man's head. Most of the time, Mav had that shit locked down as part of the forgotten past, but this whole ordeal had dragged it to the surface.

"Everyone get the hell out. Honeys are waiting on you out there. Have a fun night, boys." Copper wasn't one to hook up with any of the Honeys, at least not since Shell moved back to town six or so months ago.

Zach's heavy hand landed on Mav's shoulder as he stood, nearly sending him flying across the table. "Let's go, brother. Get you some booze and some pussy, start forgetting this shit ever happened."

They walked out together, and seconds after exiting church, Zach spotted his woman chatting with a few ol' ladies at the bar. In no time, he had her wrapped up and receiving his near violent kiss. Mav scanned the room before he had the good sense to remember Stephanie had left ten hours earlier. He'd given her his number, and she'd promised to get in contact when she purchased a new phone.

All day, he'd been twitchy, wondering where she was and what she was doing. Was she uncomfortable sitting in the car for the ride back to DC where she lived? Was she still stressing and feeling misplaced guilt over what happened with King? Her cousin had the personality of a dead fish and had whisked Steph out of the clubhouse almost before he'd had the chance to say goodbye.

Christ, he needed to stop thinking about her. None of it mattered. Not like he was going to try and keep some kind of relationship going. She'd gone back to her life. Time for him to do the same. And he could start with getting a good drunk on and finding a warm body to occupy his bed.

Speaking of…

"Hey, baby, welcome home." Carli, one of the Handlers' Honeys sidled on up to Mav. A shot in each hand, she stopped about six inches away from him. "Missed you, baby," she said in a syrupy, high-pitched voice. "Had us all worried."

Her tone was almost accusatory, as if he'd made some kind of reckless choice. Rode his bike on the wrong side of the highway going ninety instead of being held against his will and tortured.

Carli had been Mav's go-to when he didn't have time or energy to go searching for someone new. Recently, however, she'd been edging toward major clinger. Meant it was time to put the brakes on. That was the excuse he was going to give her, anyway. Nicer than telling her his dick just straight-up had no interest in her. Seemed he couldn't get it up for any woman he'd come across since meeting Stephanie. Except Stephanie herself, of course. Shit, just thinking about her gave him a semi.

"'Sup, Carli?"

She downed one of the shots then nestled the other in her ample exposed cleavage. "Thought you could use a drink. You'll have to get it yourself, though, baby."

He barely suppressed the urge to roll his eyes. "Ain't your baby, Carli." Folding his arms across his chest in a dismissive posture, he didn't make a move toward the shot.

"Oh...uh...I know." Her grin wobbled, but she wasn't deterred. "How about we move somewhere a little quieter? You're probably pretty sore, huh?" She licked her cherry red lips and pursed them, looking more like a duck than a sexpot.

Sore? She had no fucking idea. There were cracked ribs on both sides of his chest, so every breath was agonizing.

"Not tonight, Carli, okay? Got too much shit on my mind. Go find one of the other guys. One of them will take care of you." She'd been singling Maverick out lately, and that wouldn't bode well for her future with the club. The Honeys were there for the guys, all the guys. They didn't get to be overly choosy. Once in a blue moon a Honey caught the eye of a brother and ended up an ol' lady, but that shit was rare.

Might sound like a raw deal to some, but the girls got the protection and support of the club in exchange. Most of the girls came from shit backgrounds and loved life with the club. But they weren't actual members and needed to get with the program if they wanted to stay.

For a second, he feared Carli might cry. Shit. Was she really that spun up over him? He was never gonna make her his ol' lady. She had to know that. Even if he'd been interested in her, with a background like his, he didn't have the first fucking clue how to be with a woman long-term.

"Nah," she said. "Turns out I'm not in the mood like I thought I was." Pulling the shot from between her tits, she slammed it down, then stepped back away from him.

"You got a role here, Carli. Don't forget that."

"Right, Maverick." With one last puppy-dog look at him, she spun on her hooker heel and marched toward the exit.

That went well.

If he were smart, he'd grab one of the other Honeys and drag her back to his room, but he'd already proven he was a damn fool. His dick only wanted Stephanie and, lucky for him, his bed still smelled like her. So instead of searching for a woman, he'd be spending the night alone smelling his sheets and buffing the missile like some horny teenager.

CHAPTER FOURTEEN

"Please continue, Agent Little." Special Agent Maddox sipped his water and flipped to a new page in his notebook.

As if he needed to take notes. As if there would be something new she'd reveal the third time around. Unless he suspected she'd lied and was trying to trip her up. She was getting all spun up in her own head. Would it be unprofessional for her to bonk her forehead against the table a few times before answering his question?

"I fell asleep. I don't know what time it was or how long I was out. A commotion outside the door woke me up. Shark came barreling in the room and went straight for me, ranting and raving about someone showing up at the house."

The special agent watched her over the top of his square-shaped readers. He'd done that through most of the debrief which, as it turned out, was just a fancy word for interrogation. This was her first since working behind a computer in cybercrimes didn't warrant too many debriefings. "Did he say who it was that had shown up?"

Maddox's stare seemed to penetrate through her eyes and into her brain. Like he was rooting around in there and trying to determine if her account of the events was accurate and truthful.

"No. He just kept screaming, 'They're fucking here.' He didn't even glance at Maverick. Just came straight toward me, grabbed my head, and slammed it against the table."

Her reporting of the events was neither true nor accurate.

If assaulting a man and allowing him to be executed wasn't bad enough, now she'd flat-out lied to her superiors at the Federal Bureau of Investigations.

"And you were rendered unconscious?"

With a nod, she said, "Immediately." At least that much was true.

Could the metal seat be any harder on her ass? She fidgeted, trying to shift the pressure to the side of her butt instead of directly over the sore bones. As she moved, her splint clunked against the table, drawing both her and Special Agent Maddox's attention.

"How are you feeling?" he asked for the first time since they began this debrief—six hours ago. Mid-forties, divorced, with a receding hairline, growing gut, and slight underbite, he had the reputation of living at the office.

"I'm sore. My wrist hurts, my ankles hurt, my ass hurts, and my next dose of pain medication was due an hour ago. We've been at this for hours without so much as a bathroom break. If my pants were off, I'd think I was still back in Shark's basement."

He didn't so much as blink at her snippy tone. "We're almost finished. Just a few more questions."

She rolled her unencumbered hand around. "Let's get on with it."

"Tell me about when you woke up."

Since she'd already laid it out for him twice, ordering him to tell her about it was on the tip of her tongue. But that wouldn't end this debacle any faster. "I woke up when I heard voices. Two men were standing over me."

"Hell's Handlers?"

"I don't know. They never said."

Lie.

Maddox sighed, clearly losing patience with her unhelpful answers. "Were they wearing leather cuts?"

"They were not."

Truth.

"What did they say to you?"

"Asked my name. Asked if I thought I could get up once the cuffs were removed. I said yes, but when I sat up, I passed out again. Next time I woke up, I was in the hospital."

Partial truth.

"And you never saw the men again? Didn't get any names?"

"No."

Lie.

"How did you end up at the Handlers' clubhouse?" He shut his notebook, thank God, and nudged the glasses up his nose.

"Maverick came into my hospital room to check on me. He offered a room for me to stay. It would have seemed off if I refused since I had no one or nothing in Tennessee, so I said yes."

Truth. Sorta.

Resting his forearms on the table, he asked, "And what happened when you arrived at the clubhouse?"

"I was shown to a room, and I stayed there for a day. Someone brought me some food, and that was that until the Agent showed up to drive me back."

Lie.

Maverick would be in jail in a hot minute if she admitted the truth. So would Zach, Copper, and Jig. The men who saved her and sought vengeance for three murdered teens.

Her inner voice had been screaming at her since she first laid a hand on King. This debrief only made it worse. Yet she kept on ignoring it.

"And you saw nothing, heard nothing while you were in the clubhouse that could be of use to our investigation?"

"No. Nothing."

Lie.

"Come on, Agent Little. Work with us a bit here. I know this was traumatic for you, but another agent is dead. Shark's house was torched, Maverick was gone when you woke up, and we have nothing. Less than nothing. Not a single shred of evidence to link the Hell's Handlers to what happened in the woods. Those men who rescued you didn't wander up to Shark's doorstep by accident, but they might as well have since we have squat. Agent Rey's family wants answers, and so do we."

Stephanie straightened in her chair, ignoring the way her sore ass ground into the hard surface. "Answers? You want answers? I've given you fucking answers. I gave Baccarella answers when I was in the hospital. Rey turned. He was a bad agent. As bad as they come. He was responsible for the deaths of three teenage girls. He almost got me raped and killed."

Maddox had the nerve to rub a hand across his smooth jaw and sigh like he didn't fully believe her. Ironic since that part was one of the few truths in her statement. "Agent Little, undercover agents are often required to—"

"To rape and murder teenage girls? Really Maddox? That's how you're going to spin this?"

Finally, a flush rose on his cheeks, and he looked abashed. "No, of course not. I'm just saying that maybe the situation wasn't quite as evil as it seemed."

Stephanie leaned forward across the table. "He admitted to being fully loyal to Shark. To. My. Face." A hard slap to the tabletop between each word had the wound on her wrist burning. Whispered it in my ear right before he tried to rape me."

"Fuck," Maddox said as though this third time through it finally sank in.

"We still need something on the Handlers."

"Why?" She scrunched her forehead. "We were never there for them. The Gray Dragons are trafficking woman, and we now have proof. We've never been interested in the Handlers before. Why now?"

"Both Shark's and Agent Rey's bodies were found at the house, charred to near dust."

Rey's? How on earth had the Handlers pulled that one off? Nope. She didn't need or want to know. At least there was one thing she was in the dark about.

"That can't slide, Agent Little. They may have done us a favor by taking the assholes out, but it's still murder of an FBI agent. Doesn't matter if he was crooked. Please give me something. Think hard. Anything you heard, saw? Even if it seems insignificant now."

Pinching the bridge of her nose, Stephanie chuckled. "Ever spent any time around bikers?"

Maddox shook his head.

"They're all a bunch of hot-headed, macho alphas. Real men," she said in an exaggerated man voice. "They don't tell the little women anything about their business. And I wasn't even one of their women. You think they were going to let any tidbits drop around me? You think they were going to let me see anything that was going on? You're fooling yourself."

Lie.

So many lies.

"All right," Maddox finally said, pushing back his chair and rising to his full height of only five-feet-six inches.

After spending days around men who made her feel child-sized, it was odd to be in the presence of a man who only had three inches on her. Sent her on a bit of a power trip. He couldn't intimidate her with his size if he tried.

"I think that's enough for today. We'll be sending some agents down to talk to the Handlers, but that will be a big fat dead-end, I'm sure."

She nodded. None of the bikers would talk. Not for a million bucks.

"We may have some follow-up questions as the investigation goes on. You know the drill."

Another nod from her. All of a sudden, the interrogation room felt about the size of a doll's house, and she needed to get the hell out before she broke through the walls. "You know where to find me."

He opened the door and gestured for her to precede him. "Take some leave," he said. More like ordered.

"I'd planned to." She held up her casted wrist. "Not much good on a computer with this thing."

"You've been approved for two months. SAC Baccarella wants you to take it all. Make sure your head is on straight and let your arm heal. Come back when the cast gets removed."

"Yes, sir." She left him standing in the hallway staring after her. Part of her wanted to sprint back to him and demand to know if he bought her story, but that was a dead giveaway as to the falsity of her statement. So, she marched forward and tried like hell to ignore the disapproval in Maddox's gaze.

As she stepped out of the FBI Headquarters and onto Pennsylvania Avenue, a pit settled low in her gut. Two months was a long time. Under normal circumstances, she'd be thrilled with a mandatory sixty days paid vacation. Now, however, the thought of eight weeks off, alone in her one-bedroom apartment, all her friends at work during the day…it sounded like a recipe for nothing but hours and hours of obsessing over the horrendous choices she'd made in the past few days.

How was it that with just a few full revolutions of the Earth, her life could have been turned so completely on its head? Nothing made sense anymore. Not her belief system, not her career, not her attraction to a man so wrong for her and, most importantly, not herself. The thought of going home and looking at herself in the mirror turned the pit in her stomach into full-on nausea. She was petrified that the woman staring back at her would be unrecognizable.

And now she had two months to do nothing but fear arrest, drown in guilt, and pine for a man she had irrational but powerful feelings for.

Just a few things to look forward to while she healed.

CHAPTER FIFTEEN

"Sixer's dead." Zach let that bomb explode smack in the middle of breakfast, causing Maverick to choke on his cinnamon roll waffle. Sixer and Lefty had been vying for top dog in the Gray Dragons now that Shark was fish food. Took a full month, but it looked like Lefty had won.

And that meant it'd been a month since he'd seen Stephanie. Though not a month since he'd thought about her—that was about ten minutes.

"All right, brother?" Jig slapped him on the back from his seat in the booth next to Maverick. Fuck, that hurt. His ribs still weren't a hundred percent, not that his brothers gave a shit.

"Say it again?"

"You heard me just fine, dipshit," Zach said as he shoveled a forkful of pancakes in his trap. "Sifser if dead." He spoke around his mouthful. The club didn't typically discuss business in the diner, but it was a rainy Wednesday morning, so the place was uncharacteristically vacant. So empty that Toni had sent some of the servers home early, and the rest were milling around behind the diner's eat-in counter. No one within earshot.

"Jesus, man, were you raised in a barn? Swallow before you start spewing that shit all over the table. How'd it go down?" Mav asked.

Zach took a big gulp of his coffee and shrugged. "Civil war, like we thought. Lefty had the stronger backing. Sixer was found minus his tongue and eyes on the side of the road."

"Shit, that's some rage for ya." Nothing like ripping out someone's tongue and eyes to get the point across.

Across the table from Mav, Copper grunted and rubbed a napkin across his mouth. These days, his beard was much more under control, cropped close to his face. Didn't detract from his don't-fuck-with-me vibe but was much less mountain-man.

Shell's influence for sure. Last time, she'd sicced Beth on him. She'd pouted and whined about him being too itchy-scratchy. Next day his beard was well groomed.

"So Lefty's taking over? What do we know about this fucker?" Copper asked before sipping his coffee. Even though he was fully engaged in the conversation, his eyes kept drifting to Shell refilling salt shakers behind the counter.

Dark circles rimmed her eyes, and her normally put-together hair was thrown up in a sloppy pile on the top of her head like she hadn't had much time to get ready that morning. Come to think of it, she'd mentioned something about her little girl having an earache. Beth was the sweetest kiddo but, man, there was serious drama when she wasn't feeling well. Shell must have had a shit night.

Copper frowned each time Shell came into his field of vision. She worked her fingers to the bone to provide a good life for Beth and took the club up on embarrassingly few offers of help. Prideful woman.

Drove Copper batshit.

When he'd flat-out ordered her to let the club pay her rent for a few months, she'd blown a gasket. Never once had Mav seen her react in anger before or since that day but, man, when she let the temper run free, even the scariest of his brothers cowered.

If Prez wanted her to stop working and be cared for, he needed to man the fuck up and make her his woman. Until then, she'd made it damn clear the club might be her family, but they had no say in how she ran her life.

"Hate to say it, but we know dick," Jig answered. "Lefty was high up in the gang, not quite as important as King, but probably third in command, their bastardized equivalent of Sergeant at Arms."

"Hey, gentleman, how is everything?" Toni asked as she sidled up to the table wearing denim cutoffs that showed off some pretty sweet stems. Her diner T-shirt was snug and stretched across tits Zach stared at like he hadn't been all over them in weeks, when in reality it'd probably been less than a few hours.

"You tell me," Zach said, tagging her around the waist and pulling her to his lap. He captured her lips and kissed the hell out of her right there in front of the rest of them.

"Mmm, sweet," Toni said, breathless when they pulled apart. She'd come a long way in the month since she'd killed Shark. At first, she struggled to deal with it, but Zach got her through. Watching them suck face gave Mav some strange twinge of discomfort on the left side of his chest.

Something was wrong with him. Maybe he needed to see a shrink or some shit. It'd been over a month since he'd even touched a woman. Stephanie was the last, and she had done some voodoo shit to his dick because it wouldn't get hard over anything but thoughts of her and her slick heat coating his fingers.

She'd disappeared into the wind. Not a call, not a text, not so much as a fucking telegram. He'd considered tracking her down a few times, but what was the point? If she wanted nothing to do with him, who was he to fuck with her life? Whatever unhealthy obsession he'd developed for her would fade in time. Until then, he'd just have to get used to a prolonged case of blue balls.

"Get you guys anything else?" Toni asked from Zach's lap.

"We're good, babe. Actually, can you give us a few minutes to chat? Don't send anyone over." Zach gave her that pointed look that said club business, and Toni nodded.

"You bet." She started to rise, but Copper put his mitt-sized hand over hers, holding it to the table. Her eyes widened comically. Copper wasn't one to go around being all sweet with anybody. Except Shell's daughter. Whenever Beth was around, he turned into a red-headed teddy bear.

"Hold on a minute, doll." He cast an apologetic look at Zach. "Got a question for you."

Toni looked between him and Zach. Worry lines marred her forehead when she took in Zach's tense posture and narrowed eyes. "Cop," he said in a warning tone.

"What's going on?" Toni asked, still bobbing her gaze between her ol' man and the prez.

"Sorry, Zach, but it's gotta be done." He gave Toni the respect of looking her right in the eye. "You ever hear of a guy named Lefty, doll?"

The color drained from Toni's face so fast it looked like a video on fast forward. "Lefty?" she croaked. "Yeah, I know him. Knew him." As his name left her lips, she seemed to curl in on herself, shoulders slumping, arms crossed over her chest. Shit. That could only mean one thing.

"He, uh, he is—was Shark's cousin. They were close, uh, very close." She cleared her throat and stared at a tiny nick in the table where her fingernail scraped over it again and again. "Close enough to share. Everything."

Behind her, Zach growled and wrapped his arms around his woman. All four men at the table kept their focus on their plates. They all knew exactly what her statement meant. Toni had a bit of a rough past. She'd been Shark's girlfriend years ago when she was a teen and he was angling for a seat at the big boys' table. He and his banger buddies had a nasty habit of passing their women around to other gang members, willing or not. Toni had some pretty nightmare-inducing memories from that time in her life.

And now she'd basically told them Lefty was one of the assholes in those nightmares.

"He's taking up where Shark left off," Copper told her. "He someone we should worry about?"

Getting some of her pluck back, Toni straightened and uncrossed her arms. "Well, he's a sadistic, misogynistic son of a bitch. He's dumber than Shark, but also crazier. An egomaniac who always needed to be right and be number one. So, I guess I'd say yes, he'll be someone for the Handlers to worry about."

Copper gripped his coffee mug so hard his meaty fist was in danger of pulverizing the thing. Mav could relate to the feeling. No doubt Zach felt ten times worse. "I'm most concerned with him trafficking women," Copper said in full president mode. "If he tries to grow that business, they'll be snagging women from our territory eventually. It's just a matter of time."

"Snagging women?" Toni's soft echo of his words seemed to remind him he was in mixed company.

"Shit, sorry, doll. Nothing you need to worry about. Okay?"

Too bad Copper didn't know Toni better. If he had, he could have saved himself the snort of derision and "bullshit" that came from her. Her back was iron-rod straight tense, and she looked ready for battle. "Look, I'm not trying to be all up the club's private business, but as a woman who spent far too much time with those assholes, I can't possibly pretend I didn't hear that. There aren't many reasons to kidnap women, so I can pretty much guess what they're doing with them. I'd say if anyone was going to want a piece of that action, it'd be Lefty."

"Fuck," all four men said at the same time.

"Thanks, doll," Copper said.

Zach whispered something in her ear that had her relaxing and nodding. Then she rose and made her way behind the counter where Shell was wringing out a rag in the sink that looked like she'd gotten all the water out ten minutes ago. The two women shared a look, then Toni squeezed Shell's arm and disappeared into her office, leaving Shell chewing on her lip and still twisting the dry washrag.

For a moment, Maverick allowed himself to imagine it was Stephanie standing behind that counter, supporting him, worrying over him, waiting to go home and tear up the sheets with him. For the first time in his thirty-eight years, the idea of being attached to a woman wasn't terrifying.

And *that* fucking terrified him.

CHAPTER SIXTEEN

"Is this some kind of fucking joke?" Stephanie asked as she peered around the room. Of course, it was a joke. Any second now, her co-workers would pop out of the closet and bathroom with a sheet cake that said *Sorry your case went to shit in the worst way. Welcome back.*

Not that she was in the mood for a practical joke or a damn party. She was beyond exhausted. Two months of horror-filled dreams that made sleep near impossible would drain anyone.

Seconds ticked by, and the only thing that happened was the SACs pursed lips drooping into a frown. "In deference to your situation, I'll overlook your outburst, but in the future, control your tongue when you speak to your supervisor, Agent Little."

In deference to her situation.

In deference to her *fucking* situation.

Her mouth formed the shape of the *wh* in what, but the word never came out. Instead, she took a breath and stared at the ceiling until she had something nicer than *fuck you* to say.

"Please excuse me, sir," she said through a locked jaw, "but how can you justify giving Agent Rey a post-humus Medal of Valor?" The muscles at the base of her skull felt like they were being tightened by a crank.

"He died in the line of duty, Agent Little. On an undercover mission that took him away from his wife and child for over seven months. The gang is killing each other in a civil war. We haven't had any more reports of missing women. His mission was accomplished."

The air in the windowed corner office she'd once been so enamored with grew hot, stifling. The top button of her blouse was dangerously close to choking her. She needed air. Needed out. But that wasn't going to happen anytime soon.

"He was a traitor, and you're treating him like a hero. He was the reason I was grabbed. He was the reason I was terrorized. He was the reason I was nearly raped—hell, he was the one who almost did it. He's why I have ring-shaped scars around my wrists and ankles." She drew in a shaky breath and straightened in her chair. "And he's the reason I still wake up screaming every single night," she said, head high. There was no point in hiding it. The lack of sleep was evident in her pale skin, sunken eyes, weight loss.

It wasn't anything to be embarrassed about. For forty-eight hours she'd been terrorized, the threat of rape and death hanging over her head every second. It was traumatizing. No one would make it out without a nightmare or two. No one needed to know the majority of her nightmares involved the FBI arresting her for aiding and abetting, for perjury, and for murder. That her dreams were plagued with Rey's taunting face reminding her he knew what she did and would find a way to make her pay.

Did Maverick have nightmares?

Not the time. Not the place.

"So your report says." Director Baccarella leveled her a stare that had her fuming. He was in his early fifties with salt and pepper hair and a small but growing gut that spoke to his time out of the field and behind a desk. The salt and pepper hair that once made him look distinguished in a Clooney kind of way was looking much more salt than pepper since she'd last seen him.

She'd lied about so much, it was ironic one of the only truthful parts of her statement was the portion he chose to call into question.

"Excuse me?" she asked so low she wondered if she'd said it out loud. Even though she deserved so much more than a little disbelief, the sense of betrayal was so heavy on her chest she couldn't muster the power to speak louder.

"Look, Stephanie," he said using her given name for the first time in two years. "Daniel was a decorated Special Agent. He'd been in the FBI over ten years. He had a wife. Kids. He was a Boy Scout Troop leader, for fuck's sake."

Like she didn't know all this? She was the one who worked closest with him over the past two years. She was the one who sat at his family's table for Sunday dinner more times than she could count. She was the one who rushed to his house to babysit his kids when his wife cut her palm slicing an avocado and needed fifteen stitches.

"So, what? Because he looked like the poster boy for the FBI on paper, my report must be wrong? I'm lying? Maybe I'm bitter that the mission went south and I'm looking for someone to pin it on? Must be. Because I've only been here two years. I'm not married. No kids."

What a mess of a situation. Because she was lying about so much. But not about this. Not about Rey giving up everything he'd supposedly believed in for nothing but some cash and some power.

Not like you giving it up for an orgasm.

God, she wanted to vomit. She was no better than the man she hated. Sweat coated her palms, and she rubbed them on her navy slacks as discretely as possible. Why did he keep the room so damn hot?

Director Baccarella sagged in his chair, suddenly looking less like a powerful government official and more like an exhausted and overworked public servant. "No." He paused and gazed off into space as though deciding what he wanted to say. "We had suspicions for the past few months."

This just got better and better. "Suspicions?"

"I know he mostly checked in with you, but I spoke with him

once a month. He'd missed check-ins and his reports to me were inconsistent, sometimes erratic, with conflicting information. His wife hadn't spoken to him in almost six weeks."

"And you didn't think I needed to know this? The agent who was his contact in Tennessee? The one who went down there to meet with him?"

What a fucking joke.

The director's phone buzzed on his desk. He spared a moment to check it, and his face hardened. "Listen, Agent Little," he said, focusing back on her. The tired man of moments ago was gone, replaced by the sharp-minded agent who'd been one of the youngest to make director. "You've been at this long enough to know nothing is ever simple. Nothing is ever black and white. I'm going to give it to you straight. The Director of the FBI is looking to retire by the end of the year. There are two of us on the president's short list to replace him. I want that position. But a rogue agent who murdered three teens and tried to rape another agent would not only kill my chances, it'd kill my career entirely. So it stays here between the very few people who know the story."

Stephanie flew out of her chair and slapped her palms down on the desk. Pain reverberated through her wrist. The cast had been removed three days ago, but weakness in the joint kept it stiff and achy.

She loomed over the seated director as much as a five-foot-three frame could loom. "I have to attend a medal ceremony for a man who betrayed his country and almost killed me because you don't want to look bad? This is fucking bullshit."

Baccarella cleared his throat and rose. He was only six inches taller, but it still had the effect of stealing her advantage. "I warned you once, Agent Little."

Stephanie couldn't stand it anymore. She had to get out of the room. "I'm sorry, sir, but I just can't accept this outcome."

A snorted laugh was his response. "You can't possibly be this naïve after working here for two years."

Hearing Daniel's same accusation out of the director's mouth was a knife that cut the last thread she'd been hanging on by. "Guess I'll see you at the medal ceremony, sir." She started toward the door, keeping her head high and her steps long.

Just as she gripped the handle, he said, "One more thing, Agent Little."

"Sir?" she said without turning.

"We're going to need you to go back to Tennessee."

Shit. She'd known this request was coming. Somewhere in the back of her mind, in a place she'd been ignoring for weeks, she knew they were going to ask this of her.

"I'm not an undercover agent. I'm not trained for it." Did he even give a shit that she'd be in more danger than an experienced agent?

"We're pretty sure the Hell's Handlers took out Shark and Daniel but can't find a damn thing that connects them to the murders. I need to close that loop. I need the win. We also have suspicions they're taking over the drug trafficking and possibly the human trafficking as well."

Never.

Had he seen the men's reactions to Daniel's involvement with the missing girls, he'd never think that. The admission could never cross her lips, though. Not unless she wanted a free trip to prison. And really, should she say never? Her attraction to Maverick was clouding her judgement. She didn't know those men. If King flipped for the promise of a big payday, it certainly wasn't unreasonable for men already criminals to pick up the slack.

Even if her gut rejected the notion.

Stephanie let her forehead fall to the door with a thunk. "Sir, none of the information we have on the Handlers MC points to them dealing in drugs or women. All intel indicates crimes the FBI isn't overly interested in at this time."

Except, of course, murder. Multiple murders. One that happened just ten feet away from her.

"I need more than assumptions and speculation."

Back to Tennessee. Back to the Handlers. Back to Maverick. Excitement and dread warred for victory in her gut. "And if I refuse?"

Even though she wasn't looking at him, she saw him shrug in her mind. "Not sure the Pittsburg PD would take you on again considering what your father did there, but you could always give it a try."

Take the assignment or lose her job.

So Daniel earned a commendation and she earned threats to her job.

Message received.

"We'll send another agent," he continued. "The investigation would take a lot longer. You have a relationship of sorts with those people. They'll welcome you. Another agent might take months to worm their way into the club."

And another agent would discover the club killed both Shark and Daniel. Maverick would go to jail, probably for the rest of his life.

She'd use her last breath to keep him out of jail.

"When do I leave, sir?"

"Got you on a flight day after tomorrow. And you'll report directly to me."

Fantastic.

"Yes, sir." She opened the door then swiveled her head back toward Director Baccarella. "I'll go sir, but you need to know you're wrong about one thing. I'm not naïve. This is a very clear-cut case of right and wrong. You're just forcing me to go along with your wrong decision."

She stepped through and hustled past the admin's desk, avoiding the curious stare the thirty-something assistant shot her.

Tomorrow she'd be back in Tennessee. Maybe even in Maverick's presence.

Sexy, funny, protective, affectionate Maverick.

Criminal Maverick.

White and black parts of one charming man.

For the first time in her life, menacing gray clouds hovered in Stephanie's future. How was she supposed to continue her pursuit of justice when she questioned everything she believed in around Maverick?

CHAPTER SEVENTEEN

"Hey, Mav, what happened to you last night? Zach told me you were gonna stop by for dinner. I made your favorite." Toni's voice was laced with disappointment.

Shit.

Had Maverick known she'd go out of her way to make a meal for him, and enchiladas at that, he'd have forced himself to leave his own pity party and show his face at his best friend's house like he'd agreed to.

Toni slid onto the stool next to Maverick, and he waved over the prospect working the bar. "She'll have an Ultra," he said of Toni's typical beer. "How you doin', gorgeous? You gonna give me some sugar?"

Toni giggled and rolled her eyes about the same time a bulky, tattooed arm banded across her chest and yanked her flush against Zach's chest.

"What the fuck I tell you about your lips and my woman?" Zach practically growled as he lowered his mouth to Toni's neck and sucked at her pulse point.

"Zach!" she screeched, but quickly gave up the fight. "Well, okay." She giggled and bit her bottom lip as Zach trailed kisses up to her jaw.

Mav stared at the array of partially full bottles lined up along the back mirror of the bar. He sure didn't mind watching. In fact, he normally loved it. Watching two people go at it was one of the best ways to get his own motor revved. But there was something about seeing Zach and his girl get it on that made his insides churn. Probably had something to do with the intensity of the connection they shared. Too much emotional slime coated the air between them. They were so far gone over each other, it was nauseating.

Fuckin' love birds.

Something Maverick never had and never would understand. Sex? Fuck yeah, he understood that. Wrote the fuckin' book. It was his favorite pastime, after all. But being obligated to bang the same woman night after night, morning after morning, or whatever? He shuddered.

No, thank you.

He loved women too much to pick just one. Each was special and unique in their own way. Tall or short. Blond, redhead, or brunette. Thick or thin. He loved them all. Sure, there was a type that stiffened his dick faster than the others, like pocket-sized blonds, spinners, but he sure as hell didn't discriminate.

Then the image of one light-haired, blue-eyed wildcat flashed through his mind making all his former convictions feel wrong. He shoved the thoughts away. None of it mattered, she was gone.

"You two nymphos about finished, or you gonna need me to show you the best position for fucking on this bar?"

Toni swatted Zach's face away but snuggled her back against his chest. "You didn't," she said, her eyes dancing.

Mav winked. "Sure did, sweet stuff. Wanna hear the tale?"

"Think I'll pass, thanks. Can you tell me exactly where, though? Because last week I dropped a pretzel on the bar top and I still ate it. Now I feel like I need to go scrub my tongue." She picked her beer up by the neck with two fingers and looked underneath it as though she could see the Maverick-germs crawling around.

Mav threw his head back and laughed. Zach's woman was hilarious and as good as they came. Made herself a rockin' ol' lady. "Let's just say I started at that end, and I'm working my way down." He pointed toward the far end of the bar.

"You're a fuckin' animal," Zach said. "You should be required to carry papers."

Toni laughed and held her hand up for Zach to high-five. As their palms slapped together, Mav made a mock vomit noise. They'd started this little hand-slap routine a few weeks ago, and it was as dumb as it was juvenile.

"Hey, Toni," he said, not feeling very playful anymore. "Sorry I bailed on you guys last night. Didn't mean for you to go to any trouble on my account. Won't happen again, sweet stuff."

Wiggling herself out of Zach's hold, she rose and planted a kiss on Mav's cheek. Sweetness and sunshine with a backbone of pure steel. That's what Toni was. "No worries, Mav." She glanced back at her man. "I was just worried about you. You've been off since…well, you know. Where'd you end up last night anyway?"

Where had he been? At a strip club, conducting an experiment of sorts. A very failed experiment consisting of him leaving ten minutes after arriving.

When he only shrugged, Toni nodded and gave him a smile. "I'll let you boys talk. Shell's supposedly here somewhere with Beth, so I'm going to track them down."

She started to walk away but Zach snagged her hand, reeled her close, and laid a kiss on her that had her breathless and swaying when he was finished. "I won't be long, babe. We got a sunset to see."

"Uh, yeah, sure." She nodded, her eyes glassy, and stumbled toward the back of the clubhouse.

"So, how you feeling, man?" Zach asked when his eyes were no longer glued to his woman's ass.

"Good." Mav drained his beer and set the bottle down. "Great actually. Been three days since I've taken any of that pain shit. Even dropped the Motrin."

"That's fucking great." Zach ran a hand through his perfect

blond hair. The hair that helped craft his nickname. He was a dead-ringer for Zack Morris, the teen heartthrob from the nineties show Saved by the Bell. Zach hated the meaning behind the name at first, but even he couldn't deny the striking resemblance. He was a jacked version of Mark Paul Gosselaar for sure.

"Yeah. What are you up to tomorrow? I'm meeting with Rip about some ink."

Zach fell silent then said, "For your arm?"

For his arm. It nearly killed him when that brand was destroyed. The physical pain had been so intense the only thing that got him through was Stephanie's beautiful gaze locked with his, but the pain of losing something so meaningful to him ached ten times worse.

"Yeah, I'm not getting inked tomorrow, just meeting with Rip to see what my options are with the skin graft and scarring."

"Shit, man. I've got personal training sessions all day. Let me see what I can move around." Zach owned the only gym in town, and while he had a great team working for him and barely had to show his face, he loved the place and still took on quite a few clients.

"Nah, man, don't fuck with your schedule. I'm good. Not like I haven't been there before."

They both laughed. Mav had so much ink he was running low on space for new tats.

"You sure?" Zach asked.

"Maverick!" Copper bellowed from the clubhouse side of the building. "Get your scrawny fucking ass in here. Pronto!"

"Uh oh." Zach coughed in the shittiest attempt at not laughing. "Daddy's pissed. What'd you do? Have a girl in your room with the door closed?"

"Fuck off."

"Toni left the extra food in the fridge for you."

Christ, she was a sweetheart.

"Good woman you got there, Z."

"Fuckin' know it, brother."

"Still think I can get her to ditch you for me."

"Never gonna happen." It'd been a running joke since the two got together. Mav would die before making a move on the woman, and Zach knew it. But he was still a possessive monster when it came to his ol' lady, and Mav jumped on every opportunity to get under his brother's skin.

Maverick smirked then slapped Zach on the back. He moseyed on over to Copper's office. "What's up, Prez," he asked as he stepped through the door.

Seated behind his desk, Copper's scowl was fiercer than usual. Good thing Mav didn't scare easily. He might be inclined to slink out of the office otherwise. "Looking a little tense, Cop. You need me to rub your feet or some shit?"

"No, I don't need you to rub my damn feet. I need you to take this one up to your room." Cop gestured with his head as he spoke, and it was then Maverick noticed Carli standing against the wall, a hopeful smile on her heavily made-up face. "Take her to your room and fuck her until she's too tired to bring her bullshit into my office."

The smile took a dive off Carli's face, and her expression hardened.

Shit.

That girl could throw a fit like no other. And if she did so in Copper's office, there'd be hell to pay for both Carli and Maverick. Even though he was clueless as to the bullshit Copper mentioned.

Didn't matter.

If there was one thing Copper couldn't stand, it was drama from the Honeys. They could party, fuck, and hang as long as they wanted, given they didn't cause trouble. More than one had been tossed out on her well-used ass for getting too clingy and overstepping with some brother's ol' lady. This little show here was Carli's first and final warning.

"Sorry, Copper. Won't happen again," Maverick said, shooting eye daggers at Carli when she opened her mouth. She needed to pipe the fuck down until they were out of Copper's office. Being on his bad side pissed Maverick off, and being in the doghouse because of a Honey was even worse.

Humiliating.

"Let's go." He gripped Carli by her upper arm and propelled her out of Copper's office ahead of him. Without speaking, he marched through the bar area and up the stairs toward his room, ignoring the whistles and catcalls of his stupid-ass brothers.

"Mav, slow down," Carli whined as she teetered along on five-inch spikes. "I'm gonna break an ankle."

"You'll be lucky if that's all you break," he muttered under his breath, stopping outside his door to hunt for the key in his pocket.

Carli plastered herself against him, her balloon-sized, man-made tits engulfing his arm in their cleavage. Once, not even too long ago, that might have worked, but he hadn't touched her since the week before he'd been snatched off the street and had no interest in doing so now. Ever again, really. "Like you'd ever hurt me," she whispered near his ear. "You're a lover, baby, not a fighter."

That was true. He'd take fucking over fighting any day. That didn't mean he couldn't throw down when necessary. But he wouldn't harm a woman. Scare her a little? Fuck, yeah.

When the door swung open, he stepped out of her hold without warning. Since she'd been leaning so heavily on him, she lost her footing and staggered into his room, grabbing the door frame to keep from face planting on his geometric print area rug.

"What the hell, Mav? Why are you being such a dick?" She jammed her hands on her hips and stuck her lower lip out in a pout that would make most men wonder just what she could do with that mouth.

A lot. She could do a lot.

Because she was easy as spreading soft butter and had sucked countless dicks between those lips.

"I'm the one asking the questions here. You went to Copper? About me? What the fuck were you thinking? You got any idea how much the prez hates that shit?"

Still pouting, Carli strode toward him with a sultry walk meant to entice. Her tits were encased in some leather bustier type thing that showed off a mountain of fake flesh and ended above her belly button, revealing a two-inch expanse of bare stomach. With spaghetti straps and a metallic zipper down the center, it looked like some kind of oversized bra.

"I was worried about you," she said in a girlish voice, lowering the zipper as she continued toward him. Platinum hair, bleached to shit, swished around her leather-covered hips as she walked. "You've been weird since they rescued you. You haven't fucked me at all. At first, I thought it was because you were too injured. But you even turned me down when I offered to ride you. And now you're back on your bike and working, but I still haven't had your dick."

She was close, and Maverick finally felt his blood heat. But not with lust. Nope, not even a flicker down below. This was all fury.

"So the-fuck what, you haven't had my dick. You don't own that shit. Plenty other willing brothers around here to take you on."

"No one can do what you do, Mav."

He hated the sound of his own name coming from her unclean mouth. "So you went to fucking Copper? What'd you think he was gonna do? Order me to fuck you?"

Her pout turned to a mischievous grin.

Fuck.

That's precisely what Copper had done.

Conniving bitch.

Time to shut shit down. He was done with Carli.

"Ever think I'm just over it? Done with you? Maybe I'm looking for someone who ain't so broken in?" Harsh, sure, but sometimes that's what was necessary to get the point across.

Besides, he'd been in a shit mood for weeks, and it looked like he finally found someone to take it out on.

She stilled her hand and the zipper about three-quarters of the way open, and an ugly sneer crossed her face. "I think maybe more happened than you want to admit while Shark had you. Maybe you got a little taste of dick while you were there, and now you need a little something different to get you off."

And out come the claws.

Was this bitch for real?

"Okay, we're done here." He strode toward the door and gripped the handle. "You need to get the fuck out. Stay away from me and out of my shit, or I'll have you banned. You ever go to Copper about me again, and I won't need to have you banned. He'll throw you out like last week's garbage."

With that parting shot, he jerked the door open and his heart skipped at least three beats. Stephanie stood outside his door, hand raised and fisted as though she was mid-knock. She was wearing a loose purple T-shirt with a white rhinoceros across her tits and lettering that read *Help the chunky unicorns*. Skinny jeans that appeared a size too big hung from her hips.

Nothing sexy about the outfit. Nothing seductive. Hell, she didn't even look good with dark circles under her flat eyes and a pallor to her skin that hinted she'd been hiding out inside since she'd left, yet the second his gaze finished its journey over her gentle feminine shape, his dick was rock hard and ready to play.

Instant boner.

"Stephanie," he said as though she wasn't aware of her own name. Not a smooth or charming opener in sight.

"Hi," she said, dropping her hand. She flashed him the sweetest, slightly nervous smile, then her eyes shifted to a spot over his right shoulder and widened.

Carli had sidled up to him and was once again pressing into him, only she hadn't bothered to do up her top.

Stephanie's face blanched, which he hadn't thought possible, then her gaze dropped, and Maverick could swear he felt the searing heat of it wrap around his cock.

His very hard cock.

The white in Stephanie's cheeks immediately gave way to a crimson flush. "Oh, my God," she mumbled, her gaze shifting between Carli's smug expression and his hard dick.

The woman he'd been dreaming about for the past six weeks thought he had a raging hard-on for the scheming club whore.

Fuck a duck.

CHAPTER EIGHTEEN

Well, this was off to a fabulous start.

The man who'd saved her from rape, who'd murdered the bastard who nearly raped her, who'd worked her to her first man-induced orgasm in years, and who she'd lied her ass off to protect was about to have sex with a very cheap looking...*lady*, if the bulge between his legs was any indication.

And she'd interrupted it.

Full-on interrupted while his *date* was in the process of undressing.

Kill me now.

The intensity of his gaze made her squirm, made it impossible to look away and peek at his package to see if it was still hard or if she'd totally killed his mood.

"What are you doing here?"

Well, he didn't sound repulsed by her presence. Though certainly not excited either. Straight-up shocked was more like it.

"I, uh, um..."

In the forty-six hours since she left SAC Baccarella's office, Stephanie had been briefed, briefed again, and then briefed some more. She was now the FBI's official Hell's Handlers expert with a profile on each man memorized—at least as much information as the FBI had, which admittedly was not impressive. They'd also given her a cover story that she'd learned forward and backward, but now seemed unable to conjure a single word of.

Then it started to come back to her. Maverick: road captain. Owner of a private security business suspected of muscle for hire and some illegally acquired intel. Lives at the Handlers' clubhouse. Fun-loving, easygoing to a point.

Womanizer.

"I—" She cleared her throat and shifted her focus to the frowning woman. Why wasn't he shutting the door in her face and getting back to business?

He continued to stare at her like he could see straight through her skin. "You're struggling."

Not the story the FBI wanted her to use, but the truth. They preferred she act worried for him and how he was healing. Thought it would help her worm her way into the fold. Part of her wanted to deny his statement, but she found herself unable to lie to those penetrating eyes. Except for the whole being an FBI agent, of course.

"I'm struggling."

"Fuck." He nodded and ran a hand through his hair. "You look like shit."

Well, that was sweet.

The second the words left his mouth, he winced. "I didn't mean it like that."

Holding up a hand, Steph nodded. "It's fine. I haven't been sleeping all that well. Not much of an appetite." In case he was wondering why her outfit hung off her like a sack. As opposed to Miss Ginormous-Tits who wore skin-tight clothes and seemed to have lost all patience for this interaction.

"Baby," she whined, rubbing those voluptuous breasts against Maverick's arms. "Come on back inside."

Maverick blinked and finally pulled his gaze from Stephanie, gaping at the woman as though he'd forgotten she was there. "Get gone, Carli," he said sliding his arm from her boa constrictor hold.

"But—" She pouted. Actually pouted like an unhappy child.

"Nuh uh. Time's up." Mav stepped forward, dismissing her,

his focus back on Stephanie. His gaze started at her hair and took a slow, examining journey down her body, stopping at her wrists. He circled it with a touch so gentle, tears sprang to Stephanie's eyes. His thumb landed on the raised scar left from the handcuffs, and he lifted her arm as though holding a butterfly. "Shit, wildcat."

God, it felt good to hear that nickname. Stupid as it might be, it gave her a boost of confidence. She had felt nothing but weak and defeated the past two months. Hearing him call her wildcat reminded her there was someone out there who knew what she was really like.

Stephanie shot a quick glance at the seriously pissed-off skank, who still hadn't left, then said, "It's okay. Rarely hurts anymore."

"Shouldn't be there at all." Still so gently she nearly let the tears fall, he tugged her into the room at the same time his other hand nudged Carli out the door. "Told you before she knocked, Carli, that it wasn't going to happen today, tomorrow, next year, or fucking ever. This is your only warning. Pull shit like this again, and I'll see to it you're banned from the property."

Then he slammed the door, but not before Stephanie caught the way Carli's face crumpled into misery. Part of her felt a little guilty for playing a role in Carli's fate, but she'd be lying if she said it wasn't wonderful to hear he hadn't planned on sleeping with her.

"I'm so sorry I interrupted you. I can go if you want to, uh... you know."

"Heard me tell her it wasn't happening?"

Stephanie nodded.

"Wasn't saying that shit for your benefit, Steph. Not interested in her. Only seem to be getting hard for one particular woman these days."

Wait—he couldn't mean her, could he?

No, that was crazy.

"You never called," he said, accusation thick in his voice. "No text, nothing. Got jack shit from you, babe."

Unable to meet his gaze, Stephanie risked looking down. His boner seemed to have deflated. "I know. I've been a little…lost."

"Hey." He nudged her chin up with the knuckles of his right hand. Whatever it was that made her admit the truth, it was worth it. Just seeing the understanding and compassion in his eyes made her feel lighter. "We'll get it sorted."

Seeing as how her throat felt suddenly too thick to swallow, Stephanie could only nod and squeeze his hand in gratitude.

With his free hand, he pinched the excess, denim sagging around her ass. "We'll get this sorted, too."

"What?"

"Liked the way your ass filled out a pair of jeans before. We need to get you back there again. Couple visits to Toni's diner oughta do the trick."

Heat rushed to Steph's face. She'd lost almost ten pounds in the past two months, and for someone who wasn't big to begin with, it was too much. She'd known it, but the appetite just wasn't there. Basically, she'd eaten enough to survive, but had lost all pleasure in the activity. But standing there in front of Maverick, she felt hungry for the first time in months.

If only she were hungry for food alone.

While she'd been lost in thought, Mav had closed the distance between them until his front pressed against her and what she'd mistakenly thought was a diminishing hard-on was resting against her stomach. Her core clenched, but he made no move to alleviate his problem, just wrapped his arms around her and held tight. She tilted her head back and rested her chin on his firm chest, keeping her gaze on his face.

"Glad you're here, wildcat."

"So am I." It was the truth. Despite the enormous chasm of lies separating them, Stephanie felt grounded for the first time since she walked away two months ago.

AS AMAZING AS Stephanie felt all snuggled up against him,

135

and as much as his cock wanted him to do something about that amazing feeling, the rest of him was aware of just how thin she'd gotten over the past two months. It was like holding a bag of bones instead of the soft woman she'd been a short time ago.

Unacceptable.

His protective instincts flared to life, overshadowing his cock's need for release. The woman needed to be fed some goddamn grub, then needed to sleep. In his bed, preferably.

WTF?

In his bed? No. Women did not sleep in his bed. They fucked in his bed.

Sure, there'd been that one night before she left when he'd held her all night long, a night he thought about way too many times since she'd left. But that wasn't going to become the norm just because he was pissed Stephanie hadn't been taking proper care of herself.

Nope. He'd find her an unoccupied room at the clubhouse. They had plenty to spare.

With a bit of reluctance, he unwound his arms and stepped back. "Come on, let's get you fed and get you some good sleep."

Hand in hand, they made their way to the kitchen. "Grab a seat. Toni left me some enchiladas. They're the shit." As he spoke, he moved around the kitchen, first rifling through the fridge, then dishing out two heaping plates worth of food and popping the first in the microwave.

It was a novel experience, taking care of a woman, but not unpleasant. Her serious gaze tracked him as he moved around the industrial-sized kitchen. Many years ago, when the clubhouse was built, the MC wanted to be ready and able to handle a huge crowd. Hence the fifteen bedrooms, eighteen bathrooms, and a kitchen large enough to feed an army of hungry bikers. Something it did quite often.

Some of the guys lived there, like he did, while others, like Zach, had a house. Mav didn't need much—it was just him, and he was at the clubhouse all the time anyway, so why not live there?

"Thanks," Stephanie said when he dropped the plate in front of her.

"Dig in. Don't wait for me. Just take a minute to nuke mine then I'll join you."

When she took a tentative bite, her eyes lit up, and then she dug in with enthusiasm. In the ninety seconds his food heated in the microwave, Steph had devoured half her portion.

"Aren't you going to eat yours?" she asked after he'd been standing there watching her eat like an idiot for who knew how long.

Couldn't be helped. Every time she brought that damn fork to her mouth, her tongue peeked out seconds before she took a bite. It was adorable and sexy all at once and had his dick perking up in appreciation. "Yeah, getting it now."

She nodded and began to lower her focus back to her food, but must have caught sight of his rabid hard-on because her eyes widened and her mouth dropped open. Then, the damn vixen licked her lips and swallowed.

Mav groaned as he set his plate down and plopped into the seat across from her at the long rectangular table. "Maybe you could cover your mouth with your hand while you eat?"

"What?" She wiped her mouth as though worried she had sauce on her lip.

"You're fucking killing me, sweetheart. Between those lips opening and closing, and your tongue licking that lucky fork, I'm about to die. I swear if you were eating an ice cream cone, I'd have blown my load in my pants by now."

Fork midway to her mouth, Stephanie froze. Shit, had he gone too far? Then she lowered her hand and burst out laughing. The joyful sound shot straight to his dick, doing nothing to help the now-uncomfortable large erection.

"Oh, my God," she said once she'd calmed. "You have no idea how much I needed that."

Mav couldn't help but grin. She was too adorable.

137

"The fuck's going on in here?" Jig wandered into the kitchen, Rocket in tow. Jig hadn't spent much time with Steph, but as he was the one to find her tied up in the basement, he'd been concerned for her. A few times over the past two months, with about as much subtlety as a charging elephant, he'd hinted that Maverick should hunt her down.

"Well, look what the damn cat dragged in. Good to have you back, girl."

"Hey, Jig, thanks. Good to see you, too. How've you been, Rocket?"

Rocket grunted. "Fine." Then he grabbed a beer and left the kitchen.

Stephanie's eyebrows rose. Already, with one good meal settling in her stomach, she had more color in her face and seemed to perk up. "Something I said?"

Jig laughed and ruffled her hair like she was his little buddy. Kind of surprising since Jig tended to have very little to do with women. He fucked 'em, sure, but even that was an unconventional experience if rumor was to be believed. "Rocket's a loner. After about five seconds in other's company, he gets hives. Just how the dude is wired."

Holy shit. Not only was Jig smiling at Stephanie, he'd made a funny. The food in Mav's mouth thickened into a nasty lump. Did Jig have a thing for Steph? The glob of paste in his mouth wouldn't go down. Something must have shown on his face because Jig caught his eye, threw his head back, and laughed like a loon. Actually laughed. That grumpy fucker never laughed.

Shit, it was almost worth the ribbing that was sure to follow if it meant hearing Jig react like that.

"Chill the fuck out, brother," Jig said. "You're safe. Enjoy your meal."

Stephanie tracked him with her gaze as he walked out, a wrinkle between her eyebrows. "What was that about?"

"Nothing, sweetheart." Mav leaned back in his chair. He'd never admit how relieved he was to know Jig wouldn't be competition. "Just club shit."

Competition for what? He was starting to sound like a chick.

"So what's your plan, Steph?"

She rested her fork on the edge of her plate and propped her chin up with her hand. "Not sure, really. I was floundering and just needed to get away."

"You got a job to get back to?"

She shook her head. "Nah, I actually quit."

"So you can stick around for a bit?"

"Looks like it." She wouldn't meet his gaze. "Just gotta get a hotel."

"Fuck that. Stay here. We got plenty of empty rooms. Hell, you could stick around for a while. I'm sure Toni could put you to work in the diner."

Stiff as a board in the chair, she bit her lip and wouldn't meet his eyes. Whatever she'd been up to the past two months, one thing was for sure, she wasn't having a damn bit of fun. Wasn't living her life. Wasn't moving past what happened and finding things to be happy about again.

That was all going to fucking change if Mav had any say in the matter.

"Or, hell, I could use some help at the office."

Head inclined she said, "I don't even know what you do?"

"I run a security company. Some PI work, some personal protections, installation of cameras, alarms. That kinda shit."

Her eyes lit up like he'd offered her a free trip to Tahiti. "That sounds interesting. But I can definitely get a hotel room. I don't want to put you all out."

"Ain't a thing, wildcat," he said. "Save your money. Toni and Shell will be thrilled to have you around. They're always bitching about needing more women around here who don't open their legs for every male who walks by. I don't have a clue what they're talking about, but who am I to argue with a woman?" He winked, and she let out a soft laugh.

After a few minutes of studying him, she nodded. "Okay,

thank you, Maverick, I'd like to stay here. Just until I figure out what's next."

That was all it took, just her uttering his name, and Mav knew he was in big fucking trouble. Because even though he'd be putting her in a room far from his, and even though he'd promised himself he'd keep his hands off, he was so damn thrilled she was staying at the clubhouse.

What the hell was happening to him?

CHAPTER NINETEEN

Another night of tossing and turning.

Another nightmare waking her in a cold sweat.

Another time her subconscious sent her to prison, only this time Mav and his club brothers were incarcerated as well.

Another morning waking with a knotted stomach, aching jaw, and a bone-deep weariness. Usually an early riser, Stephanie allowed herself the rare luxury of lounging around in bed for a good portion of the morning. Really, it was much less about getting any real rest and more about her just being a straight-up chicken. She wasn't quite ready to start spewing lies to everyone she came across in the clubhouse. It all just felt so dirty and wrong. Especially with the warm welcome she received and the generous offer of shelter for as long as she needed it.

At ten-fifteen, a pounding on her door had her finally dragging her tired ass out of bed. When she opened the door, Maverick stood on the other side in a black wife beater, faded denim, and a beat-up pair of Vans. There was a lot of ink on display, and Stephanie found herself drawn to the colorful expression of who the man was tatted all over his body.

"Hey," he snapped. "Eyes are up here."

Heat rushed to her face, and she stopped ogling his body in favor of eye contact. The words had sounded harsh, and so in contrast with the smirk.

"Sorry. I was just admiring your tattoos. They are amazing."

"I was just messing with you, sweets. You can gawk at my bod any day any time. Hell, I can strip down and let you stare at every inch of me if you'd like." He raised an eyebrow and moved his hands to the button of his jeans.

Oh, what a tempting offer. Instead of drooling and begging for just that, she said, "That won't be necessary."

"Come on, get dressed. We're rolling out in fifteen minutes."

"What? Where are we going? And fifteen minutes? Clearly, you don't have sisters."

Something flashed across his face before he could mask it. A painful memory, maybe. Now she felt like an ass, ruining the playful mood. But Mav recovered in seconds. "You look gorgeous. A little tired, maybe, but gorgeous. We are going to grab breakfast, then I have an appointment I want you to join me for. After that, we're going to get drunk and have fun. If I'm right, and I usually am, you haven't had one lick of fun over the past two months. Time to put an end to that shit."

Well, he hit the nail on the head with that guess. Damn insightful man. Not one ounce of fun was had. In fact, she'd barely set foot outside her apartment in those two months. The walls had become her enemies, mocking her self-imposed imprisonment. Maybe he was right, and it was time to put an end to that shit. Plus, she was there to gather information, and that wouldn't happen if she hid in her room like a scared child.

"Okay...I guess. Let me just throw on something else."

"Sure." Mav stepped all the way into the room, allowing the door to close behind him, then folded his arms and leaned against it.

"Um, you gonna turn around so I can get changed?" She glanced over her shoulder as she rifled through her suitcase.

"Nope." No one could rock a flirty smirk like Mav. How it was possible for one facial expression to make her want to slap him and kiss him at the same time, she'd never understand.

"I'll just run into the bathroom and change. Give me two minutes." She gathered a pair of jeans and a casual T-shirt and started for the bathroom as Mav's laughter rang out.

"Babe, last time I saw you, I played with your tight pussy until you came all over my hand. Think you can handle me seeing you in your panties."

Stephanie stumbled as fire rushed to her face. She wasn't promiscuous, and she certainly wasn't a prude, but never had she had a man speak to her like that. She should be horrified. Hell, she should close the gap between them and give him a good crack across his face. Instead, she clenched her thighs together and prayed he wouldn't notice his effect on her.

It was a wasted prayer.

His gaze traveled straight to the portion of her that remembered precisely how expertly his fingers worked her up. "I'm...just...uh...I'll be...right back."

Clothes balled in her fist, she fled to the privacy of the bathroom and flicked the lock closed. Too bad the lock couldn't keep out Mav's howl of laughter.

Dirty rotten flirt. He knew he was more than she could handle, and he loved it.

Quick as she could, Steph stripped out of her sweatpants and oversized T-shirt and stuffed her legs into a pair of skinny jeans. She'd actually bought these right before leaving DC, so they fit better than most of her clothes. The downside was that they showed off how bony she had become. A fitted black V-neck and ponytail completed the outfit.

As she was leaving the bathroom, she caught sight of herself in the mirror and realized she had a glowing smile on her face. The first one in months. Probably the first one since Mav gave her that stellar orgasm right before she left.

With a sigh, she gripped the edge of the vanity counter and squeezed her eyes shut so she wouldn't have to look at the happy woman in the mirror who was only smiling because a criminal, hell, a murderer put the smile there. Maybe executioner was a more fitting word.

But still...

This was bad. The kind of bad that could lead to many nights of too much wine, cartons of ice cream, sappy movies, and buckets of tears...oh yeah, and unemployment and a prison sentence, too.

She could smile at Mav. She could banter with Mav. She could even flirt with Mav. Hell, the bureau wouldn't object to her sleeping with him either, but it was all supposed to be fake. Everything she did and said while with the Handlers was supposed to be in search of incriminating evidence. The FBI was counting on her to bring down the men who killed Shark and Agent Rey—*may his soul be forever tortured.* Damn Baccarella. All this because he wanted to run the FBI and needed someone to hang for Shark and Rey's deaths.

But instead of diving into the investigation, less than twenty-four hours after returning to Tennessee, she was giggling at his sexy banter and as giddy as a school girl at the thought of spending the day with him.

"Damn, girl," Mav said when she rushed out of the bathroom thirty seconds later. "We need to get some meat back on your bones, but you're still sexy as fuck." He made no attempt to hide the hand adjusting his crotch, just gave her a playful wink.

"You sure have a one-track mind, don't you?" She tossed the rumpled clothes on her temporary bed and stepped through the door he held open.

"Never claimed otherwise."

"Oh! My car keys are on top of the dresser." She turned to go back into the room, but Mav blocked her path.

With a snort, he spun her back around. "No way do you drive when we're together. And no way do I ride in a cage unless I have no other options. I've been riding again for about a week, so we take my bike. You ever ridden?"

She had, and she loved it. "Yeah, but it's been years and years."

Mav's face clouded. Gone was his typical mischievous smirk, replaced by a look of genuine displeasure. "You spent time on the back of some asshole's bike?"

It was like there was some sort of broken connection between Stephanie's brain and heart. Her intelligent side screamed at her to let the comment go, but her heart and the rest of her insides fluttered with happiness at his jealous tone. Not to mention how fun it was to be able to have a leg up on the guy that loved to tease everyone else. "Sure did. Lots of times. And he wasn't an asshole."

His ire grew, and he stopped walking about fifteen feet from the motorcycle. "How long you with this guy?"

"Long time," she said, her lips curling up. "Seems like my whole life."

"You love him?"

She bit her lower lip to keep the laughter in. "Sure did. Still do, actually." Even though she hadn't seen him in six years. Refused to see him.

"The fuck's his name?"

"My dad? His name is Steven. Steven Little, but I just called him Dad."

"You little shit." Mavs eyes glittered with mirth as he folded his arms across his chest. "Got me good, there, didn't you? Hope you're proud of yourself." He laughed and tossed her a helmet. "Get that sexy ass on the bike."

Snickering, Stephanie did as asked and had the helmet fastened before Mav mounted the bike. Once he was in position, he spoke to her over his shoulder. "You said 'called.'"

"What?"

"You said you called him Dad. Your old man not around anymore? He was a cop, right? Was he killed in the line of duty?"

Shit. He'd picked up on that. Leave it to the fun, sexy, playful biker to also be observant and curious. "He's alive." It was often impossible to get the words to cross her lips. Especially in her law enforcement circle where everyone's eyes immediately grew suspicious and their minds wandered to a place of wondering if she'd betray the badge in the same way. And look at that, she had.

Mav wouldn't judge, though. He lived a life outside the law, for crying out loud.

"He's serving a twelve-year sentence in a state prison in Maryland."

"Shit, babe, what for?" His voice was so laced with concern she found herself getting choked up. Why on earth was this man, this criminal, also the sweetest and most caring man she'd met in years?

She shook her head. "That's all I'm gonna say. I don't talk about it."

He was still for a moment then said, "Fair enough," and wrapped his large hands around the outside of her thighs. With one firm tug, she was nestled snug against his back. Warmth flowed from the hard planes of his body straight into hers.

Talking about her father couldn't have come at a more perfect time. It was a reminder that if those she trusted most could betray her, she needed to be extra careful around Maverick and his club. Usually, discussion of her father left her cold and distant. Not this time. This time the conversation was practically forgotten as the pleasure of holding Maverick stole all her brain power. She shoved the worries away. It was easy to do if she told herself she was playing a part, acting interested for the sake of the investigation.

Too bad she was lying to herself.

Fighting it was pointless. For the next little while, she had no choice but to wrap herself around Maverick as close as bark on a tree. She had no choice but to hold on. It was that or fall off, so she might as well enjoy it. At least that's how she was justifying the explosion of joy that zinged through her blood the moment she circled her arms around his taut stomach.

Ninety minutes, one belly full of the most fantastic omelet Stephanie had ever eaten, and another motorcycle ride later, Mav rolled to a stop in front of a no-frills tattoo parlor. "You're getting another tattoo? At a place called Inked?" she asked as she swung her leg off the bike—no easy feat since the thing was a monster and she wasn't exactly blessed in the height department.

Mav chuckled and swatted her hands out of the way, unclasping her helmet for her. "Yep. Shop is owned by a guy named Rip. Rumor has it, it's short for Ripshit because the dude has a temper that rivals an active volcano. Never seen it myself..." He shrugged. "But since he's the only one I trust to ink me, I ain't about to push the fucker. Anyway, he's not big on frills and fuss, so he called the place Inked. Short and to the point."

"That it is."

"Come on. Got an appointment in two minutes, and Rip is not a fan of lateness. Don't want him to tat his face on me, so we better move." He slid his palm against hers and she pretended the weakening in her knees and quiver in her stomach was just aftereffects of the motorcycle ride.

"Wait, what? He'd put his face on you?"

Mav just winked and towed her toward the door.

Above their heads, a bell jangled and alerted Rip to their presence. Or at least she assumed the tall, potbellied man with a bullring and...holy shit, were those horns under the skin of his head? "Hey, Mav, thirty seconds more and I'd be looking for a spot to add my face to your collection."

Okay, so Maverick hadn't been kidding about the lateness thing.

"Hey, Rip. Where do you want me?"

It was then Rip seemed to notice her holding hands with Maverick. T-shirt stretched across his large abdomen, he waddled his way over. "Well, well, well, who is this gorgeous creature? You bring me a virgin?"

Stephanie's eyes widened and she sputtered, but Mav just laughed and squeezed her hand. "Wipe your drool, Rip. This is Stephanie, and I have no idea if she has any tats, but it doesn't matter. She's just here for moral support."

Rip snorted and held his hand out to her. When she shook the offered hand, his fingers were long, callused, and he had a good firm grip. "Nice to meet you, Stephanie. Don't let this one cast a spell on you." He slapped Mav on the shoulder. "He ain't nothin' but trouble."

"Nice to meet you. And you're right. I am definitely a tattoo virgin."

"I can always tell by the wide-eyed wonder." He chuckled to himself. "Follow me on back, kids. Maybe you'll see something you can't resist while you're here, Stephanie."

She glanced at Maverick who bobbed his eyebrows suggestively. Yeah, she'd found something she couldn't resist all right.

CHAPTER TWENTY

Imagining Stephanie spread out on Rip's table, getting her first tat inked into her skin had Maverick rock hard through most of the consultation. Rip was hopeful that in about two to three more months Mav's skin graft would have healed enough to handle some ink.

He could hardly fucking wait. The absent brand on his arm felt like a missing limb and was unbearable some days. Like he'd lost a deep part of what made him who he was. None of his brothers treated him differently or seemed to realize how affected he was by the lost emblem, but damn if it wasn't killing him slowly.

After the appointment, he guided Stephanie back through the clubhouse. He had plans for her. As the morning passed, she'd loosened up and relaxed a bit, but there was a part B to Operation Chill Steph Out and he was ready to dive in.

"Maverick, my office. Now," Copper barked out as they passed him.

For the first time in his life, he was torn between club business and wanting to be with a woman. And that was bullshit. Club came first.

Always.

"Prez needs me." The words came out a little gruffer than he'd meant them, making Stephanie frown and take a step away from him.

"Go. I'm fine. Toni said she was going to stop by tonight, so I'll hang in my room until she gets here." She hugged her arms around herself as she turned to walk away.

With a gentle hand, Mav reached for her arm and spun her back. "Wait." He dug through his pocket, producing a key. "Make a right at the top of the stairs then the last door on the left. I won't be long. I want you waiting in my room."

Stephanie's mouth dropped open twice before she found some words. "Oh, um, okay. I can do that." She grasped the key, looking so adorable in her uncertainty. "See you in a bit then."

As she turned away, Mav grabbed her arm again and spun her with some force this time. Before he had time to consider how stupid it was, he sealed his lips over hers in a quick but fierce kiss. When he released her, she staggered so he gripped her shoulders to steady her.

She didn't say anything but sucked her bottom lip into her mouth as though savoring his taste on her lips.

"Christ, woman." Mav groaned and willed away the hard-on, but it was useless. He was destined to sit in a meeting with Copper turned on as fuck.

Steph's focus trailed down his body until it hit the very unmistakable tenting in his jeans. Her eyes widened, and a giggle escaped before she could slap her palm over her mouth.

Mav stepped forward and leaned closer until his lips hovered inches from her ear. "Laugh it up now, wildcat. I promise, in a few hours you won't have enough breath to laugh."

With that, he turned and strolled away, leaving her slack-jawed and gaping. Damn, he hadn't felt this good in months.

"What's up, Prez?" he asked as he walked into the office and shut the door.

"Got word of another missing girl." Copper tossed back whatever had been in his glass and slammed the empty cup on his desk.

"Shit," Mav said as he dropped into the chair opposite Copper's desk. It was then he noticed the exhaustion clinging to his president. The past few months had taken their toll on him. He was thirty-nine but looked like he'd aged an extra ten years. As president, Copper took his role to heart. He not only viewed himself as leader of the MC, but head of the family as well, and that extended to every ol' lady, child, and loved one in each of his men's lives.

"Lefty?"

"Think so. This one's different than the others. Older. Twenty-eight or something, but gorgeous from the pictures I've seen."

"Sounds like they might be searching for something specific," Mav said.

He sighed and rolled his neck across his massive shoulders. "Yeah, and that worries me. We thought they were small-scale in the trafficking biz. But I'm worried Lefty is gonna up the game. If they're hunting for specific women, it means they're building a return customer base and taking requests. I'm worried women are going to start disappearing all over the place. They probably already have this one marked to go to some fucker. This shit ain't gonna end well for her."

If anyone ever needed an ol' lady, it was Copper. Someone to lose his burdens in each night. Someone to make the difficult times and occasional darkness lighter. Shell was that woman. The stubborn ass just needed to realize it. Usually, Mav wouldn't be advocating for a man to shackle himself, but Cooper didn't sleep with any of the Honeys and never brought an outside woman around, so he was already chained without the benefit of a wet pussy and a soft, warm body in his bed.

"We got a plan?" Mav leaned forward, resting his forearms on his thighs. The skin graft only hurt if he put direct pressure on it, so he was careful to keep most of the weight on the side of his arm.

If he'd been looking for a boner-killer, he'd certainly found it. One hundred percent alert and ready to help, his mind started spinning with all the ways he could lend a hand.

"We gotta tread fucking lightly here. Cops are all over this shit, but it sounds like they're chasing their own asses. Screw's been banging some chick who works the front desk at the police station. She's a nosey little shit and runs her mouth like a faucet. Told Screw the cops don't have shit. Lefty's not even on their radar yet. Morons think the end of Shark was the end of the gang."

"We gonna have a sit-down with him?"

Copper nodded. "Yeah, Zach's got a line on where he's been holed up. So, I'm heading over with Zach to pay him a little visit tomorrow afternoon. Before that, I need you to pull some security footage for me. Some lacky stuffed the girl into the trunk of a car in the parking lot of a Subway, for fuck's sake. They got cameras aimed at the lot."

"I'll get right on that, Prez." Mav could do that shit in his sleep. He wasn't any kind of computer wiz, but he could hack his way into plenty of security systems. Came with the territory, or at least the less legal side of his security business.

"You want in when we visit Lefty tomorrow?"

"Fuck yeah." Maverick had a special kind of hatred for men who used their size and strength to intimidate, abuse, and violate others. He'd been on the receiving end of that and it had nearly killed him. While Zach or Copper would be the ones to hand out any justice, he'd never pass up the opportunity to watch the show.

"All right." Copper pushed his chair back and rose. He didn't have much height on Maverick, maybe an inch at best, but was about twice as broad. "You can work on my computer in here if you want. I'm off to Shell's. Something about a leaky faucet. Stubborn woman's house would collapse around her before she took a dime from anyone. Least she lets us fix the shit, even if she insists on buying the supplies."

Mav laughed and stood as well. "Like you don't pretend to have half the shit she needs lying around so she won't have to buy it."

With a shrug, Copper marched toward the door, his long steps eating up the distance in three steps. "Gotta do something or she'd end up working six jobs."

"You know, you could—" Mav started.

Raising a hand in a stop motion, Copper opened the door. "Shut the fuck up and get to work." He was gone a second later, the door slamming behind him. Sure, Prez had to be sick as shit of everyone bitching at him about Shell, but that's what he got for being an inflexible ass.

As Mav moved to Copper's desk chair, he tapped out a quick text to Shell.

Maverick: Big guy is headed your way. Looks dead on his feet. Feed him and give him some sweetness.

Thirty seconds later his phone chimed.

Shell: Thanks for the head's up.

Shell: And I'm always sweet.

Mav chuckled and sent her an eggplant emoji only to get a vomit face in return. He had the best family.

Hacking into Subway's security cameras was child's play, and within ten minutes, Mav was staring at the oblivious woman whose life was about to swirl down the shitter.

Jesus, it sucked to sit on his ass and watch, knowing what was about to go down. Even the grainy camera footage couldn't disguise her beauty. She was gorgeous, capital-G gorgeous. Tall, curvy, with thick auburn hair falling down her back in large waves. She moved with confidence, like a woman who knew she had what men craved. As she sashayed from Subway to her car across the darkened lot, Mav's heart raced.

Every instinct he possessed was driving him to warn her, dive in and save her, anything to prevent her from falling prey to a vicious predator. But of course, the tape was eighteen hours old, so nothing could be done.

"Fucking hell," he muttered as she arrived at her vehicle, parked way in the back of the lot, nearly out of view of the camera, and so damn dark it was hard to catch any details. Just as she reached the car, a shadowy figure wearing a black hoodie that hid his face seemed to materialize from thin air and was on her like a ninja. She thrashed and probably screamed, but it was a complete waste of energy. Within seconds, the attacker choked her out until she was limp and shoved her unconscious body into her trunk.

For a moment, Mav froze as he imagined Stephanie at the hands of these raping pieces of shit. If he hadn't been in that basement with her, she'd have had the same fate as this poor soul. All the pain he'd experienced, the broken ribs, the bruising, even the burn and loss of his beloved brand, was worth it to have been able to prevent Stephanie from being raped and sold off like cattle.

Nothing useful on the footage. One attacker. They used her car, which the cops were bound to find abandoned miles away from where they'd stashed her. There wasn't a lick of evidence to suggest this was Lefty's work, but Mav's gut was screaming. So was Copper's it seemed. And he'd trust their combined instincts with his life or any of his brother's lives. Even Stephanie's life.

Fuck yeah, he'd be joining them on a little visit to Lefty.

Mav stormed out of Copper's office, a nagging restlessness coursing through his blood. He needed to do something, needed action to work out the excess energy. Hell, he needed a good hard fuck. As he glanced around the clubhouse, a few of the Honeys tried to get his attention. Not even a flicker of interest on his part. The only woman he wanted was waiting for him in his room, uptight and in need of a good fucking herself. Too bad she was likely to shut him the hell down if he made the offer.

Maybe he'd get a good drunk on instead. Muddle his brain so he could sleep without visions of Stephanie being sold and used as a fuck toy for sadistic assholes.

As he walked toward the bar, his lips twitched and an idea formed. Steph needed to loosen up, and he had hundreds of questions he wanted to ask her. She'd made a few comments in the past that didn't quite make sense. Clearly, the woman had secrets. Secrets he wanted. He wanted to learn everything about her inside and out. And since she wasn't likely to let him inside, what better way to get her to relax and get a little sloppy than to spend some time with a powerful friend named Jack? At the very least, it would help distract him from the fact he hadn't been laid in over two months.

He circled the bar, grabbed the whiskey, two shot glasses, and booked it to his room.

Steph was reclining on his bed, knees bent, thumbing through her phone. She shot straight when he entered the room. "What's wrong? You look upset."

Guess his frustrations were written all across his face. "Let's play a game."

Steph frowned and swung her legs around so she was sitting on the edge of the bed. "A game?"

"Yup." He plopped down next to her, handing her an empty shot glass. "A get to know you game. I ask you a question. You either answer, or if it's too personal and shit, you drink."

One blond eyebrow rose. "I drink more than two of those, and I'll be answering anything you want to hear. Might start swinging from that ceiling fan too."

With a chuckle, Mav opened the bottle and poured himself a shot. "Maybe that's what I'm hoping for."

"Hmm," she hummed.

He tipped the bottle in her direction and waited. Silent, she stared at him for a moment, then at her empty glass, then him again. "Same rules apply to me. You can ask whatever the hell you want."

That seemed to do the trick. With a sigh, she held up the shot glass and waited for him to fill it, which he did without hesitation. "Ladies first," he said with a wink when her glass was full. "My policy in all things."

Steph snorted and rolled her eyes. "I'm sure it is." Her eyes lit with delight and an adorable wrinkle appeared between them. "Why do they call you Maverick?"

"Going easy on me, huh?" When she just shrugged he said, "I

was a little shit growing up. A hellraiser, always bucking the system, very independent, didn't like to follow the rules."

Steph smirked. "So totally different than you are now?"

"Funny, smart ass. Anyway, my elementary school principal used to call me Maverick. I spent quite a bit of time in her office. It stuck."

"What's your real name?"

"Nuh uh. My turn."

She scowled, and instead of looking fierce, her twisted mouth looked straight up kissable. "Go ahead." It sounded so resigned he wanted to laugh.

Mav leaned back on his elbows. There were a few key things he wanted to know about her but didn't want to scare her off with overly personal questions at first. "How much weight have you lost since I last saw you?"

"Eight pounds. What's your real name?"

Maverick burst out laughing. "No discussion, huh? Just jumping right to the next question? Okay, Ethan Davis. Why's your old man in prison?"

She blinked. Once. Twice. Then lifted the glass to her lips.

"Use it wisely. Start sucking that back this early in the game and you'll be wasted before you know it." As a troubled frown crossed her face, Mav felt a tad guilty for pressuring her into answering questions she'd already said she didn't talk about, but he had this drive, this need to uncover everything about her.

A heavy sigh left her, and she lowered the shot glass.

Victory.

"As I mentioned, my dad was a cop, high-ranking, a police commissioner, actually. The day after I graduated from—" She cleared her throat. "After I graduated, he was arrested for taking bribe money from the mob. He's serving a twelve-year sentence in Pennsylvania. It's halfway over."

"Shit, sweetheart. I'm sorry." Growing up with a cop father explained some of why she'd been so staunch in her opinion of right versus wrong. Her father must have set the bar high as far as always being just and staying on the right side of the law. Probably a hard-liner when it came to following the rules, then he shattered her world and destroyed her safety net by going against everything he'd taught her.

A fucking dirty cop.

She did have secrets. Probably a lot more respect for law enforcement than he did. Maybe that was why he'd had the nagging feeling she was hiding something. Had to be hard to admit to outlaw bikers that you came from blue stock.

"Yeah," she said, her voice raspy with emotion. "So, uh, how many women have you slept with?"

He watched her for a second, not surprised by her attempt at putting some levity back into the game. He'd give it to her for now, but she wasn't off the hook when it came to the tough shit. Not when he was finally figuring out what made her tick. "One."

The smile that lit her face made him feel like a fucking hero. "Okay, that's the biggest pile of bullshit I've ever heard."

He shrugged. "It's true. I have only ever slept with one woman."

Eyes wide, she huffed. "Okay, I'll play your game. Was it that Carli girl?"

She said *girl* like the word tasted horrible in her mouth. "That's another question, but I'll give it to you. No, not Carli. The only woman I have ever slept with was you."

"Me? But we...ohh, okay. I see what you did there. Very smooth."

He shrugged. "It's the truth. You are the only woman I've slept the night with."

Her entire posture softened. "Wow," she whispered. "Uh, okay, well how many women have you had sexual relations with?"

Now it was his turn to smile. "Sexual relations?"

"I'm covering all my bases since you seem to be a master at skirting the real question."

"Sorry, sweets, that's another question."

She huffed. "Oh, come on. You know that's what I meant all along."

Playing with Stephanie was fun and exactly what he needed to take his mind off the shit with Lefty. "Okay, fine, but no more cheating."

She made an X over her heart with her pointer finger.

"Well, I may not be the smartest fucker out there, but I'm sure as hell not stupid enough to answer that question." Like he even had a clue how many women he'd fucked. He lifted the shot glass to his lips and downed the whiskey. Ahh, damn good burn.

They went back and forth for a while, laughing, drinking, and learning little tidbits of info about each other. With each reveal, Mav found himself craving more of Stephanie. More of her mind, more of her history, and fuck if he didn't want her body. It was a dangerous game. He wasn't built for engaging in anything serious and wouldn't offer it to her, but he couldn't tear himself away from her.

"Okay," he said, refilling her glass after she wouldn't tell him the most orgasms she'd had in one night. In her tipsy state, she'd giggled, spilled about a third of the shot on his sheets, and downed the rest. It was no big deal; he planned to have first-hand knowledge when he blew that number out of the water at some point. "Why are you here? No bullshit, no excuses, no lies. Why did you come back to Tennessee?"

Fishing? Sure. He wanted to know if she'd returned because she thought of him as much as she'd been on his mind over the past two months.

"I—" She stared him straight in the eyes, and he saw the struggle, the indecision, and maybe even some sorrow. Then she shook her head and drank.

"Chicken," he whispered.

A sad nod was all he got in return.

CHAPTER TWENTY-ONE

Danger! Danger!

The word had been bouncing around in her head from the moment Maverick suggested the game. Drunk, she was more likely to let something slip. Let a clue about her true identity tumble out. But this was also a chance to ask questions, find out about the club. Maybe her best shot at getting in-depth information.

So she'd played along and learned that he was thirty-eight, prospected with the club as soon as he turned twenty-one, was currently the Road Captain, and had as many piercings as she had fingers on one hand. From her, he'd learned she was twenty-seven, a natural blonde, and she hated cats. Fun, get-to-know-you information, but not exactly the deep MC secret-revealing gouge she was after.

But now, four shots in, she was tipsy and feeling a little more reckless and a little less investigatory than she had at the start of the little game. "My turn," she said, scooting along the bed until her entire side was plastered against his. "You've got full sleeves and I've seen the tattoos on your chest and stomach. Just how much more of you is inked, anyway?"

His grin grew sinful, and the pierced eyebrow arched into his forehead. "All of me."

Stephanie laughed, nearly upending her shot glass. "Come on. Not all of you." His facial expression didn't change, and she sobered. Well, not really, but she snapped to attention. "All of you?"

He just kept giving her that cat-who-ate-the-canary grin.

"Oh, my God! Can I see?"

Mav's head dropped back, and he stared at the ceiling for a good minute before saying, "You realize you're killing me here, don't you?"

"I am? What? How?"

"Yeah, you're clueless. Well, you asked for it." With a sigh, he pushed off the bed and stood straight up which put his pelvis at eye level. "You sure you're ready for this? Women have been known to swoon at best and die right there on the spot at worst."

Fully sober, she'd never in a million years have requested he drop his drawers so she could verify he had a tattoo somewhere under there, but in her half-drunk state, she just giggled and waited for the show.

Slowly, like he was, in fact, putting on a show, he lowered the zipper on his faded slim jeans before shoving them down his hips. Clad only in a pair of light gray boxer briefs, his crotch was at eye level, and it was then Stephanie realized her mistake. He was aroused. Fully aroused. Largely aroused.

Heat pooled between her legs, and along with it, a rush of liquid that should have mortified the hell out of her, but her alcohol-soaked brain didn't seem to care at the moment.

"Last chance to back out." His tone was full of warning, and all playfulness had vanished.

She shook her head, tongue too thick in her mouth to release any words. It was a mistake of epic proportions, but she couldn't seem to tell him to stop. He hooked his thumbs in the sides of the boxers and shoved them to the floor with his jeans. Then, he returned to his spot on the bed, reclining on his elbows. Between his legs, legs that were covered in almost as much ink as his arms, his cock jutted straight out.

Stephanie couldn't help it, and licked her lips in a completely instinctive reaction.

"Fuck," Mav said on a groan.

Sure enough, along the left side of his shaft was a tattoo that began just beyond the head and ran the length of his cock. As though driven by a force she was unable to deny, Stephanie slid off the bed and onto her knees between his legs.

"Warrior," she read the word inked on his cock. She longed to ask him the significance, but before the words left her mouth, she noticed an abnormality in the writing. A semicolon replaced the *I*, making it read *Warr;or*.

Just as she was about to ask the meaning, she recalled an article she'd read online a year or so ago, and the words lodged in her throat. "A—" She shook her head and cleared her throat. "When people write, they use semicolons to..." Hot tears flooded her eyes. She couldn't finish the thought.

Mav had an uncharacteristically serious expression on his face. Tight-lipped, flat-eyed, no trace of the good-humored man she was so drawn to. Despite that, the pull to this man who had a difficult story to tell was just as strong. "It's used when a sentence could be ended but isn't. When the writer decides to continue on with a new thought," he said in a dead voice.

Stephanie nodded and rested her forearms on his lean but still defined thighs. "And a semicolon tattoo has come to represent a person who thought of or attempted to end their life but was saved somehow and decided to continue on." She stared straight into his somber eyes. "You tried to kill yourself."

It wasn't a question, but he nodded anyway.

God, the thought of it hurt. A giant fist squeezed her heart until she felt lightheaded. That this beautiful man once thought his life was no longer worth living made her physically ill. If anyone was needed on this earth, it was Maverick, who brought so much life and vitality to everyone he encountered. "Will you please tell me about it?"

Eyes locked with hers, he leaned forward and reached for the bottle that rested on the floor. He didn't speak as he filled the shot glass and raised it. Between his legs, his cock was now flaccid, the letters in the word warrior scrunched together.

Without thinking of the many repercussions, Stephanie rose to a tall kneel and encircled his wrist with her hand just as the shot glass reached his lips. "Please," she whispered. "You've seen me at my worst. Lying on that table, nearly naked, about to be raped. No more games. Your story is safe with me. Please give me this piece of you."

"It's not a pretty bedtime story, sweetheart." He seemed a little lost in thought. Probably reliving horrific memories. "And it's not something I talk about...ever."

Still on her knees between his spread legs, she ran her palms up the insides of his thighs then back down again. His softened cock twitched and began to fill once again. "What have you told all the other women you've been with?"

Oh, shit. Had she really asked him about other women when she was keeling between his naked legs? Like they both didn't know where this night was going to eventually lead. And now he'd be thinking of other women he'd banged.

"I've never told a soul beyond Copper and Zach. No woman has ever seen it up close enough to read it."

Wait...no woman had seen it? Last she heard, women threw themselves at Mav like he was some kind of Rockstar. And it hadn't been mentioned that he turned them down often. "But..."

"Look, you asked, so I'm going to shoot straight with you." Mav's voice changed. A bit of bite entered it. Even though he'd agreed to answer the question, he tossed back the shot of whiskey. "It's no damn secret that I've fucked a lot of women. Fucked them. As in bent them over the couch, or a pool table, kept every damn light off, and never let 'em linger. I don't let them go exploring either. So aside from you, no one has seen that fuckin' tat since I got it." He rolled his gaze to the ceiling then back down. "Ten years ago."

No woman had seen it in ten years. It was mind-boggling. It meant that in ten years—

"You think too loud, woman. Yes, I haven't had a blow job in ten years."

Her mouth dropped open, and she was afraid she'd never be able to scoop her jaw off the floor. That was going to change tonight. A huge surge of warmth and power flowed through her bloodstream. He trusted her enough to share that part of him, and she fully planned to reward him for it.

No matter the consequences to her heart.

"Tell me," she whispered.

He shook his head.

"Tell me." This time she demanded it.

He expelled a huff of air so full of pain and heaviness she felt guilty for making him recall the painful parts of his past. But Stephanie needed to know. Not Stephanie the FBI agent, Stephanie the woman who was over-the-top attracted to this man for so much more than his physical appeal.

She continued to knead his thighs while he worked through whatever shit was in his head.

After a few seconds, he tucked her hair behind her ear. "Wildcat," he whispered, "I'll tell you, but I want you to answer one question for me first."

She tilted her head and waited.

"Are you wet right now? Is that tight pussy all wet and needy for me?"

She swallowed around a giant golf ball in her throat. She'd been wet five minutes ago; now, she was embarrassingly soaked. Tell him? Not tell him? It was a crossroads that seemed so much more significant than just the state of her arousal. But how could she deny him this one question when he was about to reveal his darkest secret?

"Soaked." The word sounded like it'd been dragged from a desert-parched throat.

His eyes darkened, and he ran a thumb over one of her pebbled nipples, sending a jolt of desire straight to her core. "You do realize you aren't leaving here until you've been fucked like you've never been fucked before?"

And there it was. The crossroads between right and wrong. Good and evil. Criminal and law enforcement agent. But it wasn't that simple at all, and for the first time in her life, she truly understood what it meant to be lost in the gray zone. Her body needed the release only he could provide. It craved him. But what was brewing between her and this complicated man was so much more than a physical ache. She was forming a connection with him that she'd never had with another man. And he felt it, too. It was written all over his face.

Really, there was no choice. She'd made the decision the moment she asked her first question. "I realize," she whispered.

With that admission, he pinched her nipple through her T-shirt and thin bra, ripping a sharp gasp from her before releasing her.

He began, "My mother died of a heroin overdose exactly six months after I was born, leaving me in the care of a father who really didn't give a shit about anything but himself, his booze, and his pit-bull. That damn dog was treated better than I was, any and every day of my goddamned life. When I was nine, the old man got into a fight with some jackass who lived in the same trailer park as we did. He was gunned down right there outside our double-wide at two in the afternoon while I watched through the window with the cops on the line."

The breath that left her felt like it was torn from the depths of her soul. All she could see was a devasted, lonely, screwed-up little boy with no one to love him. "What happened to you?"

He laughed, but there wasn't a speck of humor to it. "What happens to any orphaned kid whose extended family wants nothing to do with him?"

"The system?"

"That's right. The goddamned foster system. My first house already had four foster kids, all boys, and the meanest sonsabitches you could imagine. I wasn't the youngest, but I was the smallest, the scrawniest by far. And man did they use that to their fucking advantage, not wasting a single moment to torment me. Burning my homework, eating the food allotted to me, beating the shit out of me each time the previous set of bruises healed. There I was, some little kid with no mother, who'd just seen his old man killed in front of his face. To say I was fucked in the head would be an understatement."

As he spoke, Stephanie ran the palms of her hands up and down his thighs. The movement was meant to soothe—both of them, if she was honest—but instead, it had his cock rising to full attention once again. Her mouth watered for a taste, but she wanted him to get the poison out of his system before she brought him to climax and made him forget it all.

"Keep going," she whispered as she stared straight into his haunted eyes. Agent Little didn't exist in that room any longer. Nor was there an outlaw biker. Only Stephanie and Maverick in their own world—one that felt so right despite being so wrong.

CHAPTER TWENTY-TWO

This was only the third time in his life Maverick had ever told the entire story from start to finish, and both times the old feelings of hopelessness, despair, and futility came crashing back. This time, though, a tiny blond angel did her best to soothe him and chase away the demons.

And it was working.

He could get the words out without feeling shame or self-loathing. This was part of his past, something he'd never imagined coming to grips with, but needed to if he wanted a normal interaction with a woman. In the past, that had never mattered. Fucking someone without letting them get a glimpse of his cock was easy, especially in the MC world where the women were willing to accept it however it was given.

For the first time, that wasn't enough, and he had a feeling Stephanie was the only woman he'd be able to tell this story to. While he couldn't offer her anything beyond this, it was more than he'd ever given a woman, and it was enough.

For today at least.

God, she was beautiful. Maybe not in the typical va-va-voom sense most of his brothers seemed to lose their shit over, but she was perfect in his eyes. The care and compassion on her face nearly slayed him. He didn't want her to be sad for him. He'd survived and now had a great fucking life.

He rubbed his thumb across her hard little nipple again,

unable to keep his hands off her. A small whimper vibrated through her throat.

"I lived there until I was fifteen. By that time, I'd shot up and was nearly six feet tall. I've never been bulky, but I learned to fight dirty, and when combined with my height, I stopped getting shit on every day. Then my foster mother got sick, and the family decided they couldn't continue taking in kids. So we were all shuttled elsewhere. And that's when the real hell began. The parents were all right, but they had a nineteen-year-old biological son who was a sadistic piece of shit. He made life fucking hell. So, at sixteen, I ran away."

Stephanie remained quiet, her gaze full of so much emotion it was difficult to maintain eye contact. Small gasps and puffs of air left her lips as he continued to strum her nipples. Fuck, she was so responsive, and as soon as he was done with the fucked-up story of his young life, he was going to feast on her body until she screamed his name. Never had he given a shit what a woman said or did when she came, but the need to hear his name from her lips while she succumbed to the pleasure was overwhelming.

"W-what happened after you left?" She moved her body very subtly, squeezing her legs together, leaning forward so her tits pressed into his hands. Her need was just as sharp as his. His cock was so hard it could probably knock down the wall and, unused to being denied, his balls ached with the heaviness of unfulfillment. But he didn't mind, because once he lost himself inside her, it was going to be epic. For both of them.

"I lived on the streets until I was nineteen." So much had happened in those three years. So much had dirtied him and made him into an animal, trying to survive day-to-day. The gritty details weren't something she needed. No, she had enough of her own nightmares. No need to add to them.

"I did...a lot of shit to survive. Things your beautiful mind wouldn't comprehend and should never have to think about."

She frowned. "I'm not naïve, Maverick. You might not think

so, but I know how the world works. I know what people do to survive. I've seen plenty."

For some reason, he believed her. Still, he wasn't going to tell her how he'd sold himself for food, how he'd stolen, hurt people, did whatever was asked of him, until one day it became too much.

"I had a group of friends, I guess you could call them. We looked out for each other on the street." He couldn't look at her face and continue, so he dropped his gaze to her chest where her nipples strained against the thin fabric of her T-shirt. "One was a girl who couldn't have been more than fifteen. I tried to shelter her from the harshest realities of living on the streets. It was only a matter of time before she started prostituting herself—it happened to every damn one of us, but I tried so hard to keep her free from that until she at least turned legal age. Like that would have somehow made it less horrifying."

He sighed and forged on. "Anyway, I was supposed to bring her some food one night. Neither of us had eaten in at least a day and were so hungry. But I blew her off for some piece of ass. She didn't have any money and was hungry, so she went out on the streets in search of who the hell knows what. Ended up giving herself to some piece of shit who promised to take her to McDonald's if she sucked his dick. Instead, he raped her, strangled her, and dumped her body in an alley."

"Oh, God, Maverick." Stephanie cupped his face in her hands and forced him to look at her. "You do realize it wasn't your fault, right? Has anyone ever told you it wasn't your fault?"

"Not at first. Everyone fucking blamed me, and I couldn't live with the guilt. Couldn't live with what I'd become. So, one night, I sat on an overpass, fully prepared to jump. A kid about my age rode up on his Harley. It was Zach. He handed me some fuckin' beef jerky and sat next to me. For some reason, the whole story poured out of me. He didn't feed me any bullshit. Just told me about this club his old man was part of. How it was a brotherhood, a family, and how he was going to prospect when he turned twenty-one. Told me they'd be looking for other prospects as well.

"I climbed off the ledge, learned to ride, moved to Townsend, and prospected when I turned twenty-one. Rest is history."

"Thank you," Stephanie whispered.

"You can thank me by getting up here and sitting on my dick."

She shook her head and sat back on her heels. Her eyes sparkled, and she looked so hungry he groaned. "No. No jokes, no teasing, no flirty Maverick. You gave me a gift by telling me that story. Now I'm going to give you something back. Something you've waited way too long for."

As she spoke, she had traced the soft pad of one finger down the lettering on his dick, and he nearly came right then and there. When she reached the tip, she flicked the piercing, making him fist the sheets of the bed in a death grip.

He could have stopped her if he wanted to, but fuck that. He wanted her hot mouth around his dick more than he wanted to eat, more than he wanted to fucking ride. Her grin grew mischievous as she lowered her head and tongued the piercing while keeping eye contact.

His eyes rolled back in his head as the warmth of her soft tongue licked over his sensitive flesh. Gripping him by the base of his cock, she ran that tongue over his tattoo, then pressed soft kisses along the length of it. If he were a man who could cry, he'd have teared up, because this was so much more than her sucking him off. This was her taking care of him, giving him pleasure, healing him.

"Ready?" she whispered.

"Fuck yes. Suck me, beautiful."

Passion flared in her eyes and she opened her mouth wide, engulfing the head of his cock into the warm, wet cave. Christ, it felt good as she sucked on the tip. Every instinct he had told him to grip her by the hair and ram his cock down her throat, but he had no idea how experienced she was at giving head and there was the piercing to consider. Breaking a tooth or fucking up her throat would be a guaranteed mood killer. So he turned himself over to her and let her have complete control over his dick.

And, damn, if she didn't seem to relish in it. Her lips glided down the length of him, pausing as he neared the back of her throat. Then she drew back, inhaled through her nose then descended on him again. And again. And again. A little farther each time until he eventually butted up against the back of her throat.

She gagged slightly, the muscles of her throat closing over the head of his dick before she regained control and actively swallowed, nearly strangling him with her throat. "Holy fucking shit." It was insane, the pleasure so sharp,he had a hard time formulating logical thought.

She let out a little giggle at his reaction, and even the vibrations from that shot through him like a bolt of lightning. Jesus, how had he gone ten years without this? Then again, having Stephanie be the first woman with her mouth on him in ages was fucking out of this world.

She did the whole deep throat and swallow thing once again, and Maverick lost it. He gripped her by the hair and held her face to his crotch, pumping his hips with tiny motions at the back of her throat. Just when he worried it was too much, she moaned, and his entire body jerked as he neared release.

While he loved every second of his cock in her mouth, he needed something else. Giving her head a tug, he slipped from between her lips and cursed the loss of pleasure.

"What's wrong?"

"Wrong? Fuck, look at you." Her lips were shiny and swollen, face flushed, and eyes glassy. "Not a fucking thing is wrong. I just need my dick in your pussy and your tits in my mouth. You good with that?"

She nodded, and he raised an eyebrow. "Yes, yes. That sounds good. So, so good."

A chuckle escaped him. She was fucking adorable. "So get

those damn clothes off and hop up here on my lap, wildcat."

"Oh!" She started pulling at her jeans with frantic movements as though she'd forgotten she was still dressed. Within seconds she stood naked before him amidst a pile of haphazardly removed clothing.

"Get over here." With both hands, he reached forward and palmed her ass, yanking her down onto his lap.

Her small yelp turned to a low groan as he slid two fingers into her without warning. "Maverick," she said on a moan.

"Fuck, I'd almost forgotten how tight you are. You're gonna feel so fucking good fisted around my dick."

"Yes," she said. "Give it to me."

"Soon, beautiful. Want you crazy for me first."

She rocked her hips on his hand, completely shameless in her search for pleasure, and he fuckin' loved it. "Kiss me, Maverick."

Still pumping two fingers inside her, he grasped the back of her head with his other hand and crashed their mouths together. There was nothing gentle about the kiss. Nothing exploratory. Nothing sweet. It was a full-on attack. Their tongues clashed, lips mashed together, and his tongue ring clanked against her teeth. She sure as hell didn't seem to mind his rough tendencies if the way she moaned into his mouth and ground down on his fingers was any indication.

Just as he felt a ripple around his fingers, she yanked her mouth away. "I'm close. I'm close."

"I want it now. Come, babe."

She shook her head. "No. I want to come with you inside me. Please. Please, Maverick, fuck me."

Well, who could resist a plea like that? "Jesus." He released her hair and reached to his nightstand with a fumbling hand, sending condoms flying. A sweet laugh bubbled out of Stephanie just as he managed to fist one in his palm. She watched with rapt attention as he protected her, then batted his hands out of the way. Without a word, she gripped his dick, canted her hips, and sank down on him at a slow, torturous pace.

"Oh, wow," she said as her eyes fluttered closed. "I can feel it. The metal."

"Is it good?" He wanted her to like it. Wanted to give her pleasure greater than any other man had. He held her by her hips, keeping her locked against him, unable to move.

"Yes, it's good. Crazy good." Her eyes popped back open, and she beamed at him. "You gonna fuck me, or what?"

He'd wanted to give her a second to get used to the unfamiliar sensation of the piercing, but she seemed good to go, so he gripped her ass tight and thrust his hips forward. "Trust me, babe, you're gonna be fucked like never before."

She gasped, so he did it again, then started a pounding rhythm that slid her back and forth along his dick as he slammed in and out of her. He'd known she was tight, but fuck, feeling her pussy all over his dick was another level of pleasure. As he stroked in and out, her walls squeezed him, tugging on the metal and making him lose his breath. He was gonna blow in two seconds at this rate, and he didn't even fucking care. He'd make it up to her tenfold if he needed to.

"Maverick, it's so...oh, God." She held his shoulders for dear life as their gazes connected and he fucked her with furious need.

Something passed between them. Something that wasn't physical and reached straight into his soul. Never had sex been like this for him, and he didn't have a fucking clue what was happening.

Was it just added intensity due to the circumstances that brought them together? That had to be it. They'd met when pain, fear, and adrenalin were coursing through their systems. And that intensity carried through to their fucking.

Nothing more profound than that.

Her small, perky tits bounced with every forward and back movement of her hips and Mav's mouth suddenly watered for a taste. Not huge by anyone's standards, she probably wasn't even a full B cup. But what the fuck did he care? All he needed was one of those hard, responsive nipples in his mouth and he was good to go.

Keeping one hand on her ass, he gripped her hair again and yanked her down. Her back arched, allowing his dick to hit even deeper and her tits to bounce right near his mouth.

Her moan turned into a strangled half scream, and she gripped his biceps so hard there were bound to be fucking marks. "Maverick! It's—I can—"

"That's right, baby, feel it. That metal's stroking right over your G-spot, isn't it?" Another moan was all he got, so he lowered his mouth and sucked on her nipple. Her entire body went rigid, and ten nails pierced the skin of his upper arms as she screamed out his name while she came.

Her pussy squeezed him over and over. There was only so much he could take, and he wouldn't be far behind her, but first, he needed another. "Again."

"You're crazy."

Without missing a beat, he moved to her other breast and captured the nipple between his teeth at the same time he tightened his grip on her hair. "A-fucking-gain," he growled, mouth full of tit.

"Jesus," she whispered. With him controlling the movement of her hips and her back arched over his legs, she was helpless to do anything but take what he gave her. And he gave her everything he had until he couldn't possibly keep from coming another second.

"Now," he barked, releasing her breast and increasing the force of his thrusts. "Come right-fucking-now."

"I am!" She yelled it out as her nails scored his skin once again and she clamped down around his cock. "Maverick," she cried when he planted himself as deep as possible and came inside her.

It was a pleasure-high he'd never been on, and there was no way in hell he'd survive without another fix. And soon. Gently, he released her hair and her ass and helped right her. She was soft and pliant in his arms with a slap-happy grin on her face. Come drunk. Fuck, yes.

With her still straddling him, he scooted them back and swung his legs onto the bed. Then he rolled to his side and held her tight, their bodies an intertwined mess of limbs.

"Not sure I've ever heard anything better than you screaming my name as you came, beautiful."

"Hmmm," she mumbled, making him smile. "Want me to go back to my room?"

"Wouldn't let you if you tried. Let's get some sleep so we have some energy for some real fucking later."

A soft chuckle shook her body before she settled against him. It wasn't long before Maverick felt an even rise and fall against his chest.

It took him a while to fall asleep, and as the post-orgasm glow faded, the doubt crept in. What the hell was he doing sharing his story, letting her swallow his dick, demanding she sleep in his bed? It was a recipe for disaster, because, while it was great for the here and now, he wasn't in the market for an old lady.

The club would soon wage war on Lefty. That was his priority. And he knew himself. He'd never been satisfied with one woman before, so why the hell would he be this time around?

He needed to end it and right-the-fuck away. For so many reasons. She was a cop's daughter. Didn't get much further from MC life than that. Even a fuck buddy situation wouldn't work. She'd be around the MC all the time. How would she ever except the upcoming war given her background? No, he really needed to end it.

But as he looked down at her face softened by sleep, he knew he wouldn't. He couldn't. Not until he fucked her out of his system at the very least. Something about her called to him in the most basic and animalistic way.

Looked like he was still the same selfish bastard who'd gotten a fifteen-year-old girl raped and murdered.

CHAPTER TWENTY-THREE

As it had been the other two times Stephanie ate there, the diner was packed, and Toni, Shell, and the rest of the staff bustled around at top speed. She sipped her cappuccino and stared out the front window at the parking lot. A few cars, a lot of bikes, and a truck or two filled the space.

Mav's bike wasn't one of them and he wasn't in the diner with some of his brothers. No, he was out on "club business" doing God knew what. She'd asked but was given a scowl and a "club business is not for women" BS speech. Shell and Toni had exchanged a few pointed and worried looks in the ten minutes Steph had been there, but whether they had any more information about the club business than she did was still left to be determined.

Not that she had any right to know anything. Toni was Zach's ol' lady and a fixture in his life. Shell had grown up in the club, and from what Steph had heard, she had some strange push/pull relationship with Copper where they were head over heels for each other, but neither ever made a move.

No, she was just the lying FBI agent who fucked Maverick and couldn't think about much of anything but getting back into bed with him. Or, at least, that's all she'd been thinking about right up until he'd given her that club business line and dropped her at the diner. Now, the investigator in her couldn't help but obsess about what he was doing.

Was it legal?

Did it have to do with the Gray Dragons?

Did it have to do with the missing girls?

How could she find out what it was?

Was it something she was going to have to report?

Was it something she *would* report?

That last question was the one that had her staring at a bunch of cars rather than facing reality. Because way down deep in her gut, she feared she would continue to try to protect Maverick and his club no matter the cost to her career, or freedom.

And that was as foolish as it was illegal.

Illegal. God, she was the daughter of a decorated police commissioner, a dirty police commissioner doing time for the very thing she was considering. Did the apple really fall that close to the tree? The thought made her sick. Just two months ago, she'd been so staunch in her opinions, and all it had taken was one man to upend her entire belief system.

She was so much weaker than she'd ever imagined.

"Stephanie! I am so glad to see you." Wearing a huge smile, Shell slipped into the booth next to Steph and gathered her in a tight hug. "You look fantastic. How're you feeling?"

Shell's sweetness and what appeared to be genuine happiness to see Steph had her returning the embrace with a laugh. "Considering how bad I looked the last time you saw me, I'm not sure that's a compliment."

Shell laughed as well and leaned her head back on the booth. "You know what I mean. You look good in general, not compared to anything."

"Thanks. And I'm feeling pretty good." *Having nightmares about going to prison, or at least I was until Maverick fucked them right out of my brain then held me all night.* Yeah, she wouldn't be uttering those words aloud.

"So, are you just visiting? How long are you here for?"

Oh, I'm here until I can feed the FBI enough information to arrest your entire family and the men you love. "I'm not sure yet.

Indefinitely, I suppose. I just...needed a change and somehow ended up here." God, how did agents do this undercover thing? Of course, they usually weren't smitten with one of the people they investigated. And they weren't questioning everything they'd ever believed in. And they weren't half convinced the group being investigated wasn't nearly as depraved as believed.

"Well, we are so glad to have you. We'll have to hang out soon, beyond my fifteen-minute break at work I mean." There was just genuine goodness about Shell that couldn't be overlooked.

"I'd love that. How's Beth doing?"

"Lord save me." Shell rolled her eyes. "Ever heard of the expression threenager?"

"Nuh-uh." Steph shook her head. "I don't have much kid knowledge or experience. What's a threenager?"

"It's a three-year-old who has the attitude and snark of a teenager. Basically, it's your worst nightmare come to life. That kid's lucky she's so damn cute."

Toni picked that moment to slide into the booth across from Steph and Shell. "Don't listen to the overworked mommy here. That little ray of sunshine is nothing but sweetness and love."

Shell snorted and ran a hand through her curly blond hair. It was a few shades lighter than Stephanie's, a very pale yellow. "Next time she's flailing on the floor because her strawberries are too red, I'll send her over to your house and you can witness the sweetness and love first hand."

All three women laughed, and warmth filled Stephanie's chest. The women were so welcoming, so accepting of her into their lives. She barely knew them, in all reality had only met them once or twice before, but they acted as though they were all old friends.

"Sooo," Toni said, rubbing her hands together as she looked at Steph. "Rumor has it you entered Maverick's room last evening and didn't emerge until sometime after eight this morning. Deets, girl. And don't leave anything out."

With a gasp, Shell's jaw dropped. She stared at Steph then turned and gaped at Toni. "We've been at work how long? Hours, and you're just mentioning this to me now? And I thought we were besties." She tsked and turned back to Steph. "Spill."

Heat rushed to Stephanie's face, and all logical thoughts fled her mind as the two women waited for an explanation. "I, uh, well, I..."

"She's struck dumb." Toni whistled. "That good, huh?"

A sigh slipped from Shell. "It's so unfair! The two of you are getting it from all angles, and here I am, stuck raising the threenager without any dick to make me feel better."

Steph choked on her sip of cappuccino at the same time Toni's eyes nearly bugged out of her head. "Holy shit, did you just say 'without any dick to make me feel better?' Because that's what it sounded like, but there is no way in hell those words came from your mouth."

"Oh, shut up. Just because I have to watch my mouth around Beth doesn't mean I can't speak like the rest of you from time to time."

With a wave of her hand, Toni said, "Wait a second. We're supposed to be talking about Steph getting dick from Maverick. Not your lack of dick."

"Say it a little louder, why dontcha?" Shell grumbled.

These two were hilarious and it was nearly impossible to get a word in edgewise. Which was fine because Steph really didn't want to comment on what she'd done with Maverick. For all she knew, it wasn't going to happen again. And then wouldn't that be awkward if she started gushing about him and how many times he'd made her come the night before.

The sound of a phone vibrating had Shell and Toni sobering and sharing a look. Reaching into her pocket, Toni drew out her phone. "Everything's fine," she said, and Shell visibly relaxed. "Just gonna be a little longer than expected."

Both women grew serious and seemed to have some nonverbal conversation. Even if she weren't an FBI agent, even if she was just whom they thought, the woman hooking up with Maverick, she'd be dying to know what was going on.

"Everything okay?" Steph asked as nonchalant as possible.

Both women jumped a little, like they'd forgotten she was there and listening. Toni looked at her then sighed. "Look, I'm not about to share any club business, and I'm not even a hundred percent sure what they are doing, but you have as much right to know what's going on as we do—"

"No." Steph shook her head even though her investigator voice was screaming at her to shut up. "I don't. I spent one night with Maverick. I'm just some random woman to him. You don't have to tell me anything."

A snort came from Shell. "Maverick doesn't spend the night with women. Ever. E-V-E-R. So the fact that you did is big. Huge, really. And given what you went through, I think you have a right to some details." She glanced at Toni, who nodded.

"This does not leave the table," Toni said, all fun and games gone.

"Of course," Steph said, the potential lie souring her stomach.

"Shark's cousin is trying to keep what's left of the gang alive. He's a sadistic asshole whose interests seem to lie in the skin trade. Another girl has gone missing. Actually, not a girl this time, a woman quite a bit older than the others. The guys are working on getting her back." Shell shuddered. "They're fine. We just worry."

As soon as the words were out of Shell's mouth, Steph's brain churned through the many possible outcomes. None of them good. "Why don't they go to the cops, or just let the cops handle it? Or the FBI even? Why take matters into their own hands? They can't just go around hunting these guys."

"Can't they?" Shell propped her head on her hand. "There are quite a few reasons to leave the law out of it, actually. First is that in the eyes of the cops, or even FBI, the Handlers are no different than the Gray Dragons. Now you and I know what crap that is, but the authorities don't give a shit."

Well, Steph couldn't argue with her on that point. Wasn't that the whole reason she was there? Because the FBI thought the Handlers were no better than the Dragons? Of course there was the whole her-boss-was-an-ass-who-wanted-to-run-the-FBI thing.

"And," Toni chimed in, "the cops are bound by so many rules and regulations, by the time they cut through all the red tape, who the hell knows what would happen to this girl? Consider this, the cops have to get a warrant, get evidence, make arrests, interrogate, then hope they'll get accurate information as to where this girl is. After that, it goes to a trial where the Dragons put the fear of God in the jurors or, hell, make them disappear altogether. Next thing you know there's a mistrial or hung jury and they're back out there to start again."

Shell was nodding along as Toni spoke. "She's right. So instead, our boys go and rough up some Dragons, get the necessary information, save the girl, and go after Lefty. It may not be legal, it may not technically even be right, but you ask that girl who's rotting away somewhere, terrified and waiting to be sold to the highest bidder, and I'll tell you which option she'd pick."

Fascinated by the women's staunch support of the Handlers, Steph rubbernecked back and forth between them. What did it say about her that she understood where they were coming from? That she actually agreed with them? Because they were right about a few key things. It would take law enforcement too long to secure all the necessary evidence. And they would have to play by the rules. If they found the woman, who the hell knew what would be left of her? And that was a big "if" because women were lost to the horrors of human trafficking every day while investigators worked to bring down the ringleaders.

If the Handlers could bypass all that, save the victim, and eliminate the source, was it really that wrong?

Yes! It was wrong. What the hell was happening to her? She shouldn't have come to Townsend. It was a huge mistake. But as she looked into the determined eyes of both Shell and Toni, she found herself saying, "Is there anything I can do to help Maverick?"

"Just be there for him." Toni's green eyes were windows to her love for her man. "This stuff is hard on all of them. Sure, they aren't saints, but they are nothing like Shark or any of the Dragons. Trust me. I have very first-hand knowledge of that."

Stephanie knew none of the Handlers had anything in common with Shark. Had never even questioned it, but the girls were right, in the eyes of the law, the Handlers were no different than the Dragons. Illegal was illegal, wrong was wrong, killing was murder. Even when it saved the lives of others and rid the world of evil.

Suddenly, her breakfast threatened to make a reappearance. She was the one who thought that way, who'd refused to see the complicated nature of the world. Who wouldn't listen when others told her there was no such thing as black and white. Now she had no idea what to think, how to act. She had all these conflicting feelings and emotions tying her stomach in knots.

Toni must have sensed Stephanie's inner turmoil because she smiled and lightly smacked her palm against the table. "Okay," she said. "That's enough heavy for the morning. We've got three minutes of break left, and I want to hear about the good stuff."

When both women focused their attention and curious stares back on Stephanie, her face heated. It had to be as red as the bottle of ketchup at the rear of the table. "What do you want to know?" she squeaked.

"Well," Shell said, "for starters, does Maverick really have a pierced dick?"

CHAPTER TWENTY-FOUR

Mav waited astride his bike for Copper to do his thing. About a minute ago, they'd rolled up to the small warehouse Lefty had claimed as his headquarters, and so far, nothing had happened but a staring match between Copper and some punk kid with an AR-15 who thought the assault rifle was a representation of his dick. With his hair shaved down to stubble that contained some kind of symbol on each side, the kid couldn't have been a day over eighteen. Little did he know, the Handlers could wipe the floor with this crew of pissants and Gray Dragon rejects.

"The fuck you want?" Rifle-boy broke the silence first. Not surprising, but a stupid move on his part. Even if most men couldn't handle Copper's particular brand of laser-stare, he should have held out a little longer.

Weak sauce.

"Here to see your boss, little boy."

On his bike between Copper and Maverick, Zach chuckled, and Rifle-boy seethed and turned a furious shade of crimson. Seemed he'd yet to learn the simple sticks-and-stones lesson most learned as kids. If some childish name-calling got him that hot, it'd be easy as fuck to get him to lose his temper and do something stupid.

"Only little thing here is your dick, old man," Rifle-boy responded.

This time, Mav joined Zach in a good, loud laugh because,

come on. Thirty-nine did not an old man make, and Copper was six-five, two-seventy. There was just no way in hell the man had a small dick. It was a physical impossibility or something.

Unlike Rifle-boy, Copper let the insult roll right off his massive shoulders. "Wasting my time, boy. I ain't here to look at your ugly fuckin' face. Get. Me. Your. Boss."

Copper's voice held so much command even Rifle-boy seemed to grasp the urgency of the matter. But, seeing as how he was a stupid shit, he clenched his jaw, held his weapon tight across his chest, and didn't budge.

Idiot.

"Jesus fucking Christ," Copper muttered. Prez had little to no patience for morons, and this guy topped the charts. Whether in a gang or an MC, if you're low level, you're a soldier for the cause. That meant you didn't make decisions. This kid's job was to take the request to his leader and let the big boys make the decisions. If Lefty had already banned Copper from the premises, bullets would be flying. But Mav had a sneaking suspicion Lefty was going to try and buddy up to Copper.

The Handlers had the numbers, which meant they had the muscle. Lefty did not. All he had were disloyal men who didn't give a shit that Lefty killed the man who should have succeeded Shark. If they'd had any loyalty, any pride in their gang, they'd have walked when Lefty murdered Sixer. Instead, they just attached themselves to whoever promised a quick buck.

The door to the warehouse opened, and out strode a man who had to be Lefty. Average height with messy black hair, a black wife beater, camo pants, and a rolled bandana tied around his head, this joker looked like some kind of Rambo wannabe.

Zach tried to cover his snort with a cough but failed miserably.

"Stand the fuck down, Whip," Lefty said, then whispered something in the kid's ear. "Copper and the fuckin' Handlers are always welcome here." He waved them toward the entrance. "Come on in gentlemen. Least I owe you for getting Shark out of my way is a drink."

Three guys walking into enemy territory with nothing more than a couple of handguns and a baseball bat wasn't typically a smart move. In this case, however, Lefty wanted to kiss their asses, get on their good side, and he was also smart enough to realize that if something happened to Copper, Zach, or Mav, his entire baby gang would be slaughtered within hours. Nothing was going to happen here but the laying of some ground rules—Copper-style.

"Guess we're drinking," Zach muttered as he pulled out his phone. He shot off a quick text, presumably to let Toni know they might be a while. Steph had planned on a late breakfast at the diner where both Toni and Shell were working today. Hopefully, the women would keep her company and filled in on the timeline so she wouldn't worry.

Jesus, there he went thinking like she was his ol' lady. They'd fucked, multiple times throughout the night, but still, it was only fucking. Just because it had been the most intense fucking of his life and he wasn't nearly ready to give that shit up, didn't mean he owed her any explanations about him or his life.

Then why can't you think of anything but her all day every day?

"Thanks, Lefty. We're a little parched after our ride," Copper said, all friendly-like as he climbed off his bike.

The trio followed Lefty into the building past Rifle boy, who looked like he'd love nothing more than to ram that gun up their collective asses. As they passed, Zach went out of his way to slam his shoulder into Rifle-boy, nearly knocking him to the ground.

"Well, shit, you okay there, buddy?" Maverick asked. He slung his arm across Zach's shoulders. "Sorry about my friend here. His vision ain't so good. Can't see anything under five feet ten inches. What are you five-six? Five-seven?"

Rifle-boys nostrils flared, and he snarled but held his tongue. Whatever Lefty whispered to him must have been some good shit.

The warehouse was pretty sparse inside. A half-built bar lined the left wall and a card table with four folding chairs was the only piece of furniture in the place. The walls were cracked and bare, and the floor was covered in a combination of sawdust, leaves, and trash. Place was a dump.

"Please excuse the appearance. As you know, we're just getting up and running. Have a seat. Beer okay?"

Mav didn't give a fuck what they were drinking. He wanted this meeting over and done as fast as possible. He didn't like being a fly in the spider's lair even though he knew Lefty's web was flimsy at best.

"That works," Copper said, taking a seat. His colossal frame looked hilarious on the rickety folding chair. Any other time, Mav would have been tossing out some great one-liners to get under Copper's skin.

"Want to thank you boys," Lefty said after a Hispanic guy with an eyepatch delivered their drinks. "Shark had been losing his shit at a rapid clip. Getting sloppy, losing business, making enemies." He gave Copper a pointed look. "He needed to be taken out."

"Didn't do it for you," Copper said. "He was moving in on our territory, kidnapped one of my men." He didn't glance at Maverick or give any indication he was the one Shark had taken. "Fucked with my enforcer's woman." This time, he jerked his thumb in Zach's direction.

As enforcer, Zach often had the privilege of beating the shit out of assholes who owed the Handlers significant sums of money. His preferred method of delivering those love taps was Louie, an aluminum Louisville Slugger. As Copper spoke, Zach rolled Louie back and forth under the palm of his hand. His face had darkened, no doubt at memories of the abuse Toni had suffered at Shark's hand flooded in.

"Uh, right, of course." Lefty squirmed in his chair, his eyes shifting between the Handlers. Tough pill to swallow, realizing you weren't top dog in a meeting in your own house.

"Wanted to come by today to lay down a few ground rules. You know, so we can coexist peacefully," Copper said before taking a swig from his bottle. Lounging back in his chair, he gave the appearance of a man who was relaxed, enjoying his beer, chatting with friends. Mav and Zach both knew he was anything but. Copper didn't miss a trick and was in complete control at all times. Except when it came to Shell.

"Sure, sure. What'd you have in mind?" Lefty squirmed in his chair then adjusted his ridiculous bandana.

"First, stay the fuck out of our territory. That means no drugs, no bullshit, no anything. I don't want to see any Dragons dealing on my corners or driving through my town. Hell, I don't want to see 'em walking through the park eating a fucking ice cream cone. Don't give a shit what you do on your own turf, but you don't set one single toe in mine. Get me?"

Lefty's posture grew stiff and he leaned forward in his chair. "Of course. We got nothing but respect for the Handlers. Don't want to make any trouble with you guys. We stay on our turf, you stay on yours." He gave Copper a questioning look.

With a nod, Copper said, "Goes both ways. After today, we'll stay out of your territory as well."

It had to be killing Lefty to agree to the terms, but the fucker had no choice. As of now, he didn't have the manpower to go against Copper. That might change in the future, but that was a worry for another day. "That all?" Lefty asked.

"Let the fucking girl go," Copper said.

Any remaining friendliness vanished from Lefty's face, replaced by a hardness that made him the leader. "Don't know what the fuck you're talking about, Copper."

Copper leaned forward and rested his thick forearms on the table. None of the Dragons could tell from looking at him, but Zach and Mav knew him well enough to recognize he was seething inside. Seconds away from blowing. It didn't often happen. In fact, Mav could only recall one instance when Copper truly lost his shit, but it sure as fuck wasn't pretty. "You know exactly what I'm talking about, asshole. Skin trade is over. I will not tolerate it, and you won't survive a war. Let the girl go."

Lefty's face grew an unhealthy shade of red, but what could he do? He was backed in a corner, and he knew it. Still, he shifted his eyes to a man behind Mav. The guy transferred his weight from one leg to the other, ever so slightly, and slid his hand between his shirt and his jacket.

Having spent most of his life peeking over his shoulder for an attack, Mav was prepared. He had his pistol out and a foot from Lefty's head in seconds. When Zach slammed Louie against the metal table, the ear-splitting bang made Lefty jump.

"Skittish much?" Mav asked at the same time Zach said, "I wouldn't do that if I were you."

Lefty froze and shifted his gaze to Zach, who stared at the man behind Lefty. The man who hadn't had enout time to draw his own weapon.

"Mav will have a bullet lodged between your eyes before your weak little army gets a shot off. Then you'll have the entire Handlers MC up your ass within an hour. I promise it won't be a fun way to go," Zach said.

Copper rose and slapped a hotel key down on the table. "Sweetwater Motel Six. Room ten. The girl is there, unharmed, by midnight, or I'll be riding around with your head on my fender."

The warehouse grew quiet, nothing but the sound of Lefty's frustrated breaths hitting their ears. "She'll be there," he said through clenched teeth.

Copper nodded. "Pleasure doing business with you. Let's ride boys."

Mav and Zach trailed after him as he walked from the building like he owned the fucking place.

When he reached the door, Copper called out. "I hear another girl's gone missing, and you won't get a warning. I'll slit your throat in your sleep."

Time to head back to Townsend where Stephanie awaited.

Mav smiled as he mounted his bike. As much as he wanted to watch the life drain from Lefty's eyes, that wasn't the way the world worked. They couldn't go around killing every motherfucker that crossed their paths. Now, if Lefty didn't stick to the game plan, all bets were off.

They did good today. Stephanie might not see it that way with her let-the-police-handle-it fairytale view of the world, but even she had to realize some things just needed a little MC justice.

CHAPTER TWENTY-FIVE

Stephanie emerged from the shower to the buzz of a cell phone. Not her personal phone, but the secure burner the FBI had given her.

Frowning, she fished it out of the tampon box she'd hidden in the bottom drawer of her dresser. She'd been staying at the Handlers' clubhouse for five days and wasn't supposed to check in with the powers that be for another two days.

After retrieving the phone from under some yoga pants, she closed herself in the bathroom attached to her room. No one would likely hear her since it was eleven on a weekday and most of the guys were downstairs or at work, but she wasn't taking any chances.

"Little," she said in a low voice.

"Agent Little, it's Baccarella," her SAC returned.

She pulled the phone away from her ear and stared at it in disbelief for a beat. Why was he calling her? She was supposed to check in with him, not the reverse. It wasn't protocol. Shit. Had something happened?

"Good morning, sir. Is everything all right? I'm not scheduled to check in for another few days?"

"Another girl went missing a few days ago. Older this time. She turned up at a hospital in Monroe County, shortly after midnight," he said, not wasting any time on small talk. "I got a witness who says he saw a girl who matches her description, but looking like she went five rounds with a heavyweight champion, get on the back of a bike at a Motel Six in Sweetwater."

Shit. Her stomach dropped to the ground. There was no way. Toni and Shell had already confirmed the Handlers had nothing to do with it. But it might not even matter. With Baccarella's mission to become the FBI director, he'd likely dig until he found something, even if he had to stretch the truth. He couldn't be trusted to conduct a fair and unbiased investigation. She almost snorted into the phone.

The last thing *she* was doing was conducting an unbiased investigation.

"Were they wearing Handlers' colors, sir?" she asked, trying hard to sound professional and not like her world was crashing down around her.

If Baccarella found a way to pin this on the Handlers... God, she couldn't even think about it. How could he even think the man who'd allowed himself to be burned with an iron to save her from being raped was involved in the buying and selling of women? Then again, Baccarella probably didn't think it was the Handlers. It just fit with his agenda.

"Handlers' colors?" Baccarella laughed. "Really getting into the biker chick role, huh?"

Shit. She was walking a fine line. All eyes would be on her, especially after Agent Rey flipped. The FBI could award him all the accolades they wanted, but they had to be feeling the sting of his betrayal. And here she was playing a game that was just as dangerous, just as wrong. There was a need inside her, a deep-seated need to protect Maverick and his brothers. If the FBI felt she was getting too close, they'd pull her. But that wouldn't be the end of it. Someone else would be sent in, someone who didn't give a shit what happened to any of the Handlers.

"Isn't that the point? Assimilate while I'm here? Make them believe I'm here for them?"

"Fair enough," he said. "And to answer your question, the witness said there weren't any identifying marks on the biker.

He wore a helmet with a face shield, so a description is out of the question. All the witness said was 'big biker.' Doesn't exactly narrow it down."

Relief hit her hard. She wasn't quite sure what she'd have done if Baccarella told her the rider had worn a Handlers' cut. Devastating wouldn't begin to describe her emotions.

Shit. What a mess. If she were smart, she'd ask, no beg, Baccarella to pull her before she got sucked in any deeper. Her feelings for Maverick were genuine, and causing her to make fatal errors in judgment. But she couldn't walk away. She needed to protect him. She needed to ensure that when she was called back to DC, Mav and his brothers would be free from prosecution.

Because she'd officially dived into a pool of gray, and there was no end in sight.

"I'm staying right at the clubhouse, sir. I truly don't believe the Handlers are involved in human trafficking. It just doesn't add up." Lefty's name was on the tip of her tongue, but she had no idea what the Handlers had done to him or had planned for him. The FBI digging around Lefty would potentially lead them right back to Mav's club. No, she needed more information before she divulged that tidbit. And that meant leaving Lefty's fate to the Handlers, for now at least.

"Well, I know they killed Shark and Agent Rey. We just can't prove a damn thing. I can feel it in my goddamned gut. Start digging, Little. When you check in in two days, I want something concrete—unless you're looking to give living in a cardboard box a whirl."

"Yes, sir," she said as her mind spun in a million directions. How on earth was she going to satisfy her boss and keep Maverick out of jail?

What a nightmare.

"Stay safe, Agent Little," he said before disconnecting the call.

Clad in nothing but a damp towel, she shivered. The air in the bathroom had cooled since her hot shower, leaving her chilled.

After hiding the phone once again, she quickly dressed in jeans and a Hell's Handlers' shirt Shell had gifted her. Not surprising, it had quite the low neckline, showing off the small amount of cleavage she had, also thanks to Shell and "the best bra ever invented." The two women were similar in size, but Shell had a few more curves.

As she made her way down the stairs, her stomach growled. If she kept hitting the diner for their mouthwatering and sugar-laden meals, someone would have to roll her back to DC. Maybe a breakfast of coffee and fruit would undo some of the recent damage she'd done.

Hushed male voices came from the kitchen, making her slow her stride. The men were always careful to keep talk of club business behind closed doors. Maybe they'd forgotten she was in-house.

"She get a look at your face?" Copper murmured.

"Nah. Kept my helmet and face shield on." That was Rocket.

Stephanie almost threw up right here in the hallway outside the kitchen. Her breath started coming in pants, and she struggled to keep quiet. Shit. They had been the ones to rescue the woman. While she was relieved the woman was safe and being cared for, worry for the Handlers ramped the anxiety right back up. They were too close to this. Too close to being a casualty of Baccarella's blind ambition.

"She was in some bad fucking shape, Cop. Beat all to shit," Rocket whispered.

"Fuck."

Oh God, that was Maverick's voice. Any hope he was uninvolved dissolved on the spot.

"Raped?" asked Copper.

Rocket growled, like an animal issuing a warning. "She didn't say much, but she whimpered when she lifted her leg and climbed my bike."

"Sick bastards," Copper said. "Did I not tell Lefty I would bring war to his doorstep if she were harmed?"

War? Jesus. Baccarella would have a field day with this information. Hell, he'd probably sit on it and watch it play out just to swoop in at the last minute. Arresting Lefty and Copper at the same time would make him the Golden Boy of the FBI. Hello, new director.

It couldn't happen.

"Tell you what, Cop, she was one tough broad. I offered to call a prospect to bring a car so she wouldn't have to ride an hour on the bike, but she said she didn't want me to risk myself any more than was necessary. Somehow, she made it the whole way then walked into that ER with her head held high. Lefty may have tried, but he sure as fuck didn't break her."

"Took her to the University ER?"

Steph imagined Rocket nodding in the severe manner he had. "Figured the trauma center was so used to seeing horrible shit they'd be less likely to dig too deep."

"What the fuck are we gonna do about Lefty?" Maverick asked. He sounded hungry, eager to go after Lefty. "Feel like it's a fucking test. He's calling our bluff. We got the girl, no one wants to start a fucking war unless absolutely necessary. So he fucked her up to see what we'd do."

"I need to give it some—what the fuck was that?"

Shit. Shit. Shit. Steph had leaned her head against the wall, making the softest of thuds. But these men were all hypervigilant, probably more so when not wanting to be overheard. Time for damage control. She turned and speed walked back toward the stairs just as Copper stuck his head out of the kitchen.

"Stephanie," he called.

She froze and spun around plastering a cheerful smile on her face. "Oh, Copper, hi. I was coming to get something to eat, and I heard voices. Sounded serious so I was just on my way back to my room. I'll come back later."

He flattened his lips and stared at her—hard.

She held her breath. *Please buy it. Please buy it.*

She held her breath. "Come on in here a minute. Wanna run something by you." He jerked his head in the direction of the kitchen before disappearing.

If he'd told her he had a million bucks waiting for her in the refrigerator, she wouldn't have been more surprised. He was bringing her into a discussion about club business?

She hurried into the kitchen. Maverick's eyes lit up the moment he spotted her, and he came right to her. Wrapping one hand around the back of her neck and the other across her lower back he hauled her against him and kissed the hell out of her.

Everything faded away but the firm pressure of his lips, the scrape of the metallic ball over her tongue, and his arms around her.. He was her drug of choice, and like so many addicts, she'd traded her soul for a fix.

"Ahem, could you two horndogs keep it in the fuckin' bedroom?" Copper asked. "Didn't call you in for a live sex show, darlin'. Not that it wouldn't be a good one, but we got shit to talk about."

Oh, my God. She wanted to die. She tried to wiggle away, but Mav's grip on her neck held her close. "Mav," she whispered, "let me go."

"Copper can wait for one more fucking second. He's just cranky cuz his dick spends way too much time with his own hand these days." He didn't even try to muffle his voice but antagonized his president right out in the open.

Steph giggled as he pressed one more kiss to her lips then released her, tucking her close to his body. She wrapped her arms around his waist and held tight. Why, oh why did it have to feel like she belonged right there at his side? "What did you want to talk to me about?" she asked Copper.

He ran a hand down his face, pausing to scratch his beard. "You're aware of the Gray Dragon's involvement with trafficking girls." He shifted his gaze to Maverick, who squeezed her tighter, before returning his attention to Steph. "We'd hoped taking Shark and King out of the equation would put an end to that operation, but it hasn't. One of his lackeys has taken up the cause. Last night, Rocket rescued a twenty-seven-year-old woman who'd been snatched and was slated to be sold to the highest bidder."

Stephanie hung on every detail. This was it, the entire reason she was in Tennessee. She was torn between begging him to talk faster and pleading with him to stop. Any information he divulged could be used against him. Though, who was she kidding? She'd already proven her willingness to perjure for this group. Now, knowing they were fighting to save and protect the women from sexual slavery, how could she do anything but support them?

They were still breaking the law. Killing people, taking justice into their own hands. It was all wrong in the eyes of the law.

But the FBI had nothing. And one of their own agents had been integral in the kidnapping and deaths of three teenagers after letting them be used and abused. And just the previous year, in a similar case, jury members were bribed and threatened to coerce a favorable ruling for the defendant, a sick bastard who preyed on innocent women. The Handlers could take this scum out without ever involving the law.

Stephanie wouldn't stand in their way. Instead, she'd help keep the FBI off their backs.

Hello, gray zone.

"What do you need from me?" she asked.

"She's on board with keeping quiet about who rescued her, just a random biker whose face she didn't see, which is the truth anyway. She gave a detailed description to the cops of a bike different from Rocket's. We also had to ask her not to seek out any local psychological help. Those people can be bought or threatened by Lefty into spilling what they know. But the girl's gotta be fucked up after all she went through."

"I'll do whatever you guys need."

"We forced Lefty to give her up with threat of war. Can't help but feel somewhat responsible for the rough treatment she received, since I'm pretty sure Lefty was trying to send us a message. He'd wanted an alliance, and we shot that chance to shit. She suffered through more than you did, but I thought maybe she could talk to you. Maybe you could help her."

"Jesus, Prez," Mav spat out. "You're asking Stephanie to relive some nasty shit. A little heads-up would have been nice, brother."

She gave Maverick a squeeze. He was sweet to care, but there was no way she'd turn down this request.

These were good men. Not everything they did was on the up and up, and not all the money they made was legitimate, but when she dug down through a few messy layers, the core of this club was solid. They cared about family, about women, and about the community. Never in her life had she imagined herself able to overlook things like loan sharking, muscle for hire, or even murder, but there she was. Tolerating it and even condoning it.

"Of course, I'll speak with her. Just let me know when."

"Thank you," Copper said. "She'll be in the hospital for a few more days. I'll get her info to Mav after she's released so you can set something up."

"I'm happy to help." And she was. If she could give that poor woman even a few moments of peace after what she'd gone through, it would be time well spent.

"All right. We're out." Copper slapped Mav on the back as he strode out, Rocket not two steps behind.

The instant both men were gone, Maverick gripped her waist and turned while lifting her at the same time. In the next instant, her ass slammed down on the long rectangular table, and his mouth descended, claiming her lips in another air-stealing kiss. "That fucking shirt," he ground out against her mouth.

She barely had enough breath to keep her brain working, let alone process the statement. His mouth moved to her neck where he nipped the sucked at the tendon running to her collarbone. Her head fell back, and she let him go to town.

Damn, when his lips hit the spot right where her neck curved into shoulder, she wanted to scream to the women of the world that this man was hers and she was never letting him go.

Foolish and oh-so incorrect.

"M-my shirt?" she finally asked after that semi-sobering realization.

Licking along her collarbone, he moved his hands to the button of her jeans and went to work opening them with deft fingers.

"Mav, wait," she said on a gasp when his fingers brushed the skin of her lower belly, causing a surge of goosebumps all over her stomach.

"Makes me fucking insane seeing my club's name scrawled across your tits." He kissed her lips then met her gaze with a shit-eating grin. "Need you, babe. Now. You gonna let me have you?"

She tried to swat his hands away, but he was like a man on a mission, somehow working her jeans and panties down her hips despite the fact she was sitting on them. The cold table meeting her bare ass and thighs made her yip and jump. "There are people here." She'd never been one for indecent public displays. Clearly, Maverick was not of the same mind.

"Cop and Rocket are the only two people in-house. And they won't be back, trust me. They know exactly what's about to happen in here." He palmed her ass and tugged her so far forward she teetered on the edge of the table and had to grab his sides to keep from pitching face-first to the tile floor. The feel of his large hands kneading her ass cheeks had her pussy dripping with need.

"They know you're about to fuck me on the kitchen table?" How on earth would they know that? Some sort of alpha biker telepathy?

"Fuck you? Wildcat, it's the kitchen. You don't fuck in the kitchen." He winked. "You eat in the kitchen." In the next instant, he dropped to his knees and pressed his face to the junction of her thighs, inhaling with a low groan.

"Oh, my God," she whispered as his nose bumped her clit and his tongue took a maddeningly slow journey through her folds. That warm, skilled tongue was magic and had her moaning in seconds.

"Shit, Steph. All this delicious cream is just for me, isn't it?" He slid his tongue over her again, this time the steel ball of his tongue ring rimming her entrance.

"Wow, that feels...really different." And really fucking wicked. He was completely destroying her for all other men. After the FBI pulled her back to her real life, she wouldn't be satisfied with a man unless he was covered in ink and decorated with all kinds of metal. And even then, he wouldn't be Mav. She'd probably remain celibate for the rest of her miserable life.

He chuckled against her pussy, and even that had her whimpering in response. "Different good?"

"Different fucking amazing."

"Damn straight, baby." He brought his tongue up and circled it twice around her clit before flicking her hood. The day before leaving DC, she'd gotten waxed—which showed exactly where her head was in this game—and his wet, slightly rough tongue on her smooth skin elevated the pleasure to mind-blowing.

When he gently, feather-lightly, ran the ball of his tongue ring over her clit, she cried out and shoved her hands in his hair. A growl came from deep within him as she held his head against her pussy and squeezed her thighs around his head. Just when she worried she'd smother him, he gripped her ass harder, pulled her tighter to his mouth, and switched from gentle to aggressive in his assault on her senses.

Stephanie's head fell back on her shoulders, and her mind muddled as she gave into the full body pleasure this man wrought from her.

When this was all said and done, there was a good chance she'd be going to hell or prison. At least she'd have the memory of this man eating her straight to heaven.

CHAPTER TWENTY-SIX

Steph rubbed her arms as she shivered and bounced on the balls of her feet. A surprise cool front had blown in overnight, stealing the sun and the warm days that had made early fall in Tennessee a pleasant experience.

Now, after wandering about fifty feet out into the woods, she was regretting her clothing choice. Should have worn more than the Hell's Handlers' hoodie she'd pilfered from Mav. She lifted a way-too-long sleeve to her nose and inhaled. Smelled like Maverick. A hint of smoke from the clubhouse, whatever deodorant he used, and sex appeal, if that had a scent.

The combination of comfort and excitement from being wrapped in his essence made up for the shivering and foolish lack of a jacket.

Geez, she was becoming a sap.

From its home in her back pocket, the Bureau phone vibrated. She glanced at the screen as she tugged it out. Five p.m. on the dot. "Agent Little," she answered.

"Tell me you've got something for me, Little. And tell me it's something that will make up for all the shit I've been in since Daniel screwed everything up. I'm chomping at the bit to tear down these mother fucking bikers. The girl who appeared at the hospital has been closed-mouthed as a fucking mime. Can't get her to say shit. The bikers must have scared the piss out of her. Threatened to come after her again or something."

Steph waited, letting him rant until he ran out of steam. Rocket wouldn't have threatened the girl. Just told her like it was. It might take some time, but the Handlers would end Lefty. They'd make sure no one ever came after her again. But she'd have to keep quiet about both Lefty being the kidnapper and the Handlers' role in rescuing her.

And she'd be just as guilty as the MC. Hell, she knew what the end result woudl be and she'd had the resources at the tip of her fingers to make Shark and King pay through legal and just measures. Yet, she didn't utter a word of it.

Turned out, the promise of revenge was a powerful motivator and trumped what she'd once called justice.

"Little? Fucking talk to me."

Shit. "Sorry, sir." She cleared her throat. "The Handlers didn't take the girl. They aren't involved in any way with human trafficking. They don't even run prostitutes. Haven't since before Copper took over as president."

Her statement was met with nothing but frustrated breaths. "Don't tell me you have nothing for me, Little. Your ass will be riding a desk until it chafes."

"Sir, with all due respect, there isn't anything here. These men don't run women." What made this so frustrating was that it was the goddamned truth. But she couldn't admit they'd rescued the woman because she'd have to admit to knowledge of their plan to go after Lefty and eventually knowledge of what happened to Shark and King.

"Fuck," he spat out. "What about the biker who brought the girl to the hospital? You're telling me that wasn't a Handler?"

"That's what I'm telling you. There are thousands of tourists here this time of year. Many come to ride their motorcycles through the mountain roads. It wasn't the Handlers, sir. First off, they don't ride without their colors, and second, there isn't any evidence, or even any thread to pull ,indicating they are involved."

She could practically see his face turning red and a cartoonish vein popping out of his head. "What a clusterfuck. What about Shark and King's murders? Tell me you have something to pin on the Handlers."

Here's where it got tricky, because this was where nothing but lies began. She'd worked it all out in her head, but had to word everything with care. Baccarella would look into anything she gave him to the best of his ability, and if things didn't add up, her ass would be roasting over hot coals faster than Mav could make her come. And he was damn gifted. Suddenly, she was no longer feeling the cold but sweating with apprehension.

"Sir, I know this isn't what you want to hear, but it's not looking like the Handlers are the ones who killed either man. From all accounts, they arrived and discovered Maverick passed out in front of Shark's cabin. There were a few other dead Dragons as well, one was probably King, but no one here knew him. Maverick woke in the hospital and told them about me. Jigsaw and Screw went back and found me in the basement. Just like I've been telling you all along."

"Christ, Little, you're a shit undercover agent."

She *wasn't* an undercover agent, and he fucking knew it. She bit down on her tongue to keep the scathing retort inside.

"We need to pin this on the Handlers, Little. *Need* it. Do you understand me?" There was an air of desperation to his claim.

"Why, sir? Why the Handlers? The Dragons have multiple enemies. Hell, Shark was kidnapping teenage girls and selling them. He worked with the lowest of low. The timeline doesn't add up. We know the Handlers were in church until late on the night Maverick and I were rescued." Lies, but since they didn't keep written records and every MC member had the same story, it couldn't be disproven. Plus, they'd burned Shark's cabin and surrounding area to the ground, so time of death wasn't certain. And thankfully, Stephanie honestly couldn't speak to the timeline since she'd been in and out of consciousness.

"Because we have a dead Agent, Little. A dead agent with a wife and parents who want answers. And we have a president who doesn't like the Bureau looking like a bunch of bumbling idiots who can't solve the murder of one of their own. I want the director position, and I won't have fucking bikers stealing it from me."

Stephanie stared up at the leaves rustling as a soft breeze blew by. It calmed her somewhat. At the very least, it kept her from screaming that Agent Rey was a murderer himself, that he'd been responsible for the deaths of three teens, that he'd jumped teams and was Shark's go-to man. They'd had that conversation already, and it didn't seem to matter to anyone but her. All that mattered was that the Bureau put on a good front, looked shiny for the politicians, and Baccarella got his promotion.

"We need to shift focus off the Hell's Handlers, sir. It's a waste of time and a dead end."

"To whom?" he barked. "The Gray Dragons gang is destroyed. It's the Handlers. I can feel it in my fucking bones. I don't care what you have to do, Little. You get me some goddamned evidence by this time next week."

He disconnected, leaving her staring at the phone in horror. He didn't care what she had to do? Was he suggesting she falsify evidence? Plant something to make the Handlers guilt obvious?

How could he ever think she'd do something like that? She'd never do something so wrong, so illegal...

"Listen to me," she muttered to the trees. She'd lost her shit. There she was, shocked and horrified that her boss would ask her to plant evidence to make an MC who was guilty appear so. But she had no problem lying, covering up, and even assisting that same MC in its criminal activities.

When the hell had everything gotten so fucked up?

The moment you let Maverick kiss you, touch you.

It was true. Before that, she'd been able to pretend there wasn't an intense connection between them, but once it'd turned physical, she could no longer deny her feelings.

For the first time in almost six years, she longed for her father. Finally, after so long, she understood his dilemma. Understood how it was easy for him to make a choice the world might see as wrong, but he saw as beneficial and worthwhile. If she could go back in time, she'd do everything in her power to help him fight for his freedom.

Feeling the weight of the coming week pressing down on her, she started the trek back to the clubhouse. The brothers were all in church. That was how she was able to sneak out into the woods unnoticed. Tonight was the vote to patch Screw into the club. Apparently, he'd been prospecting for a little over a year, so it was time. If he made it, which she had no doubts about, they'd do that barbaric branding ritual then there'd be a monster of a party.

She wasn't sure she was up for a party unless it was a private party for two. Her and Maverick, preferably sans clothing. Never having been overly promiscuous or even sexual in the past, Stephanie had basically become a slave to his cock, and his tongue…and even his talented fingers.

For the past few days, they'd gone at it two, three, hell, even four times a day. She couldn't get enough of the man, and he seemed to feel the same. Rough, gentle, fast, slow, playful, intense. Name it, they'd done it, and she'd loved every second of it.

There wouldn't have been a problem if that's all it was, but no, they stayed up well into the night talking, sharing secrets and painful stories from their pasts. Maverick was flirty, fun, and could make her pass out with pleasure, but there was so much more under the surface. He'd revealed a protective streak a mile wide, and he was loyal, caring, and even quite dominant at times. There wasn't an aspect of him that she didn't like—if she overlooked his criminal activity, of course.

But even that made him who he was. A little bad, a little naughty. A little forbidden. And hella sexy.

Stephanie was so lost in thought she hadn't noticed the woman hovering at the edge of the woods in a shimmery metallic dress with a plunging neckline that showed off everything but her nipples. It was a mini dress, but that didn't prevent it from having a slit that went so high, it was obvious she wasn't wearing panties.

She had to be freezing her ass off.

Whatever she had to say, it certainly wasn't going to be an apology or a welcome to the club speech, that was for sure. Steph had glimpsed her around the clubhouse a time or two over the past few days and, though she stayed away, she'd shot death glares at both her and Maverick.

"What do you want, Carli?" she asked as she stopped about two feet away from the woman. Far enough that she couldn't get bitch slapped but close enough to notice that there were indeed goosebumps all over the crazy woman's skin.

"Heard you on the phone," she said with a smirk.

Stephanie's heart skipped a beat. This stupid club whore could ruin everything. Copper would order her death if they found out she was FBI. And now her fate rested in the hands of a jealous Honey. Sweat broke out along her hairline despite the chilly air.

"And? I have a life, Carli. And people in my life that I like to speak to. Sorry if that's a problem for you." She put her hands on her hips and tried to portray a don't-give-a-shit attitude.

Carli tossed back her head and laughed. "What, are you married? Got a boyfriend back home who thinks you're on a little work trip while you came here to get some biker dick?"

Stephanie's knees went weak with relief. She could have grabbed the stupid woman and kissed her. That's what Carli thought this was? She hadn't listened very carefully if she thought Steph was fucking Baccarella. Just the notion of it made her want to hurl. "Look, Carli, I'm not about to get into a catfight with you, no matter what bullshit you vomit at me. So just get out of my way, stay out of my business, and keep the fuck away from Maverick." As she walked past Carli, she slammed into her, and although she was a good three inches shorter, even more if you counted Carli's stilettos, she managed to make the other woman stumble.

Okay, maybe she was up for a catfight. Just a small, teensy one.

"See you at the party tonight, bitch," Carli called to her back. "It will be fun to tell Maverick he's getting someone's sloppy seconds."

Don't take the bait. Don't take the bait.

"What do they call it when you've been fucked by every guy in the club? Sloppy twentieths just doesn't sound right."

Whoops. She took the bait. Really not wanting to have her hair pulled and face scratched, Stephanie picked up her pace until she was practically jogging toward the clubhouse. She couldn't resist one peek over her shoulder. Carli stood at the edge of the woods, hands on her hips, in that ridiculous excuse for a dress. Her eyes were narrowed and Stephanie could practically see the venom dripping from her fangs.

When she reached the clubhouse, she ran around the side of the building and bent forward, propping her hands on her knees. Her breath came in quick gasps, not from the jog, but from the close call. She had to be more careful. Not all the Honeys were as dumb as Carli. And the Handlers themselves certainly weren't fools. If someone else had tracked her, she'd be halfway to a grave right now.

Too close.

Hopefully, Carli would keep her trap closed, but just in case, Stephanie needed to come up with a story for Maverick.

About why she was out in the woods.

Talking on the phone.

To a man.

Piece of cake.

CHAPTER TWENTY-SEVEN

"Congrats, brother," Maverick said, slapping Screw on the back.

Screw smiled, though he looked a little green and halfway to shitfaced. "Thanks, Mav. Jesus fuck, that shit hurt. I don't know how you survived—oh fuck. Shit. I'm sorry, man. I didn't mean anything by it."

Even though his insides clenched and his arm felt like it was burning all over again, Mav waved him off. He wasn't about to ruin Screw's big night over a thoughtless comment made after the guy downed a shit ton of moonshine. "No worries, brother. It was fucking rough, I can tell you that much." And even worse was the pain of seeing a blank forearm every day. I'll walk you in. Get your shirt on, get some more booze in you, and find you some pussy."

"Thanks," Screw said. "Might make me a pussy to say this, but I'm feeling like a fucking baby horse with wobbly legs."

Mav laughed. "Been there, man. Totally normal."

The Handlers' initiation ritual for new patches was brutal. Not only did they get their arm branded, but it happened with the entire club watching, and the brother had to take it standing up, without screaming, without puking, and without passing out. No easy feat. More than one man had made it through the prospecting period only to cry like a baby during branding and be booted from the club.

As they walked away from the raging bonfire and into the

clubhouse, the prospect tending bar, Little Jack, caught sight of them. He'd started prospecting about two months after Screw and they were close. "Congrats, man!" Little Jack tossed Screw his shirt and poured him his favorite scotch.

"Thanks. Can't fucking wait until you gotta go through this shit." Screw slid his left arm through the shirt sleeve, careful not to brush the charred skin of his forearm. In the morning, he could treat it, but part of the fun—for the rest of the MC—was making the new member walk around with it open all night. The pain would fade fast as he drank and fucked.

"You got any of the Honeys in mind for tonight?" Little Jack asked. Contrary to his name, he was a big fucker and Zach's prospect. Hard worker, loyal, gonna make a great brother soon, like Screw.

"Like to work my way through all of 'em at some point," Screw said on a laugh. "You know, gotta find my favorite." Prospects weren't allowed to dipp in the well of club whores. It was something the Honeys got quite a kick out of. They loved nothing more than taunting the poor assholes with teasing touches, dirty whispers, and future promises. Poor guys complained about having PBBs, or prospect blue balls. Screw had more than a few women to punish for that tonight.

Little Jack handed Mav his favorite whiskey, but his eyes kept flicking to some woman Mav didn't recognize. She was across the bar, chatting with Shell. She was a looker, all right, tall with long, sleek, amber hair, perfect posture, and clothing that screamed professional, not biker.

"Who the fuck's that?" LJ asked.

Screw snorted. "Someone way the fuck out of your league, dickhead."

"Gotta agree with my new brother, LJ. That's some expensive pussy over there. Maybe a tourist who was looking to slum it during her mountain getaway," Mav said.

"You gonna go after her, LJ?" Screw asked on a laugh as he polished off his scotch and held out the glass for another.

"Fuck, yeah," LJ said.

"Good fucking luck."

This was gonna be good. "You know what?" Mav asked. "I'll give you five minutes to pick that classy pussy up. You go get her. I'll watch the bar for you." Prospects couldn't have any of the Honeys, but visitors and woman partying for the night were fair game.

The cocky grin left LJ's face, and he frowned. "Really? You think I should. I mean, I can, but should I?"

Screw was doubled over with laughter. "Don't get cold feet now. You talked a big fucking game. Come on, I wanna see you banging that one in a dark corner tonight."

Shit. Mav would love to fuck Stephanie at this party. Find somewhere just out of sight where they could be caught at any moment. He fucking loved the thought of nerves and lust battling it out inside her. And when she finally caved and let him do whatever the fuck he wanted to her within earshot of his brothers...fuck yeah, that was happening tonight.

"Yeah, all right," LJ said. "Just give me a second." He stretched his arms and bounced on the balls of his feet like he was preparing to enter the ring, not pick up a classy broad.

"The fuck you doing?" Screw asked.

"Just getting ready. Shut the fuck up."

Mav sipped his drink and laughed. Never once had he regretted his decision to join this brotherhood. Just as LJ walked from behind the bar, Jumper, a member in his late forties who'd been around since he was twenty ,sidled on up to the woman LJ had his sights set on. She smiled at him and, within seconds, was in his arms, dancing to hard rock blaring from the speakers.

"What the fuck?" LJ said, sounding shocked.

Screw choked on his drink. "Looks like you're flying solo tonight, man."

Mav grinned at him. "You know what they say, brother—he who hesitates masturbates. Have fun with your hand tonight. I'm sure Jumper will let you know all about her classy pussy tomorrow."

Grumbling under his breath, LJ stomped back behind the bar. This time, he poured himself a double, slamming both the glass and bottle as he worked. Screw was laughing so hard Mav thought he'd fall right off the barstool, but then he blinked and sobered in an instant.

"Incoming," he whispered. "I'm outta here. Good luck, brother."

"What the..." Mav looked over his shoulder and let out a groan.

"Hi, handsome." Carli strutted up to him with her back arched and tits sticking out even farther than normal. "Share your drink with me?"

"The fuck you want, Carli? Thought I told you we were done. There shouldn't be anything you have to say to me. You know damn well I'm with Stephanie."

Before he could stop her, she grabbed the glass out of his hand and brought it to her lips. A red crescent lipstick stain remained after she'd taken a sip. Her half-lidded eyes promised sex as did her scrap of a dress. Yes, in the past he would have been all over it, but only because it was easy and he wanted to get off inside a woman rather than his hand. Her whole vibe didn't hold much appeal to him. "Finish it," he said when she tried to hand it back to him.

Her sultry smile turned upside-down for a moment before she tried another tactic. "You know," she said, pouting her ruby lips. "You should be nicer to me. I have a gift for you."

If that lip thing was supposed to make him think of getting head, it didn't work. Okay, maybe it did, because he was suddenly remembering Stephanie's tongue trailing up and down the ink on his cock. Man, that was some good shit. Bore repeating. Soon.

"Don't want it, Carli. Get lost." He turned his back on her. "LJ, need another drink. New glass."

"You got it, Mav." LJ shot Carli a nasty look then poured

Maverick's drink. Maybe it was time to talk to Copper about having Carli move on. Seemed many of the brothers were tired of her drama.

When he turned around again, Carli was right there, lips pressed against his ear. "Your woman is fucking another man," she whispered.

His muscles froze, and he squeezed the glass so hard it should have shattered. The logical side of him knew Carli was probably full of it. She was a master shit-stirrer. But the other side of him, the rasher, less controlled side that went apeshit at the idea of another man even thinking about Steph's pussy, was winning out.

"What the fuck are you talking about?"

Looking so proud of herself, she stepped between his spread legs. "Heard her on the phone with a guy." She dropped her hands to his knees and started to slide them up his thighs. "She was hiding in the woods for her conversation. Very suspicious," she said in a sing-song voice.

"Get your fucking hands off me, or I'll have LJ toss your ass in the parking lot." Every muscle in his body was rock-hard and raring for a fight. Even if there were another man in Stephanie's life, he wouldn't be there for long, because Mav was going to rip his dick off and run over it with his bike.

Carli let him go and stepped back, clearly stunned by the hatred in his voice. Her lower lip trembled, and this time Mav didn't think it was an act. "I just don't want to see you get hurt, baby," she whined. "You know how I feel about you. I could—"

He stopped listening as his gaze locked with Stephanie's. She stood near the entrance to the bar wearing a denim mini skirt and a stark white tank top that said *Handle This* in black cursive across the chest. He'd seen Toni wearing something similar not long ago. The back of the shirt had the Hell's Handlers' symbol.

Fuck, there was just something about seeing her in his MC's shit that made him want to fuck her right then and there. But they had something to discuss first. Hands on her hips, her gaze shifted to Carli, and her eyes narrowed. She was pissed. And fuck if it wasn't hot as hell.

What the hell was wrong with him? There was a fair chance she was fucking another guy, and all he could think about was how much more he was going to want to fuck her after he watched her lay into Carli.

Looking like a pissed-off little fairy, she marched over to where he and Carli were. Something was different about her. She'd curled her hair into waves that framed her pretty face and had gone a little heavier on the makeup. She looked fantastic, like a biker's ol' lady.

Like his ol' lady.

Clearly, he wasn't drinking enough.

When she stopped within arm's reach, she only looked better up close. That's when the anger hit. No other man was allowed near her. Didn't matter they hadn't had a conversation about being exclusive. Didn't matter he didn't have relationships or wasn't looking for an ol' lady. No man was to touch her.

He opened his mouth at the same time she held up her hand. "Look," she said, shooting daggers at Carli with her eyes before turning her attention to Maverick. Then it was like everyone else in the room disappeared. She gave him one hundred percent of herself at that moment. "I don't know what she said to you, but I'm pretty sure I know the gist of it. I'm not a child, and I'm not a whore, so I'm coming to you straight and killing this right now."

Carli gasped and looked at him like he should scold Stephanie for what she said. Please, it was taking everything he had not to laugh.

"We haven't known each other very long," she continued. "It goes without saying, we still have a lot to learn about each other. There are people in my life and things in my life that you do not know about. I needed to speak to one of those people in a private conversation that I didn't want to have inside a clubhouse full of nosey men and catty whores."

Shit, he was going to lose it. He bit the inside of his lower lip while Carli seethed.

"I am not married. I do not have a boyfriend or a man in my life in any capacity beyond friendships and collogues. Before you, I hadn't had sex in two years, three months, and seven days."

Carli snickered, and if she weren't a woman, Mav would have smacked her. He fucking loved being the one that broke Stephanie's fuck drought. He loved the way she faced this head on without drama and without taking Carli's shit.

Wildcat.

"Whatever she thinks she heard," Steph went on, "is A, not her business, and B, not accurate."

"Okay," he said. He believed her and respected the fact she tackled this without excuses or bullshit. Or maybe he just wanted to believe her. Could she be hiding something from him? Part of him wanted to push it further, but he was already three drinks in and Carli was right there. Not the time or the place. A drunken blowout was exactly what Carli was banking on.

"Like I need any more dick than I'm getting from you right now. I couldn't even—wait, what?"

He chuckled. "I said okay."

She frowned, her small, unintentional pout a million times more effective than Carli's could ever be. "Okay?"

"Yes, okay. I believe you. And you could probably use a little more of my dick, dontcha think?"

Carli still stood way too close, her mouth open and her arms crossed. Stephanie turned to her. "If you don't get your fucking hands off him, your hair extensions are going to be all over this floor."

"Easy there, wildcat," Mav said as he laughed. He grabbed Stephanie by the ass, ignored her yelp of surprise, and hoisted her up into his arms. As he walked them both away from Carli, he fused his mouth with hers.

Wrapping her legs around his waist, she kissed him back, full and deep. He loved the taste of her and the feel of her as she gave herself over to him. "Let's get you a drink," he said, walking to the opposite end of the bar. "What do you want?"

"Gin and tonic with lime please," she said.

"Hear that, LJ?" Mav asked.

"Yeah man, give me ten seconds."

Her drink appeared, and she took a huge gulp.

"Forget it, babe. It's done." For now, she was there in his arms, and he'd rather soak her up than pick a fight.

She nodded and took another large sip. "Forgotten. Just trying to catch up to you."

He laughed and nuzzled her neck as she drank. "You look fucking hot tonight, wildcat. Not gonna be able to keep my hands off you for long. You wear this for me?"

"Mmmhmm. Worked out pretty well for me last time I wore a Handlers' shirt. Thought I'd find out if it was a fluke or a trend."

"Fuck, a trend. Definitely a trend. You wear that shit, and it's pretty much a guarantee you're gonna get fucked. LJ, get her another," he called out as she drained her first drink.

"Hmm, seems like you fuck me pretty much all the time, no matter what I'm wearing."

He chuckled. "Good point."

Once she had her next drink, he took her hand and led her to a dark table in the back of the room. It was a booth with a bench seat along the wall and two chairs in front of the table. He slid onto the bench, drawing Stephanie down to his lap. The majority of the partygoers were outside at the bonfire, but since it was cold, a few people were milling about inside. No one paid any attention to them in the back corner, though, and it was dark and loud enough, most people probably didn't even realize they were there.

With a soft sigh, Stephanie settled onto his lap. He realized how fucking much he loved his life at that moment. His girl on his lap, brothers partying all around, family intact. Sure, there was some trouble on the horizon, but for the night, everything was perfect.

And most of it was because of the woman in his lap. She brought meaning into his life he'd never had before, a connection and trust with someone he genuinely liked and respected, as well as had the hottest sex of his life.

Was this what it was like for Zach and Toni? For his other brothers who had ol' ladies?

If so, he was fucked because he just might be making a commitment to Stephanie in the very near future.

And then what the hell did he do?

CHAPTER TWENTY-EIGHT

It was a lie of omission, but it didn't feel as gut-wrenching as lying to Maverick outright.

Stephanie settled her back against Maverick's chest, letting the tension of the day drain away. He'd believed every word out of her mouth. No questions, no demands, no asking who the hell she needed privacy to speak with. He'd taken her word over Carli's.

Just. Like. That.

It warmed her from the inside out, this trust he put in her, but at the same time, it was like a knife to the heart. She wasn't cheating, would never cheat, and had been truthful in stating the pitiful length of time she'd gone without sex. He was right to believe those words, but the real sin was so much worse.

Even when she spoke the truth, it felt dirty. Every word out of her mouth was tainted by the pile of lies she'd already told. The truth couldn't be revealed now. It was far too late. Even if Maverick somehow were able to forgive her, Copper wouldn't let her live. She knew it deep in her bones.

Mav slid his hand under the hem of her shirt, resting it against her stomach. His long, warm fingers spanned most of her width, and her eyes fluttered closed. She vowed then and there to soak up every look, every touch, every delicious sensation, and take those gifts to whatever dark place awaited her.

"Missed you this evening," he whispered, his breath as heated as the liquor flowing through her veins.

A smile curved her lips. "You did not. You were out doing your macho thing with your biker brothers. Bet you didn't think of me once."

He nipped her earlobe just shy of too hard and said, "You fucking kidding me? Thought of you at least ten times. This right here? You, all soft and warm in my lap, relaxed from your drink, my hands on your silky skin, best part of my day, beautiful."

And there he was, the genuinely fantastic man behind the fun, flirty, good-time guy he showed everyone else. Was it any wonder she was falling so hard and so fast?

"Best part of mine, too."

She opened her eyes and sipped her drink as his mouth started to play against the skin of her neck. It only took a second for goosebumps to rise up and a tremor to run through her. Her pussy throbbed and grew slick, so used to getting what it demanded of Maverick.

Eight or so people milled around the large open area of the clubhouse. Three sat at the bar while LJ chatted them up. A few were in a heated discussion at a table on the far side of the clubhouse.

Then there was Screw.

He'd been playing pool with one of the Honeys—Steph never could keep their names straight—but they'd abandoned the game in favor of a vigorous make-out session. She and Maverick had a perfect profile view of the pair and Steph couldn't tear her eyes away from the sight of Screw basically dry humping the woman against the pool table. One hand was under her shirt on her breast while his other held her thigh up around his hips. With a rhythmic motion that seemed to jive with the pounding beat of the music, he ground himself against her.

"You like it?" Mav said, jolting her out of her captivated state.

"W-what?"

"Watching them go at it. Do you like it?"

"Oh, no, of course not. I can't believe they're doing that right there in the middle of the room. Do they not care people might be watching?" She polished off the last of her drink and set the glass down. Now she needed a large glass of ice water. Maybe she'd dump it over her head.

Or on her crotch.

Mav's chest vibrated against her back as he laughed. "They care, babe. It's part of the fun."

Hmm. He was probably right.

The Honey with Screw started to sink to her knees as her hands went to his fly, but he stopped her with a tug on her hair. When she'd stood straight once again, he turned her and bent her over the pool table, keeping his hand on her back as she flattened against the felt. Then he worked her tiny leather skirt over her hips, exposing a bare ass.

The sight of his tanned hands roaming over the pale globes of the woman's ass did nothing for Steph. Nope, not a thing.

At least, that was her story, and she was stickin' to it.

But clearly, it did something for Mav. His erection was unmistakable as it rested between their bodies. "Do you like watching them?" she asked.

"Fuck, yeah," he said, totally unabashed. "It's hot as fuck." He pressed his hips up, grinding his erection against her ass, and she let out a puff of air. "But this? It was there before they even got started. That came on the moment you walked into the room."

She smiled. The man was good with the words.

The hand on her stomach slid downward at a snail's pace. Reclined against his chest, she held her breath as he slipped his fingers behind the waistband of her skirt and into her panties, then farther until he encountered her shamefully wet pussy.

"Hmm," he said in her ear. "I think you're lying."

Even though she knew exactly what he was talking about, hearing the accusation had her tensing all over.

"This sopping wet pussy tells me you like watching them quite a bit." He circled her clit with a wet finger, and she bit her lower lip.

"I like your hands on me," she replied as she wiggled her ass against his cock. Her heart raced. Not only did she like his hands on her, but she couldn't believe the rush of excitement that consumed her at the thought of being in the open. Never would she have imagined she'd do something like this, yet she was practically ready to beg for it. The life she was living now was so far from her life in DC she barely recognized herself.

But damn if her current life didn't feel spectacular in that moment.

Mav groaned. "Fuck, babe, I like hearing you say that shit."

While the Screw and Honey show continued, Mav played with her pussy. Nothing that would get her off, just light strokes and teasing flicks designed to make her a pile of needy goo in no time.

In the next second, Screw shoved his pants to his ankles and fisted his dick in his hand, sliding a condom down his length. A large part of her wanted to look away. It felt strange, wrong, staring at another man's cock just twenty feet away, but she couldn't make her head turn, even as he pushed it into the Honey.

"Watch her take every inch of him," Mav whispered as he slipped his middle finger inside her. "Look at her face. She fucking loves it."

Stephanie moaned, the combination of the visual and physical stimulation overwhelmed her senses. Who knew she'd like watching so much? She could have been watching porn all these years. Although she had the suspicion the only reason she liked this was because of the man behind her.

Screw gripped the Honey's hips and fucked her with hard, rapid strokes. Her fingers curled into the felt of the pool table, and her mouth dropped open. She had to be moaning, maybe even yelling, but the music was so loud Stephanie couldn't hear a thing.

Inside her, Maverick worked his finger at a faster clip,

mimicking Screw's pounding. Sweat broke out across Steph's forehead, and her breathscame in pants. She squirmed in his lap, unable to sit still. Any minute now, and she'd shatter into a million pieces.

Mav sucked her earlobe into his mouth then released it with a groan that sounded pained. "I need your pussy, babe," he said in a gravel filled voice. "You gonna give it to me? You gonna be my wildcat?"

"Here?" she squeaked.

"Right fucking here. This ass has been rubbing all over my dick for ten minutes while we've been watching Screw fuck like a damn rabbit. I need inside you."

She glanced around the room one last time. Screw and the Honey were still going strong, and everyone else was wrapped in their own business. No one even flicked a glance in their direction.

With a shaky breath, Stephanie squirmed her way around until she straddled Mav once again, but facing him this time. She rolled her hips against his length and stared straight into his eyes.

"Jesus," he hissed, grabbing her hips and holding them tight against him. "Fucking killing me, babe."

She ached for him and saw the same true need reflected back at her. Everything but Maverick disappeared. They could have been on a deserted island for all she cared at that moment. The only thing that mattered was feeling Maverick inside her and experiencing the intense connection she'd only ever found with him.

"Fuck me, Maverick," she said. "Right here."

"There's my wildcat."

IT WAS EVEN hotter than he'd fantasized, the mix of trepidation and lust in her eyes with desire winning out.

Her denim skirt had worked its way up over the curve of her hips as she'd done that cruel wiggle and spun in his lap. Now, all that separated them was a flimsy thong and his clothing. Getting straight to work, he unbuttoned his jeans, slid the zipper down, then shifted until the pipe he'd been rocking since Stephanie walked into the room was free and primed for action.

The second he'd bared himself to her, Stephanie glided that drenched pussy up and down the length of his dick, making him hiss out a curse. "Fuck, that's so hot it almost burns. Babe," he said, stilling her movements and chuckling when she whined, "condom."

Her eyes widened, and her mouth formed the cutest surprised O. "I don't have one."

"Fuck, me either." Of all the times not to be packing any rubber.

"I'm clean," she said. "And I have an IUD, so if you're clean…"

Jesus Christ, was she about to suggest…

She shrugged.

Mav swallowed hard. There was a strong chance he was about to feel all that wet heat directly engulfing his cock. He could die five seconds after getting into her and wouldn't give a shit. The knowledge of taking her ungloved would carry him to whatever afterlife awaited with a big fuckin' smile on his face. "I am. Got tested at the hospital and haven't been with anyone but you since."

Her radiant smile said it all. With a soft hand, she gripped the base of his dick and sank down on top of him, one blistering hot inch at a time. Mav hadn't fucked without a rubber since he was a stupid kid, and the memories had long faded. He knew one thing, though. He'd be damned if he'd wear one inside Stephanie ever again. It was so much more intense. The heat, the wetness, every tug of her tight pussy on his piercing. His eyes nearly crossed from the pleasure of it.

When she'd taken all of him, she stilled, and they both sighed. He leaned forward and closed the inch gap between them, pulling her into a kiss that was deep and drugging. "It's fucking different, Stephanie," he said when he drew back. "It's different with you. Never felt anything this good in my life." He flexed his hips, and she yelped. "And it's not just this tight pussy. It's you. You're wrapping yourself so tight around my insides, baby. Tell me you feel it, too."

She had to. This couldn't be one-sided. For the first time in his life, he was vulnerable. While she held his dick deep inside her body, she also held his heart in her hands with the power to crush it to dust. Something he'd never thought he'd feel. And while he wasn't ready to profess his love—he wasn't sure he was capable of that kind of thing—he sure knew it would hurt like fuck if she wanted nothing more than a hard ride.

Her eyes were saucer-wide, and she nodded. "I feel it too, Maverick."

The fact they were in public should have made the conversation awkward, but it had the opposite effect. It was more intimate, as if they were in their own little bubble, stealing time from the real world that continued around them.

"You need to hash it out? Talk about where we are?" He wasn't sure what the hell that even meant, but he'd try to have that conversation if it'd keep her in his life and his bed for the foreseeable future.

An almost sad look overtook her sweet face, and she shook her head. "No, I don't want to talk about it. It's enough that we're both feeling it."

That should have been an enormous relief. He didn't want to slap a label on this shit, and neither did she. But he was reminded of what she'd said earlier about having people and parts of her life he knew nothing about, and a feeling of uneasiness came over him.

Stephanie didn't let it last long, though.

"Think we can get to the fucking now?" she asked, rolling her hips and giggling.

A laugh burst from him. "I think we can manage that."

He gripped her hips and pushed up into her hard, holding her tight and grinding his pelvis against her clit.

Her mouth dropped open, and her eyes rolled up. "Holy shit," she whispered as her hands flew to his shoulders.

Even though she was on top, she let him take complete control of her much smaller body. He lifted her hips with his hands, then slammed her back down on his cock. "This what you had in mind?" he asked.

"Y-yes, that'll do."

He did it again and again, setting the pace and plunging up hard into her as he worked her hips along his length. She hung on for dear life, curling her fingertips into his deltoids and whimpering with every fierce thrust. The prick of her nails only ramped up his need.

He loved watching her tits bounce up and down under his club's shirt. That shit was turning into some kind of fetish.

She was so fiery and taut around him, and combined with the thrill of being in public, he wasn't going to last nearly as long as usual. He sucked on her neck, keeping the brutal pace as her cries grew louder and longer. Thank God for the insane volume of music, because he might like to fuck in public, but he didn't exactly want every eye in the room on them. And if they all heard Stephanie's screams of ecstasy, there'd be a horde of bikers jacking themselves off and watching the show.

"Oh, my God, Maverick," she said after only another thirty seconds. "I'm going to come already. Fuck, it's gonna be big."

"That's right, baby. Come hard. All over my cock. Let me feel that come all the way to my balls."

"Shit," she cried out as their hips slammed together once again. This time, when he tried to lift her back up, she resisted and ground herself into his pelvis while she squeezed his sides with her surprisingly strong thighs. Her head dropped back, and she wailed as her core fisted him in wild pulses.

She was fucking gorgeous when she came.

There was no way in hell he could hold off after that display. The next time her pussy squeezed him, he buried his face in her neck and shouted out his own release. Whatever it was, taking her bare, the quick heart to heart, or thrill of being in public, it was fucking intense. For a second, he worried his insides had melted when his abs clenched so hard as he rode the wave to paradise.

Stephanie collapsed against him, warm, liquid in his arms, spent. "I'm not sure I'll be able to walk for a few days," she mumbled into his neck.

He grunted out a laugh and stroked his hands over the round curve of her ass. They stayed that way for a few moments, quiet despite the chaos of the clubhouse around them. Just when he was about to check if Steph had fallen asleep, she sat straight up and looked over her shoulder.

With his softening cock still inside her, he gasped at the sensation her movements caused. The mingled mess of their fucking trickled out of her and down his dick, coating his balls. After that monster orgasm, he shouldn't be able to get hard again for a week, but damn if feeling their come dripping all over him didn't have him halfway there already.

He followed Stephanie's gaze to where Screw and the Honey were righting their clothing. Well, the Honey was trying to fix her shit, but Screw kept coping a feel. She swatted his hands away from her tits as she tried to adjust them in her top.

Steph turned back to him with a playful glint in her eyes. "I think we need to leave now."

He arched his pierced brow. "Oh, yeah? Where we going?"

"Well," she said, reaching out and playing with his nipple rings through his T-shirt. "I'm thinking your room. I'm feeling the sudden need to be bent over something and fucked from behind." She tilted her head and gave him the cutest damn smirk. "Wonder why?"

"Fuuuck," he said, blowing out a breath. She wanted to reenact what they'd watched Screw do with the Honey.

Mav was fully hard and aching again the instant the words left her mouth.

He stood so fast, Stephanie stumbled and almost knocked the table clear over. Not giving a single shit about the table, Mav yanked her skirt back in place and tucked his sticky dick back into his jeans.

Wrapping a hand around the back of her neck, he drew her against his lips. "You feel me on your legs?"

"Yes," she whispered.

"Good. Get used to it." He grabbed her hand, and together they raced toward the stairs and up to his room.

He owed Screw a cold one, that was for damn sure.

CHAPTER TWENTY-NINE

Patience had never been Maverick's strongest suit, and waiting for Steph over the past forty-five minutes had been hell. Especially since Rocket hadn't said a damn word the entire time. So there was nothing to distract him, nothing to keep him from watching the house and worrying about Stephanie.

"Jesus, fuck," Rocket said on a growl. "Just fucking stop already."

With a scowl, Mav turned to his brother. "The fuck's your problem? You haven't said two words since we got here, and now you got shit with how I'm handling myself?"

"Your woman is fine. Stop the damn fidgeting." Rocket was on his bike alongside Mav. Dark glasses concealed his eyes, but the crossed arms and glower made it clear he wasn't pleased.

Mav glanced down at his left boot, bouncing off the ground like he was itching to get up and dance. What could he say? He was high energy and jittery when he was stressed.

Rocket drew out a pack of cigarettes. "Here," he said. "Do something the fuck else, will ya?"

It wasn't often Maverick smoked anymore, usually just if he was crazy tense. Last time he'd had one was after the meeting with Lefty. Needed it to calm his nerves and squash his desire to murder the man. When he'd kissed Stephanie afterward, she'd wrinkled her little nose and demanded he brush his teeth before getting his mouth on her again. "Nah, man, I'm good. Sorry 'bout the tapping."

Rocket snorted and lit a smoke, mumbling something under his breath.

"What was that?" Mav asked. At least this frustrating conversation was some kind of distraction. He glanced at the house again then back to Rocket.

"Said you're fucking pussy-whipped." He blew out a stream of smoke and tilted his head. A loud crack came from his neck. Rocket might hold it in better than Mav, but he was anxious as well.

Rocket shouldn't even be there. It was too damn risky to have him lurking down the block from Chloe's house. She was the twenty-seven-year-old redhead Rocket had driven to the hospital the week before. True to his word, Copper had asked Stephanie to pay her a visit today, a check-in to make sure she wasn't running her mouth or losing her shit.

Not that anyone would have blamed her for it if she was coming apart at the seams. The situation was fucked all around.

Mav refused to let Steph go unless he tagged along for protection. Copper wasn't thrilled with the idea but understood, so he'd okayed it as long as Mav stayed out of sight. Down the block. Last thing they needed was for Chloe to freak if she saw a biker, and it took her back to her captivity.

For some reason, Rocket had demanded to go as well. When Copper refused, Rocket did something Mav had never seen one of his brothers do before. Ever. Rocket got right the fuck in Copper's face, toe to toe, chest to chest, and told him to fuck off. That he was going. Period. Prez could have made a thing of it, but something in Rocket's expression must have changed his mind. Rocket had been strange, even quieter and more standoffish than usual, since that night. Whatever happened between him and Chloe, whatever he saw when he rode her from the hotel to the hospital, it had affected the bastard.

So there he was with express orders to "stay far the fuck away from her." Copper told Rocket he'd have his patch if Chloe so much as caught a whiff of him, and he'd put Rocket six feet under if she recognized him as the biker who rescued her.

"I ain't fuckin pussy-whipped," Mav spat out. "This shit just makes me twitchy. We don't know jack about this chick. She could be going off the rails, and we sent Steph in there blind. Plus, we don't know if Lefty's got eyes on this place."

"You're the security guy," Rocket countered. "No one followed us, you scanned for cameras and saw nothing, we've had eyes on her place since I got her from the hotel, and no one has been lurking around. It's all good."

Mav grunted and resumed his watch on the house. What the fuck was taking so long?

"Your girl's smart," Rocket said then. "And observant. I think she sees a lot more than any of us realize. She'll be fine."

Mav cast a side-eyed look at Rocket. "What do you mean by that?"

He shrugged and tossed his cigarette into the road. "Not totally sure, to be honest with you. Just think there is more to her than meets the eye."

There are people in my life and things in my life that you do not know about.

Shit. Maybe he needed to start finding out a little more about Stephanie's life. Her shit was her shit, so he hadn't pried much, but she'd been at the clubhouse nearly two weeks now. Maybe it was time to talk. Find out if she planned on sticking around and what exactly her life was like in DC. Hell, he barely knew what she did for a living. All she'd said was that she had a tedious government job and had quit after the kidnapping.

"Here she comes." Rocket stuffed his hands in his leather gloves and waited. The air was nippy and keeping a grip on the handlebars with frozen, aching knuckles was a bitch and a half.

Steph had borrowed a leather jacket from Shell, but even with it on, she'd burrowed into his back to escape the wind on the thirty-minute ride to Chloe's sleepy neighborhood.

He tracked Steph as she strode toward them, jacket open

despite the chill and flapping with each step. Once again, she'd worn a Handlers' shirt, this one long sleeved with a shallow V-neck and the logo on the front. He'd like to think she wore it because she knew what it did to him, but it could be that she just liked the clothes.

"Well?" Rocket's impatient voice cut through the intimate eye-connection he had going on with Steph.

She glanced between the two of them before zipping up her jacket and stuffing her hands in the pockets. "Well, first off I'll say that you're good. She doesn't know your name or what you look like. Only that you're a Hell's Handler. She stuck to the story that you came up with for the cops and hasn't talked about it with anyone else in her life. She hasn't seen a psychologist. Said she wouldn't even if she could tell the whole world what happened. Just isn't her thing. And she has absolutely no intention of changing the story with the cops now or in the future."

Rocket grunted and opened his mouth.

"And yes," she cut in before he had a chance to get a word out. "I'm fully confident she was telling the truth. And yes, I asked the questions in a clever way, so she didn't think I was just fishing for that information."

With a smirk, Rocket turned to Mav and arched a brow. All they'd told Steph was that they'd wanted to check in on Chloe, make sure she was dealing and not slitting her wrists in the bathroom.

"Figured out what we were really looking for, huh?" Mav asked as he grabbed her hand and tugged her against him.

She shrugged. "It wasn't exactly a mystery. Sure, Copper doesn't want anything to happen to her, but his top priority is and always will be the club. Chloe has information that could be used to take you guys down. If I were him, I'd want to make sure she wasn't going to blab. Both for her own safety and the club's."

Another grunt from Rocket, this one full of grudging respect.

After knowing the guy for years, Mav could decipher his grumbles pretty well.

It was pretty impressive, the way she'd seen inside Copper's head and straight to the heart of the matter.

"And how's she holding up?" Mav asked as he gave Steph a chaste but lingering kiss on the cheek. For all the dirty they'd done that week, Stephanie melted in a special way when he did something as simple as kiss her cheek or hold her hand. Once in a while, it seemed even more intimate than the drugging kisses they usually shared. He was at the point where he'd do damn near anything to sink his hooks even farther into her.

Shit. Maybe Rocket was right, and he was pussy-whipped.

"She's a little hard to read, to be honest. On the surface, everything seems good. House is clean, she is clean, seems to be eating. Saw an empty carton of ice cream sitting on top of her trash." She drew in a breath, then reached up and smoothed her hand over Mav's head. "Helmet messed it up. Anyway, she has some dark circles under her eyes, but you can hardly fault her for not sleeping well. She told me she's gone back to work and appears to be functioning well."

"So what's the problem?" Maverick asked. Rocket just sat on his bike, stone-jawed and clenching his fists at his sides.

"Well, I could totally be reading into things, but her nails were bitten down to nothing. And her eyes were all shifty like she kept expecting someone to jump out of the pantry or something. I think she's scared out of her mind and just really good at hiding it."

Mav stared at her. Damn, she really was perceptive. Saw things that most people wouldn't even think to notice, let alone put meaning to. Maybe those powers of observation came from growing up with a cop for an old man. She'd be an asset to Mav's security company for sure.

Another reason to find out what her plans were going forward. Offering her a permanent job might make her more willing to stick around in his life and in his bed.

Down at the end of the block, a man in a dark suit emerged from his house and slid into a BMW sitting in his driveway. It started up three seconds later.

"Time to get the fuck out of here," Rocket said.

With a quick nod, Mav fired up his bike and waited for Stephanie to climb on. She threw her short leg over the seat and hoisted herself up like it was nothing, wrapping her arms tight around him.

"Let's roll," she said as though she'd been a biker's woman her whole life.

Mav smiled as he shot off after Rocket. Steph was badass. Never seemed shocked by his lifestyle, didn't blink at being asked to help his brothers. Hell, she'd been in the room when he killed someone and she still wanted him. Was it any wonder he fuckin loved her?

The revelation hit him like a ton of bricks, making him swerve and nearly run off the road.

Fuuuck. Bitch of it was, it was true. He could fight it, deny it, but in his gut, he knew it was true. He was in love with the damn woman.

Now, what the hell was he supposed to do?

STEPHANIE INCHED CLOSE to Maverick's ear the second the engine ceased rumbling. "Everything okay? You did this crazy swerve thing back there."

Over his shoulder, Mav gave her his customary grin, the flirty one that never failed to make her knees weak and her stomach all warm and squishy. The fact that he seemed to only be sending that special smile her way these days made it extra potent. "All good, sweetness."

"Where exactly are we?" They'd pulled into the deserted parking lot of a bar that she wasn't even sure was open. The name was plastered across the roof in neon lights, but the only part still lit was Bar, so she couldn't even read the name. Aside from Rocket and Mav's bikes, the lot was empty.

Rocket hadn't bothered to wait for them either. He'd hopped off his bike and trudged into the bar before they'd even rolled to a stop.

"Buddy of Rocket's owns this joint. Not exactly the Four Seasons, but they serve alcohol, play music, and keep their mouths shut. The owner is good people."

A drink would hit the spot. Talking to Chloe put her in a bit of a funk. The woman had been through hell, making what Stephanie endured seem like a walk in the park. She'd politely asked Steph not to return and to make sure the Handlers never contacted her again. Most likely, Copper would honor it, but he'd probably keep eyes on her in some capacity for a while. Until they were sure they could trust she wouldn't freak out and blab to the cops.

Jesus, now she was encouraging victims to keep their experiences from law enforcement.

She couldn't fall much farther.

"Hey, babe, you hear me?"

Blinking, she focused on Maverick's handsome face. "What? Sorry, zoned out for a second."

He cupped her cheek and kissed her softly. They didn't do soft frequently, and that made those moments he gave it to her that much sweeter. "That was hard on you, wasn't it? Talking to her."

She bit her lower lip and nodded. For more reasons than he'd ever understand. It only highlighted the choices she'd made, the decisions that were taking her so far from what she'd always stood for, always believed in. "It was a little rough," she whispered, suddenly feeling choked up.

"Babe, talk to me about it." His thumb brushed a tear she hadn't been able to control. "Don't let it turn to poison inside you. Trust me on that."

Because he knew. And he thought *he* was full of something toxic. "There is nothing poisonous about you, Mav," she said. She meant every word of it. He was an outlaw. Had done things both the general public and law enforcement saw as wrong. But he was a good man. And those things didn't define him. Everything he did, everything his club did, was done for a good reason. They weren't about senseless violence, killing, or hurting others.

Maybe she was just justifying it to make herself feel better for leaving everything she'd stood for behind. "You hear me?" she asked him.

"Yeah, babe, I hear you."

"Good," she grabbed his biceps and gave him a little shake. "Now, let's get inside and have a drink."

Ten minutes later, she was working her way to the bottom of her gin and tonic at a back table in the rundown bar. Part of her wanted to ask the bartender to leave the bottle of gin and bring her a straw. If she sucked down the entire thing, maybe she'd forget what was coming. Forget what tomorrow was.

Check-in day with Baccarella. The end of her rope, her job, possibly her freedom, or the Handlers'. Even though she shouldn't ask, shouldn't have the knowledge she was dying for, she had to find out. She'd fallen in so deep with Maverick she'd never be able to stop thinking and worrying about him when she was back in DC. Possibly living in a cardboard box because she had no job.

Better than prison.

Fuck it.

"Can I ask you guys something?"

Rocket hadn't said much since they'd arrived, which was no surprise. He seemed to talk business with the guys when necessary, but otherwise preferred to observe. And he did it well. The man seemed to see straight into her head, which was unnerving to say the least. "What?" he replied.

She lowered her voice and leaned forward even though the bar was completely devoid of any customers but them. Even the bartender had disappeared behind a closed door about five minutes ago. "Is there a plan for Lefty and the gang he's trying to build up? I mean, I know you guys threatened him, but do you think he's done with the sex trade?"

Mav and Rocket exchanged a look that had her narrowing her eyes even though she understood it. This was a boys' club at its core. Women weren't technically in the club and weren't privy to the information. It had still been worth a shot.

"Club business is for club members," Rocket said in that gruff voice of his.

Steph nodded. As she'd thought.

"Usually," he continued.

Her mouth fell open, and she blinked. Was he going to answer her question?

"Women are disappearing. We'll protect you ol' ladies as best we can, but shit happens. Figure the more you know, the more you can protect yourselves."

She'd almost missed everything he'd said after ol' lady. Face heating, she risked a glance at Mav. Where she'd expected a look of panic, all she got was a wink.

Shit. Did he think of her as his ol' lady? They'd never talked about exactly what they were to each other. Was she going to break his heart when she left? The thought made the gin in her stomach turn to lead. She pushed the nearly empty glass away and focused on Rocket.

"Plus," he said. "You've seen some shit with us. Shit you didn't try to stop. We go down, you're coming with."

"Fuck, Rocket. Could you be more of an asshole?" Mav asked. "Babe, he didn't mean—"

Steph held up her hand. "I know exactly what he means. And I'm not offended." It was a warning. Don't fuck with his brothers. While the subtle threat was aimed at her, and therefore uncomfortable, she appreciated how he had Maverick and the others' backs.

Mav flipped Rocket off then took her hand. She shifted in the booth until she was facing him.

"Lefty's gang is a mess of leftover Gray Dragons and dipshit kids who have something to prove. They're weak at best right now. The Handlers could wipe them off the map, but no one wants a war. People get hurt on both sides, brothers get arrested, shit gets ugly. We told Lefty we'd stay out of his shit if he brought Chloe to that hotel and got out of the trafficking biz. Plenty of other ways he can make his dirty money."

Steph nodded as it all ran through her head. Good, this was good. It could all die out if Lefty stuck to his side of the deal. Though that was a big "if". "Think he'll play nice?"

Mav fiddled with the fingers on her right hand. "Well, that's the problem. The other condition was that Chloe had to be unharmed, or at least not harmed worse than she was by the time we got to Lefty. We're pretty sure he went extra hard on her as a fuck you to Copper who made it pretty clear he had no intention of any kind of alliance."

"Shit." Steph sucked in a breath and looked at Rocket. His jaw ticked and his eyes blazed with anger.

"So now you don't know if you can trust him. And now you need to figure out if it's worth starting a war over one woman or if you wait it out and see if he stops selling women."

Mav blew out a harsh breath. "I know it sounds harsh, babe, but—"

She held up a hand again. "I get it. I do. It's not black and white." Her eyes widened as the words left her mouth. It wasn't something she'd ever thought she'd say. But there she was.

Rocket studied her with those eyes that saw too much. "I know you had a tough time dealing with the shit that went down with King, but you're awfully unfazed talking about this," he said. "Deal with a lot of this kinda shit in your everyday life?" he asked.

She was the worst undercover agent ever. Being too comfortable with the details hadn't even crossed her mind. Rocket's stare had her squirming in her seat. Was she about to blow the whole damn thing right then and there?

"Hey, back the fuck off," Mav said, meeting Rocket's suspicious stare with an equally pissed one. "Whatever the fuck's been up your ass this last week, either spit it out or keep it in, but don't project your shit on her."

Stephanie reached for her drink and sucked back the rest. "My father was a cop," she mumbled into the glass. "I've heard it all."

As the alcohol burned its way down to her stomach, she felt fire lighting her soul as well. One lick of the flames for each lie she'd told over the past two months. She'd be a pile of ash in no time.

CHAPTER THIRTY

"Gin and tonic, sweet thing?" LJ asked from across the bar. When she didn't respone, he said, "Steph!"

"What? Oh, sorry. Yeah, that's fine."

"No worries. I get it," he said with a wink. "All this is a lot to take in. Flusters a girl." As he spoke, he flexed his admittedly impressive biceps, pressing a kiss to the left one.

Steph grunted at the same time a Zippo lighter went flying past her head. It bounced off the very bicep LJ had his lips on, leaving a red welt.

"What the fuck?"

"Stop makin' eyes at my woman, dickhead," Mav said as he came up behind her. He circled her waist with his arms and zeroed in on her neck with his lips.

Instant arousal. Every. Damn. Time. Even when her insides swirled with anxiety. The man was some kind of sexual magician.

"Wasn't making eyes at her, man. I was showing her what she was missing, being with a scrawny fucker like you."

Even though it was all weird macho fun and games and Maverick was laughing like a loon, Steph's hackles rose a bit. Mav was no slouch. Just because he wasn't a brute. "Thanks for worrying about me, LJ," she said, "but it's not necessary. His biceps may not be as big as yours, but I guarantee he's even bigger than you where it counts."

"Oooh," at least four different voices chimed in.

"Man, LJ just got schooled by a girl. Damn, boy, how's that feel?" Jig threw back his head and cracked up. It wasn't often that man laughed, and Steph was happy to be the one to put a smile on his face.

"Seriously, LJ," Copper said, chuckling as well. "Might not be willing to give you a patch if little five-foot-nothing girls can get the better of you with one sentence."

For a second, Steph froze. He was joking, right? He wouldn't deny LJ getting in the club because of some silly teasing, would he? But Copper winked, and she relaxed. These men and their vicious senses of humor.

"Hey, man, just looking out for her. She's part of the fam now, ain't she?" LJ asked.

The men grunted their agreement then went back to their drinks. How it was possible for her heart to both soar and sink to her feet at the same time, she'd never know, but that's precisely what happened. Being treated as part of this big, loud, gruff family of bikers sounded like heaven.

But it was fake. And this was probably her last day, her final party, her last chance to spend time with Maverick. Because in two hours she had to call Baccarella. And even though she'd come up with a plausible lie, pinning Shark and Agent Rey's murders on Lefty, she had no proof. She'd be pulled out of Tennessee, and the most she could hope for was that the FBI dropped the case due to insufficient evidence and never found out about her role in the charade.

"Trust me, LJ," Mav said, "my woman has no complaints. In fact, I'm having trouble keeping up with her demands." He squeezed her and nipped her earlobe as her face heated.

"Mav, shut u—"

The door to the clubhouse flew open, smacking against the wall with a loud bang that had her jolting in Mav's arms. Every man turned, tense and ready for action.

"Get down! Now! Down on the floor," a male voice yelled

above the loud pulsing music as at least twenty people in blue FBI vests flooded into the room.

"Face down. Hands on your head. Right fucking now!" The first man in the clubhouse held his gun level with Screw's face as the newly patched brother shoved his Honey behind his back. "You too, ma'am. On the floor. Now!"

Stephanie froze. She couldn't breathe, didn't blink, didn't so much as twitch. What was going on? What the hell was happening? She'd had no warning. No clue the FBI was about to raid the Handlers' clubhouse. And for what? Was this it? Were they going to cuff her and yank her out like she was under arrest? That's how they did it. To maintain cover. After the initial arrests, the agent was released and their character supposedly arraigned for some bogus charge, disappearing into the system until, eventually, someone worked out that they were a plant. Jesus, she wasn't ready. This shouldn't be happening. It wasn't right. There was nothing to find there. No one to arrest. Did they somehow discover the information she'd been hiding?

Mav spun her around and gripped her shoulders, hard, giving her a little shake out of her stupor. "Stephanie!" he barked at her.

"W-what?" she asked. She didn't have to feign shock or pretend to be terrified. She was both those things and more.

"Listen to me, wildcat. Do what they say, but don't say a fucking word to anyone. You with me?"

She nodded and swallowed as tears welled in her eyes. Mav's face swam before her, concern for her written all over it. This was the last time she'd see him. The last time he'd hold her or touch her or make her feel alive. It might be foolish, but she had to tell him how she felt. She grabbed his face and kissed him hard on the lips. "I love you, Maverick," she said before dropping to her knees then laying on her stomach with her hands over her head.

She'd probably never know his response, but it didn't matter now. It was over.

Maverick lay on her left, hands on his head as ordered. About six feet away on her right, Copper also assumed the same position. Waves of fury poured out of him so strong they were palpable. He wasn't one to follow orders, but to give them. And he'd be ripshit over the invasion of his family's safe zone. Especially since Shell was upstairs putting Beth to sleep. There'd be hell to pay over this.

But Steph would be long gone.

Within minutes, every man and woman in the clubhouse was on the floor in the position of surrender. Special Agent in Charge Baccarella waltzed into the clubhouse like he owned the place, papers in hand. Hatred welled up inside her. Hatred for being put in this position, hatred for being left in the dark, contempt for the smug grin he cast her way when he made eye contact. How many times had she been on the reverse of these raids? Too many to count.

"Killian Murphy. Which one of you scumbags is Killian Murphy?"

Beside her, Copper growled low in his chest. She tried to send him a telepathic message, begging that he cooperate and make it easier on himself.

"Why the fuck are you in my house?" Copper asked without changing his position.

Baccarella strode closer until he loomed over Copper's prone form. "Murphy?"

"Hmph."

"Well Mr. Murphy, we've been tipped off that your motorcycle gang is running drugs across state lines." He tsked. "You know that's not allowed."

"Then why the fuck are you pussies here and not the DEA?"

Good question. And drugs? Baccarella knew damn well the MC didn't traffic drugs. Hell, the SAC wished they were pushing dope, because he could have passed them off to the DEA and been done with them.

"Not your job to ask the questions, Mr. Murphy." He had to know how it would grate on Copper to be called Mr. Murphy and to have his MC called a gang. Baccarella was especially gifted at the underhanded jabs and digs. "We have a warrant here to search the premises for illicit drugs. If you ladies and gentlemen don't mind holding your positions, we'll conduct our search. We find nothing, we'll leave you alone. We find something, well, most of you will get to enjoy a free ride to our Knoxville field office."

"And if we do mind?" Copper ground out.

Baccarella laughed, and Stephanie had to restrain herself from jumping up and smacking him across the face. Arrogant asshole. There was a way to do this that wasn't demoralizing and mortifying. Especially since he wasn't going to find so much as a dusting of cocaine.

"Guess I really just don't give a shit, Mr. Murphy."

Baccarella looked at her and winked before strutting off to join the men and women already tearing through the clubhouse.

"The fuck was that?" Mav asked from her side.

What the hell was Baccarella thinking? He needed to watch himself before he blew her cover straight out of the water.

"Guy's just an asshole," Steph said.

A child's cry followed by a woman's shout could be heard from upstairs.

Copper reacted instantly, pushing up from the ground, but an agent was on him before he could fully rise to his knees. "Back on the fucking ground! Now!" the agent screamed, gun to Copper's head.

"Swear to Christ," Copper muttered, resting his forehead on the ground. His body was so tense, like a caged tiger growing hungrier by the second. One wrong move by the agent, and he'd spring into action, consequences be damned.

"They'll be okay," Stephanie whispered. "They probably just woke Beth and pissed Shell off. You know what a mama bear she can be."

He turned his head and stared into her eyes. She'd never encountered anger like she witnessed in his gaze. With a nod, he seemed to unwind, just a smidge, and said, "Thanks."

Time passed so slowly it felt like they'd been there for hours when in reality it had only been about twenty-five minutes. Stephanie's elbows ached from being curved for so long, and her chest was sore from being flattened against the grungy wooden floor.

About five minutes later, Baccarella strode out of Copper's office with a neutral expression on his face. This was going to go one of two ways. Either they found nothing or they planted something. She feared it was the second. Otherwise, they'd have no reason to pull anyone into jail and separate her from the club. She held her breath, waiting for Baccarella to speak. Even though she knew full well what was coming, hearing the words would pierce her heart.

"Well, boys, looks like it's your lucky day. We tore this place apart, so sorry about the mess, and didn't find a damn thing."

Wait. What? They found nothing. Where was he going with this?

"Big fucking surprise," Copper grumbled.

"Huh, looks like we had a bad tip. Happens sometimes. Here's how this is going to go. We're going to file on out now. You all remain on the floor until we are out of sight. Don't want any sudden moves spooking one of my agents into shooting, now do you?"

It made no sense. What was happening?

When he was the final remaining agent—meaning no witnesses to whatever happened next—Baccarella started toward the door then snapped his fingers and turned around. "Oh, almost forgot one thing. Agent Little? Stand up, please."

Stephanie's blood ran cold, and she swore her heart stopped beating for five seconds before it kicked up so fast she was instantly dizzy.

"Agent Little, I gave you a direct order."

Tears filled her eyes and spilled over completely unchecked. She didn't care if it was childish or unprofessional; they couldn't be stopped. This was not protocol. This wasn't procedure. This was punishment at its very worst.

"Y-yes, sir," she said, rising on legs that shook like palm trees in a hurricane.

Beside her, Maverick whispered, "What the fuck?" And she could feel Copper's laser stare burning into her.

"Agent Little, it appears you have been withholding vital information from the Bureau. Since you have been unable and unwilling to fulfill your role as an undercover agent with the Hell's Handlers Motorcycle Club, you have been relieved of duty."

Blood rushed in her ears louder than Niagara Falls, and her breaths came in choppy spurts. Why was he doing this? Did he have any idea what would happen now? They'd kill her. Even if by some miracle, Maverick stood up for her, Copper would never let her live.

"It's unfortunate things had to end this way. But don't worry, this entire case will shed light on the sacrifices agents are willing to make in the pursuit of justice. We can't win them all, can we, Little? You'll receive the same medal as Agent Rey."

A posthumous medal.

She was a problem for the Bureau now. An agent who'd defected to the criminal underworld. A scandal and an embarrassment. Someone to be dealt with. Baccarella had known precisely what he was doing with this stunt. By now, he'd probably learned all about Lefty and his trafficking business. There was his arrest, and he no longer needed the Hell's Handlers. The Handlers would deal with her, saving the FBI embarrassment, time, and lots of cover-up work. They'd spin it like a tragic accident while serving her country. Then he'd swoop in, arrest Lefty and his gang, and Baccarella would be handed the director position all wrapped up with a shiny bow.

That self-serving bastard just signed her death warrant.

CHAPTER THIRTY-ONE

A fed? A fucking fed? A sickness like he'd never felt before rolled through Maverick's gut. He'd welcomed her into the club, into his family, around his brothers, and their women. Jesus Christ, he was going to vomit.

Was it true? Any of it? How had it happened? Did she get herself kidnapped by Shark on purpose? Or was that just a happy accident that worked in the FBI's favor to infiltrate the MC?

This raid was bogus. Plain and simple. A ruse to pull Stephanie, if that was even her fucking name, back to the legal side of the world. But it didn't make sense. Why would he out her in front of the MC? They knew what she looked like. Copper would be out for blood. They could search her out easily.

As his mind spiraled out of control, he'd almost missed what the FBI douchebag said to Stephanie.

Fuck me hard.

The piece of shit was leaving her there.

The moment that realization hit, two other insights came to light. No one was being arrested, not a single one of his brothers. Stephanie had information that could put a good number of them away forever. She was in the room when Maverick shot a man in the head for fuck's sake. So why weren't the feebees slapping cuffs on every man in the clubhouse and hauling 'em in?

Only one reason.

Stephanie hadn't squealed.

The other lightbulb that went off had to do with her feelings for him. No way were they faked. At least not the orgasms. She came, and she came hard. Sure, some women could put on a good performance, but they couldn't fake the out-of-control spasming of their pussies or the gush of arousal that coated his dick every damn time. That was as real as the ink on his skin.

So, she withheld information from her superiors, and she loved his cock.

What the hell did it mean?

Well, it meant the FBI was walking the fuck away from her.

But surely, this asshat of an agent knew, right? He knew what would happen to her if he walked out and abandoned Stephanie to the MC?

Copper would end her.

One glance at the tears rolling down Stephanie's face, and Mav's heart clenched. She knew. She knew her fate.

He should hate her, and at that moment, part of him did, but it didn't change what was in his heart. Up until two minutes ago, he'd been ready to tell her he fucking loved her. Those feelings had been developing over the months since he first met her. He wasn't someone prone to frivolous emotion, so these feels for her? They were deep-seated.

And wouldn't disappear in an instant.

Mav sprang to his feet in one smooth motion, ninja-style. "You can't fucking leave her, man," he shouted at the smug agent.

Shoulders slumped and the saddest look of defeat in her overflowing eyes, Stephanie whispered, "Maverick, get back down."

He couldn't look her in the eye. His brothers needed him now, and if he stared into her sorrow-filled gaze, he'd lose his shit, grab her, and run for the hills.

"You can't leave her here," he said, speaking slowly like the man was dense.

The agent just stared him down with a half-smile. "And why's that?"

Fists clenched, Mav locked his knees to keep from charging the arrogant piece of shit. "You know damn well what will happen to her if you walk out that door."

"Hmm." The agent stuffed his hands in the pockets of his navy FBI jacket and rolled back onto his heels. "Not quite sure what you mean. You trying to tell me you have knowledge of an impending criminal act?"

The urge to rip this man's throat out nearly overwhelmed Maverick. He wasn't a violent man by nature, but there had been a few times in his life where a leashed beast broke from its chains and ran wild. This couldn't be one of those times, but the creature was yanking pretty hard on the fucking shackle.

When he didn't respond, the agent shook his head. "Didn't think so. Stay outta trouble, boys. We'll be closing the case on Shark's murder. It was a tragedy, the FBI losing two agents during this operation, but it looks like Lefty killed Shark." He tsked. "Damn shame."

Wait, two agents?

Mav exchanged a look with Copper. Who the fuck was the second agent?

With a mock salute, Baccarella turned and walked out the door. The room was so quiet, you could hear an ant fart. Then slowly, the men started to rise. Within seconds, an entire MC full of pissed-as-fuck bikers were staring at Stephanie.

She ignored them all, turning to face Maverick. Black streaks tracked down her face, and her legs trembled. He wanted to run to her, gather her in his arms, and promise it would all be okay.

But it was so far from okay, it might never be okay again. His chest hurt, ached like he'd taken a hit from Zach's beloved baseball bat.

Stephanie sucked in a shaky breath, squared her shoulders, and gave him the respect of eye contact. Unable to stop the trembling in her legs, she vibrated and quivered. She offered no explanation for her actions, no justification, no apologies that he wouldn't have believed anyway. "What I told you before lying down? I meant it with my entire soul."

I love you, Maverick.

Fuck that. She loved him?

Anger burned low in his gut, spreading through his limbs and finally kicking him into gear. The only problem was, his mind was still a fucked-up mess. He lunged forward toward her, not sure if he was going to wring her neck or kiss the hell out of her just to see if her responses were real.

Stephanie's eyes widened with fear, but she didn't so much as take a shuffling step back. Copper darted between them and shoved Maverick with a hard palm to the chest. Pain speared through his ribs, and he staggered back.

"Zach, get her the fuck out of here. Take her to The Box."

Stephanie gasped, and Zach hesitated.

"Gave you an order, Zach," Copper barked.

The Box? Jesus, he couldn't let this happen. Not to Stephanie. She'd been held in a basement once before. She'd be fucking terrified. "No," Mav said. "Don't—"

Copper shot him a look that had him freezing in his tracks. "Get the fuck in my office, Maverick." When Mave didn't move, he said, "Now!"

"Let's go, Agent Little," Zach said as though the word felt disgusting in his mouth. He guided Stephanie from the room.

No one spoke, suddenly looking at any and everything but Mav or Steph. It was no secret what The Box was used for. And it certainly wasn't to hold presents.

She didn't put up a fight, letting those silent tears slide down her cheeks. Mav felt his world shrinking to a pinpoint as he watched her walk away, head held high but devastation all over her face.

"Maverick," Copper growled.

He nodded and trudged toward Copper's office. The last thing he saw before disappearing into the office was Stephanie's tearstained eyes staring at him with so much pain and longing it was like a punch to the gut. With a hand on her lower back, Zach guided her out into the night.

Zach was gentle with her, and for that Maverick would owe him a debt of gratitude. She'd been hurt not long ago and still had some residual discomfort. She didn't need to be manhandled. She was going to be terrified enough.

Jesus, listen to him.

His brotherhood was the most important thing in his life. He'd always thought himself loyal to his MC above all else. Never once did he think he'd feel for a woman what he felt for Stephanie. And now he felt like a disloyal son of a bitch for not immediately condemning her to hell.

"Fuuuck!" he screamed as the door slammed shut. He rubbed at his arms while he paced the length of the small room, feeling like coarse sandpaper was being dragged over his skin. It was slow torture, not knowing the whys and the hows. And not knowing what was happening to Stephanie was akin to having hot needles shoved under his toenails.

Copper erupted into the room with an expressionless face, but his body language spoke to his fury.

"Prez," Maverick began.

But Copper shook his head and pointed to the chair. "Sit the fuck down."

While following orders was the last thing he wanted at the moment, Copper was due all the respect Mav possessed, so he dropped into the seat. Immediately, his leg bounced, and he drummed his fingers on his thigh.

"I'm not gonna fucking hurt her," Copper said as he took the seat behind his desk. With a weary sigh, he rubbed a hand down his face. "Just want to start with that. I ain't in the business of brutalizing women. This is fucked to all hell, but there are at least three of us that should be in the back of those POS FBI sedans right now. Only reason we aren't is that woman."

Mav nodded as an ounce of the tension he carried evaporated.

"She's gotta go though, Maverick. Don't know if you have an enchanted cock or what, but the only reason I can think she didn't turn us in was you. Can't risk keeping her here and her getting an attack of moral fucking conscience one day and turning on us."

That could still happen with the information she already had.

The unspoken words hung between them because neither wanted to admit the risk Copper was taking. He may not be in the business of hurting women, but if Mav hadn't had a relationship with Stephanie, Copper would make her disappear. Permanently.

"You gonna be able to live with it?" Prez asked.

Live without Stephanie? He wasn't sure anymore, but he nodded. What the hell choice did he have? She'd lied repeatedly. Lied about who the hell she was. She'd put his entire club at risk, his family at risk.

Christ, they'd all loved her. Every last one of his brothers had fallen just a little bit in love with her.

Even Toni, and Shell, and some of the ol' ladies raved about how fun, helpful, and supportive she was. Somewhere along the way, he'd forgotten why his hit-it-and-quit-it-attitude worked so well in the past.

This reminder would be tattooed on his soul.

"I'm gonna talk to her, see what I can get outta here before I give her the boot. Don't want you to see her again. I'll tell you what I find out. Okay?"

Maverick grunted. Okay? Fuck no. None of this was goddamned okay.

"Go get drunk. Find some easy pussy. Start getting the fuck over her. Bitch ain't worth it, Mav."

"Just—"

"Told you I wouldn't hurt her. You ever known me to break my word?"

"No, Cop."

"Ain't gonna start today."

Maverick

Maverick watched Copper leave. Once he was alone in the office, his entire lifeforce seemed to drain from his body. Darkness settled into his heart, a blackness he'd only ever experienced once before. It was like a demon sucking his soul from his body, making him care about nothing but ending the pain.

Back then, the only thing that saved him from ending that pain at his own hand was his brother.

He slumped in the chair, staring at a large twenty-four by thirty-six framed picture hanging over Copper's desk. It was him, Zach, Jig, Rocket, and Copper. Shell had given it to Copper last Christmas. Those men were who mattered. Nothing else.

He felt himself teetering on the edge like he'd been years before. His brother's would have to be the ones to pull him back once again.

Shoulda known better than to let a woman worm her way under his skin.

Lesson learned. He'd toughen that skin so nothing or no one would ever pierce through it again.

CHAPTER THIRTY-TWO

"Sit."

Her legs were shaking so hard Stephanie wasn't sure she'd be able to control her knees and lower to a sitting position.

In the basement with the drain in the floor.

The basement that King died in.

On a chair that looked an awful lot like the one King died in.

The faint bleachy smell tickled the hairs in her nose making her sniff and causing her stomach to lurch. If by some miracle, she survived this fiasco, she'd never buy that particular cleaner again.

When she reached the chair, she turned and forced her legs to bend. Basically, she crashed down onto the metal chair, whacking her tailbone. Though the pain was intense, she didn't bother reacting. Zach, with his folded arms, spread legs, and hateful scowl, wouldn't care about her discomfort. In fact, he'd probably revel in it.

Seated, her legs finally stopped trembling, but not her insides. They shook like she was made of Jell-O.

Preparing for impending pain wasn't an easy feat. When Shark held her, there was always the chance she'd be rescued, the chance something would happen to keep the men from hurting her. But now? Well, now she was SOL, and the pain was coming. Her mind didn't seem to fully grasp that fact.

Maybe because the pain was already there. Sharp, deep,

powerful, and centered on the left side of her chest. Would they allow Maverick in the room? Would she ever be able to apologize, to try to explain? At the very least, she didn't want him to feel guilty for bringing her into the club, and she wanted one last chance to tell him she loved him.

Even if he never fully believed it.

Her arms felt like hundred-pound lead weights as she lifted them and placed them on the armrests. Being tied up in a basement again wasn't something she'd ever thought would happen, and panic started to crawl its way to her chest, making her breaths come in shallow gasps.

"Not gonna tie you up." Zach spoke for the first time besides giving one-word orders of walk, sit, wait.

"W-what?" Brilliant, question the man who said he wasn't going to restrain you.

"You gonna try to run?"

Despite the gravity of the situation, a harsh laugh escaped her. Where the hell would she go? She'd have to eat spinach and do pushups all day, every day, for the next ten years to even have an ounce of the muscle mass Zach had. "No, I'm not going to try to run."

He nodded and walked across the small square room, leaning his back against the wall. The minutes ticked by slowly, leaving Stephanie to wonder when someone would burst through that door and her interrogation/torture would begin. Maybe they'd be kind and just end it swiftly.

A shudder rolled through her, catching Zach's attention. "My woman fucking loved you, you know that?"

Tears filled her eyes. "She's amazing. I love her, too. I care about everyone I've met here." She purposefully used the present tense.

Zach snorted. "You can cut the bullshit now, fed. You're lucky you're not a fucking man." He cracked his knuckles and rolled his shoulders. "I'd be allowed first crack at you if you were a man."

The sound of the door opening was followed by the heavy tread of boots clomping down the steps.

Copper.

She swallowed and tried to keep from sobbing and begging for her life. Anything he wanted to know, she'd tell him. She owed him that much. Owed it to Maverick.

When he reached the end of the steps, he walked straight to the corner of the room where another chair rested and dragged it over to her. The scraping of metal along the concrete floor scored her eardrums and raked along her spine.

"You fucked my boy up," he said once he was seated, his forearms resting on his massive thighs. "Never thought I'd see that guy go in for anything more than easy pussy, but damn if you didn't wrap him around your little finger."

Even if they weren't planning to physically torture her, this emotional agony just might be worse, because, while they all thought it was an act, she was just as destroyed as Maverick.

"They teach you that shit in fed school?"

"N-no." Geez, it sounded like her vocal cords had been dragged behind Copper's bike for miles. "It wasn't an act."

Copper laughed. "I know they tell you to say that shit."

Tears filled her eyes once again. Crying was utterly useless, but she couldn't seem to stop. There were so many volatile emotions swirling through her, and it seemed her eyeballs were the only places to release them.

"Got a few questions for you," he said as he scratched his trimmed beard.

"I'll tell you anything you want to know."

He raised an eyebrow as Zach muttered, "bullshit" under his breath.

"I assume your boss was counting you as one of the dead agents, but who is the second?"

A chill ran down her spine as Copper talked so callously about her death. Like it was a foregone conclusion. "It was King."

Both men reacted to the news with shouts of, "What the fuck?"

Not bothering to wait for further questions, she just launched into the story. "The Handlers have never really been on the FBI's radar. No one really gives a shit that you're suspected of loan sharking and money laundering when the Dragons are running drugs and women one county over. We always planned to leave your stuff to the local PD."

Copper watched her with curious eyes, relaxing into his chair somewhat, while Zach stood sentry near the steps like there really was a chance she'd make a run for it.

"Keep going."

She nodded and took a breath. Her voice sounded stronger, less full of terror. At least they weren't going to attach electrodes to her earlobes to get her to talk. "King was my partner in the Cybercrimes Unit. He had an extensive undercover history but wanted something that would keep him home, since he had a wife and kid. About a year ago, the Bureau needed someone with his background, and he was placed with the Dragons. I had no undercover experience, but they used me as his contact in DC. I still worked Cybercrimes, but I was his handler, basically. Just over two months ago, he missed a few check-ins with me. The Bureau sent me here to make contact. I was scouting around in the woods outside Shark's cabin when I was caught."

As though that day happened only last week, the helpless feeling of fear tightened her gut. "I ended up alone with King, or Agent Daniel Rey, for about five minutes. He could have easily let me go, but it was then I discovered he'd gone all in with Shark."

"Shit. That must have stuck in your craw, huh?" Copper asked with a smirk.

"Well, he nearly raped me, and the only reason it didn't happen was because Maverick pissed him off enough to divert his attention. And that ended up with King burning the fuck out of Maverick's arm, so yeah, I guess you can say it stuck in my craw, asshole."

Whoops. Perhaps not the best time to get all snarky and belligerent.

Instead of reacting with anger or violence like she'd half expected, Copper chuckled. "Feisty, ain't ya? Think I'm starting to see what Mav saw in you."

She narrowed her eyes and bit her tongue. Past tense again.

Assholes.

"Here's my real question. You could have ended this shit two months ago. You were right here in this fucking room. A fed, witness to a murder. You didn't say a fucking word to the FBI then and obviously haven't said anything since. Why?"

It was time to get real and admit she'd left the world of black and white months ago. "Two reasons. First, because he deserved it. He was responsible for the deaths of three teenage girls, and he'd have walked on those charges."

Another chuckle. "That's one of the reasons I had him killed. Hard to believe a fed would feel the same. Ain't you supposed to believe in the system?"

A heaviness came over her. "I used to. Shit's happened to change my mind."

"Huh." Copper leaned forward again. "And the second reason?"

She cocked her head and stared at him, pressing her lips into a thin line. It seemed too personal to voice.

"Ahh," he said. "Guess I should thank Maverick for being so good with his cock."

She flinched. Of course Copper would reduce it to that, reminding her all the women who'd been on the receiving end of Mav's cock. "It was more than that," she said through clenched teeth.

Copper studied her for a few moments before giving her one curt nod. "Yeah, I'm starting to think it might be. What happened after you went back to DC?"

"I was debriefed. For hours on end. And I lied. Then the

bureau gave me two months off to heal. When I returned, I was told to come back here."

"And like a good little fed doggie you trotted right down here, huh?"

She was getting sick of his attitude, which was ridiculous because, if that's all that was hurled at her, she was pretty damn lucky. "If it wasn't me, it would have been someone else. Would you have preferred that?"

Copper grew quiet, studying his feet for a few moments. "You continued to lie since you got back here, didn't you?"

"Yes," she answered in a small voice. Every answer was like admitting how much she loved Maverick only to have that love tossed in the trash like a bag of garbage.

"Guess in some twisted way, I owe you a thanks. Feds snuck anyone else in here, and I'd be sitting in a four-by-four cell right now."

Was this a trap? Copper saying thank you seemed like the least likely thing to ever happen.

"Ain't gonna give that to you, though."

Ahh, there it was.

"Loyalty's the most important thing in my club. That goes for the ol' ladies, too. Lying ain't loyalty. I want you gone. Your purse and suitcases are already in your car."

Her heart stuttered. "Y-you're not going to k-kill me?"

"No. You earned that for lying to your boss. And I can't do that shit to Maverick. He'll be fucked up enough as it is. Go straight to your car and get the fuck out of my life. Leave my boy the hell alone so he can get the fuck over you. You hear me? No calls, no texts. I want you to be nothing but a bad memory."

The relief of being allowed to live was overshadowed by the tremendous pain of never seeing Maverick again. For the rest of her life, she'd regret the way this ended. Would he always wonder if any part of their relationship was real? That seemed almost as cruel as dying. "Will you…" She cleared her throat. "Will you tell him something for me?"

Zach scoffed while Copper grunted.

As good of a yes as she was going to get it, seemed. She looked Copper straight in the eye and spoke with as much conviction as possible. "Please tell him that he made the right choice all those years ago. And that he's ruined me for anyone else." She gave Copper a small smile and stood. "I'll go now."

With her heart still on the floor in The Box, just waiting to be washed down the drain, she climbed the stairs, walked through the woods, and right to her car.

She hadn't realized she was crying until the clubhouse was no longer visible in her rearview mirror. The flood of tears made it impossible to drive safely, so she pulled over about three miles from the clubhouse.

The first choking sob wracked her entire body. The torrent that came after was born of a pain so deep she worried there wasn't any pain reliever in the world that could touch it.

CHAPTER THIRTY-THREE

Two days, a carton of ice cream, and three bottles of cheap wine later, Stephanie was still in Townsend, holed up in a motel. After eating and drinking her troubles away, she was faced with the fact that she was officially pathetic.

Not to mention sticking around town was moderately dangerous. Copper sure wouldn't take too well to stumbling across her. But seeing as how she'd only gone from the hotel to a convenience store and back once, she was pretty much in the clear.

After the last of the wine had been consumed, she finally slept, waking sometime after the sun had set.

Why hadn't she driven as far away as possible?

She'd tried to deceive her inner self with bullshit excuses and weak reasons, but the truth was as hard to ignore as it was pitiful. Staying in Townsend made her feel connected to Maverick in some way.

"Ridiculous," she muttered as she rolled over and sat on the edge of the bed. Through the slatted blinds, the blinding lights of the motel's vacancy sign filled the room.

Maverick hated her. And she didn't blame him. So, staying in Townsend to feel close to him was just a step away from creeper town.

She had to face it. It was time to go home.

Decision made, there wasn't any point in hanging around the

hotel until the morning. After shoving her belongings into her suitcase and dragging it out to the car, she made her way to the motel reception desk and returned her key.

Five minutes later, motor running, she couldn't make herself shift the car into gear. Her hand and her foot just would not budge to get the car moving. She sucked in a breath that caught in her chest. The walls of her Honda Accord started to close in on her, compressing the air and stealing all the oxygen.

Her vision grew gray—very fitting—and as the panic attack steered her toward unconsciousness, she smashed the window button down at the same time she turned the key and killed the motor. Cool, fresh air flowed into the car and she finally filled her lungs.

She'd dated before, been in relationships before, and even thought she'd had her heart broken years ago. But she'd been wrong. Dead wrong. This was a broken heart. The inability to figure out what to do next. The feeling of being adrift in the sea, no land in sight. The beauty of the world surrounded her, but nothing mattered because she'd lost the most important thing in her world.

She had to pull it together. At least enough to drive out of town and back to DC. When she arrived in her own town, to her own home, she could lose it. Lock herself away for weeks. Hell, she didn't have a job at the moment.

The sound of men's voices made her jump and pulled her out of her head. Grateful for something besides her own misery to focus on, she glanced out her window. Four parking spaces over, two large dudes hovered near a dark sedan.

It was midnight, shadowy, and quiet in the near-empty parking lot. Neither man seemed aware of her presence.

"What room did Lefty say? Eleven?"

Stephanie shoved her balled fist in her mouth to stem her cry of shock. Not fifteen minutes ago she'd checked out of room eleven.

"Yeah, don't know why he's got such a hard-on for her, but he said we're looking for a little blonde spinner in room eleven."

Stephanie pressed herself against the backrest of the seat, trying to flatten herself into invisibility. She wanted to sink down below the window but was petrified they'd hear her clothing rustle. As it was, they might be able to hear the pounding drum of her heartbeat.

"She's one of the Handlers' ol' ladies," the other man said. "It's all part of his plan for the MC. He gave them a chance to work with him, but they shat on it. Now they pay. He's got Marco working on bombs now. Gonna snag this bitch then blow the fuck outa their clubhouse while they're going outta their minds lookin' for her."

Blow up the clubhouse? She bit her lip to keep a scream of hatred inside.

"Hey man, look." The larger of the two men pointed toward a tiny coupe that just turned into the lot. His voice was low, so deep he almost sounded like a caricature. "That bitch is blond."

Risking discovery, Stephanie leaned an inch forward and peered out the window with one eye. Sure enough, a woman with long, curly blond hair was stepping from a little two-seater sports car.

"Don't know, man. Lefty said she was a little bitch. That one looks tall," the shorter, but pudgier man said.

"Fuck off. How many blonde bitches you think are staying in this shithole by themselves? That's gotta be her. Besides, he didn't tell us to bring a fuckin ruler. Grab her and shove her in the trunk," the big guy whispered.

The clueless woman teetered across the gravel parking lot on five-inch heels. She was way too close to Lefty's goons for comfort. Walking as though she never considered that strolling through a parking lot alone at night could be dangerous, she paraded toward the line of rooms.

"Let's go," Short and Stout said.

The two men wandered out into the lot toward the woman. On reflex, Stephanie reached for her center console where she'd been stashing her service weapon while with the Handlers. Without making a sound, she lifted the cover and stuck her hand into the console.

Empty.

Goddamn bikers!

No weapon. Nothing but her five-foot-three-inch self with some basic FBI hand-to-hand combat training. Probably no match against two large thugs. She could call the local PD, but by the time they got there, it would be too late for the woman who was unlucky enough to have the same hair color as Stephanie.

Well, as dangerous as it might be, there was no way she could sit by and let another woman be shoved into the trunk of a car. Especially when the intended victim was her.

"Hey!" she shouted as she sprang from the car and charged toward the men whose backs were now to her. Element of surprise was the only thing she had going for her.

"What the fuck?" Both men stopped advancing and turned toward her.

Waving her arms like a lunatic, she ran straight toward Lefty's thugs. "Run!" she screamed at the woman. "They're going to fucking kidnap you. Run to the office!"

The shorter man grunted and launched toward the woman. Eyes wide and mouth gaping, she let out an ear-splitting shriek, kicked her stilts off, and sprinted for the motel's lobby. Screaming her face off, she was just a few feet ahead of the goon, but it should be enough to make it. No way would he run into the office where the receptionist and her boyfriend were there to witness.

"Fuck!" the other thug said as he stared at her. "It's you we fucking want."

Stephanie skidded to a stop, turned, and started to run back to her car. Lefty's man reached her before she'd taken two steps, grabbing the hood of her sweatshirt and giving a hard yank. As she flew backward toward him, panic started to cloud her thoughts.

If they got her in that trunk, she was beyond fucked. They'd try to use her as a bargaining chip to get something out of the Handlers.

She almost snorted out loud.

Like that would work.

On instinct, she leaned forward to counteract her body's backward momentum when she realized she hadn't zipped her sweatshirt.

Both arms slipped right out, sending her sprawling toward the ground. She hit with the force of a monster truck, sliding forward through the gravel. Her chin smacked against the ground, rattling her head, and bits of dirt and rock tore into her palms. Her knees and stomach burned like she'd been dragged across a carpet naked.

Shit. That was gonna hurt tomorrow.

She sure as hell hoped she lived to experience it.

"You fucking bitch," Big and Tall growled, and advance on her again. Scrambling forward on stinging hands and knees, she managed to rise to her feet and race the final few feet to her car. Her heart pounded so wildly she felt it in all her pulse points like a chant, urging her forward.

Thank God, the keys were in the ignition. She slammed the door shut and started the ignition in one move. Just as the engine turned over, a hairy fist reached through her open window and grabbed her by the ponytail. The thug wrenched her sideways like he was trying to pull her through the window. Her head jerked and slammed against the window frame.

"Fuck!" she cried as tears filled her eyes, a combination of pain and intense fear.

Stretching her right arm as far as she could, she was just able to wrap her hand around the gear shift. She slammed the car into reverse and jammed her foot on the gas as hard as possible. The Accord screeched backward, kicking up dirt and gravel.

The thug screamed when his arm smashed into the window

frame. Stephanie bit her lip to keep from crying herself as her head moved with his arm. Within seconds, he was unable to maintain his grip against the moving car, and he released her. It wasn't time to celebrate yet. She shifted into drive and peeled out onto the road as fast as possible.

Both men stood in the parking lot, shouting obscenities before jumping in their car and shooting off after her.

As she drove thirty miles above the forty miles-per-hour speed limit, she fought to control her breathing and keep from completely freaking out. At that moment, she had three choices. Drive straight out of town and hope she could lose them. Drive to the local police station. Or drive to the Hell's Handlers' compound.

It was a no-brainer. Literally. She didn't even have to think about it. Her body took over, and she realized she was steering onto the highway that would take her to the clubhouse. Lefty's thugs wouldn't be stupid enough to follow her straight into enemy territory.

Would they?

Five minutes of breakneck speeds later, she'd navigated the winding road in a way she'd never have done if she'd been thinking logically. One missed curve, and she could have gone careening off a cliff into the abyss. She'd been closely followed the entire time, but when she exited onto the road that would take her directly to the Handlers' clubhouse, Lefty's guys continued past.

"Oh, thank God," she said, rolling to a stop in the middle of the road. Her entire body shook with the adrenaline rush as she rested her head against the steering wheel. Now that the imminent threat of capture had disappeared, her body came alive in the most unpleasant of ways. Both hands were clenched tight as a boa constrictor around the steering wheel, and the abraded palms screamed for relief. The knees of her skinny jeans were torn to shreds and tinged red with blood. The left side of her head throbbed with a dull ache.

Shit, she was a mess.

But she was alive.

Going to the clubhouse was hands down one of the stupidest decisions she'd made as of late, and she'd sure made a lot of them. But she owed it to the Handlers to let them know what was coming. Clearly, Lefty was waging war. Not only was he willing to kidnap who he thought was one of the Handlers' ol' ladies, but he was also planning to blow up the clubhouse.

A blatant declaration of war. They needed to be prepared and know what was coming for them, even if it put her at risk.

The Stephanie of three months ago would have gone straight to her bosses with this information. But so much had changed. While in her heart, she knew this was wrong, she couldn't deny the Handlers their version of justice and safety. And she'd learned the system was beyond flawed. Hell, it had chewed her up, spit her out, and left her for dead in a biker clubhouse. A little MC justice was just what the situation called for.

With a shuttered breath, she tried to ignore the aches and pains and drive the last mile to the clubhouse. When she arrived, a sick feeling came over her. She'd been warned not to return. Warned what would happen if she did return. And their parking lot was littered with rows of bikes. There was a party going on.

"Just do it," she said. "Get out of the damn car. You made it this far." Her body decided to listen to her. It took a few tries to get her trembling fingers around the door handle, but she got it open and started toward the prospect serving as bouncer for the night.

Each step sent an agonizing jolt of pain through her knees that seemed to throb in time with her headache. She was almost finished. All she had to do was deliver a message, then she could get back in the car, drive to a new hotel out of town, and nurse her wounds.

Alone.

"What the fuck?" LJ was on door duty tonight. He moved his large frame across the entrance and folded his arms across his sizable chest. "Are you out of your mind, lady? I ain't letting you in there."

"LJ," she said, though it sounded more like a sob than his name. "I'm not here to cause trouble, but it's really important that I go in there."

"What the fuck happened to your face? And your pants are all ripped up. What the hell, Steph?" His facial expression morphed from one of indignance to one of concern. That was the Handlers, tough as nails one minute, but putty when it came to their women.

"My face?" She frowned. What had happened to her face?

"Yeah, your chin is fucking bleeding all down your shirt."

It was as though him saying the words enabled her body to feel the pain, and the entire lower half of her face lit on fire. She lifted a hand to her chin, and it came back red. Shaking her head, she said, "It's fine. I'll deal with it later. You have to let me in LJ. It's a matter of life and death."

He ran a hand down his face and sighed. "Fuck, Copper's gonna have my balls for this one. I ain't never gonna get my damn patch now." He opened the door. "Tell 'em you knocked me out or some shit. I'd rather have them thinking I got my ass beat by a tiny slip of a woman than let you walk in."

"Thank you," she said. "Thank you, thank you, thank you. You made the right decision. And I owe you a big one."

He snorted at that and turned his back on her.

Stephanie steeled her spine and marched into the clubhouse. Much as it had been when she'd attended their parties, the bar was packed, people in various stages of undress undulated against each other all over the place, and the music was a notch above a roar. Immediately, as though connected by an invisible force, her gaze found Maverick. He sat at the bar, drink in hand, with Carli yammering in his ear.

Stephanie's stomach soured. He didn't appear to be enjoying or even aware of Carli's attention, but when she leaned in and whispered something to him, Stephanie saw red. This was a mistake. She should leave. Call with the information. Text. Hell, send a friendly email. But she shouldn't be there.

And then it was too late.

The music cut out, and she blinked at the rapid loss of volume. All around her, chatter came to a halt as hundreds of eyes turned her way. For the second time in a week, she was the sole focus of an entire room of pissed-off bikers.

"Um, I need," she said, then cleared her throat and spoke louder. "I need to speak to Copper."

The moment her voice rang out, Maverick's head popped up, and he spun around on his barstool. His expression was unreadable for about a second before it transformed to shock, and he shot off the stool and walked in her direction.

"Jesus, Fed, you must have some fucking balls of steel." Copper's voice drew her attention from Maverick.

He stood in the center of the room, hands on his hips, looking like Hell's welcome wagon.

Shit.

Here went nothing.

"I know I'm the very last person you all want to see. I need ten minutes of your time, then I'll disappear from your life forever," she said, unable to make eye contact with Maverick who'd stopped moving forward. "I have vital information for you. About Lefty."

CHAPTER THIRTY-FOUR

Carli had been running her damn mouth in his ear for way too fucking long. All he wanted was to continue doing what he'd been doing since the FBI raid, and that was drink himself stupid. Or until he forgot.

It was going to take a hell of a lot more alcohol than he'd already consumed. Stephanie would not leave his mind. Her scent, her voice, the gentle swell of her slender hips, the way she arched her back when he sucked on her tits, but most of all, the look of total bliss on her gorgeous face when she came.

He was in some sorry fucking shape, and there appeared to be no end in sight. Hell, he didn't even have the energy to give a shit that Carli was annoying the hell outta him.

Then she leaned too close, and her heated breath hit his ear. Just as he was about to tell her to take a flying leap, he heard it.

Stephanie's voice.

Shit, I'm losing my mind.

But then he realized the music had cut off, and all chatter died. What the hell?

He spun around and stared at the woman he loved.

She looked like road kill. "What the...?" He hopped off the stool, ignoring Carli's outraged, "hey!" and started toward his woman.

But then Copper said something about the size of her balls, and he froze in his tracks. Why was she there? She'd been explicitly warned not to return. And what the fuck had happened to her?

She didn't so much as blink when she informed Copper she had news on Lefty. His wildcat had guts, he'd give her that. Had Lefty done that to her? He swallowed down the desire to demand the information. Lefty and his crew were sick sonsabitches if what they did to Chloe was any indication.

Oh, Jesus, he hadn't even considered that Stephanie might have been sexually assaulted. Nothing would matter, not his patch, not the fact that she'd been a fed, not the lies, nothing. If he found out Lefty'd had laid his hands on her, he'd kill the fucker and everyone Lefty worked with himself.

"I'll give you ten minutes of my time, so I hope that's enough to say your piece," Copper said. "Jig, grab the first-aid kit and meet us in the spare room at the top of the stairs. Let's go, Fed."

Without an invitation, Maverick followed Copper and Stephanie up the stairs. She knew where all the rooms were and went straight to the empty one.

"Sit," Copper ordered before turning to Maverick. "Don't think so, brother."

Mav never, *never*, went against his president's orders. It was less about the pecking order and more about the deep respect he had for the man and his position.

But there was a first for everything.

"Listen, Prez, there isn't a damn thing you can do to keep me out of that room."

Copper chuckled and leaned against the door frame. "You don't think so?"

"No."

"Fuck." Copper blew out a breath. Part of what made him such a good leader was his innate ability to read and understand the men under him. He threw his arms up as he turned, muttering, "Now I've gotta deal with an ex-fucking-fed in my house," before entering the room.

Steph sat on the edge of a bare queen-sized bed. Dried blood coated her chin and ran down the front of her shirt. It had slowed to an ooze, but the wound looked dirty and gaped about a half inch. Dark smudges of exhaustion rimmed each eye, her skin was pale, and her hands trembled slightly, making her appear scared and defeated. Not the wildcat he was used to. His heart ached at the sight.

Now that Mav was in the room, he didn't know what the hell to do with himself. Go to her, glare in anger, fall to his knees and profess his love, shake her and demand answers? He could have done any one of those things, but Jig showed up, and the decision was made.

Sit on the sidelines and watch while another man patched her up.

"Check out her face and anything else she injured," Copper said.

Jig walked in, knelt at her feet, and opened his kit. After working his hands into a pair of too-small gloves, he gently raised her chin. "What the hell happened?" he asked. "This thing has a few chunks of rock or something in it."

"Yeah, it's gravel," Stephanie said in a tight voice. "I fell in the parking lot outside the Townsend Motel."

"You fell, huh?" Copper asked.

A feminine grunt was the only response.

"Well," Jig said. "I'm gonna have to pull them out, and you'll need a few stitches. Let me numb you up before I clean it; otherwise it will hurt like a bitch. I'm no doc so it might leave a small scar." He rummaged around in his kit as he spoke. "Shouldn't look anything like my ugly mug, though," he said and winked at her.

A small chuckle left her, and Mav had the inexplicable urge to ram his fist into Jig's face. God, he was such a psycho. There wasn't a single sexual or inappropriate thing about Jig's handling of Stephanie, yet the green-eyed monster barged his way into the room.

After a few more seconds of sifting through the bag, Jig pulled out a small vile of liquid and a long-needled syringe. Steph's eyes grew wide, and despite the gravity of the situation, Mav chuckled. His tough woman had once confessed a panicky fear of needles.

"Sorry, just one or two pinches," Jig said.

Mav moved to the bed and sat next to her, taking her hand. She flinched when their palms met. Gently, he released her and turned up her palm up. The fleshy part had been torn to bits, probably by the same fall. "Jesus, Steph, what the hell happened to you?" Instead of holding her hand, he rested his on her thigh. She stared at the spot where they touched for a moment, then looked him in the eye.

Longing, fear, regret, and sorrow all stared back at him. But what he saw above all was love.

"Maverick, you can make fucking moon-eyes at her when we're done. I want to know what the fuck she's doing here."

"Lift your chin," Jig said. He glanced over his shoulder at Copper. "Can she talk while I work?"

"Yeah, get to it."

Stephanie did as asked and tilted her chin toward the ceiling. Mav got the impression it was easier for her to tell the story without actually looking at any of them.

"I've been staying at the Townsend Motel for the past few days and—"

"Why?" Copper asked. "That Baccarella asshole have a change of heart? And I swear to God, woman, if you lie to me, my boys will be rolling you out of here in a body bag."

Maverick ground his back teeth together. Copper was pissed and mouthing off, but he'd never do it. Still, it made Mav want to rip the man's red beard right off his face.

"Change of heart from basically giving you guys license to kill me?" She laughed, but it was an ugly sound. Not the tinkling sound of happiness he loved to hear. "I don't think so. I haven't spoken to him. And that's the truth. You can check my phone if you don't believe me." She ended the sentence on a high-pitched *me* and jumped as Jig injected the needle into her skin.

Mav tightened his grip on her leg.

"Go on," Copper said. "Why did you stay?"

Even though her head was tipped back, Mav could see the blush that stole across her cheeks.

"I couldn't go," she whispered.

"What?" Copper barked.

"You can relax your neck until that kicks in," Jig said.

Stephanie lowered her chin and stared at the ground. "I couldn't make myself go." She turned her head and looked at Mav.

The utter devastation in her eyes speared his heart like a harpoon.

"I couldn't sever my last connection to you." The words were spoken low as though she'd only wanted Mav to hear them, but the room was small, so everyone knew.

At her declaration, Copper lost some of the antagonism in his stance. He looked resigned. Almost as though he knew Mav wasn't going to let her go without at least trying to hash it all out.

"So what happened?" Maverick asked.

"Bad timing happened, I guess you could say." She frowned. "Or maybe good timing, I don't know." Her shoulders rose and fell with a shrug. She went on to tell them what transpired that night as Jig stitched up her chin, then moved on to clean her palms and knees. With each word that left her mouth, all three men in the room grew more and more tense.

When she got to the part about Lefty's thugs being sent after her, Mav's vision clouded. The only thing that kept him from losing his shit entirely was Stephanie's subtle twitch and slight whimper of pain when Jig pulled a small chunk of gravel out of her knee.

"Fuck," Copper breathed out.

"It gets worse," she said, shifting her gaze between the men.

"Just give it to me straight." Copper said.

"They were planning to take me because they thought I was an ol' lady. Thought it would send the club into a frenzy and have you all out searching for me. It would leave the clubhouse vulnerable, and they plan to blow it up. One of the guys said someone named Marco is working on bombs."

Mav's blood ran cold while Copper's fists clenched and a vein visibly throbbed in his neck. Jig froze and hissed out a curse.

"Church in an hour," Copper said. "First step is to beef up security and organize a watch schedule. Mav—"

He drew out his phone with trembling hands and tapped a text to two of his brothers that worked for him. "On it, boss. We'll add more cameras, alarms, beef up the locks, the works. We're gonna need to secure the perimeter as well."

Copper nodded. "We'll discuss it all in church." He focused on Steph once again. "I got one more question for you."

"Okay," Steph said.

"I'm done," Jig cut in.

With a nod, she gave him a smile. "Thank you for doing that. I figured I'd end up stuck in a walk-in clinic all night somewhere between here and DC."

At the mention of her leaving, Mav's stomach tightened.

Stephanie kept her focus on the prez. "What was your question, Copper?"

"You could have taken this to the feds, probably worked your way back in their good graces. Hell, you could have gone to the local PD. But you came directly to us. Why?"

"The same reason I withheld information from the FBI this whole time." Her voice was low, almost shy as she ran her fingers over the bandage Jig had applied to her palm.

Copper grunted, seeming satisfied with that cryptic answer. Mav hadn't been privy to the conversation where he'd ordered Steph to leave town. Apparently, they'd talked about some things the prez hadn't passed along.

"You did a good thing tonight, fed. A couple of good things. Saved that girl, saved yourself, gave us the information we need to keep our family safe. And you did it knowing there was a chance I wouldn't listen, or fuck, a chance we'd shoot you on sight."

She shrugged, the motion full of defeat. "Everything I thought I understood about the world was tossed out the window when my partner turned. For years, I tried to deny the truth, but I've had the harsh reality that the world isn't black and white shoved in my face over and over again. Finally, I've accepted it. Now I know that protecting family and loved ones is important above all else. And it needs to be done by any means possible."

Copper gave her a curt chin lift. "You're loyal." He looked to Mav ,who was practically bursting with all his questions. But he'd have his time when the prez and Jig left the room. Stephanie wasn't going anywhere. Not that night, not ever if he had his way. Sure, they had some shit to work out, but as Copper said, she was loyal, and her loyalty lie lay with the Handlers.

"Gonna take some time to build the trust back up with the folks around here," Prez said.

Stephanie's eyes widened. The look of shock on her face was almost comical. She'd genuinely come expecting to be given the boot once again.

Loyal and selfless.

Copper's lips quirked at her laughable expression. "You up for the challenge?"

She cast a quick sideways glance at Mav, probably gauging his reaction, but he kept his face neutral. "Yes," she whispered while nodding. Good thing her chin was numb or that probably would have felt like shit.

"All right. Guess I'll leave you guys to it. Just don't fuck too loud, okay? You can hear every damn moan from this room downstairs."

Mav smiled for the first time in three days. "Not making any promises, Prez." Then he grew serious. "Cop, you know what all this shit means, don't you?"

Copper started twoard the door. "Means that piece of shit,

Lefty, thinks his dick is about nine inches bigger than it really is.

Mav and Jig chuckled.

"Like I said, church in an hour. Looks like we gotta prepare for war."

CHAPTER THIRTY-FIVE

Once he was alone with Stephanie, Maverick's emotions went haywire. Anger, desire, sadness, relief, and happiness all warred for top dog, making his head spin and his heart flip over in his chest.

Little by little, the anger crept to the surface, passing all the other sensations. He pushed off the bed and stalked a path to one side of the room then back again.

Stephanie's lower lip trembled, and she looked close to tears, which only made him feel like a shit. She'd been hurt, again, and the last thing she needed was a furious biker snarling at her. But, damn it, she'd lied. Over and over again.

Lied while he poured his heart out to a woman for the first time in his life. And that's where this resentment really stemmed from. It was less about the fact she was an FBI agent and more about the fact that he'd allowed himself to be vulnerable around her. No one saw that side of him, especially not a woman. But he'd given it to her.

While she gave him lies in return.

"Was your old man really a cop? Is he really in prison? Is any of that bullshit story true?"

Stephanie reared back as though he'd slapped her, and he felt lower than dirt. But didn't he deserve to be pissed off? *She* wronged him.

"The story is completely true," she said. "The only thing I lied about was my job."

Mav snorted. "Right. And who were you calling the day Carli caught you in the woods?"

She flinched at the mention of Carli's name. So far, he was two for two with his questions hitting her like bullets. "Special Agent in Charge Baccarella. The man who led the raid a few days ago."

"That piece of shit who left you here to be killed?" That was her contact? Christ.

"Yes." She kept her gaze trained on the floor.

"Look at me, dammit." He stopped directly in front of her.

Her head lifted, and her gaze met his. There were so many times her mouth had lied, but were her eyes capable of the same untruths? Because he'd seen deep into her soul through those eyes. Or at least he thought he had.

"It hurts too much," she mumbled turning her head and averting her gaze once again.

"Sorry. Thought Jig said your chin would be numb for a few hours."

Her voice was so soft he almost didn't hear her. "It's not my chin that hurts. It's my heart."

A sick part of him felt triumphant. That he could make her hurt as he did, but the feeling was fleeting and followed by regret. "When you freaked out back when I killed King, that was because you truly believed what I did was wrong, wasn't it?"

Her head slowly shook back and forth. "It was because I was conflicted. Caught between right and wrong. It wasn't a place I knew how to live in. It was a gray zone, and I'd fought against them my whole life."

"Why didn't you turn me in? Why did you lie to the bureau? Look what it cost you."

"I couldn't do that to you. It didn't matter what my conscience said, what my training said, or what protocol said. I couldn't do that to you. Not with how I feel for you."

The urge to kiss her, to lie her back on the bed and fuck her until the past few days blurred was growing hard to ignore. But he resisted. "And you never told them anything about Lefty?"

"No. Never."

"What did you expect to happen between us?" He needed to see her face so he could read the truth in whatever answer she gave.

She looked at him again, this time right in the eye and he breathed a sigh of relief. "I thought the bureau would pull me out eventually. I'd go back to DC. The club would fall off their radar. And I'd try to put the pieces of my broken heart back together alone."

Trust wasn't something he handed out like candy. Steph had damaged that trust. Normally, he'd be done. Their relationship would be dead in the water, but everything inside him screamed to give her some of that trust back.

She rose from the bed and walked toward him. On instinct, he backed up a step, but she kept coming. When she reached him, she circled both his wrists with her small hands and glided them up his forearms to his biceps. The crinkly bandages on her palms scraped over his skin. His gaze was drawn to the stark contrast between them where her arms rested against his.

Ink covered almost every inch of his skin, where hers was creamy, smooth, unmarked. Kind of like the difference between their souls before she'd been sent to Tennessee. She'd been clean, on the right side of the law, working for justice, then she became involved with the club and him. Now, some of what he was bled across the lines. She'd shined some of her goodness into his world, and he'd darkened hers a bit. Maybe not truly darkened it, that would come as things heated up with Lefty, but he'd shown her more of his reality. And it had changed her. Changed them both.

She might have thought the world was black and white, but Mav had been born in the gray zone and lived there his entire life. Who was he to condemn her being stuck between two worlds?

"I missed you," she whispered. "I keep dreaming about your

hands on me. Your mouth on me. The way you feel inside me. Every time I fell asleep, I woke up wet and aching for you."

Jesus, the woman played dirty.

"Was any of it true?" He hated how exposed he felt, like his heart was on the outside of his body, defenseless and so easy to harm.

Sliding her hands across his shoulders then down his chest, she tilted her head. "Any of what?" She toyed with the hoops through his nipples. He'd had little to no sensation there before the piercings, now every tug on the metal rings shot straight to his dick, even through his shirt.

"Any of us."

She froze. "Every single thing that happened between us was completely true. From the second you told me to stare into your eyes in Shark's basement until I said I love you during the raid. Every second of what happened between us was real."

He wanted to believe it so badly, wanted her back, but how the fuck did he make his head get on board?

"I want a chance to show you. I want a chance to love you, Maverick. Because I do. I love how protective you are, how you smile, laugh, and flirt. I love how you are with your family, with your brothers. I love how you smell." She pressed a kiss to his shirt, right over his racing heart, then inhaled a long breath. "I love how you taste. I love how you make me come alive."

Her forehead rested against his chest. "Please tell me there is some part of you that doesn't hate me for what I did. Is there some part of you that still wants me? I will work every day of my life to show you that I can be trusted."

STEPHANIE HELD HER breath.

Well, she'd laid it all on the line. It was up to him now to decide if he still wanted her. And if he did, was he willing to give her a chance?

"It's not about wanting you, Stephanie. I wanted you from the moment I saw you dragged into that basement hissing and spitting like a pissed-off cat. You were terrified, but so brave and sassy. Then you broke your fucking wrist trying to get King to stop burning me."

He paused and shook his head as though trying to puzzle through a riddle. "Why did you do that? At that point, you had no idea who I was, and you were committed to the FBI."

She shrugged and resumed playing with his nipple rings. Every so often, with the right tug or flick, his body would twitch. And somewhere along the line, his cock had gotten in on the action and stiffened between them.

"I couldn't bear the thought of them doing that to you. Especially not when you'd kept King from raping me."

"I want you, Stephanie. So much. I want what I thought we were building. I'm just not sure it's there anymore. Part of me is angry. Fucking furious with you for lying to me. Part of me wants to h—" He shook his head and flattened his mouth into a hard line. "Never mind."

"No, say it. Part of you wants to what? Hurt me?"

"Just drop it, Stephanie. That's not what I meant. You were injured tonight, for fuck's sake." He stepped back as though her touch was too much to bear.

"Fuck that," she said making him laugh. "My face is numb and I'm a little scraped up, but I'm hardly the walking wounded. Tell me what you meant. You want to hurt me? Want me to hurt like you did?"

His eyes darkened. Maybe it wasn't the best idea to goad an already pissed biker, but she needed to break through to him.

"Go ahead, Maverick, hurt me. I can take it. Do your worst." Christ, anything to get his hands on her.

"Steph, drop it. I'm warning you."

"What are you gonna do, huh?"

"Stephanie." This time the words were snarled.

She got right up in his face. "Hurt me, Maverick."

In the next instant, she found herself flat on the bed with a furious Maverick looming over her. Her body thrilled at the feel of him lying along the length of her. Damn, his weight felt glorious.

"You better watch it, wildcat," he growled from above her. "The FBI used to own you, but they handed you over to my club. Copper walked out of this room and gave you to me. You know what that means?"

She shook her head. Was it sick for her nipples to harden at the menace in his voice?

"It means I own your ass. You're mine to do with as I please. If I want to tie you to this bed and keep you on the edge of orgasm all damn night, no one's gonna come to save you. Maybe after hours of being a sopping wet mess, begging for release, you'll finally understand some of what you put me through." As he spoke, he ground his cock against her clit. She was already a sopping wet mess.

He might be covering it with anger and sexy talk, but Stephanie still heard the underlying pain, the kind of pain that wrapped itself around a person's heart and soul, squeezing the life out of them. And she'd done that to him with her actions. With her lies.

All of a sudden, everything crashed down on her, the loss of her job, the callous way her superior tossed her aside, being sent away by Copper, losing Maverick's love and trust, the impending confrontation with Lefty.

Giant tears rose up and spilled from Stephanie's eyes before she had a chance to try to stem them. Her breath hitched, and a sob tore through her chest. "I'm s-sorry." She finally said the words that held so much more meaning than just those seven little letters strewn together.

Above her, Maverick froze.

Great, not only was she melting down, but right when they were about to get to the sexy time. Nothing said *come fuck me* like a hysterical woman.

"At first, I-I was afraid to say a-anything. I t-thought S-shark would kill m-me. Then K-king almost c-called me A-agent Little when h-he was in The B-box. And I l-lost my shit on him. Then y-you killed him. It was t-too late to s-say anytthing about who I w-was."

"Shhh, Stephanie, take a breath. You can barely speak." He framed her face with his hands and landed a soft kiss on her lips. Even though it was nothing more than a peck, his flavor seeped into her system, calming her.

"I left here planning to never see you again even though I had all these insane feelings. I thought they'd go away. They were just because of the high-intensity circumstances we met under. Then they ordered me to come back. Someone else would have been sent if I'd refused. Coming myself was the only way to make sure you and your club were safe from arrest. I was already in so deep, and then…" She looked up at his motionless form. "And then I fell in love with you. It wasn't supposed to happen. I'm so—"

"Shhh." He kissed her again. This time longer and deeper, his tongue playing with her lips until she yielded to him. As their mouths tangled, relearning each other after days apart, she felt the shattered pieces of her heart bonding back together. He was her missing link, the one thing she needed to be whole.

After a few moments, he pulled back, and like a shameless hussy, she followed him with her mouth, trying to get more. He chuckled but denied her further kisses. "I always wondered what flipped your switch and made you go all attack dog on King that day."

Heat rushed to her cheeks as she recalled the loss of control that resulted in her beating her old partner. "Now you know. Now you know everything."

Mav's smile died. "I'm sorry for all you went through."

She shushed him with fingers over his mouth. "You have nothing to be sorry for. This was all on me."

He kissed her hard one time. "Okay, here's how this is going to go. Since we already established I own your ass, you just have to follow orders, okay?"

Oh lord, she'd created a monster. A sexy, flirty, tatted, and pierced monster. "Okay…"

"I've never wanted a steady woman in my life. Then I met you, and I barely survived the past two days without you. All the shit that's happened? It's forgiven and in the past. Yes, Copper was right about how it's going to take the brothers and probably the ol' ladies some time to build trust again, but between you and me, the past is done. Over after this conversation. We won't talk about it again. I will give you my trust. You will give me your trust. You'll be my ol' lady. You have no choice about that. I'm never fucking letting you go anyway. You get any pushback from my family, you bring it to me, you hear? You're mine to protect, and that includes from my stubborn, asshole brothers."

She sure as hell didn't deserve it, but somehow, she'd gotten exactly what she'd wished for. What she needed. A smile that felt like it was splitting her face in two curled her mouth. "I love you, Maverick."

He kissed her until she felt starved for air then whispered, "I love you, too, Stephanie. Now take your top off then lie back so I can fuck you so hard the entire club hears us from downstairs."

CHAPTER THIRTY-SIX

Mav watched as his woman pulled off her—actually his—Hell's Handlers' shirt and reclined on a stack of pillows. She wasn't wearing a bra, and her perky tits greeted him with hardened nipples he couldn't wait to get his mouth on. He fucking loved the fact she'd stolen his shirt and wore it against her bare skin.

Even when she thought they were over.

It was one more clue that her feelings were real.

Never a grudge holder, he'd meant what he said. They'd hashed it out. He loved her and believed she felt the same. He also trusted her. There may have been lies, but she'd proven her loyalty to Mav and his club with actions. Hell, she'd put herself at risk of arrest and worse while trying to protect him.

Putting herself in harm's way to protect him was becoming a pattern, and while he appreciated the fierce way she loved and how it extended to his family, they had one thing to get straight before this went any further.

"Keep your hands at your sides. Don't give a fuck if you rip a hole through the sheets, you don't move those hands. Yeah?"

Eyes ablaze with desire, she nodded and curled her fingers into the white sheet. "Yeah," she said on a breathy exhale.

Mav grabbed her knees and parted her legs enough to wedge himself between them. Keeping his eyes on hers, he unbuttoned her jeans and lowered the zipper. "Lift your hips."

She obeyed, bridging her hips. Mav couldn't resist pressing

his nose to the junction between her legs and inhaling the scent of her arousal as he worked her jeans and plain cotton panties over her hips. Before she had the chance to lower them, he licked a quick swipe up her pussy then nipped at her mound.

She yelped and jerked her hips, knocking him in the chin with her pelvis. "Sorry," she squeaked.

With a chuckle, Mav lowered her hips and yanked the damn tight jeans off her legs, tossing them over his shoulder. Then he crawled up her body and hovered his lips over her right tit. He paused, suspended an inch above the tightened nipple. Every time he breathed out on the needy bud, Stephanie squirmed. Eventually, she arched her back, bringing the nipple against his closed lips.

"Jesus, Maverick." A frustrated growl rumbled through her chest.

"Something wrong, baby?" As he spoke, her nipple brushed against his lips. Out of the corner of his eye, he could see her hands tugging on the sheet.

"You're messing with me."

"Sure am," he said on a laugh.

"Well, stop it!"

"This better?" He snuck his tongue out and circled the nipple again and again. Every now and again, he licked but never gave her the suckling pressure she craved.

"Maverick," she whined. "Please give me more."

Abandoning the nipple and ignoring her moaned, "nooo," he dropped a long kiss to the valley between her tits. Then he licked his way to the other nipple and started the torture all over again.

"I'm not gonna survive this," she whispered.

Mav loved her like this. Completely at his mercy, redy to beg, but willing to give herself over to his control. He reached his hands between her legs and swirled his finger around the opening of her pussy.

"Fuck," she whispered.

"Don't know what you're complaining about, sweetheart.

Your pussy seems to love what I'm doing to you. You're soaking the fucking sheets." He dipped his fingertip inside her, providing much the same torment he was giving her nipple. Just enough to make her crazed.

He had her right where he wanted her. Willing to agree to any demand he made of her as long as he deepened the pleasure and gave her relief.

"You're not in the FBI anymore, babe. You hear me?"

"What?" Her shocked exclamation had him laughing. No doubt, she didn't expect him to bring this up when he was about to fuck her.

"There's no reason for you to try and protect me anymore. You hear me? Thought we sorted this shit in the hospital, but apparently you need a refresher. You don't put yourself out on a limb for my club or me. I can take care of myself, beautiful. It's my fucking job and my brother's fucking job to keep you safe."

"Maverick," she said, blinking at him as if trying to get with the program.

He kept at her pussy with light, teasing circles, occasionally slipping nothing more than the tip of one finger into her. Between sentences, he lapped at her nipple then blew on the wet skin.

She could barely concentrate on his words, so desperate for him, but she wasn't getting a damn thing more until he got what he wanted.

"I love you, Mav. I'll do anything to protect you."

"No!" He scored his teeth across her nipple, and she jolted beneath him. "You'll never beg some fucker to turn his attention to you. I don't care if he's burning every inch of my skin off my body. You'll never put yourself at risk of being arrested. And you'll never fucking charge into a clubhouse full of bikers when you think they might be out for your blood. You fucking promise it now, or I'll walk out that door."

Yes, he might have sounded like an asshole, but the thought of losing her to a sadistic lunatic, to prison, or any-fucking-thing had him out of his mind.

"Mav, I can't make that promise." Her breaths came in ragged pants.

"You need more, don't you, baby? You want me to give you more? Deep? Hard?" Christ, his dick wasn't going to last through his own teasing.

"Yes, yes, yes," she said, nodding.

"Then you give me what I fucking want."

With a frustrated cry, she sagged against the pillows. "I love you, Maverick," she said in a voice full of need.

"Then you trust my club and me to take care of you. Any problem, any trouble, you come to me. I'll take care of it. What'd I tell you?"

She rolled her eyes. "You own my ass."

He gave her a wicked smirk. "Damn straight, baby. Now give me what I want, and I'll give you what you want."

STEPHANIE'S ENTIRE BODY was on fire with need for Maverick. Never had she felt so on edge, so out of control, so needy she would agree to sell her soul to quench the desire. But what Maverick asked of her, she wasn't sure she could give.

Protecting and defending those she loved was in her blood. It's what she'd been trained for, worked for. And while, when push came to shove, she'd try to protect Mav or any of his brothers, she got what he was asking. No unnecessary risks. Come to him with problems.

Trust him.

And he was giving her his trust when she barely deserved it at this point.

So the decision to give him what he needed was easy.

"Okay," she said. "You win. I won't try to protect you. I won't put myself out there. Now, please—"

The words were barely across her lips when Maverick closed his mouth around her nipple and roughly shoved two fingers into her pussy. She let out a loud cry and arched her back as white-hot pleasure shot through her blood.

Fuck, it was so damn good.

He curved his fingers, scraping over the bundle of nerves that had her shouting out his name. "Fuck, Steph." He kissed and nipped his way up to her neck. He sucked at the pulse fluttering her skin.

"I know," she said, then moaned as he dragged his fingers across her G-spot yet again. "Mav, I need you to fuck me. Please."

"Want you to come first," he growled into her neck.

She shook her head back and forth. "No, I want to come on your cock."

"Jesus, can't fucking resist that." His fingers left her body so fast she whimpered at the loss.

Mav pretty much threw himself off the bed, yanking at the button of his faded denim. "Fucking boots," he muttered under his breath as he struggled with the laces.

Stephanie threw her head back and laughed. God, it felt so amazing to be here with him again. She felt free, elated, loved. "I'm not going anywhere, Mav. Take your time."

He snorted. "You may not be going anywhere, but if I don't get inside that pussy in the next ten seconds, it's all gonna be over, and you're gonna be washing some dirty sheets and polishing yourself off."

With another laugh, she shook her head. By then, Maverick had all his clothes removed and stood before her in all his inked glory. His body really was a work of art. He crawled back over her and placed his hand on her sternum, above her breasts. Then, he trailed it down so it rested against her stomach.

"Fucking love the way that looks," he said. "All my ink against your naked skin. You're so beautiful, Steph."

"Mav," she whispered as tears filled her eyes.

He winked. "How hard do you want it."

"Hard, Mav. I want to feel you for days."

His playful grin grew predatory. "Your wish is my

command."

Fast as lightning, he was off the bed again, dragging her to the edge by her ankles. He flipped her onto her stomach, and she landed with a yelp as he yanked her hips back. Feet on the floor and torso flat on the bed, she barely had time to process the change in position before he was slamming inside of her. "Holy shit," she cried.

He never gave her a chance to adjust. Never let her take a moment to get used to the sensation of being full of him before he was pulling out and shoving himself back in again. He fucked her like someone had hit a turbo button, thrusting with a brutal power she hadn't known he possessed.

In this position, his piercing hit a different spot than usual, sending off a spark of intense sensation. Within a minute, she couldn't keep up with his pummeling, so she took what he had to give.

"God damn, this pussy," he said as he went to town on her. "Milks me so fucking good. Every. Damn. Time. I could watch my dick disappear into you all fucking day."

All she could do was moan in response because a tingling had started along her spine and spread out to her fingers and toes. Her mind went fuzzy ,and an orgasm barreled into her without any warning.

"Maverick," she screamed as she came, and came, and came.

"That's fucking right," he said, not letting up the pace.

She sagged into a pile of mush as he continued to fuck her. A few more thrusts and he gripped her ass so hard she was sure she'd have marks for a week. "Fuck, fuck, fuuuck," he yelled as he planted himself deep inside her. With each spurt of his release, the ball of his piercing ground into her, sending off aftershocks that had her whimpering and twitching.

"Fuck, that was intense," he said as he pulled out and collapsed next to her.

Part of her wanted him to stay inside her body forever, as unrealistic as the thought was.

He scooped her up and scooted down the bed, positioning her so she sprawled along the length of his body. Then he ran a hand over her ass, and she kissed the first thing she could reach, which happened to be his chest.

"Shit," he said, still palming her ass. "You're gonna have marks. I was rougher with you than I've been before. Did I hurt you?"

"No. Not at all. I loved it. Hope we can do it again very soon."

He gave her his flirty smile. "We can do it every day, babe." His lips hit her forehead as he gathered her even closer. "I'm never letting you go," he whispered into her hair.

"Good," she whispered back. "There's nowhere I'd rather be."

Just as her eyes were drooping closed and the sweet pull of sleep was drawing her in, there was a pounding on the door.

"Damn good performance, you two," Zach yelled.

Stephanie giggled. Copper warned her it might take time to rebuild trust with the club. That was all right. She was there for the long haul and willing to put in the work to form that trust again.

As long as Maverick had his arms around her, nothing seemed impossible.

EPILOGUE

Stephanie glanced around the prison meeting room and wished she'd taken Maverick up on his offer to accompany her. Actually, it had been more a demand than an offer, and he'd been pretty pissed when she insisted it was something she needed to do on her own.

"There's not a fucking thing in this world you need to do alone, babe," he'd said. "We're a fucking team. We do every damn thing as one."

"I pee alone," she'd pointed out, to which Mav had muttered something about stubborn women and deserving a blow job for his patience.

In the end, he'd agreed to wait outside with his bike.

And at some point, he'd drag out of her how he was right and she could have used the backup.

After exactly three minutes of sweating and tapping her toes, her father walked into the meeting room of the medium-security prison where he'd resided for the past six and a half years.

This was the first time Stephanie had seen him since he was sentenced. He looked different. So much older, grayer, tired, but fit and strong.

Guilt hit her square in the chest. If she hadn't been so rigid in her views, borderline obsessed with the notion of right versus wrong, she would have visited him all the time.

"Stephanie." He gasped and halted halfway to her. The guards must not have told him who his visitor was because the look of joyful shock on his face was one hundred-percent genuine. "W-what... Why?" He shook his head and continued to walk to the small table set up for visitors.

She rose, suddenly unsure of herself. What had they said when she arrived? Was she allowed to hug him or not? Once again, she wished for Maverick's supportive presence to get her through.

"H-hi, Dad," she whispered. He reached out and grabbed her in a hug so tight her spine cracked.

"No hugging!" a guard barked as he strode toward them.

"Sorry," her dad said as he released her.

"Oh, sorry," she parroted.

"Sit," he said, his eyes full of a watery sheen. "Tell me everything about you."

God, how did he not hate her? She'd abandoned him for six years. And he looked at her like she hung the damn moon. "Dad, I'm sorry. I'm so, so sorry. I should have—"

He held up a hand. "But you couldn't. I get it. You weren't ready. I always knew something would happen one day to shatter your illusion of the world. That's when I knew you'd come to see me. I only hope you weren't too hurt in the process."

"A little banged up," she said with a shrug. "But I had good help gluing myself back together."

One of her dad's light gray eyebrows rose. "Male help?"

She huffed. Why was it a girl always felt like she was twelve when talking to her father about the men in her life? Maybe this was worse because her dad had left just as she was coming into full womanhood.

They talked for the full hour that was allowed by the prison. In that time, she tried to jam in every detail of the past six years, leaving out anything that she might not want prison officials to overhear.

Her father wasn't exactly thrilled to hear she'd hooked up with an MC and demanded she bring the "hoodlum" by on her next visit.

By the time she walked out of the prison, she felt lighter than she had in years. She hadn't even realized how much of a weight her non-existent relationship with her father had placed on her shoulders.

After she walked out of the building, she jogged to Maverick and threw herself into his waiting arms. She kissed him all over his face and mouth, muttering, "thank you," after each one.

He laughed and grabbed her face, holding her still for one of his patented bone-melting kisses. When he'd sufficiently liquefied her insides, he pressed her tight against his chest.

God, she loved everything about this man.

"Not that I don't appreciate the gesture, but what are you thanking me for?"

"For encouraging me to do this. For coming with me." She gave him a sheepish smile. "And you were right. I was a nervous wreck in there and could have used you."

MAV THREW BACK his head and laughed. Stephanie loved to act all tough, but inside she was a marshmallow. He'd known she'd be a hot mess before seeing her old man, but gave in when she begged to do it alone. Next time he wouldn't be so accommodating.

"Huh, guess you owe me one, dontcha?"

Stephanie snorted. "Like there's a lack of blow jobs in your life."

Nope, that wasn't something he was missing out on, that was for sure. His girl loved all things about his cock, including its taste. "Can never have too many of those."

She giggled, and the sound lifted his heart. Already, just a few minutes out of seeing her father, she seemed lighter. That was good. Necessary. Things back home were fucked, with the animosity between the Gray Dragons and the Handlers at an all-time high.

"Let's grab some grub then start the trip back," Stephanie

said. "I know it was difficult for you to get away right now. I don't want to keep you from your brothers for too long. They need you."

"One more minute of this." He held her tight against him. It had been nice to be away, even for two days. It was the first time in months he didn't have to worry about Stephanie's safety all day every day.

But he just transferred the worry to his brothers, who did, in fact, need him.

One of the things he loved most about Stephanie was her love for his brothers. As predicted, it had taken some time for them to come around, but since she was a naturally easy person to love, it really hadn't been too bad.

"All right, babe, what are you in the mood for?"

She raised an eyebrow and wiggled her hips against him, making him laugh again.

"Not that, you horny wench. I need to feed you. You were too nervous to eat, and I won't have you passing out and blowing off the back of my bike."

"There you go with the blowing again." She let out a dramatic sigh. "Pizza. I think I want pizza."

"Yes ma'am," he said swatting her on the ass and handing her a helmet.

"Oooh, I like the sound of that. I think I should hear it more often."

Mav snorted. "Don't get used to it."

She giggled and started to climb on the back of the bike. Mav snagged her wrist as she lifted her leg and yanked her back to him. "Hey," he said against her lips, "proud of you, babe. Love you."

"Love you too, Mav."

Not everything in Maverick's world was roses, but from the moment he accepted Stephanie back into his life, at lease part of every single day was perfect.

Thank you so much for reading **Zach**. If you enjoyed it, please consider leaving a review on Amazon or Goodreads.

Other books by Lilly Atlas

No Prisoners MC Sereis
Hook: A No Prisoners Novella
Striker
Jester
Acer
Lucky
Snake

Trident Ink
Escapades

Hell's Handlers MC
Zach
Maverick
Jigsaw

Join Lilly's mailing list for a **FREE** No Prisoners short story.

Lilly Atlas

www.lillyatlas.com

Join my Facebook group, **Lilly's Ladies** for book previews, early cover reveals, contests and more!

Jigsaw Preview

"Isabella Monroe, do not make me ask you again! Bring me the suitcase from under your bed and do it now!"

Izzy sighed and dropped her sketchpad on the deep purple comforter. Three was her mother's limit. Three times of asking and being ignored by her thirteen-year-old daughter, then she'd storm in and let her Latina temper flare. And that usually ended up with Izzy being grounded.

Not that she cared. Where did she have to be? Who did she have to hang out with? All her non-school time was spent hiding out in her room with her sketch pad and worn-down charcoal pencils, *doodling* as her mother called it.

With another sigh, she flopped back onto her pillow and stared at the cracked white ceiling while she counted to five. Then, she rolled over and hung off the edge of the bed while searching for the giant suitcase her mom had stashed there a few months ago.

Their two-bedroom Bronx apartment didn't have much in the way or storage space. Or living space for that matter. Her room was smaller than some rich lady's closets.

"Got it, mom. I'm coming." Izzy rolled the empty suitcase down the short hallway and into the master bedroom which was only about two square feet bigger than her own shoebox. "What do you need it f—"

She stopped dead in her tracks and blinked as though the

scene before her would change after if her eyelids dropped and opened again.

Nope. Of course not.

Izzy's heart sank. "He's leaving?" she asked, barely above a whisper.

"Don't you sound sad for that *pendejo*, Isabella. You do not know what he did, *mija*."

"What did he do, mama?" Isabella asked because it was expected of her. She knew the routine by now. Her stepfather committed some heinous offense in her mother's eyes—though Izzy never quite saw things from her mother's hysterical perspective—then Catalina would rant and rave like in a frenzied fit until she ran out of steam. Afterward, she'd sleep for two days straight. Izzy asking usually got the ball rolling and the faster she got it out, the faster it would blow over.

But the packing of the suitcases was a bad sign. This was the third time in Izzy's memory that the suitcase packing happened. And each time, it resulted in divorce. Three divorces in less than thirteen years, because really, Izzy didn't remember much before age five. Actually, her mom packing a bag and running Izzy out of the house without her beloved teddy bear was her first full memory at age five.

So three spectacularly dramatic divorces in eight years and she'd never bother to ask her mother if she'd been married to Izzy's father. Part of her was afraid to know.

"What did he do? What did he do?" Catalina stopped haphazardly flinging socks and boxers into the luggage and faced Izzy. Her dark, nearly black eyes, the eyes she'd passed on to Izzy, were wild, as was her ink-black hair, currently frizzing out of its messy bun in every which way. "He stuck his dick in that fucking teenager next door. That's what the *bastardo* did."

"Mama, Juliet is twenty-two," she said like that would make a difference in her mother's eyes.

"And this makes it okay?" Her mother shrieked as she shook her head and stomped her foot like a petulant child. "We took vows, Isabella!"

Again with the vows.

Tears filled her mother's eyes then spilled over unchecked.

Here we go again.

Izzy bit her tongue to keep from blurting out that she was pretty sure there was no way in hell Juliet would have sex with a balding fifty-year-old toll-taker who was lumpier than a bowl of cold oatmeal. Juliet worked her ass off at a minimum wage job while taking night classes online and raising her two younger siblings. She had no time for a fling with an unsexy married man.

But those words would just send Catalina further into a tizzy. So, another approach it was.

"Mama," she said, softly. Izzy had learned over the years to approach with a soothing tone and delicate step when her mom had one of these irrational episodes. "Can I make you a cup of tea? Maybe, if you sit and relax for a while, you'll feel better, and you can talk to Len when he comes home. How does that sound?"

"Tea? My marriage is falling apart, and you want me to have tea? Isabella, don't act like a child. Hand me that suitcase and start filling it with anything in that drawer," Catalina said pointing to the drawer where Len kept his shirts.

A lump formed in Izzy's throat. Len might be fifteen years older than her mother, and not the most attractive of men, but he was kind and worked hard to provide for them. Best of all, he loved Izzy like she was his own flesh and blood and she felt the same about him. So many nights, she'd fallen asleep watching reruns of Friends with her head on his shoulder. He hated the show, though he claimed to love it and sat through countless hours just for her.

Her chest started to ache, and her eyes stung. God, she was going to miss him.

Two hours later, all his belongings were stuffed into the bulging suitcases and waiting by the front door when he came home from work.

The oblivious smile that curved his mouth the moment he laid eyes on Izzy cracked her heart in two. Shame filled her, and she looked everywhere but at his happy-to-be-home-after-a-long-day grin. She could have told her mother no. Could have refused to help her stuff those suitcases. Could have demanded her mother stop giving into her raging insecurities and use her brain like a rational adult.

But she hadn't. She'd kowtowed to her mother's wishes like she always did. Long ago, she'd learned standing up to her mother when she as in one of those irrational fits was pointless. She'd just be screamed at. And not yelled at like a frustrated mother whose child did something wrong. No this was an intense, lost of control, screeching like a banshee kind of screaming. Once, in a haze of mania, she'd even slapped Izzy across the face. Never again had she argued in those moments.

Suddenly it was too much. The ensuing fight between her mom and Len, the sadness and pain on the horizon, the loneliness of the apartment once it was just her and her unstable mother. Izzy sprung from the couch and flew at Len. Her arms locked around his hefty waist, unable to meet in the back.

"I'm sorry," she sobbed into his soft stomach.

"Shh, Izzy-bella," he whispered into her hair. He sounded resigned like he knew this was coming and wasn't a bit surprised.

But he did sound sad.

"I love you," she said, the words muffled by his girth.

"Oh, girl, I love you too. And I will miss you so much. But you're strong," he continued. "And you're caring, and a beautifully talented artist. You have so much to look forward to in your future." He stroked a pudgy hand over her hair. "Make sure you turn that art into something someday, you hear me?"

She nodded against him as he held her tight. "Will you be okay?"

"Sure, Izzy-bella. I'll heal. Now you go on and get out of here.

No need to stick around for the rest of this."

One last time, she squeezed her arms around him as hard as she could. Then, without making eye-contact, because she couldn't bear to see his pain, she kissed his cheek and ran out the front door, grabbing her backpack on the way.

She ran until her legs cramped, and her lungs burned before finding a private park bench to settle. Losing herself in her sketch pad, she drew her hopeless feelings until the sun vanished behind the high-rise apartment buildings.

Just as she was about to make her way back to what was bound to be a depressing apartment, laughter rang out.

"Look, it's Frizzy Izzy." Paula McLean, the most popular girl in the eighth-grade, strolled down the sidewalk with her ever-present bitch-posse. For some reason, Paula had taken an instant disliking to Izzy the moment they met, in Kindergarten, and made it her mission to make Izzy's school life miserable ever since.

The hair insults were the most frequent. Izzy had inherited her mother's ridiculously thick hair and had yet to learn to tame it.

"Hi, Paula. Have a good evening." She rose and started to scurry off, but one of Paula's little puppies, Krista, yanked the sketch pad from under Izzy's arm.

"What do we have here?" she asked in the whiny tone she was known for.

"Give it back!" Panic filled her. No one looked in that book. No one. Not even Len and she'd even talked to him about what she drew. But showing him, or anyone, was a different matter entirely. It was so personal, she had a hard time looking at some of the sketches herself. It was where she poured her pain when life became too much, and she needed an outlet.

Pages of agony, frustration, teenage angst.

Krista flipped the book open and started on the first page. Without looking, Izzy knew exactly what it was. A self-portrait she'd drawn after enduring a particularly rough day of bullying at school.

She's chubby. No guy will ever want her.

She's so poor she wears the same clothes three times a week.

All her mom's husbands run out because Izzy's so ugly.

And the insults had gone on and one. So, Izzy did what she did best and drew her pain away in a self-portrait of herself wearing her insides on the outside. Exactly how she'd felt that day. Exposed, vulnerable, ashamed.

Kind of like she did at that moment.

Krista lifted the next page. "Oh, my God." She giggled. "Look at this one What the hell is wrong with you Izz—"

Without putting an ounce of thought into it, Isabella pulled her arm back and rammed her fist into Krista's nose. Crushing pain like she'd never experienced shot through her knuckles all the way up to her elbow. But it was a good pain. A satisfying pain. A powerful, life-changing pain. And the feeling only intensified as she looked up and saw the blood gushing from Krista's purple nose. Eyes wide and horrified, Krista shrieked and started balling. "You crazy fucking bitch," she screamed in a nasal voice then started spitting and gagging as her mouth filled with blood.

Paula and the other bitch looked as horrified as Krista and started backing away.

That's right bitches.

Izzy stared down at her aching hand, and she flexed and extended her fingers. She glanced back up at the popular crew and smirked.

Never again.

Never again would she be bullied.

Never again would someone take something from her.

Never again would someone leave her alone and lonely.

Never again would she allow her heart to break.

She'd become strong both physically and mentally.

She'd harden her heart and learn to fight because it felt damn good to be the one on top. To be the one inflicting the pain instead of receiving it.

About the Author

Lilly Atlas is an award-winning contemporary romance author. She's a proud Navy wife and mother of three spunky girls. Every time Lilly downloads a new eBook she expects her Kindle App to tell her it's exhausted and overworked, and to beg for some rest. Thankfully that hasn't happened yet so she can often be found absorbed in a good book.

Made in the USA
Middletown, DE
28 May 2021

40617396R00176